THE
COGNOMINA
CODEX

BOOKS BY D. ERIC MAIKRANZ

THE REINCARNATIONIST PAPERS

The Reincarnationist Papers
The Cognomina Codex

THE COGNOMINA CODEX

D. ERIC MAIKRANZ

BLACK STONE
PUBLISHING

Printed in the United States of America

First edition: 2023
ISBN 979-8-200-98771-9
Fiction / General

Version 1

Blackstone Publishing
31 Mistletoe Rd.
Ashland, OR 97520

www.BlackstonePublishing.com

To RC, JZ, and IS

AUTHOR'S EXPLANATORY NOTE

Readers of *The Reincarnationist Papers* will recall that Evan Michaels's story started as three notebooks, handwritten in Bulgarian and purchased by chance in an antique store in Rome at the turn of the millennium. After finding a translator and transcribing the notebooks into English, I fact-checked as many details of Evan's story as I could, entered them as footnotes to the text, and published the work as *The Reincarnationist Papers*.

It might be fair to say that I found that first work, but the book you now hold is a different matter entirely. The most accurate description of events is to say that this work found me this time.

I was in Paris at the end of a two-week vacation when a large, flat package arrived for me at the front desk of the hotel. It was wrapped in sturdy brown paper with my name elegantly handwritten across the face. I unwrapped the mysterious package to find an oversized, hand-bound leather tome with gilded silver at the edges of the cover. The crisp pages felt handmade and were filled with the same elegant English handwriting as on the package, and those delicate pages contain the story you now hold.

As with *The Reincarnationist Papers*, I simply transcribed the handwritten text, gave the work an apt title, and fact-checked items in the story to verify their historical accuracy—which I have added as footnotes.

I do not make any claim as to the veracity of this story and the existence of the Cognomina and its members. I will leave that to the reader to decide.

D. Eric Maikranz

1

The image of the hotel haunted him. He saw it when he closed his eyes on a well-deserved cigarette break or during a rare shower on the road. He saw it clearer each night when he laid his tired head down in a new encampment along the trek from Syria to central Europe. The hotel's white stones were always clean, cleaner than anything his waking eyes had ever seen in his young life. But its black front door beckoned him—like a mystery where somehow *he* was the key to unlock it.

He'd hated the visions when they first sneaked into the narrow confines of his teenage mind, playing and replaying like clips from someone else's favorite movie.

Later, he tried to keep the strange visions of the hotel locked in his mind so that he could study every detail of the beckoning building. He would back away from the front door to see the complete structure, and then down the cobblestone driveway to the narrow side street, and then back farther to see the snow-covered, needlelike church spires of an unknown city that held the hotel like a secret. And then sleep would come to his weary body once again.

THE YOUNG SYRIAN REFUGEE LOADED CRATE after crate into the back of the yellow commercial truck, the kale greens and tomato reds barely visible in the thin predawn light. He didn't mind the work. The mindless labor reminded him of carrying artillery shells in a remembered war or of working alone in empty and doomed warehouses—the labors of other men that he somehow knew.

He had befriended every driver that visited the farm, and he learned that each one serviced a different route of farmers' markets. He chatted with each one in his broken German to learn their destinations. This truck he loaded, the yellow one, was Kurt's.

"Basil or Bern?" he asked as Kurt passed with a mug of fresh coffee steaming into the cool morning air.

"Zurich," Kurt barked back without turning.

The refugee laborer loaded the last of the heavy onion crates and then crawled into the cargo box of the truck where he restacked the open vegetable boxes to create a hidden space to sit. He stepped back out of the truck, grabbed the small backpack that held everything he owned, and lit one of his last four cigarettes. He ran his thumb over the military lighter and remembered how the occupying Russian soldiers had laughed at him when he had traded his father's gold ring for it. But the lighter reminded him of something before his father, something that he needed to get back to.

He drew in the warm smoke and looked at the other men loading trucks in the dark—men from Africa, men from Iraq, two from his native Syria. These were men with fractured pasts and focused futures. He had traveled with several of them to get to this sanctuary of a farm they had heard about on the road. It was a place that would work you to exhaustion, but would take you and feed you and not report you.

He flicked a long ash onto the dark earth and studied each stern face in the pale light of a promising dawn. He saw hard faces that had forsaken families and homelands to make it this far. He saw faces that he had shared stories, dreams, and lies with. He had held the wire open for several of them to cross into some already forgotten frontier that lay behind them now. Each of them had their own dream destination beyond this farm. Stories of Paris and dreams of Amsterdam and distant London filled the conversation around every makeshift evening campfire. But he was headed for Zurich, back to a past he was beginning to piece together.

He wanted to say goodbye to these men who had been his companions and fellow dreamers on their shared migration, but he knew he could not. Goodbyes are too common a currency to have any value among refugees. He drew on the cigarette and said a quiet farewell to each face in turn as he watched them in their darkened labors. Then he climbed into the back of Kurt's truck, took his hiding place amid the fruits and vegetables, and fell asleep.

THE DOORS OF THE TRUCK SWUNG OPEN to reveal blinding sunshine as the young man sprang to life and picked up the apple and pear cores that had been his stolen breakfast. He grabbed and placed heavy crates on the back deck of the truck, as though every farmers' market load came with a prepacked porter. Here, Turkish and Albanian immigrants did the lifting. When Kurt returned with another coffee, the refugee had stepped out of the truck and became another bending back in the buzz of premarket activity. He unloaded the last of the carrots, grabbed his pack, and looked for a street sign he might recognize from his jumbled memories of this city. The sign at the edge of the plaza read "Helvetiaplatz."[1]

Find the train station, he thought. He could probably figure out how to get there from the train station. If he really had been here before, perhaps he had arrived by train. He had planned this a hundred times in his head, planned how he would find the white hotel, what he would say, who he might recognize, how they might welcome him. It had been over a year since he had begun to remember this place, a place he had never been to, yet felt he had visited before. He stopped to look at himself in the side mirror of Kurt's truck and wiped smudges of farm dirt from his dark, sunbaked skin.

His teachers back in Syria had all marveled when he had picked

---

1. This plaza in Zurich's fourth district stands at the corner of Langstrasse and Stauffacherstrasse and hosts produce markets twice weekly.

up English in a matter of months, but he hadn't learned it so much as remembered it. It would certainly help him here. He straightened his back and stood tall as he started walking with the confidence that he would need to fit in here. In Zurich, with his perfect American English, he would be just another dirty, weathered backpacker moving from coffee shop to youth hostel, and not a young veteran of caravans and clandestine border crossings.

He saw two backpackers a block away and practiced the lines in his head before speaking. "Hey, man, do you know how to get to the train station?"

FROM THE BUSTLE OF THE STATION, he saw his first remembered landmark of this city. The twin spires of the central cathedral stood against a blue sky as though they protected some promised kingdom. He had definitely seen them before. From their base, he thought he might remember the way to the white hotel. Corner by corner, the avenues narrowed, and black asphalt gave way to gray cobblestones as the streets became more familiar to him.

Turning down Augustinerstrasse, he saw it. The hotel was smaller than he had remembered, but the brightness was right. It gleamed pure white like a proven truth. He stood on the sidewalk opposite it and studied its every detail. He lit his last cigarette and recalled the countless times he had imagined himself standing right where he stood now, ready to walk up and enter a half-remembered world. His legs barely obeyed him as he took his first nervous steps up the cobbled drive toward an envisioned new life that was tied to a dispossessed past.

The sign, Hotel St. Germain, stood in bright gold letters beside the large black front door, and a smaller weathered, hand-painted plaque hanging under it read Voll belegt in German and No Vacancy in English. The imposing entry door offered no doorknob or handle—just as he knew it wouldn't. He looked to the side and saw the golden decorative rope pull. Again, it was right where it should have been. He ran a rough, calloused hand over it, feeling its welcoming smoothness. The farm dirt under his fingernails curled as dark crescents as he grasped the cord and pulled. A bell chimed deep inside the mysterious white building, and he felt as though an hour passed before he heard the bolt move on the other side.

The refugee tried to recall the faint feelings of how the men and women on the other side of this door had once accepted him. Hazy visions of smiles, embraces, tattoos, and banquets had fueled his fantasies about what he might claim on the other side of this black door after they would throw it open and welcome him.

A man in his late twenties wearing a dark suit slowly drew the door open to reveal an entryway with a marble floor and the carved stone walls of a larger lobby behind him. The man had wide shoulders and a thick neck that hinted at a background in athletics or military service. He asked a question in German, but the young traveler couldn't understand it.

He stood there, shaking, as he repeated the opening sentence he had been practicing for over a year. "Hello, you don't know me, but I had to come here," the young Syrian said in English. "I cannot explain it, but I have traveled a long distance and I feel like I belong here in this hotel."

The doorman stepped forward into the open doorframe to get a closer look. "It might be that we do know you," he said in English with a clipped German accent. "But my first question to you is, do you remember your name?"

The young man stood stunned. He hadn't practiced anything beyond his opening, "I am Yousef, but also not Yousef—I mean, I think I am more than Yousef. I think I had another name . . . from before . . ."

"Tell me that name, if you please."

Tears welled up in the young Syrian's eyes as he grappled with the crowd of strangers' memories running through his head. He could see their actions and could even recall images of their faces reflected in mirrors of a distant past, but he could not remember their names. He only knew from the last one that he should find this place. "I, I," he stuttered, "I try, but I cannot remember his name. But I can see him here, in this hotel."

The doorman narrowed his eyes for a moment before stepping back to close the door. "I'm sorry, but we are full. I would need a name in order to check the hotel reservation log."

Yousef's heart pounded in his chest as this mystery world started to slip away from him. "But I belong here," he protested as the doorman's hard face withdrew behind the narrowing crack in the door. "I came all this way to find you. Please listen to me," he pleaded as the door and his future began to close in front of him.

"I'm sorry, but we have had a lot of impostors recently. Feel free to come back when you remember the name that your reservation is under. I wish you good travels, sir," the man said through the crack as he closed the door and slid the securing bolts back into place.

2

Yousef faced the closed door as the shock of the rejection washed over him. He had come to the hotel hundreds of times in the visions that haunted him, and never once did they deny him. His mind raced through different courses of what to do, where to go next, but every path led him right back to this black door and the beckoning gold cord.

He looked back down the narrow street, but the only thing he could see were the weary faces of all the other refugees who had walked with him on the road here. The Syrian turned away from their empty stares and reached out to pull the silken rope again.

He heard another man's voice, also in German, speaking to the doorman. The voices of the two men rose in disagreement. Yousef's pulse quickened when he heard the locking bolts slide free again. *What could he say to make them understand that he belonged inside, that somehow this strange hotel was home to him?*

A different man opened the door this time. His thick hair was gray, and his tall frame was stooped from a long life of looking down at others. This man seemed familiar but older. *Of course he would be older,* Yousef thought.

"Do you speak English?" the taller man asked as he stepped into the open doorway in front of the scowling doorman.

"Yes," Yousef blurted out.

"Excellent," the older man said with a nod. "Do you speak any other languages that you didn't study in school?"

Yousef nodded.

The older man turned back to his younger companion, whom he seemed to regard as an apprentice. "Sometimes they arrive quite confused about why they are here, so we need to welcome everyone with an open mind." He turned back to Yousef. "Do you remember this hotel?"

The refugee swallowed his fear and focused on making the most of this second chance. "I have a memory of this place, and it drew me here. I remember being here, being inside, being welcomed by others," he said, closing his eyes to summon the visions that had driven him. "I remember some faces—I remember yours. Your name ends in a Z," he said, straining and then opening his dark eyes. "Diltz," he shouted like an answer to a contest. "I remember that your name is Diltz, Mr. Diltz."

"Many people know that is my name," the man countered coolly. "What else do you remember about me?"

"I remember that you did not have the tattoo on the hand like the others had, like I think *I* had. I remember that you were kind to me. You sat and talked with me." Yousef took a half step toward the crack in the doorway. "Please show me that kindness again, sir."

"Good morning, Mr. Diltz," said a third man who approached from inside the hotel. "And who is our guest?" This new man looked to be in his early thirties—tall, rail thin, and Mediterranean. He wore a gray suit tailored to his lanky frame.

Yousef stepped forward, wiped his eyes, and took a long look at this stranger. "I don't remember you."

"Hmm, nor I you," the suited man answered, tilting his head from side to side, examining the bedraggled guest, "but that may be irrelevant."

"Sir," Mr. Diltz said, "this young man is called Yousef and claims to belong here in the hotel, but he cannot remember the name of his reservation."

"I see," the third man said as he turned toward the first doorman. "Should we invite him inside, Mr. Pianosa?"

The apprentice kept his stern eyes on Yousef as he replied, "Normally, I would, sir, but we have seen more and more of these claims after the notebooks became public."

Yousef froze in place as he quickly sorted through his clouded mind to remember notebooks and writing a message to someone in the future. *Were they talking about him?*

"I'm afraid it's true, sir. I see one or two of these a month now," Mr. Diltz continued. "There are a lot of unbalanced people out there, so we've become more cautious about outsiders."

"I understand," the thin man said, stepping forward to face Yousef. "Come inside, and let's have a look at you." He took Yousef's head in his hands with the familiarity of a family physician and gently turned it while studying his reddened eyes. "Stick out your tongue, please," he said as he examined Yousef's mouth and teeth. "Where were you born?"

"Syria."

"Was it a long journey?"

Emotion rose in Yousef as he nodded.

"Let me see the soles of your shoes," the thin man said, turning the refugee around. "Do you remember your room number here?" He let the question linger as he studied the bottoms of the man's military boots worn smooth from his trek.

"Twenty-nine. I remember twenty-nine."

The third man turned to Mr. Diltz, who nodded with raised eyebrows that the room number could be a correct response.

"Did you come from Damascus?"

"Yes."

"Did you walk?"

"Most of it," Yousef replied in a cracking voice.

The third man nodded. "Yes, you look like it. You look weary and dirty, but healthy," he added. "The young male body is a nearly inde-structible thing. You'll be fine with a bath, a breakfast, and some rest."

Relief washed over the refugee, and Yousef wrapped his arms around the surprised man in a flood of pent-up emotion.

The man in the suit stiffened at the embrace. "It's all right,

Yousef," he said, slowly returning the hug. "We'll find out if you belong here with us."

"Am I crazy for feeling so drawn to this place?" Yousef asked, stepping back and wiping his eyes.

"You might be crazy, and you might be something more," the man answered. "I'd like to examine you further to find out."

"Are you a doctor?" Yousef asked. "I don't remember a doctor here."

"I am a physician," he corrected. "I was likely not here when you were here before. This is not unusual. If you do belong with us, we will soon know." He took the room key produced by Mr. Diltz. "I will take responsibility for him, Mr. Diltz. What he needs is a good breakfast with eggs, a hot bath, and a long rest. Mr. Pianosa, please start the breakfast now and bring it to Room Twenty-Nine. I will show our young guest to his room—perhaps there are some items inside that will help his memory. Feed him now please, then let him sleep most of the day. But prepare a dinner for us and bring enough wine from the cellar for us— or enough for me at least," he said with a chuckle.

They walked down a long wood-paneled hallway until they arrived at Room 29. The physician presented a key attached to a small golden tassel that hung from his open hand. Yousef took the key and turned over the doctor's hand to reveal a distinctive black tattoo on the back between the thumb and the forefinger. It was the same black tattoo of three joined peaks that he had seen on his own hand in the disjointed memories of another man.

The physician let him study the tattoo for a moment before speaking. "My name is Galen. In time, you will remember your name."

"Galen," Yousef repeated, holding on to the man's tattooed hand. "Are you like me?"

"Take some time and get yourself cleaned up. Pay attention to your surroundings here, sometimes things from our past can reach out to us and trigger memories that can help us remember who we were," Galen said, placing a hand on his shoulder. "I will meet you for dinner tonight, and we will talk more. Rest now. I will take care of everything."

3

When he awoke, it felt like the other side of a dream. Last night he had fallen asleep in a barn, thinking once again of this hotel. But now that he was here, Yousef couldn't help but feel like he would wake at any moment to find himself still wandering, still on the road, still alone in this world.

While he slept, someone had placed a package outside his door: new shoes and three sets of clothes—a suit, jeans and a shirt, and an ornate robe and matching pants. The clothes seemed well made, but dated, with no tags to indicate where or when they were made. They also left two packs of Turkish cigarettes.

Yousef dressed in the suit pants and shirt and then studied some of the items in Room 29. A decorative sword hung on the wall next to a strangely shaped dagger. A decorative watch with a jeweled face whose hands never moved and a pair of very old dice were tucked away in the top dresser drawer. He held the dice and the watch in his hands like talismans and felt a faint memory of these items being presented to him by tattooed hands. "Not crazy," he said to himself, gripping the items in his hands. "I am supposed to be here."

He walked into the bathroom and placed the strange watch and dice on the cool tile of the countertop as he opened a pack of the cigarettes and examined the familiar orange-and-white label and Lendts logo. *Should I remember this brand? Was this his?* he wondered. Yousef placed a cigarette in the corner of his mouth and looked in the mirror as he brought the flame up to illuminate his face. He studied his reflection as he drew in the smoke and blew it at himself, as though that could help conjure the spirits that haunted him. The fair skin of his youth was tanned and hardened now from the road. His black eyes, square jaw, and short-cropped black hair conveyed a determination more at home in an older man. He had never thought of how appropriate his face was to his identity until he started seeing the faces of others whenever he closed his tired eyes.

Another man's face was first—whiter than his, young, and with light hair cut short. He smoked and smiled with a sidelong glance as though he held a secret he would eventually share.

Yousef looked down at the strange watch and dice. He slipped the other man's odd watch onto his wrist and clicked the clasp closed. He held the dice tightly in his right hand as he closed his eyes and tried to summon another reflection in the mirror.

The man's light face slowly came to him. Yousef concentrated on that man and his intruding memories as the corners of the dice dug into the calluses on his hand. They had been a gift, as was the watch. There had been other gifts presented to him on a special night—the night he joined their ranks here.

Yousef focused his mind and saw the man walking down a long flight of stone stairs, walking down into the earth where the others from this place waited for him, where they would accept him. *Will they be waiting for me in that secret place again?* Yousef wondered as he squeezed the gift in his hand. He went from watching the man descend the stairs with flickering torches on the walls to seeing through his eyes as he neared the bottom of the steps, and then the memory faded and was gone.

GALEN HAD BEEN RIGHT ABOUT THE FOOD and the sleep. Yousef felt new and refreshed—and famished again. He took the cigarettes, left his room, and instinctively walked to where he had recalled eating with another man, the fat man whom he had trusted.

Galen sat alone at the great communal table, reading. Two half-filled wine glasses stood in front of two open bottles. The tall doctor looked up and burst into a smile as he set two large, ornamented journals aside. "You look like a new man. How do you feel?"

"Yes, new. I feel new." Yousef smiled to match Galen's.

"I knew it. Are you hungry?"

"I'm starving."

"A good appetite means good health," Galen said to Yousef before turning to shout past the door to the adjoining kitchen. "Mr. Diltz, we are ready!" He turned his attention back to the young man. "I am so pleased I was here to receive you. I am speaking at a medical research conference in Davos next week, but I decided to stay a few days here to prepare my presentation."

"A medical conference? So are you a real doctor?" Yousef asked and then caught himself and rephrased the question. "I mean, are you a real doctor now, in this life?" He motioned to the back of his right hand where Galen's black tattoo was.

"I know what you mean," he assured, "and yes, I am a licensed physician. But my passion is medical research to improve the human condition, including my most recent breakthrough."

"What is that?" Yousef asked, eager to learn about this man who offered a welcome kindness.

"Senescent cellular rejuvenation therapy."

"Ah, that sounds fascinating," the refugee said, pretending to understand.

Galen laughed. "Forgive me, I have been living and breathing this new research for a long time now, and I likely need to practice my pitch to the layperson." He paused for a moment to reset the conversation. "I am presenting on human life extension. The work I will present next week could give each person the ability to live to nearly one hundred and fifty years old."

"One hundred and fifty? What would that be like?"

"Well, it wouldn't be like adding on another sixty years of old age. I am treating normal aging as a disease itself and have found a way to beat it at the cellular level."

"Now that *does* sound fascinating."

"Come and watch me next week if you want. In the meantime, let's talk about you."

Yousef searched the dining room for items he recognized. The long wooden table could seat over two dozen people, and its worn surface had witnessed many shared meals. He ran a rough hand over the grain as he looked at the two ranks of ornately carved wooden chairs that rose to the height of the dark wood wainscoting.

Mr. Diltz opened the heavy swinging door for the younger Mr. Pianosa, who brought in two new bottles of wine and directed two hotel staff members as they set plates on the table in front of the men. Yousef watched the dishes as they arrived—beef with carrots and onions, salmon with kale and fresh dill—and he couldn't help but wonder if his now-clean hands had helped bring those vegetables to this kitchen.

Galen motioned for him to start, and Yousef overloaded his plate with large spoonfuls that had been missing from the road. "Where were you born?"

"Damascus."

The physician smiled as the staff server poured wine for both of them. "I know the city—from a former time," he corrected. "It is a shame what has happened to your country."

"Yes, it was like watching your world burn down around you," Yousef replied.

"Did your family survive?"

"I have not spoken to my father since I left, and I have not spoken to my mother since I crossed into Europe."

Galen grabbed his wine glass and swirled the purple into graceful waves. "What about your brothers and sisters? Did they survive?"

"I am the only one, the only child."

The physician sipped and savored the wine. "That is rare in Syria, is it not?"

Yousef shrugged his strong shoulders as he continued his focused eating.

"It is easy to understand how that violence and destruction could lead you here."

Yousef chewed and swallowed hard. "I wasn't fleeing that place," he said, leveling his dark eyes at Galen before looking to the left and the right. "I was coming here."

The doctor froze with his glass halfway back to the table. "What does this hotel mean to you?"

Yousef took a sip of wine and then drew in a deep breath. "It sounds crazy to even say it out loud, but I know this place. I mean, I think I have been here before"—he paused as he weighed his words—"when I was someone else."

Galen set down his glass and looked over at the young man, who exhaled in relief as he opened up. "It does *sound* crazy, but it doesn't mean you *are* crazy. You might have landed in the exact right place. Tell me, what drew you here? Tell me everything so that I might help you."

Yousef closed his eyes. "I can see him. Sometimes he smiles at me," he offered with a slight laugh. "He has so much confidence, like he knows what is in store for me and can't wait for me to find it." Yousef opened his eyes to see the physician staring at him. "I see him walking to this hotel. I see him pulling the rope and stepping inside. I see him meeting others here, but the only one *I* recognize is the old man who greeted me with you."

Galen nodded and leaned forward in his chair. "What else?"

"I heard him speaking a different language—a language I had heard on the television, but it sounded strange to me when I was a child. Just over a year ago, I began to understand it, and when I could see and hear him, the sounds of his English returned to me as though I had known them all along." He paused to rein in the emotion that rose at sharing this part of himself.

"It's all right, Yousef," the physician said in a soft voice. "You're not the first one to ever feel this way."

"I know I have changed somehow, but I feel like I am trying to put together a puzzle when I don't have all the pieces."

Galen smiled. "Perhaps you haven't had— Maybe you just

can't— Let me try to start again—" Emotion choked the words as he tried to form them.

"I feel like I have lived before, and that is why I can speak English with no training. And I suspect that is why I remember the hotel too," Yousef said before the doctor could find his words. "Was I here before, as someone else?"

Galen let out a long sigh of relief as though a protective wall had fallen away from them. "There is a way to find out, Yousef," he said, smiling. "Do you remember something called the Ascension?"

"It happens underground, doesn't it?" Yousef asked, but he already knew the answer.

"Excellent. What else do you remember?"

"I think there are questions, but I just remember the stairs down into a dark place, then the memory ends, and I am left with nothing further to go on," he confessed.

"Do you remember the risks involved?" Galen asked.

"I remember feeling afraid, but then it's gone," he said with a sigh. "It is frustrating. I feel like I am missing something or not doing something right. I know it is important that I understand this and that I get it right, but I just can't recall anything more."

"What if I told you that I knew exactly, I mean *exactly* what you are feeling right now, Yousef? How would that make you feel?"

Yousef ran a rough hand over the short black stubble on his head. "I guess I would feel like I was on the right path."

"You could be, my new friend. This thing you are feeling is possible, but it must be proven to the others for you to stay here. It can be proven, and the Ascension is part of that process, but it cannot be rushed and should only be done when more of these things return to you. Sometimes it takes many months to remember everything, other times recalling a few key memories can unlock more, and sometimes unlocking just one or two can bring all the memories back at once. It can be like opening the matryoshka, the Russian nesting dolls, where one is locked inside another and then another, but where there is only a single face on the outside," he said, looking into Yousef's eyes. "We are all just a series of people hiding behind this face. It can take time, and you should be easy on yourself and let the voices of the past come to you."

Yousef nodded as his tight shoulders relaxed. "Why didn't I remember these others until now?"

"As a man of medicine, I have studied this for a long time. The remembering usually starts at seventeen or eighteen for male bodies and up to a year earlier for females." Galen held his glass up to the elegant eight-armed antique light fixture to study the color of the wine. "I theorize it has something to do with the last stages of brain development tied to the final stages of puberty. But the truth is I still don't know why," he continued. "Yousef, what I do know is how to help people understand and reconcile these memories. I developed a process during the many times I have found myself emerging from the fog of distant and disjointed memories you are experiencing now. It can ease the confusion, tumult, and emotion that are common with remembering. This confusing time is difficult for us mentally. And I believe our mental health is the most precious thing we have."

"What do you mean?" Yousef asked.

"If you *do* belong here with us, it will be because you have lived before and can recall those lives. And if you have lived before, then we must assume you will live again in a new body, a fresh body. For us, physical injuries may not be permanent," Galen said, looking at his hands like medical specimens, "but the mind endures. Any mental injuries or psychological traumas might transcend and wait for us in a troubled future. That is why I developed a way to help people through exactly what you are feeling right now."

"Does it work?" he asked, hope creeping into his voice.

"Yes, it does. Everyone I have helped reports that it eases and accelerates this recall phase."

"How long does it take?"

"For most, it takes a day or two. The more lives, the longer it takes. I find it most successful for those with fewer lives."

"Do you have time to help me before you speak at your conference?" Yousef straightened and composed himself to make a more formal request. "Galen, would you help me with this? Will you help me make sense out of what I am remembering and feeling right now?"

Galen recognized the courage in the young man's earnest plea. "Yes, I will. Let us start tomorrow. Eat a bit more food. Eat the almond tart—almonds are good for sleep—and don't take any more wine tonight. Leave that for me." He smiled.

Yousef reached for the tart. "Thank you."

"*Fraternitas ante omnia.*[2] You are my brother in this place and beyond. It would be my pleasure to serve you as a physician."

"How did you get into medicine and healing?"

Galen took a long drink from his glass. "I know it is against the rule that we are not to discuss ourselves until you have passed the Ascension trial. But I don't like rules. And besides, if I don't tell you about myself, then what in the world would we have to discuss over dinner?"

Yousef took his cue. "You said you have been a doctor before."

"I am a physician," Galen corrected. "A doctor specializes in a single aspect of health. A physician focuses on all aspects of health—from diet to exercise to surgery and now gene therapy."

"What is the first thing—the first person," Yousef corrected, "that you remember?"

"The first thing I remember is Rome, ancient Rome. I was a physician in Rome." He raised his empty glass. "I was a Roman citizen, but Greek by birth and by good fortune," he joked as his thin lips cracked into a sly smile. He took the Syrian's glass and poured the red contents into his own. "Thinking back now, it is a fantastic story and hard to believe. I started with what today we call sports medicine. Yousef, I started my career as a physician to gladiators."[3]

"Gladiators?"

"Yes, I told you I date back to Roman times. But the real story goes back to my pet monkey, Jobo. My father brought home a baby monkey from the market one day. He regularly spoiled me with gifts, but Jobo

2. Latin—Brotherhood above all
3. History has much to say about an ancient Roman named Galen being a physician to gladiators. (See *The Prince of Medicine* by Susan P. Mattern.)

was special. He clung to me like a child, and we were inseparable. Jobo was fascinated with the scrolls I was always studying. One day I was at my studies, and little Jobo was on the table and into everything as usual. I remember the monkey standing on the edge of the table . . ."

4

The monkey stood on the edge of the table and sent his small simian hands in search of the interior edge of the scroll. It was their regular game. Galen always kept an extra scroll fragment around, and Jobo preferred the stiffer, springier papyrus scraps from their time in Alexandria. Galen automatically slipped his fingers onto the edge to hold it in place as he read from another scroll. This was the monkey's cue. Jobo reached his small, furry hands into the curls and then slowly pulled against the tension as the coil unwound. He inched away from Galen's anchoring fingers, edge grasped in tiny fists. Both contestants felt the tension build as they stretched the small scroll flat. Galen glanced at the monkey's face. The monkey focused on the physician's fingers at the opposite edge of the taut scroll.

Galen popped his fingers away first, and the scroll snapped back toward the primate before he could react. The furry imp leaped straight into the air and shrieked. He landed on the floor and squealed in a primitive cry that seemed half laughter and half protest.

Galen resumed his reading in the brief respite before Jobo jumped back onto the table. Galen again automatically placed two fingers to pin down his end. He read while the monkey studied him and slowly rediscovered his courage. Eventually, Jobo crept toward the scroll and began gently probing until he found his edge. He had pulled the scroll halfway open when a call came from outside. "Galen, it is Petros. Are you inside?"

Galen stood from his studies, and the scroll snapped back at Jobo. His shrieks once again filled their sparsely furnished small room, this time more complaint than laughter.

Galen greeted his friend at the door. "Thank you for coming. I would enjoy some company today."

"Me too," Petros said. "Are you hungry?"

"Sure, I should eat something. Shall we go to the forum shops?" Galen asked.

"Can we take him with us?" Petros asked, pointing to the monkey with an air of expectation. "I am hoping Jobo can work his magic again. I mean, maybe not for you, but think of your friend. The ladies love him."

Galen chuckled and smiled at his handsome friend. "Sure, why not." The physician turned to his pet. "Jobo, get your toy. Get your toy, Jobo."

The monkey grabbed the scroll from the floor and ran to the door.

"Well, somebody's ready," said Petros.

Walking into the center of town with Jobo always cheered Galen up. He felt like an emperor with an entourage as all eyes fell on him. Well, all eyes watched Jobo and then him. Today was no different. Petros walked at his side with the monkey in the middle. Children bolted from their mothers' sides, old men stopped their bickering, and clutches of girls whispered and giggled as the three of them passed together in the street. Galen took it all in. Jobo liked to walk out front at the edge of his silver-chain leash. Other pedestrians turned at the approaching murmurs and then instinctively stepped back from the small striding beast. The effect was dramatic, and the perpetually parting crowd lent a regal air to their strolls. There is no subtlety in a pet monkey.

Galen enjoyed the celebrity. It took his mind off the pressure of his interview the following day. Petros went off to find some food while Galen took a prominent seat near the forum's central fountain. When Petros returned with fruits and half-eaten sweet cakes, he had to push his way through the edge of the crowd that surrounded Galen and

Jobo. Galen took a few dates from Petros and hid them in the waist of his tunic. He split a fig and shared half with Jobo, who chattered with glee as he ate.

"Don't give him any of the bread," Galen told his friend. "It is bad for his digestion."

"Well, how about you? Is it all right for your digestion, Doctor?" he said, handing Galen the uneaten half. "There is a wine vendor. Do you want some wine to relax you?"

"You go ahead. I don't like wine that much, and I want to keep a clear head," Galen replied.

"As you wish. Do you feel prepared for tomorrow?"

Galen sighed. "Sure, as prepared as I could be for the most import-ant day of my life. I interview with one of the most powerful men in the Eastern Empire tomorrow for the most prestigious medical position outside of Rome, which I have traveled from Alexandria to apply for, oh"—Galen paused for a second—"and which my main rival is already *doing* in the asiarch's[4] court, albeit a poor job in my opinion. So in that context, no, I am not prepared."

"You think stitching up sweaty, bloody gladiators in Pergamon is a high-prestige job?"

"I believe it is a high-profile job."

"Look around you, my friend," Petros said, waving an arm to high-light every eye on them. "You've got high profile perfected, Monkey Man."

"You know I don't like it when you call me that."

Petros reached down to stroke Jobo's chin hairs and spoke to him in an endearing, high-pitched voice. "You lead an ambitious human around on a silver chain, do you know that?"

Galen smirked. "This job could be my path to Rome."

"Aah, there it is," Petros laughed. "Reattach enough arms and legs

4. Galen uses the terms *asiarch* and *high priest* interchangeably in his story. The title is used to describe a high ranking (Roman) official who would organize gladiatorial games and spectacles and who would own gladiators as part of running an academy for such combatants. (See "*Archiereis* and Asiarchs: A Gladiatorial Perspective" by Michael Carter.)

here in dusty old Pergamon, and you'll find yourself reattaching bigger arms and legs in the Colosseum, I get it."

"Why are you pestering me about this? I thought you wanted to cheer me up."

"I do, Galen. Listen, you have studied in the best medical schools in the Eastern Empire: Smyrna, Corinth, even Alexandria. You are certainly more qualified than what's-his-name—Philo?"

"Philon," Galen corrected.

"You're more qualified than Philon. Honestly, as your friend, I think you're overqualified for this job. You could be on your way to Rome as a physician already." Petros turned to face Galen. "Here's my point, tomorrow might be an opportunity for you, but it doesn't define you. Sure, take it seriously and do your best, but don't overthink it."

"I know I can do a better job than Philon and his predecessor have done. They have lost what, fifty or sixty fighters in their time? Most of those died needlessly from superficial wounds. Remember Apollon? He should not have died from those wounds. He could have been saved."

"Yes, Apollon's death was an event. You should have been here to see it. I wouldn't have believed an entire city would have mourned a gladiator."

"Champion gladiator," Galen corrected before biting into his half of the fig.

"Regardless, you know combat is not my taste," Petros said, shaking his head. "The whole town shut down. They paused the games for a month. It is likely why you and the other promising physicians were summoned here. Apollon must have been worth a fortune to the old man."

"It was Philon's fault. I'm sure of it."

"Well, perhaps you can prove that tomorrow, but it could still be a sensitive topic for them," Petros said, flicking a blond forelock to the side of his boyish face.

"I'll try to keep that in mind."

Petros shifted on the bench and lowered his voice. "Hey, do you think we could get him to, you know"—he stroked Jobo's chin again—"help us meet someone new?"

Galen knew the request was coming. "You know he understands every word you say."

Petros leaned in close to the monkey and stared into the small soulful eyes, like black pools in a face of golden fur. "Does the little master wish to find me a curly haired beauty today?"

Jobo chattered twice as though agreeing to the request.

"By Jove, you're right, he does understand. Shall we then?"

Galen looked sideways at his friend. Petros knew the judgment in Galen's look, but he also saw a bit of mischief there too. "Come on, think about Jobo and me."

The young physician paused, then nodded. "Sure, let's take a walk." He stood and looked down at his furry friend. "Up, Jobo, up." The monkey jumped into Galen's cradled arms and then hauled up his leash in a quick hand-over-hand motion.

As they began walking about the large spraying fountains and open shops and bazaars of the buzzing forum, the crowds changed their reaction to Jobo. No longer was he striding toward them on the end of a chain—now he was cuddled like a child, approachable, welcoming. They walked until they saw a group of young women standing together. Galen walked past them once to make sure they saw him, but he knew that *everyone* sees a man cradling a monkey. On the second pass, he caught the eye of a woman with long blond curly hair. As he approached her, he pinched the hairless skin on Jobo's stomach, and the monkey let out a screech that stopped the women's conversation.

"What, this one?" Galen asked Jobo as they both looked at her. "Are you sure?" He gave his companion another secret squeeze to prompt the small actor to his cue.

Confusion crossed her face as Galen and Jobo stepped closer to her. "Hello, this is Jobo, and he very much wants to meet you. I am Galen. What is your name?"

"Eleni," she said, looking back at her friends for reassurance. "Can he really understand us?"

"Oh yes, so if you don't greet him, his feelings will be hurt," Galen stated. "Here's an idea. Hold out your hand."

She complied, and Galen found one of the hidden dates in the rolls of his sash and placed it in her hand. "Offer him this. It's his favorite."

"Mine too," she said, taking it. "Does he bite?"

"Oh, not in weeks," Galen countered and looked back at a startled Petros.

"He's joking," Petros interjected in an attempt to put Eleni at ease. "He's gentle. I bet he would love to touch your hair too. He loves curly hair. Hi, I'm Petros." He introduced himself, Galen, and the monkey to all the ladies.

Eleni mustered her courage and offered the date to Jobo, who took it gently and began eating while looking at her with his warm black eyes. He tossed the pit aside and reached a tiny hand toward a dangling strand of curly blond hair.

"Just stand still—he won't hurt you." Galen whispered, "Gently, Jobo. Nice and easy."

Jobo reached for her hair, took it in a delicately closed hand, and pulled it just enough to straighten the strand before releasing it to watch it spring back into place. Eleni smiled as she watched him gently pull and release her hair. "He's playing," she said.

"Yes," Galen reassured her. "He loves curly things or anything that has a spring to it."

She moved closer to them to let Jobo grasp another strand higher in her flowing locks. Petros was deep in conversation with the other ladies.

"He's fascinated with you," Galen said, encouraging her further. She stroked the soft fur on Jobo's slender arm as he reached for another curl. "He has a favorite game. It involves a scroll. Would you like to see him play it?"

"He's so cute. Sure, I want to see him play."

"Let's sit over here, and I'll show you." Galen moved to a nearby bench and set Jobo down at one end. The monkey crouched in anticipation when he saw the familiar scroll.

"Look, he's getting excited," Eleni said.

Petros brought the other ladies with him to watch.

"Oh yes," Galen replied. "This is his favorite thing." He moved to the opposite side of the bench. "Now you stand here in the middle and you're the official, agreed?"

She nodded and took her post.

"Here's how the game works." Galen raised his voice so that all the ladies could hear, knowing each would have their turn after Petros's careful coaching. "We place this blank scroll in the middle between us like this." Jobo inched forward. "Then I place two fingers on my edge of the papyrus to anchor it."

Petros urged the ladies in closer.

"Jobo will then approach and grab his end of the coiled scroll and begin to pull it back." Right on time, Jobo moved close and reached in with his tiny hands. "When he pulls it back, it will create some tension, like a spring, because it is a new scroll and still very tightly wound. He will pull it to the end until it is almost flat and he can feel the tension in his hands." Jobo found his edge and began his steady pull. "You have to hold it for a second or two. It is a game of nerves. Jobo watches my fingers, while I watch him to see when he will release. Whoever releases first and springs the scroll back to the opponent is the winner."

The crowd fell silent as Jobo pulled back, building the tension until the scroll was almost flat. Galen waited, intending for Jobo to win the first round, but he still jumped in surprise when Jobo let go and the stiff scroll snapped back at his fingers. Jobo chattered with delight and backflipped in celebration of winning. To Galen's delight, the gathered ladies began clapping.

"Winner," Eleni proclaimed and raised an indicating left arm.

"Again," said Galen, placing his fingers at the edge. Jobo crept in for the rematch and began pulling with his tiny hands. Galen waited until Jobo just got to the end and then released his fingertip grip, sending the scroll speeding toward his small opponent. Jobo leaped back to the edge of the bench and let out three plaintive shrieks in protest.

"Winner," shouted a laughing Eleni as she raised her right arm this time.

Galen rose and took Eleni's right hand in his before she could lower it. He pulled her toward his end of the bench. "Take my spot." He stopped her for a moment and moved his mouth next to her delicate ear. "Let him win the first one," he whispered warmly. "He doesn't like to lose two in a row."

She returned his smile with a look of partnership as she took her spot on the bench.

Petros moved a tall brunette woman into the referee spot as Eleni put her index fingers on the paper.

Galen looked over at Petros, who was in his element. He had engaged everyone in the group and had them all riveted to the action. Eleni was fixed as a statue as Jobo pulled the scroll back and let it fly at her. She squealed in shock and then started again with an excited Jobo.

After two more attempts, Galen moved the referee into the contestant's spot and then turned to Eleni. "You're a good sport. It's fun, isn't it?"

"He is so much fun. Is he always like this?"

"He will play all day, so long as he wins enough. He will play longer with women. He loves the company of women," Galen said, "but he seems to tolerate me."

"How long have you had him?" she asked, her eyes fixed on her brunette friend. "Maybe let him win the first one, Georgia," she shouted.

"About ten years. My father brought him home as a baby, and I raised him. We've traveled to a lot of places together."

"Have you visited many places?"

"Yes, we went to Corinth, Ephesus, Alexandria."

"You've been to Alexandria?"

"Yes, I studied medicine there, and he was with me."

"Wait." She turned to face Galen. "You're that new physician that came to interview for the position with the high priest of the games?"

"I am he," Galen said, bowing to her. "Do you like the games?"

"I like the combat games, but I hate the animal hunts. They're barbaric. I liked Apollon. I met him once. It was so sad when he died."

"It was unnecessary too. He shouldn't have died. I believe he would have lived if I could've treated him."

"Really? What could you have done differently?"

"I studied about this in Alexandria. We did experiments with sheep on the very problem that befell the fighter." He placed his hands on her shoulders and turned her to face him. "They say Apollon was slashed here by the other swordsman." Galen reached out a flattened hand and ran it across her toga. "If the wound is more than, say, this deep," he said, holding her finger between his to show the size, "then internal organs will be affected and they need to be addressed first. If the smaller inside wounds are not treated properly and cleanly, they will begin to rot and the patient will die. This is just one part of the new techniques in medicine I hope to bring if I get the job with the asiarch. It is stupid for men to die needlessly."

"Is that why you studied medicine?"

"I have a passion for healing people and helping them to enjoy their lives with good health, but the most satisfying thing to me is to save a human life. There is no feeling in the world like saving someone from the darkness of death and seeing them healthy and happy again."

"How many people have you saved?"

"So far only two: a boy who was gored by an ox, and a woman who had a bad stomach disease. The boy's wound was like a gladiator's injury, and the new techniques saved him. Our life is the most important thing to each of us, even gladiators, and I know I can save more of their lives in the future if I get the chance to prove it."

"*When* you get the chance, you mean," she countered. "When is your interview?"

"Tomorrow morning."

"Tomorrow? Why are you playing games with us? Shouldn't you be making your preparations?"

"I'm as prepared as I can be," Galen said with a sigh. "I guess I just needed a break today. I needed some fun."

She grabbed his hand. "Then fun it is. I want to play the game with him again."

Galen smiled, found the remaining dates, and placed them in her open hand. "Take these. Share them with him."

TRUE TO HIS WORD, PETROS WAS WAITING outside his house before sunrise. Galen reviewed the scrolls he thought he might need to reference or read from to make his points in the interview. He loaded his bag and threw it over his shoulder.

"Petros, can you get Jobo's leash?" Galen asked.

"You're taking him?"

"No, I want you to take him. I can't leave him here. We don't know how long this will last. He has needs, you know."

"Sure," Petros replied. "Come on, Jobo, come on, little master. Time to walk the humans."

They left in silence and walked toward the stadium and adjoining gymnasium where the asiarch and other officials would await them.

The three of them walked through the forum, but the focused morning crowd did not part ways in regal deference. Busy workers carried loaves of bread, fruits, and slabs of meat to the bazaars lining the square. The fresh lamb racks, quarters, and organs—alive only an hour before— lay in disordered parts, their ruminant blood thick in the air as the trio passed.

The overpowering smell of offal reminded Galen of his first medical studies in Corinth. Without the possibility of autopsy or any form of human vivisection, anatomy professors preferred the morning butcher shops to show young students the inner structures of bone, muscle, and sinew. Young and old butchers alike were hardened and indifferent to the normal horrors of their red art and were easily coaxed into removing organs or whole muscles still pumping and twitching in their final protesting labors. It weeded out the weakest of the students and inspired the most inquisitive of them. Near the end of Galen's time in Corinth, the younger butchers would severely wound a live goat—or a pig for a few coins more—to see if a student could save it with his new surgical skills. Galen had been too junior to join the surgery students in their efforts, but senior enough to know which specimen to bet on for recovery when the laughing butchers wagered on the fates of the injured beasts.

Galen and Petros stopped for morning bread and fruit, with Jobo only too happy to assist in their selections, then entered the empty stadium next to the palaestra. Galen sat on the stone bench away from Petros and Jobo and watched the morning sky receive its color as he ate. He imagined the sounds of the crowd as he sat next to the high priest in the royal box. He imagined watching the combatants in action, noting every wound or injury that would require his attention after the combat had ceased. He saw himself leaping from the stands onto the sand, rushing to the aid of a gravely stricken man who would live only minutes without his help. He envisioned himself as a new part of the life-and-death drama of the games, the advancement of care for man.

Petros approached Galen, breaking him from his concentration. "I hear people moving in the square. I think it is time."

They entered the colonnaded open square of the palaestra. Two long tables stood in one corner facing four stone rows of spectator seating. Custodians and stewards from the high priest's staff cleaned the benches and set out wine and two chairs for the tables. Galen greeted each man individually, ignoring customs of rank and station. He sat at one of the two tables and set out his scrolls and surgical tools for ready display. A few more officials trickled in and took seats on the sides.

Galen said softly to Petros, "I want you to sit at the edge there, near the exit so that leaving with Jobo won't disrupt the group."

Galen heard them before he saw them—boisterous talking dotted with deep laughter. Philon, the acting physician, walked beside the high priest, both smiling widely as the younger man continued his story, ". . . and then the priest said, 'You're in the wrong temple, sir.'"

Philon smiled but leveled cold eyes at Galen as the old priest, stooped with age, led the rest of the entourage in laughter as they walked in and took their seats around him.

Galen had expected Simon, the asiarch, to introduce himself, but now he stood alone on his island of a table as the group settled in. He was not the first candidate to challenge Philon for the permanent position, and he imagined this was how the incumbent had structured the other interviews as well. Galen arranged his materials once more to occupy the awkward silence. Annoyance stiffened into resolution as he turned to address the group only to be cut off by the high priest.

"Thank you all for joining us here on this fine day." The asiarch's voice was thin and brittle sounding. "Interim attending physician, Philon of Ephesus, we all know. Joining us today, we have Galen, once of Pergamon and now returning to us from distant Egypt." He paused to collect his breath before addressing Galen directly. "Welcome home, native son of Pergamon, and thank you for answering my call. I should mention that it was my honor to have met your father, a fine citizen whose signature remains on beautiful parts of our good city."

Galen bowed in gratitude, giving the priest a chance to collect his sparse breath.

"Philon will start today, and Galen will go second with Philon having a final rebuttal."

Galen figured Philon would structure it this way—to give himself the advantage of speaking during the cool morning and leaving Galen to deal with the strain of sun, speech, and wine.

Philon cleared his throat. "Your Excellency and esteemed gentlemen"—he glared at Galen quickly—"this will be my fourth such dissertation for the role of attending physician for His Majesty's gladiator academy, and since the second of my presentations, I have chosen a different topic to keep things interesting and allow me to demonstrate the full scope of the abilities I bring to this court."

He walked around to the front of his table to address his audience. "Today I will discuss the spiritual health of the warrior and how that is fundamental to overall health. I believe, and will continue to instill once in a more permanent role, that worship of the old gods like Mars, Pluto, and even Diana are better spiritually for the fighting man than the encroaching Asian, Egyptian, and Jewish cults of Mithras, Isis, and Christos. Adherence to our traditional gods will make for a more obedient and more easily managed school of men, and better and easier management could mean a larger school and more money."

Galen noticed the asiarch brighten and nod as he followed Philon's words.

"You see, the principal danger with Mithras,"[5] continued Philon,

---

5. Mithras was originally an angelic figure in ancient Zoroastrianism, but was adopted as the basis for a Roman Mystery Cult that was popular with soldiers and gladiators in the first century AD. (See *The Roman Cult of Mithras: The God and His Mysteries* by Manfred Clauss.)

"though the other new gods offer the same promise, is an afterlife where the gladiator's situation and station will be improved. This has the potential benefit that a promised second and better life could convince him not to hold on to this life too dearly, perhaps making him a better combatant, freed of the fear and terrors of death. But the danger is that this can introduce a mental laziness of deferred application, where the man turns away from perfecting himself in this life through discipline, exercise, and training. This deference in desire for a second life can leave us with an inferior man and an inferior combatant."

Galen settled in and noted the position where the sun met long shadows on the stones of the palaestra's open square. He listened and made mental notes of rebuttal. About an hour into Philon's speech, Galen noticed his opponent wore a jeweled dagger tucked into the sash about his waist. It seemed a bit ridiculous, but still it fascinated him, and he began focusing on the way the jewels danced in the strengthening sunlight as Philon paced.

The wine stewards made regular rounds, filling cups with red, white, or sweetened wine. Galen watched the high priest and his acolytes drink as his rival prattled on. Philon was a good speaker, and Galen could see why they kept him on in the role, but he also couldn't help but wonder why they had not chosen him already. *What was that weakness, that failing they found that still gave them pause after the first three interviews?* He saw how Philon kept their attention, how he flattered them. Galen looked over at Petros and found him fast asleep, chin on his chest with a sleeping monkey curled in his lap.

The sun pushed the cooling shadows from Galen's table, and he was forced to shield his eyes at times to follow his opponent's movements as Philon kept mostly in the shade as he spoke. Galen moved his array of display bandages and wraps over the top of his metal surgical tools to keep them cool to the touch. Stewards brought refreshing wine around again as morning gave way to climbing midday heat.

Galen mused that Philon would end at midday to ensure that his competitor would also need to deal with a lunch break. Philon began his summation just as the shadows of the table legs were about to disappear at high noon.

Petros snapped upright as the asiarch spoke. "Philon, I thank you for that amazing and enlightening lecture. Let's take a short break. Lunch will be brought in."

Petros tried to stay at the edge of a crowd that inched ever closer to him and Jobo. Slowly at first, the younger men from Simon's entourage approached and began petting the monkey as they fed him small fruits from the lunch buffet. Simon, Philon, and the older guard kept their distance.

Galen ate first and readied his notes as the others started. He noticed Philon followed directly after the high priest and all the others followed him. Philon filled his plate with larger fruits, then produced his dagger to dissect them into portions for the others. A younger staffer marveled at how the blade parted the fruits into neat sections.

"A surgeon must keep his equipment sharp," Philon said, laughing.

"I, too, would like to thank Philon for his detailed lecture," Galen began in a voice loud enough to refocus them from their lunchtime conversations. "Your comprehensive review of Mars's and Pluto's blessings for the modern warrior and the infectious influence of the new faiths certainly highlights a portion of the balance in caring for men of combat. That balance is one of art *and* knowledge," Galen emphasized before continuing. "The art looks back and instructs us on how to live our lives, on how to conduct ourselves. While new knowledge is a light, a light that pushes back the darkness in front of us and allows us to advance."

"What manner of knowledge are you referring to?" came a young voice from the shadows.

The question startled Galen. Not once in the three droning hours of the opening lecture did anyone interrupt Philon. He paused and continued, "New medical knowledge—specifically, advances in anatomy, medical botany, and most importantly new techniques in surgery in dealing with injuries to the vital organs. I bring with me the latest techniques from the schools of Rome, Corinth, and Smyrna."

"Studied in Rome, have you?" asked a different voice this time.

Galen shielded his eyes against the glare but could not identify his interrogator in the shadows of the gallery. "Ah, no, not personally. I mean, not yet," he struggled. "I studied under Roman professors and surgeons while at school in Alexandria."

"Oh, very prestigious. Thanks for bringing this new knowledge to the dusty east. We must be certain to pay attention."

Simon, visible to Galen in the front row, turned to admonish the anonymous questioner and to hail the wine steward once again.

Galen took a breath. "Better care for combatants means more money can be earned."

Simon looked up from his drinking cup. "More money, you say? Please explain."

"With the advances in surgical techniques, we can save fighters from more serious injuries in the arena. This equates to a longer life span for the fighting man and a longer career to build a fan base that will pay to see him. With these advances, we can save fighters from more serious injuries, and this could allow you to stage more dangerous games—such as those with sharpened edges,[6] for example. We know these types of games are more popular and profitable, yes?" Galen left his question hanging over them.

"Please continue," the old man said, motioning him back to his presentation.

From memory, Galen detailed how to repair injuries to flesh, to bone, to stomach, to intestines, and to lungs. He detailed how to stop bleeding, when not to, and why. He pulled his clean bandage dressings out and explained the use for each one. Then he picked up some instruments from those he had laid out, selecting those he expected Philon and Simon had never seen before. He fielded additional questions designed to throw him off balance, but Galen kept his focus on Simon. "Closing wounds to skin, flesh, and organ, while critical, is but a first part of—"

A loud yawn echoed from the shaded gallery, interrupting Galen.

---

6. Galen hints here that not all gladiatorial combat used sharpened weapons or were necessarily to the death. Brock University Classics professor Michael Carter drew the same conclusion in his paper on gladiators in 2004.

Galen looked at the high priest but found no comfort in his fatigued glare. He could feel that he had lost the others and would soon lose even the old man's attention if he didn't do something dramatic to turn the tide rising against him. "When a gladiator from this school picks up a sword or a spear and enters the arena, he faces two foes: one seen, ready to strike him down in front of cheering crowds, the other unseen, waiting to strike him down through lingering sickness and take him into darkness at some later hour." He paused, ready to strike at his relaxed rival. "Tell us, Philon—which of these foes took beloved Apollon away from Simon and this city?"

The gallery erupted in coughs and protests. Petros's laugh startled a sleeping Jobo. The color drained from Philon's face as all eyes landed on him. He rose in anger. "His death was not my fault. He sustained a severe injury, and that is what took him."

Simon glared at a smiling Galen, who asked, "Is that what he told you, Your Excellency? If his wounds were that severe, he would have died that day or even later that night. Do you disagree, Doctor? But how many days after the injury did he live?" He didn't wait for an answer. "Six days, yes?"

Simon struggled to his feet and raised both hands in protest. "Apollon was like a son to me. I had him from a boy when he came to me with no family. We trained him to be a champion. And he was. Twice I freed him, and twice he returned to the school and this city. His death was a tragedy that still affects us all. I ask that you do not dig at such a fresh wound for us."

Galen stood down but only halfway, convinced he could now prove his case. "I understand, Your Excellency, but if I may, I would like to ask you some questions about this tragedy. How much did his death cost you in the canceled games and the poorly attended games that followed? How has Apollon's death affected how the people view your office? You know they don't trust him," he said, pointing to Philon, "which is why you haven't yet named him permanently."

The high priest sat and stared at Galen, his lips locked in a tight grimace.

Galen turned back to face his reddening rival. "Do you remember what condition his wounds looked like on his final days?" He reached for one of his scrolls. "I have illustrations to show what the progression of those fatal sicknesses looks like, Doctor. Let's see if you can identify anything on it."

"You were not here," Philon scoffed in protest. "You don't know the situation."

"Who gave you the opinion that he could be saved?" shouted one of Philon's supporters from behind Simon.

Galen strode to his table and grabbed a scroll, eager to demonstrate his knowledge and turn the skeptical audience back to his favor. He began to unroll it to the hand-drawn illustrations, but before he could find it, Jobo bolted from Petros's lap and jumped up onto the edge of the table, tiny hands reaching into the curls next to Galen's.

The laughter of the gallery took Philon by surprise as he looked back at Galen, who tried to find his illustrations while pushing back on his insistent pet.

"Maybe the monkey told him that Apollon could have been saved," a voice cried out in laughter.

"Did he draw the illustrations for you as well?" came another shout.

"Perhaps it is a package deal. Hire one surgeon and get the other for free," called another laughing voice.

"Yes, but which one is paid and which one is free?"

Philon moved next to the struggling Galen to get in on the joke. "I see. Yes, you two would make quite a team," he whispered before breaking into a laugh.

A helpless Galen looked on with rage and embarrassment as even Simon joined in the laughter before standing to get control of the interview. "Please, gentlemen, please. Let us give them"—he chuckled and checked himself—"give *him* a second chance."

Galen looked at the familiar face of his playful friend. He felt the opportunity slipping away from him, and only one bold chance remained. Galen closed his eyes for a second against the small horror he harbored.

He then turned toward the old man. "No. It is not me who gets a second chance."

Galen turned to face his rival standing next to him. "It is your second chance, Doctor," he said, reaching back and cupping a hand over Jobo's face. "I believe Apollon's wound was right here," Galen shouted as he grabbed Philon's ornate dagger from his waist and slashed back across the stomach of his innocent pet.

Blood sprayed onto the opened scroll, and the monkey's piercing scream stunned everyone into silence. Philon blanched white at the ghastly injury.

"This is your second chance, Philon," Galen said, prompting his reluctant rival to action. "This is the same wound in the same place. Save your patient this time, Doctor."

Simon, Philon, Petros, and the others watched in horror as blood and viscera spilled from the open gash. Galen thrust a surgical tool into Philon's shaking hand. "Please begin. Petros and I will stabilize the patient for you." Petros rushed forward and grabbed Jobo's leash to pin him to the reddening table. "Please, Doctor, do us the honor of showing us your superior skills."

Philon recoiled in horror and dropped the tool beside the bleeding monkey. "I don't know how to work on that beast."

"His body is like that of a man. Heal your patient, sir."

Philon looked to Simon for help and found none. "I will not!"

Galen looked away from Philon and back to Simon. "Then let me show you how to save him as I would save a man," Galen said, "as I would have saved Apollon had I been here in your service, Your Excellency."

Galen cleared the remaining items from the table that was now a surgical table and positioned it right in front of the high priest, who did not look away. Galen addressed the entire crowd as he worked. "Don't worry about the bleeding yet—the letting of blood will cleanse the wound of contaminants. The body can lose a lot of blood."

Jobo *was* losing a lot of blood. "First, I open the wound wide and cleanse it with white wine," he said as he poured from a nearby pitcher. "Then I look for damage to internal organs. Aha, see? We have a puncture to this part here." The asiarch pushed forward to see the work. "If I don't treat this while it is open, the patient will die—not from the injury, but the disease of uncleanliness some days later." He shot a glance at Philon, who looked on in disgust, as though repulsed by the bleeding wound.

Galen took the wine pitcher and poured again to wash around the opening in the tiny intestine. He expected it to be small, but he didn't expect anything like this. He stitched the squirming monkey's gut closed, washing as he went. "Once any internal injuries are repaired," he said, trying to contain his emotion to continue in his normal lecture voice, "only then should a physician begin to close the wound and try to stop further blood loss."

Jobo's breath came in short gasps, all the color drained from his simian face. He no longer cried but only whimpered. The officials watched Galen's hands with fascination as he stitched the wound closed, washing as he went, always washing. After the final stitch, he washed once more, placed a clean bandage over his handy work, and wrapped the monkey's torso tight.

Galen washed his hands with the same white wine and wiped them dry on another bandage. He then gave Jobo a splash of sweetened wine. "I give him sweetened wine to help build up his blood supply. I will check the dressing in two hours to ensure the bleeding has stopped. Then I will wash the wound again and apply boiled honey to it after it has dried a bit." Galen looked around at the faces in the gallery—some were impressed, while others sat stunned. He leveled his eyes at Simon. "This is how you save a man with a sword wound."

The high priest looked into the rolling eyes of the tiny beast before facing the confident surgeon. "Impressive, very impressive how fast you worked. If the beast lives," he said, turning to leave, "the job is yours."[7]

The rest of the staff followed the high priest, leaving Philon facing Galen. Rage radiated off Philon as he stared into Galen's eyes. Galen

---

7. Many historians have recounted Galen eviscerating a monkey and challenging his rival to save the animal as the way he won the post at Pergamon. (See *The Prince of Medicine* by Susan P. Mattern.)

returned his stare as the group turned to watch the tension building between the two men.

"Oh," Galen gasped, breaking the silence as he reached for the bloodied dagger on the table. He rinsed it quickly and presented it back to his rival. "Your knife, sir."

5

"I rinsed it quickly and presented it back to him and said, 'Your knife, sir,'" Galen said, reaching for a fresh bottle.

Yousef sat riveted, waiting for the rest of Galen's story. "Did Jobo survive?"

Galen looked back at him with a shocked look on his face. "Of course he survived. It took just over a week, but he made a full recovery. The news got out quickly of what I had done and that I had done it to prove Philon's incompetence. The whole city rallied around Jobo like some new champion. They brought flowers and fruit to the house. Everyone wanted to see him, and they even cheered the first time Petros and I took him for a walk into the forum again.

"I walked him over to the palaestra to show the asiarch, and true to his word, he presented me the position right there on the spot. And do you know what the funniest part is?" Galen sat back down with his fresh glass. "He made Philon give me the dagger back."

He enjoyed a long laugh. "I didn't know it at the time, but it turned out that ridiculous dagger was the symbol of station given to the attending physician to gladiators of Pergamon. So not only had I publicly demonstrated that Philon could not do the job, I had done it with the very tool that identified him as being able to do the job. Oh, he was raw as onions. *Facit indignatio versum,* or 'Indignation creates poetry,' as Juvenal used to say. But I wore it with pride for the next five years."

"Were you able to save more fighters as you promised?"

"It felt like it was as many as there were stars in the sky. I lost only two men in all that time: one had his neck broken and died instantly, the other received a mortal wound to the heart and died within a minute. I was able to save all the others. But you have to understand gladiator combat was not like in the movies today. The combats were very rarely to the death in Pergamon. Those deadly combats were saved for Rome, but Rome is another story altogether."

Galen noticed Yousef was growing tired. "But enough of my ancient history. Let's get you off to bed for some more rest, weary one. We will start your work first thing in the morning."

YOUSEF HEARD THE MAN BEFORE HE COULD SEE him clearly. The man walked with a cane that tapped the floor with each soft step of a bandaged foot. He heard the cane clicking on the stone steps as the man descended the dark stairs down to their secret place. He heard the voices of others talking in groups of fours and fives and then falling silent when the man found the last step and walked into the cavern-ous room for the first time. Yousef kept his eyes closed tight as he tried to understand what this man was sharing with him. He could hear their questions—hundreds and hundreds of questions—and he could hear some of the man's replies and the scratching of someone writing in an oversized leather-bound book. He heard the questions stop and the vaulted room held a silence as one spoke for all. "Members of the Cognomina, I present to you our new brother—"

Yousef blinked awake and held the name in his head like a precious offering. He rose and found a note slipped under his door.

Meet me in the study when you are ready. —Galen

Yousef took the doorknob in his hand and closed his eyes, feeling the cold of the polished brass in his palm, wondering if a more complete version of himself might somehow await him on the other side of that door. He took one deep, calming breath and pushed against its weight.

The low light inside bathed the wood-paneled room in a welcoming warm glow. Galen sat near a burning fireplace in one of the many dark leather armchairs gathered in twos and threes around small cocktail tables in the study. The physician rose to greet him. "How are you feeling?"

"I feel much better, physically. I feel recovered from the journey." Yousef noticed another man, dressed in a white robe, sitting at a table in the corner of the room. He silently opened a large tome and turned to the first blank page.

"Excellent, excellent. Don't worry about that," Galen said, motioning to the third man. "We almost always have one of our scribes with us to document our activities for posterity, *in bibliothecis loquuntur immortales animae*.[8] Are you ready to start the recall work we discussed?"

"Yes, I am eager to start. I feel like I need some help there. I feel scattered—not myself but somehow becoming myself." Yousef struggled to put the words together to describe his mental state.

"It's all right. That is very natural. Just accept it for now, and then let's come back to that thought at the end of our day. Take a seat here." Galen motioned him to the leather chair opposite him. "Please close your eyes and make yourself comfortable. I will start by describing what we will do today, how it works, and what we hope to accomplish. I will ask you questions throughout the day. Please think about your answers for a few seconds before answering. We will likely get the best results if you keep your eyes closed."

Yousef nodded and closed his eyes.

"We will spend this day calling up the thoughts and memories that have been coming to you recently. When they come to you today, we will capture them and place them all in their right location. And after they are in their right place, we will then order them in sequence based on when those things happened. Yousef, some of these thoughts and memories might be emotional, some might be very personal. You can keep any detail to yourself if you don't want to share it.

"I want you to imagine walking into a large house by a lake," Galen

8. Latin—Immortal spirits speak in libraries, Pliny the Elder

started in a low, hypnotic voice. "The house is beautiful and has many rooms. This is your house. You selected it from the many you had to choose from. You selected it because it appealed to you, because it felt comfortable and inviting to you. This is your place, but it has many rooms. I want you to enter your house and walk into the main room. This is the part of the house you know best. You know there are other rooms to visit and explore later, but this large main living room is where you will start. Now I want you to recall the first memory you have from this life as Yousef in Syria. Do you remember it?"

He nodded.

"Tell me about it, please. Tell me about this very first memory."

Yousef swallowed. "I remember being a small boy. I was in a stroller, being pushed around a city. The first thing I remember is the shock at seeing an African man for the first time. He leaned down to look at me, and I remember the awe of seeing his shining dark face. It's funny—I don't remember seeing my mother's or my father's face—I just knew that his face was very different, very beautiful. I felt like I stared at him for minutes, just fascinated that no one had informed me that people like this existed. I remember feeling like this was the first thing I discovered on my own."

"That is a great example, and it belongs in this room. Keep that image of this man in your mind as you walk to one of the walls in this room. I want you to place the image of this man on the wall in the way you would hang a portrait. Once you have put that memory on the wall in its place, I want you to step back and admire it." Galen waited on Yousef's cue to continue. "Tell me, what is the next memory you have as a boy?"

"I remember sitting on my father's shoulders, feeding a long carrot to a donkey. My father made sure I held it by the end, and he wrapped his calloused hand around mine to protect it as we offered it to the animal. The donkey came and began biting off parts of the carrot. I remember how its lips moved ahead of its teeth, feeling first, then biting and chewing. When it was done, it brayed very loudly for another one, but my father only had one carrot. That was it."

"Now take that memory of the donkey and place it on the wall right next to the portrait of the man," Galen said and waited for a moment. "What do you remember after that?"

Yousef recalled event after event from his childhood in Syria, and one by one Galen instructed him to put them on his imaginary wall. After the first two dozen recollections, Galen questioned if each newly remembered event happened before or after the last posted portrait to define their sequence.

After he had recalled the first years of this life as Yousef the boy, Galen changed the question. "You have done a great job recalling and ordering your memories as Yousef, but as you think back over the past year and the flood of strange memories that have washed over you, are there some that are more powerful?"

The young man closed his eyes and took a moment before answering. "Yes."

"What is the most powerful new memory you remember from the past year?"

Yousef turned in the chair, as if pulling away from something, but kept his eyes closed. "Fire, I remember fire."

"Good, tell me about that if you want. Take your time."

"I remember the flames rolling like gentle waves over the ceiling, creeping like a tide. I felt the heat coming down like a hot, oppressing hand," he said as he sank back into the chair. "The scene feels dangerous, but I know I am not in danger. I can't explain it, but I feel in control in this room, like I belong there with the fire."

"What does it look like?"

"It is orange, but darker red at the back. It looks like it is breathing—swelling and relaxing. It looks . . . familiar to me, like something, almost like someone you think you recognize."

"It is a powerful feeling, isn't it?" Galen asked. "You know this powerful memory belongs to you, but you know it does not belong in this main room of the house, don't you?"

Yousef nodded.

"I want you to capture that image of the breathing orange fire in your head, and let's walk upstairs," Galen said in a soothing voice. "There is a beautiful marble staircase leading up to the other rooms in your house, rooms you know are here but that you haven't visited in a long time. At the top of the stairs lies a long hallway. That hallway has many doors, and those doors are open to you. Now see the familiar image of the fire in your hands and walk down your hallway and step into the first open door. You remember this room, don't you? You have been here before. Look around the room and place this portrait of the fire memory on the wall. What do you remember after that?"

Yousef took a deep breath. "I remember a painting—I was stealing a painting. A trash can—I remember hiding inside a small trash can. It felt like I was in there for a long time. I remember feeling nervous and uncomfortable. I can see the painting—it is of a woman, and she has the tattoo on her hand."

"Does this memory belong before or after the fire?" Galen prompted.

"After. It is after."

"Please place it on the wall and admire it there next to the other one. This room is yours too, but different from the room downstairs. You remember how it feels to be here, don't you?"

Yousef nodded and took a deep breath.

"What else do you remember that belongs in this room?"

He sat up straighter in the chair. "I remember the poppies. Vivid tattoos on soft skin. I remember her turning around to look at me. And I remember how I felt when I saw her." He paused as if savoring the moment.

"Can you see her face?"

Yousef smiled at the passionate memory.

"What was she like?"

"Irresistible," he said with a smile, "but dangerous somehow."

"Take that image and put it on the wall in the proper order." The physician waited a moment until his young subject seemed ready to continue. "Whose room is this? Who do these memories belong to?"

Yousef sat fixed in the grip of the leather chair and felt his mind opening to the voices that had been waiting patiently for him. "I know his name now. He is smiling at me again. These memories belong to Evan. These are Evan's memories. This is Evan's room."

Galen smiled and let out a long sigh. "Excellent work—just relax and let it come to you. Do you remember the name he used with us in this place?"

Yousef opened his dark eyes, which now blazed with a feeling of accomplishment. "Evan Michaels."

"That's right," Galen affirmed. "I often find it is helpful to fully embrace the past we have with this place by using the name you chose when you joined us. Do you wish to be called Evan again?"

A familiar smile graced the young man's face as he thought about the visions that had led him here. "Yes, let's try that for a while," he said with newfound confidence.

"Excellent, Evan. Let's continue with a new memory."

HOUR AFTER HOUR THEY CATALOGED a fresh string of memories that came rushing in from that previous life. There was the Cyrillic-lettered lighter; the dingy Iowa hotel; his friend Henry; his capture, imprisonment, and physical torture; and finally, writing the journals as a message to himself. He *had* done that.

"Let's try to find another memory, Evan," Galen prompted.

"I see another fire," he said, "one that I started. It is already on the ceiling, and the curtain on the wall is on fire. This fire feels different, bigger somehow." His face tightened as the memory came back to him. "No. It is not that the fire is bigger—it is that I am smaller. I see my hands as I raise them to cover my face. My hands are those of a child."

"This belongs in another room, doesn't it?" Galen asked.

Evan's nod was exaggerated, like a boy's. "Yes, this is the wrong place."

"That's all right. We are now ready to move to a new room," Galen directed calmly. "Step out into the hallway and find another open door. Enter it now. Do you see how the colors and furniture in this room are different?"

Evan calmed down a bit as he moved his head from side to side, his eyes still closed.

"It's fine now. You are in the right room for this memory. It cannot hurt you now, but you need to recall it and make it your own again. Tell me about this fire—this first fire."

"It was Bobby's fault. That was my name then." Evan choked up with emotion. "She's gone now, and it was my fault. This was the first time I encountered it, summoned it."

"The fire, you mean?"

Evan nodded. "It was my fault. I was playing with matches I had found. I was trying to see in the dark without turning on the lights and getting in trouble. It started so innocently—just a tiny little flame, enchanting and fascinating like a small dancing sprite—but it saw my fear and it grew. Like a living thing, it climbed up the curtain and spread out down the wooden rod. In less than a minute, it was on the ceiling, standing over me, pushing me down with its hot hands."

Galen watched in fixed silence.

"I remember shouting for her, for my mother. My shouts brought her into the room, and that's when it turned and took her." Evan's voice wavered. "I saw the flames reaching out for her as soon as she opened the door. They wrapped around her, and she screamed in pain. And then she was gone. Seeing her fall to the floor in flames is the last memory I have here."

Galen pushed down his own emotion and waited a moment to ensure Evan was ready to continue. "Please take that image and place it at the end of the wall." He waited for a change of body language and decided to give his new patient some needed relief. "I think we are done in this room for now. Please step back into the hallway and move down to the next open door," Galen instructed. "What do you see in this room? How does it feel different to you?"

"It feels older—dated, like a grandmother's house."

"What else?"

"It sounds different in here. When I remember her voice, it sounds different to my ears."

"Whose voice are you hearing?" Galen asked.

"Vanya—her name was Vanya. She was my wife, and we lived in another place."

"What was your name in that place? Whose room are you stand-ing in?"

"Vasili. This is Vasili's place—these are his memories."

"What is the most powerful memory from Vasili?"

"Artillery shells. I remember moving artillery shells, mountains of them. They were too hot to touch in the summer sun and too cold to handle with bare hands in the winters. We moved them as a team, toss-ing high-explosive rounds to each other in a human chain of jugglers. I remember not caring about the danger. None of us thought we would survive to be old men."

"Where were you?"

The young man kept his eyes closed tight in concentration until the past gave up another secret. "Bulgaria."

"Take that memory from Bulgaria and put it on the wall." Galen paused. "But you did live to become an old man, didn't you?"

Evan turned in the leather chair. "I did. I moved to a new land, alone. It was after Vanya left me, after she died."

"Do you remember how she died?"

He moved his head back and took a deep breath, as though sifting through the unsorted catalog of scattered memories. "I cannot recall how she died. I only remember that I was away from her—like she might have died while I was in prison."

"Tell me about that prison. Was it large or small? Do you remem-ber where it was or why you were there?"

"I remember we were both arrested. That was the last time I saw her. She was crying and reaching out her hands for me, but uniformed men—soldiers—held me while others dragged her away."

"Please take that image and put it on the wall," Galen directed.

GALEN WORKED WITH EVAN INTO THE NIGHT, sorting memories and placing them in order, moving from room to room until the disjointed memories were sorted.

"Evan, I want you to walk through each room one more time—starting with Vasili's, then Bobby's, then Evan's—then walk back down the stairs and look around Yousef's room. When you are done, I want you to open your eyes slowly."

The physician waited some minutes until Evan flicked his dark eyes open. Galen smiled and took a long drink from his wine glass. "That's quite a day, isn't it?" The man before him, who had entered as a confused refugee, now sat comfortably, confidence building beneath a coalescing mind.

"Yes. But I feel better. It's hard to describe exactly, but I feel like I am beginning to understand the puzzle."

"You've made excellent progress today, Evan. This session was truly remarkable."

"So what's next?" Evan asked as he lit up a cigarette.

The physician nodded at his enthusiasm. "Now that you understand your timeline and how the memories fit together, I want you to focus on how you feel when you review them. Think about how you feel as a combination of four lives. In my experience, this is one of the keys to success in the Ascension trial, which you should be thinking about, but we can discuss that tomorrow," he said, standing and offering a slender hand to Evan, pulling him to his feet. "Let's call it a day."

6

Yousef squinted his sleepy eyes against the pain of the blows the prison guards rained down on the man between their questions. He could feel the damage each punch delivered and how each strike stretched the man's thin will to continue. Each physical impact was like another small weight placed on one side of a scale, and he knew the man was wasting away. Yousef felt the man's feet dragging over the hard-packed dirt floor as they carried him back to his cell. After the prison guards dropped him beside the fetid chamber pot, the man struggled to rise on his elbows to look at his battered reflection on the surface of the stinking slop. He probed a gentle fingertip at a swollen and rapidly closing eye as his split and bleeding lips parted into a burst of low laughter, revealing a freshly chipped tooth. The man marveled at his grotesque mask as his croaking laugh grew louder. The man knew that someone else would eventually remember this night and all the other nights like it that chronicled the destruction of a man. He stared at his now unrecognizable face in the bucket and imagined another one in its place as he chuckled about this bitter part of the gift that he would eventually offer.

EVAN WALKED DOWN THE LONG HALLWAY to the study. Galen sat in the same chair as yesterday, and a low fire was already burning in the stone fireplace. The same scribe sat patiently in front of the blank pages of his large leather-bound tome.

"Good morning, Evan," Galen said, getting to his feet. "Is it all right to call you Evan?"

"Yes, it is. I feel like it is getting more right all the time."

"We had a full day yesterday. How do you feel?"

Evan nodded and looked up at the taller man. "It feels like a lot, and more memories keep coming."

Galen grinned. "Excellent. We can continue the work today if you want," he said, motioning for his patient to take his seat again.

"I think so. I feel like I am coming together, like the pieces are starting to fit."

"We can begin if you are ready," Galen offered but sensed hesitation on Evan's part. "Or we could just talk for a while."

The fire crackled and popped with a familiar rhythm that beckoned him. Evan looked down at the floor as he collected his thoughts and then let his gaze drift over to the low fire. "How am I doing? Am I normal compared to the others you have helped?"

The physician sat quietly and studied the man's square jaw and darkly tanned face in profile. "Quite normal. You're right where you should be."

Evan turned his head back to the doctor. "Should I be here?" he asked sharply. "Do I belong here? Do I belong in the same way that you and the others do?"

"Yes, I believe you do," Galen said without hesitation, "and I believe you are nearly ready to convince the others of that."

"I think you mean to say that I am nearly ready to convince the others—again," Evan emphasized with a slight smile.

"That's the spirit," Galen said, breaking into a satisfied smile. "That attitude can help you in your upcoming test, but I anticipate the possibility of acceptance might not be as straightforward as you remember with the last one."

"Because of what I wrote when I was Evan?"

Galen nodded.

"But I wrote it for myself. I remember writing it so that he"—Evan stopped as though struggling for the name of his cellmate—"so that my cellmate Reginald wouldn't know."

"Oh yes, we know." The doctor chuckled. "We all know. But your creation escaped its captor and is now in the wild," Galen said, shifting in his chair. "Do you remember when Mr. Diltz said he sees one or two a month?"

Evan nodded but wasn't putting it all together.

"People, normal people, have read your papers. Your notebooks were discovered and translated from Bulgarian for the world to read. As a result, there have been a few impostors who have knocked on our door claiming to be you. So what that means," Galen continued and held up a calming hand toward his companion's rising anxiety, "is that you will likely need to do something more than last time."

"More? What more can I do than tell the truth?"

"You might need to find facts and details from your past that weren't in your notebooks but that are in *our* scribe-written version of your recall," Galen said, nodding toward the white-robed scribe who continued his writings. "And there is something else. Impostors might be able to read a series of notebooks and memorize details, but they cannot explain the feeling of living multiple lives nor can they communicate the conflict with emerging personalities you are feeling right now." The physician leveled his dark eyes into Evan's. "That, my friend, cannot be faked. *That* is what I would focus on if you want to pass their judgment."

Evan's mind flashed back to a new memory from that dark grotto below. A lean man with a snarling smile held a spear to the man's chest. *Do they kill the ones who don't pass?*

Evan shook off the feeling of dread and turned toward the comfort of the fire. "I feel excitement," he started, "but it is a mix of excitement. I feel excited that I found this place. I feel excited that I found the courage to pull the cord and announce myself. I feel excited to have found you and that you believe in me enough to help me. But I also feel another excitement." He paused and looked back at Galen. "Or perhaps it is more accurate to say that I feel another's excitement next to mine."

"Tell me about that."

"I didn't want any of this, Galen. I had a life planned as Yousef Azmah. I was going to join the Syrian Intelligence Service." Evan stopped to consider the desires of his younger self. "I wanted to protect our nation," he said with a cynical laugh, "a nation that barely exists anymore and, as it turns out after remembering three others, is not even my home country. It's like the dreams of my youth are suddenly obsolete," he said, leveling his eyes at his physician.

Galen watched him for several seconds to ensure he was finished. "It's like that for me too. I wake up at seventeen or eighteen, and the young person I had been growing up to be is nothing more than a skin to be cast away, as the real me, the transcending me, reawakens."

"That other excitement I feel is the validation of another man's faith. I see it now when the vision of him comes to me. He met a dreadful and violent end in his last life. I can feel his desperation for an exit, any exit from his condition then." Evan looked up at Galen to steady his emotions. "Near the end—his end—he believed he would get another chance. It was as though he knew he had a ticket to Syria, a ticket to me—here and now. He was excited about that, and amid his despair and brokenness, he still held hope for the future with an expectation for me to come and remember. It's like he has been sleeping and waiting for his chance to reawaken and live again."

"He knew that once we come back that first time, we always will," Galen answered. "It changes the way we live our lives. For some, it means they are released from consequence and are free to do whatever they want. They live without fear. For others, like me for instance, it means we are empowered over longer timelines to work on things we are passionate about."

"Like medicine?"

The doctor tilted his head. "I think healthcare is a better term. I have been doing that for centuries." He stopped for a moment and seemed to survey a sum of lifetimes. "I suppose I have been doing this from my first life, and in all the lives that have followed."

"And you work on this during each new life?" Evan asked but struggled to make his point. "I mean, each time after you remember that you have been other people before?"

Galen smiled. "I know what you mean. And yes, I work on this in each new trip."

"Do you ever work on the same research over many lives?"

"Oh yes, in many cases you have to. Some work is just too big to complete in one lifetime. My current life-extension work is an example of that. This is why many of us here feel that our *condition* is a gift of sorts. It gives us a longer timeline to work on things. I find the awakening is easier if you have some task or work or passion to continue. I imagine others in our ranks who focus on art or a craft or even a conflict would feel the same."

"I wonder if I will ever find any focus beyond the flame that seems to call me."

"You're just getting started," Galen countered. "Go easy on yourself. I took some time this morning to read your last account in our archive," he said, motioning to a second silver-gilded tome that rested next to the scribe. "You lived in Bulgaria in your first life?"

"Yes, I think so," he replied with hesitation. "I mean, I remember it. I began to remember it a few months ago. But the most powerful memories were from this hotel and from Los Angeles when Evan was starting fires as an arsonist."

"For some of us, the most recent lives are the ones we remember first, as though they were somehow the most legible words on a page that has been erased and written over many times. For others, there is one dominant life that comes back stronger and usually comes back to us first."

"There are memories from before Evan, and I feel like they are still coming. I mean, I continue to learn or remember new things about him and the other two before him."

"Those are not others," Galen said, leaning forward in his chair. "Vasili, Bobby, Evan, and now Yousef, all these men are you—the same person." Galen remained silent for a moment to let Evan think about the implications. "The sooner you can reconcile that, the easier this will be for you."

Evan stood up from the embrace of the leather chair and walked toward the flickering glow from the large stone fireplace as he thought about Galen's statement. *All these men are you—the same person.* He stepped around the scribe, who wrote in silence, and peeked over his shoulder at the text filling the heavy vellum pages. The fancy handwritten script looked like old German. *Am I really written into their pages?* he wondered.

"I have so many questions for you," Galen continued, "but it is best if I keep them for when we have some others present. We should keep working on your recall, but some things we should reserve until your test. I look forward to your Ascension, and I believe the others will too. In fact, some of them have found out about you already and are on their way here."

"The others are coming here?" Evan asked as he carefully placed two new logs on the growing fire. "Those with the tattoo?"

"Yes. I imagine some will arrive later today."

"But how did they find out about me?" Evan asked nervously.

Galen laughed out loud. "An interesting question from the man who outed us to the world. Besides, this hotel is full of secrets, but it has never been very good at keeping them."

"Who is arriving?" Evan asked as he raced through his coalescing memories for faces from another man's past. *Will the flower woman be among them?*

"I think it best if I save that information for when you meet them. Recognizing them in this new body would be an excellent first step toward passing your Ascension."

"And what if I don't recognize them?"

"Don't guess, whatever you do," Galen instructed. "Just share what comes to you. If nothing comes to you, then share that. Just be yourself."

"Yes, but which self?"

The doctor smiled at the question. "Let's continue our work from yesterday and see if we can get you into better shape by the time they get here. I think we should work on the most recent memory you recall."

Evan nodded and closed his eyes to the calm surroundings of the study. "I remember the unrelenting heat of the prison in Tunisia and the impact of the blows on him," he said, blinking his eyes open for an instant before correcting himself, "on me."

"That's right. Capture all of these physical sensations, but how did it feel to you mentally to endure that?"

Evan closed his eyes again as the muscles in his jaw clenched against the memory. "I was afraid at first," he confessed. "I had just been arrested and I was fearful of what would happen to me. I can remember weighing the risks as part of his offer." He paused for a moment as though trying to recall a name or a face. "There was a man, a fat man. I remember that he was kind to me and helped me, but I also remember that it was because of him that I was in that prison in the desert."

Galen sneaked a glance over at the dutiful scribe who captured Evan's words as he spoke.

"My fear of those brutal guards slowly grew into anger," Evan continued, "but that anger eventually turned from them to the man who had talked me into taking those physical risks for him. But as strong as that hatred became, it was nothing compared to the rage I felt at myself for landing there. I remember feeling that it didn't have to be that way. I could have spared myself that abuse and the painful memory of it that I will carry like a scar on my mind every time in the future when I sit with you to do this again." He closed his eyes tight against the remembered pain. "After that, I just felt stupid for being talked into doing it, when time would have allowed me the same reward I was chasing. In the end, the only thing left was that hope of a new chance and the resignation of a peaceful and well-earned sleep." Evan slowly opened his new eyes and looked at his new friend. "That's how that life ended."

The physician bowed his head slightly to Evan. "Thank you for sharing that. It must be difficult to relive that time."

"The more we work, the easier this is for me."

"Excellent. Close your eyes, walk upstairs, and place these emotions on the wall next to the image. The emotions should be like a description of the work on the nameplate next to the image. Now, I want you to try to remember anyone from your time here at the hotel—anyone with the tattoo. Just share the first image that comes to you."

Evan grinned and tilted his head back as though looking up at someone. "I remember getting on a private jet with a large man, bigger even than the fat man. The plane was his. He told me that he won it through gambling. We flew together, but there was another man with us, an older man. I remember going to a remote place."

"Good. More like that. Give me another one, please," the doctor ordered as they worked hour after hour to bring up and refine the slightest detail of his interactions from before.

GALEN WAS NEAR THE BOTTOM of a bottle of red wine when a light knock at the door of the study broke their concentration.

"I am sorry to disturb you, sir," said Mr. Diltz through the closed door, "but you did ask me to inform you when they arrived."

The physician held up a lone finger to ask for a momentary break from Evan. "Are they all here?"

"Not all, but most of them are."

"Very well. Please tell them I will arrive shortly and to get some wine ready."

A nervous rush raced through Evan's body as he thought about the opportunity of meeting others. *Do they trust me enough for me to meet them?*

"As I said, this hotel doesn't keep its secrets for very long. There are some people here who would like to meet you."

"Is it allowed?" Evan asked, swallowing hard. "Do you think I am ready?"

"It is," Galen answered, "and I do think you are ready. I think it could help you further. Besides, they may not take no for an answer. Come on. You can take it at your own pace," he said, unfolding his long frame from the comfort of the chair. "I want to see what wine they picked for me."

They left the study together and walked down the long wood-paneled hall toward the large dining room. Evan heard the voices and laughter of the others as he and Galen approached the swinging door. He stopped for a nervous moment and listened to the voices on the other side.

Galen turned to him. "It's fine, come in. They want to see you."

Evan shook his head and craned his ear toward the half-opened door. "Is that man called Samas?" he asked in a rush of emotion, after hearing one loud bellow behind the door.

Galen smiled. "Very good. I think our work today is already helping you. Do you recognize any others?"

"Give me a second." Evan closed his eyes. "That sounds like the large man with the jet. Chance."

Galen nodded. "Now you are just showing off. Come on. Come and meet them again." He smiled and pushed the door open to reveal four men and one woman sitting at the near end of the long banquet table. The physician strode in first, and all conversation turned to him.

7

"Good doctor!" came the first shout.

"Is he with you?" came another voice.

"What have you done with him?" came a third. "Let us see him."

"Physician," Galen corrected as he extended a long arm back through the open doorway. "Yes, he is. I have been working with him for a few days now, and I think it is time you all meet him. Gentlemen and lady, I present to you our long-lost Evan Michaels."

Evan exhaled twice to purge the nervous energy from his trembling body before taking his cue and walking into the boisterous dining room. They rose in turn and stepped forward.

A short, unfamiliar man was first—young with a mop of curly black hair, only a few years older than Evan. "I don't believe we know each other yet," he said, offering his hand to Evan. "But I have read your notebooks, and I do hope you are who you claim to be. I will give you my name as your brother if you pass your Ascension and rejoin our family. Until then, you can call me Cy."

The woman was next. "Do you remember this face?"

He gazed into her steel-gray eyes and marveled at her long, sharp nose. She was familiar but older and now had touches of gray hair at her temples. *Of course older—his memories of them would not have aged and he would need to adjust for that.* He closed his eyes as if to bring an image into focus. "I remember a café. I had a cane, and you recognized it. Your name is Ramsay."

She reached her arms around him before he could continue. "We heard about Tunisia and assumed the worst. I tried to get you out, but by then it seemed you had made your choice. Welcome back. Where did you come from this time?"

"Damascus."

"You don't say. I've been spending a great deal of time in Syria recently. Let's talk about that later." She stepped aside, and a tall, angular, professorial Middle Eastern–looking man stepped forward.

"And me," he said through a jumbled row of irregular teeth. "What do you remember of me?"

"The tattoo," Evan said without hesitation, imagining this man twenty years younger. "You gave me that tattoo"—he reached out and took the man's dark hands in his own—"with these hands."

"That's right. I am Auda," he said as he moved forward to embrace him, but Evan cut him off.

"And you were going to kill me with a spear," Evan said as the memory came back to him, "with a spear that hangs on the wall downstairs."

Giant Chance burst into laughter. "Ha! With all the others who've darkened our door, how do we know if you're the real Evan?" He brushed Auda aside and grasped the young man's shoulders in his massive black hands. "Let's have a look at this one," the oversized man said, stepping back to admire him like a statue. "Wide shoulders, a strong jaw, decent height, straight nose—I bet all the girls in Damascus chased you. But you have serious and stern eyes, like those of a killer," he offered, looking over at Ramsay.

"Or of a gambler," she countered with a laugh.

The last person in the room was the man who had been the focus of so much of Evan's emotions. He stood behind the table and propped himself over a cane held with a fat left hand. The man was even more rotund than Evan remembered. His bulk hung over his two short legs like an architectural marvel. He moved slowly around the table in cautious triptych steps with the supporting cane. He opened his arms, but Evan thrust out a single open hand to greet the man as some yet-to-be-identified distrust prevented him from accepting the embrace.

Samas stopped and took the offered hand. "Is that really you in there?"

"I remember you. I remember our deal now," Evan countered. "And I remember what it brought me."

Samas tried to brush off his tone with a smile. "Do you remember that you are a very rich man now?"

"That part is not clear to me yet," he said, looking back at Galen. "Other parts are clearer."

"Perhaps this will be clear to you," the overweight man said as he snatched up the cane and presented the carved dragon-head handle to the younger man.

Evan took the walking stick and admired the intricate carving on the scales that surrounded blue gem eyes and sharply carved ivory teeth. *He had walked with this when he descended into the grotto below, and it was with him when he was arrested.* "But this was gone," Evan said, confused. "How did you—"

"It came up in a Swiss police auction, and I recognized it. I thought you might eventually want it. Take it. You will know if it is yours. I trust that more will come to you in time, my friend. If you pass your Ascension, you really should check your account balance to see what your inheritance looks like," Samas said, retracing his steps back around the table.

Galen spoke up to break the tension hanging in the air between the two men. "Who has wine for me?"

Chance thrust a full glass into Galen's hand, and Auda pushed one into Evan's. "Let's see if he drinks like one of us."

Ramsay spoke first. "So when does his Ascension begin? Galen, have you reached out to all of us to get this started? Has he chosen his judges and his advocate yet?"

Galen ignored the questions as he admired the wine's color in the light. "Wait a minute, is someone trying to stump me with this bottle?"

"I told you he'd know it," Auda said.

"Let him try on this one," Samas replied.

Galen swirled the amber liquid in his glass, took a sip, and mused on its origin. "Light yet firm, some chalk, definitely the Loire Valley. It is Anjou wine, is it not? Within the last year or two, I should think."

"Told you so," Auda said, holding out an open hand to Samas to collect his wager.

"Now to your questions, my friend," Galen said, turning to Ramsay. "He has only returned to us a few days ago. And we have begun work on his recall." Galen slipped an arm around Evan. "And yes, I have called everyone to let them know. Many more are coming in the approaching days. Evan has the right to start his Ascension whenever he is ready."

Cy spoke up. "You are wise to work with Galen on your recall. He has helped many of us."

"How are your memories coming?" Ramsey asked.

"He is progressing quite well," Galen interrupted on Evan's behalf, "but I think we need at least another day before he faces a panel of his choosing."

Evan leaned forward at the table. "I don't remember being able to choose my panel of judges last time." He looked at Auda and then at Ramsay. "I did not choose you, did I?"

Samas spoke up. "The first time a candidate comes forward, he is unknown to all of us and a panel is chosen for him. Returning candidates have the right to choose their own panel. As you now claim to be Evan Michaels and are returning to us, you can choose whichever five of us you like."

"He is right," Galen said. "You should think about who would best be able to know you and identify you clearly from your past interactions with them."

"How long does the Ascension take for a 'returning candidate' like me?" Evan asked, rubbing his hand over the dragon-head handle, trying to recall its feel in his palm.

Galen looked over at Auda. "Sometimes it can be as short as a day."

"It has happened before," Auda dismissed. "Part of it depends on how ready you are to recall everything and have it match what was written before, another part is who you choose as your judges. Some judges are easier than others, some who you have a history with might hold a grudge and make it harder—or even impossible," he said, glancing at Samas. "But your case is different now because of the notebooks. Others have read your account and know some of your facts," Auda chastised. "Anyone claiming to be Evan Michaels—and you are not the first— would need to provide new information that outsiders could not have learned from those journals."

Everyone nodded at Auda's comment, including Galen.

"His words have caused me to be recognized for my tattoo," Samas said.

Evan leaned forward and spoke, cutting off Samas as he prepared to interject. "Galen, I understand that I made a mistake in writing down my story, even with the precaution I took by writing it in Bulgarian so that the cellmate I asked to keep it for me wouldn't be able to read it. I apologize for that, but I would like to start the process to rejoin as soon as I can. How long would it take to assemble it?" He asked the question to both Galen and Auda.

"Well, many more are coming tonight and tomorrow. It would be enough, but the better question is who?" Auda asked. "Who knows you, or better stated, who knew you well enough last time to be able to verify your claim to us?"

Evan gripped the cane like a new talisman as he tilted his head back and looked at the ceiling, trying to remember faces from the collection of memories he had placed on the wall today. He looked around the room at each face in turn. "Samas would know me. I spent time with him. He would remember details no one else could know. Chance might know me. When he flew me to Yemen, we spoke on his plane. I think he would remember that." He turned to look at Ramsay. "We only spent that afternoon together at the café, but I think you already recognize me," he said to her.

"That leaves two," Galen said.

Evan lowered his eyes to his wine glass on the table. "The woman with the flower tattoo—she would know me again."

"Poppy! She is on her way," Auda interrupted. "She should be here later tonight. She was most interested to hear of your return to us."

"Really?" Evan asked, a curious tone in his voice. "What did she want to know?"

"She asked if you were male or female, and what you looked like. Diltz gave me a description, and I passed it on to her."

Chance looked over at Evan. "Just wait until she gets her nails into you. I imagine she'll know if you are our returning brother."

"That's four," Ramsay said, looking around the room.

"Count me out, I was gone," Cy said, shaking his shock of black curls. "I didn't know you."

"Well, me neither, technically," Galen said.

"I should likely be excluded as well," Auda added with a smile. "I only interacted with you at your Ascension festival, and memories are always a bit fuzzy from those events."

Evan thought back to the sharpening memories of an old man standing alone next to a stone lighthouse. That man would know him and would help him.

"The old man at the lighthouse, Clovis," Evan stated solemnly. "He would know me for sure, but I left him rather suddenly—and rudely—when I saw him last. Is he still with us? Is he still alive?"

"He is," Chance affirmed in his bass voice. "But he cannot travel. He is not well enough, or at least he pretends to be not well enough, so he could not participate."

"That is not entirely true," Auda said. "Remember when Kress came back to us the second time. She needed Jens as a judge, but he was in the Bastille. Kress went to visit him, and he presented his judgment as a letter to the other four." He took a long sip of wine from his glass. "There is a precedent for judging remotely."

"It is true. I remember that," Galen said. "We could start here, and then Evan could travel to see Clovis and spend time with him to get his testimony."

"I have a way to make the transmission of his testimony back to us secure," Ramsay said, glancing at Evan. "Not that we don't trust you, but we have to respect the Ascension process. There is a language that both Clovis and I can still write, speak, and understand. We can ask him to write it to me in that language, and I will present his judgment to the assembly."

"Cuneiform?" Cy asked, stifling a laugh.

"Funny. Nineteen hundred years old and you somehow find an age joke that can still sting," she said, narrowing her gray eyes at him. "Aramaic."

"I can fly you there again," Chance offered. "There is a war on now, but I have my ways to stop in and check on the old man from time to time."

"Well, this almost sounds like a plan," Ramsay said, looking around for another bottle.

Evan stood up and looked at Samas. "With all respect that is due to you for last time," he said before turning to address Galen, "Galen, I ask you to be my advocate for my Ascension."

Galen walked to him. He had anticipated this but wanted to give the moment all the weight the young man's request deserved. "I accept," he stated proudly and opened his arms to embrace Evan.

Evan's mind flashed back to those nights around campfires on his refugee walk from Syria. *How many nights had he dreamed of being in this hotel, of being embraced by this family again?* An emotional Evan eventually pulled himself away from Galen and composed himself enough to raise a near-empty wine glass. "I know I was only with you for a short time last time, but I hope I can join your ranks again and stay there this time."

"*Amicitia pares aut accipit aut facit*," Galen said, draining his glass to the toast.

Chance squinted at Galen as he translated his rusty Latin. "'Friendship either accepts equals or makes them so,'" he said as he thought about the origin of the quote. "Juvenal?"

"Aristotle," Galen answered with a proud smile.

"You Greeks," Chance challenged, shaking his head. "Oh Greece, how you recaptured your savage victors."

"It is a plan then," Ramsay shouted, rising to her feet. "Now let us cement these plans with some more wine. I assume you would like to choose, Doctor."

"Physician," Cy countered.

"Soldiers, advance!" Ramsay shouted, leading them out to the wine room.

Samas leaned forward in his chair. "Evan, may I speak with you for a moment?"

Evan stayed behind as the others left in search of their quarry.

Samas started as soon as they departed. "Evan, I have thought about what I would say to you hundreds of times, but now the only thing I can think to say is that I am so very happy to see you again, my friend."

The familiar cane shook in his hand as a flood of fresh memories of prison and torture crashed over Evan while Samas continued, "I can imagine how you feel about me right now and how you felt then in Tunisia—I would never discount that—but I want you to know how I feel first. I missed you. I worried about you. I couldn't wait until you came back, even if it meant weathering a deserved wrath. If you feel anger and hatred for me, that is understandable and perhaps even justified. But after you ascend and embrace an improved life, I hope you will remember that I, for all my flaws, made part of that new life possible." Samas paused for a moment. "I also want you to know that I will judge you fairly, even after your collusion with her against me for our prize."

"The painting was *your* prize," Evan snapped.

"My prize," Samas conceded. "Evan, have that confidence that I will judge you fairly and that I look forward to having you back with us, but I will give you your distance."

"My God, how I hated you," Evan spat at him in a swell of emotion that surprised him as more memories of the Tunisian prison came back to him. "It is just now returning to me how much I hated you for what I endured in that prison. I may hate you for a while yet."

"I told you the risks and your way out should the worst happen."

"Oh, and I faced them, didn't I?" Evan flared. "I faced those risks and those consequences when you would not do it, could not do it.

And you couldn't do it, could you? From that cell, during that torture, I tried to imagine you in my place and never could. You hired me as you would purchase courage from some vendor of valors."

Samas raised his head on a stiffening neck. "True. My specialty is hedonism, not heroism. I did use you for that, but you agreed to your price, didn't you?"

Evan nodded slowly. "I did, but now I wonder if it will ever be enough." He let the sentence hang in the air between them as he heard the others walking back toward the dining hall, glass bottles clinking.

"Well, they are still here," Auda said.

"And in one piece," Ramsay added. "Our good doctor has made some excellent selections for us."

Mr. Pianosa helped them carry the bounty of wine into the dining room, and they placed ten different bottles on the table. Galen turned each faded label to face the front as though preparing a tasting.

Evan joined the discussion. "Galen, how did you come to know so much about wine? When you told me of your time at the gladiator academy, you said you didn't like wine then."

"That was true. I developed my taste for the grape on a medical mission of sorts and in doing so found the best wine the world has ever known."

"What? The Palatine cellar story again?" Ramsay asked.

"Yes," Galen declared with pride.

"I want to hear it," Evan said.

"The best wine the world has ever known?" Cy repeated. "*This* I want to hear."

Galen filled their glasses. "I was telling Evan yesterday about my time in the eastern part of the Roman Empire, but my real goal was always to get to Rome, which I did a few years later. If you never saw it, it is hard to describe how impressive, how impactful, the Eternal City was at its height. You just felt dwarfed by everything, with no reference for how things could be so big. Rome was like a giant magnet that attracted the best of everything from all corners of the empire, including wine."

"And doctors, no doubt," young Cy joked.

Galen smiled. "Precisely, but I struggled at first in Rome, as many other physicians didn't like my attitude about new treatments. My first big break came when I was summoned to Palatine Hill for a meeting. When I got there, I found two of my most vocal rivals waiting in a royal reception room. They greeted me coolly and didn't reply when I asked them why we had been summoned there. I soon found out when an attendant brought us into an opulent room where Emperor Marcus Aurelius reclined on a sofa. He looked terrible. He was pale as plaster, and his breathing was shallow and rapid.

"The oldest and, in my opinion, the worst physician examined him first. 'Surgery,' he declared. 'The emperor must have surgery at once.' The second physician prescribed bloodletting, vigorous bloodletting to balance the humors. I went last. I remember it felt odd that I was not the least bit nervous at approaching our Emperor. His eyes struggled to focus as I worked over him. I inspected his pupils and tongue and pressed my fingers into his abdomen to test his reactions. I was satisfied that it was a digestive problem—not life-threatening. I pronounced my diagnosis to the group and prescribed that a solution of herbed white wine mixed with pepper be drunk four times a day for three days and that he eat no other food. The others scoffed at my diagnosis, but His Majesty mustered enough strength to accept my direction and start the treatment.

"I went to the market to get the wine, herbs, and pepper that I needed, then I returned to the palace for my preparations. He drank it but didn't appear to like it very much. I didn't think much of it because he was in a lot of pain. His aides moved me into a room at the back of the palace so that I could attend to him. He improved and recovered fully, and on the last prescribed treatment, he asked me to stay beside him for a while."

Galen poured wine for all of them as they listened. "He was as nice as you would think he would be," the physician said as he continued his story. "He thanked me for healing him. Then he looked at me sternly and told me that my medical knowledge was excellent, but that my taste in wine was shit. The emperor actually used that word. He said if

I expected to stay on as his staff physician, I should prepare my treatments with the best wine in the empire.

"What was I supposed to do? I had healed the most powerful man in the world with market wine that his Praetorians wouldn't drink. I agreed to his offer to have someone show me around the imperial cellars under Palatine Hill with the hopes that he would keep me on as his personal physician. He summoned a guard, who led me into the darkened depths that lay under that noble hill.

"The cellar structure itself was massive. Amphorae-lined, hand-carved tunnels ran in every direction, and the five levels were connected by stairs crudely cut into the red earth of that hill. The clay wine vessels were stopped with wooden corks coated in thick beeswax. These proved to be excellent seals, and even the oldest wines I found were well preserved. Every group of amphorae had a sign hanging above it, noting the region, grape variety, and year. I knew I had a large task on my hands and I would increase my chances of winning his favor as staff physician if I could detail my notes on the best wines, and so I began my thirsty labors of cataloging the imperial wine cellar. The younger wines were at the lowest levels and I assumed, incorrectly, that they would be best suited to my needs.

"On my word, the lowest levels of that place, noble as it might have been above, were like scenes from Hades. There was no light, save my single lantern, and *remnants*, to be charitable, from previous tasters fouled the air. But the worst were the spiders—so big you could hear them crawling around. I saw them, more than once, trap, envenom, and slowly devour small rats, and they often worked together in teams of two and three. It was ghastly. But I persevered quickly through that lower-level drinking, writing my notes, developing a palate for average and good wine of all varieties.

"I would work, tasting and drinking really, to the point of exhaustion or inebriation, whichever came first. Some nights I slept on the floor, but never on the lowest level. Most nights I climbed back up and made it to my small room at the back of the palace.

"I worked for the better part of two months, and at the end of that time, at the end of the longest corridor on the first level covered in dust,

I found the Falernian.[9] It was a revelation of what wine could be, what enjoyment and pleasure could be. The wines got better as I rose through the levels, but nothing prepared me for what I found in the amphora under the handwritten sign titled Opimian Vintage.[10]

"That taste changed my life for better and, in some ways, for worse. Like an addict who chases that first fleeting high, I have pursued that wine's equal through the ages and found none to match it. I drank out of that one vessel alone for five full days, savoring and writing. I knew my work was done. I compiled my notes and ordered a guard to bring up my opened amphora. After recovering for a few days, I asked to see His Majesty and presented my findings as we shared glasses of Falernian.

"The emperor sipped it for a long time without speaking, but eventually turned to me and said, 'Now how much more pleasurable would my recovery have been had you treated me with this? Well done, the position is yours.' And he dismissed me with a wave of his hand, but I had to leave my cup and *his* amphora behind."

"I have heard of that vintage," Samas said, holding out an emptied glass for an attentive Pianosa to refill. "What do you think most compares to it today?"

"It was a white wine but the color of aged scotch. The closest I have found to how it can age so well are some of the balanced Chenins from the Loire Valley, wines like Jasnieres or Quarts de Chaume, but you have to let them age for fifty to one hundred years to find out, and even then only some years will be close to that magical."

"Do you know where to find some of these near-magical vintages?" Samas pressed.

---

9. Falernian wine was a favorite in Roman times. Galen wrote about it and its virtues in *De Antidotis* (*On Antidotes*) as did Pliny, Marcus Aurelius, and Columella. Supposedly, it was grown on the lower slopes of Mount Falernus in what today would be in the Lazio region. It may well exist today as the Aminean grape or the Aglianico blanco.

10. Named after Roman consul Lucius Opimius, who rebuilt the Temple of Concord in Rome, this famous vintage from 121 BC was well known and well chronicled in its time. This is the very vintage that Petronius describes drinking at his dinner banquet in the Satyricon, and Roman historian Pliny wrote that it was served to the Emperor Caligula.

"I know some families in the region who have archives," he teased.

Diltz knocked lightly and poked his head around the door for a second. "Yes, the young gentleman is here," he said to someone still behind the door.

In an instant, a striking Asian woman elegantly pushed Diltz aside and entered the room. She wore a stylish gray evening gown that opened in the back to reveal bold orange tattooed flowers. Two long silver hairpins anchored rolls of black hair into a tower atop her head.

Auda was closest to the door and rose first to greet her. "Poppy darling, how are you, my dear? So glad you could make it tonight. A bit overdressed, aren't we?"

"For you perhaps," she quipped. "I was at a fundraiser in Paris." She stepped forward to embrace him, but her eyes kept searching the faces in the room for Evan.

Ramsay stood, and Poppy extended a strong hand. "Hello, shooter," Poppy said dryly.

"If you say so," Ramsay countered with a sly smile.

Cy stepped forward, and she embraced him. "I heard you were here," she said. "So nice to see you, my friend. Let me know if you want to fly back to Los Angeles with me."

"Doctor!" she said to Galen as he stood, her eyes still looking over the room.

He stifled a grin and embraced the petite woman.

Mr. Pianosa stepped forward with a fresh glass for her, "Wine, madame?"

Poppy looked at the new innkeeper and then back at Galen. "Is this him?"

"That's the new innkeeper, Poppy," Galen corrected.

"Marcelo Pianosa," the young apprentice said as he extended a hand toward her tattooed one.

"The new innkeeper," she repeated. "I need to attend more of our meetings." Poppy took the apprentice innkeeper's strong hand and held it for a moment before turning him from side to side to admire the taper of his frame from broad shoulder to trim waist. "You'll do nicely, Mr. Pianosa," she said before spinning to face Diltz. "Are you leaving us?"

Mr. Diltz straightened his stooped posture and smiled. "Yes, my dear. I am retiring."

"Aww," Poppy said, moving toward him for a tender hug. "I didn't know."

"I've been planning it for a while now, and we are fortunate enough to have Mr. Pianosa to take my place. He has been studying under me for the past six months since he left his position in the Swiss Guard and passed his background check."

"How much longer do we have you?" she asked Mr. Diltz, casting a longing eye back at his replacement.

"Mr. Pianosa will be ready to assume all duties in a matter of weeks," Diltz replied confidently.

"We should have a celebration for you," Poppy said with her arms held wide before turning to the others. "Don't you think we should honor him before he moves on?"

She scanned the nodding faces in the room until she landed on Samas. He didn't bother to get up out of his burdened chair, and she didn't take time to recognize him. "Now, where were we?" she asked no one in particular as she scanned the room and locked eyes with her target. The room fell silent as she walked around the table toward Evan. Her eyes met with his as she stood in front of him. Her gaze followed his fit frame until she saw the walking cane clutched fast in his left hand. "Has he had this the whole time?" she asked the others.

"Samas just gave it to him to see if it helps him with his recall," Ramsay offered.

Poppy took his right hand in hers and opened it. She examined his palm and ran a delicate finger over hardened calluses. "You have worked hard to find us, haven't you?"

Evan stood transfixed, his voice failing him at seeing this woman from his visions. She turned his hand over and traced the prominent veins on the back of his hand with a long, silver-painted fingernail. "Do you remember our fun together?"

The emotions of seeing her paralyzed him. *How many times had she come to him in those early memories?* She looked younger than he thought she should have. She was more beautiful, more alluring, more *everything* than he remembered.

She looked back up into his dark eyes and ran her fingertips along the edge of his clenched jaw. "Is that really you in there, lover?"

"His recall with me is very promising so far," Galen said as if trying to help his stunned patient.

She tightened her grip on Evan's hand as she faced the physician. "I will know if it's him," she said, pulling Evan with her toward the door. "Let's go reacquaint ourselves, shall we?" A compliant Evan willingly followed. "I will let you know in the morning if we have our man," she shouted back to the group.

"*Nihil difficile amanti*,"[11] Galen said, raising a glass to toast them as they walked out hand in hand.

Poppy grabbed a silver purse she had left outside the door and led him toward the guest rooms. "Do you remember your room number?" she asked.

"Room Twenty-Nine," Evan just managed to say.

She turned to look at him and smiled widely, her eyes warm and welcoming. "Good." She moved close to him and rested her head on his shoulder as they walked. "I missed you. Did you miss me? Do you remember me yet?"

Evan nodded as he unlocked the door to Room 29, and they both stepped inside.

"Give me a moment, will you?" she said, stepping into his bathroom.

She emerged a few minutes later, naked and with her hair down. A narrow band of red circled her left arm where the rubber tube of the tourniquet had held her. She placed a small leather pouch on the nightstand before lying on his bed. "Come to me, lover." She ran her hands over his taut chest and encircled his narrow waist as she drew closer.

---

11. Latin—Nothing is difficult for lovers, Cicero

He stiffened in her arms and looked at her but could not find the words.

Her eyes widened as a giggle rose in her throat. "You haven't been with anyone in this body, have you?"

Evan blushed and squeezed his lips together.

She reached out and ran her hand over his short-cropped black hair to put him at ease. "Well, that just means you haven't been with anyone since you were last with me. Use this young body to love me the way you did in Los Angeles." She locked her dark eyes with his and pulled him on top of her. "Show me the man I knew then, and I will burn for him."

8

When Evan woke up, there was no trace that Poppy had been in his room, and he had no idea when in the night she had left. He tried to recall her scent as he replayed the fresh memory of her in his bed. He walked into the bathroom and saw *I vote yes* written with her red lipstick on his mirror. He smiled and touched his finger to that red edge of validation. She had been one of the first people he had remembered, and he had hoped to see her in this place. It felt good to connect with her as a lover, as another touchstone to his past, as someone who recognized him and accepted him. But he still felt some caution about her well up from some unremembered place.

He showered, dressed, grabbed the cane, and left his room to find a handwritten note placed on a chair in the hallway next to his door. His heart quickened in anticipation of what other note she had left him, and he picked it up.

Meet me in the study to begin our preparations. —Galen

Evan folded the note into his pocket and walked to meet his advocate.

Galen sat in the same chair; the familiar scribe sat in his usual chair. Evan walked over to the low fire that burned in the large hearth and tossed the note onto the starving flames. "Good morning," Galen said.

"I trust you don't require the cane today after your reacquaintance with Poppy last night?"

"I just felt like bringing it with me," he said, settling into the chair facing the physician. "Did you see her this morning?"

"Yes, briefly. She will be rejoining us tonight. I saw to that."

"Good," Evan said, watching the flames for a moment before turning to the silent scribe and then to Galen. "I am ready to begin."

Galen smiled. "Evan, I am honored that you chose me as your advocate to represent you and guide you through your Ascension. I have organized everything and would like to review it with you before we begin today.

"Our family, the Cognomina, is ready to begin your Ascension tonight. Per your request, I have seated Chance, Samas, Ramsay, Poppy, and Clovis as your judges. You will see an empty seat tonight in the middle of the panel, which is Clovis's honorary seat. You will be judged by four starting tonight, and Chance has agreed to fly you to meet Clovis at his home the day after we have finished. He will stop for you on his return to Zurich four days later. That should give you plenty of time with Clovis. The panel and assembly will stay together and await your return, where Ramsay will read out Clovis's notes and judgment of you."

"I understand."

"As your advocate, I need to review the rules and structure of your Ascension with you, even though you have completed one. Your first one was a neophyte Ascension, and those are quite rare. Yours was the first one in nearly a century. Those neophyte Ascensions are very detailed and take a long time for the judges to corroborate because the Cognomina has no relationship or shared experiences with the candidate. The normal ones, after a member has ascended one time, are often more straightforward affairs because you will know things only Evan Michaels would have known from those shared experiences with those who will judge you."

A light knock came at the door ahead of three kitchen staffers carrying platters of food and bottles of wine.

"Do you remember the risk involved in declaring your intent for the Ascension trial?"

"You mean the spear they threatened to kill me with after I passed last time?" Evan asked.

Galen smiled. "Yes, I heard about that." His face became serious again. "I am required as your advocate to communicate the risk around failure. If you fail this test, we *will* kill you."

"I remember Diltz told me before that other neophyte candidates had failed and had been killed, but no neophyte who failed and was killed ever returned to claim the Ascension."

"That is true. Regrettably, I participated in two of them."

"Were you their advocate?"

"I was. As a physician over these centuries, I have treated both physical and mental afflictions and in doing so have encountered and discovered many new members of the Cognomina. I have found and sponsored the most by far," Galen said, raising his glass toward Evan. "To all the ones like us who are still out there, undiscovered."

"Do you think there are many more out there like us?" Evan asked.

Galen lowered his nose to his glass and closed his eyes before he spoke. "I believe there are many more of us out there—alone, undiscovered, misunderstood, misdiagnosed, medicated, institutionalized."

"Confused," Evan added, "and wrestling with madness."

Galen nodded solemnly. "And how many of them, out there alone without our help, will lose that battle?"

"I would likely have been one of them, had Poppy not found me last time," Evan said, remembering her fierce eyes from last night. "Do you think those undiscovered others go mad if they don't find us?"

"They could," Galen mused. "They could even stay that way, possibly carrying that madness into their next remembered lives like a series of recurring tragedies."

"Well, there is at least one who is out there, alone," Evan said as a memory from his previous Ascension came back to him. "The one excommunicated by the Cognomina."

Galen froze, only his eyes looking up from his glass to Evan. "That was a long time ago, and it was something you were not a part of." The doctor let out a long sigh as if remembering something painful. "That person was someone that I knew and loved like a sister until she lost her bout with madness," Galen said as he moved his eyes toward the glass again, "and stayed that way."

Evan regretted bringing up that painful topic and decided to change the subject. "How did it feel when you watched them die, the candidates you sponsored who did not pass their Ascension?"

"Well, I didn't just watch them," Galen answered in a cold voice. "I killed them. It is the advocate's responsibility to dispatch his failed candidate. This is why I am taking this time to detail the risk." He opened his hands toward the younger man. "These hands are for healing, not killing."

Evan froze with the chill of Galen's unflinching words. *Will this man kill me if I fail their test? Is it worth everything to try to come back here?* "Has a returning candidate ever failed an Ascension?"

"Never, but that does not mean you should not prepare as we have done these past days. Evan, there is one final item I would like to review with you before we start tonight. I want to focus on getting the details of any interactions you had with the five judges around the time of our last Ascension. Let's refine the detail on those shared experiences you had with them, even if they were only brief."

Evan nodded and set down his plate. "All right, I'm ready."

GALEN QUESTIONED EVAN INTO THE EARLY EVENING until a knock at the door interrupted their final preparations. Diltz poked his head around the door. "They are assembling, gentlemen. It is time."

Galen gave Evan a warm smile. "Are you ready?"

Evan nodded. "Can I bring this?" he asked, tapping the brass tip of the cane against the polished hardwood floor.

"Sure. Since you had it before, I think it is appropriate," the lanky physician said as he rose and led Evan out of the study, turning right toward the long hallway of guest rooms. "Evan, if they ask you a question that you don't know or cannot recall the answer to, just take a moment and try your best to recall it. If you cannot, just say you don't remember." He motioned back to the scribe, who followed them ten paces behind with his oversized volume. "As you might have noticed, we write a lot of things down here, and the last thing you want is to have inaccurate or, worse, fictitious information in our archive."

"I understand."

They walked past Poppy's room, and Evan thought he heard a male voice inside as a cold knot rose in the pit of his stomach. They walked past Evan's room near the end of the corridor and stopped in front of the last guest room door on the left. Galen turned the doorknob and urged Evan inside. Evan looked around the plain guest room and instinctively walked to the closed bathroom door that disguised a hidden world below. "I remember what is beyond this door," Evan said, his voice cracking.

"After you," Galen said, motioning for Evan to go through the door first.

Evan opened the bathroom door and looked down at the amazing sight he knew he would see. Before him lay not an ordinary bathroom, but instead a narrow, ancient stone staircase that descended into the darkness of the earth. Small torches hung on the walls at regular intervals and cast flickering warm light down the carved stairs.

He ran his hand along the cold stone masonry of the walls and thought not of the one time before when he had felt their texture with another man's hand, but instead his mind wandered toward all the future times he would descend these stairs. He imagined each new time would be filled with anticipation and doubt like today. *How many more times would he do this? What would those bodies look like? What would those new people have to say and recall about him and his time now? What treasures or experiences would they wish for him to collect now as a waiting inheritance?*

He listened to the click of his cane against stone and Galen's steps behind him and felt comfort that he had succeeded at this once before. Faint voices echoed up the stairs once they were halfway down the roughly one hundred steps to the open cavern he knew from the visions would greet them at the bottom. He heard the voices clearly as he reached the last of the torches and turned at the landing to see the impressive grotto open before them.

Evan had not remembered the immense size of the room. The ceiling was over twenty feet high, supported by double rows of thick, ornately carved stone columns that rose out of an open expanse of polished black stone floor that shone like moonlit waters in the flickering firelight of large silver braziers. Evan turned to the right to view the heavy, floor-to-ceiling black velvet curtain that ran the width of the room and divided it in two. Spectators settled into two rows of seats on a small, elevated platform in front of that massive black cloth. He struggled to see their faces in the low torchlight but could see the outlines of the distinctive black tattoos on their hands. A lone table and two chairs stood near the middle of the room, facing a long judge's bench with five high-backed chairs along the back wall.

Galen directed Evan to the table, and they both sat down. A pitcher of water, two open bottles of wine, and a crystal ashtray sat on the table. Evan's eyes slowly adjusted to the low light. He looked above the empty judge's bench and admired the spear that still hung there. It was as long as a man, and the large black tip capped what looked like stained brown blood on the white wooden shaft.

Galen instinctively turned his head toward the curtain at the first mechanical clanging sound, which was the chain-operated pulley that moved the massive shroud away from the wall to create a small passageway.

Evan turned and watched Chance step through the gap, followed by Ramsay, then Samas, and finally Poppy. He couldn't take his eyes off her. She wore a dark suit crisscrossed with widely spaced vertical and horizontal white stripes that formed a sharp windowpane pattern against the black. Her straight hair was down, framing her pale face like a black border. She strode into the room in black high heels with white trim that tapped lightly against the stone floor with every deliberate step. Ramsay took a seat at the far end, and Chance sat next to her. Samas left the middle seat vacant as he sat at the other end.

Poppy peered around the edge of her hair to see Evan watching her. She paused in her parade to the bench and stepped toward her lover with a quickened pace. All eyes followed her as she approached Evan's table and ran a long silver fingernail along the bottom of his jaw before stepping behind the bench. She passed the empty seat next to Samas and stooped to whisper to Ramsay, who rose and offered her seat before moving down next to the large man.

Chance looked over at Poppy. "Are we ready to begin?"

"Oh, I started my trial with him last night," Poppy replied, not missing a beat. "I'm a yes."

Several laughs came from the gallery. Chance kept his gaze on her for a moment before continuing, "As our brother Clovis cannot join us here today, I take the responsibility of directing this trial tonight. Galen, would you please begin for us?"

Galen rose, bowed to the gallery, bowed to the bench, and put his hand on Evan's shoulder. "I present to you Evan Michaels, a returning brother who wishes to rejoin the Cognomina."

Chance raised a hand to silence soft murmurings from the gallery. "Does the candidate know the risks involved?"

"Yes, he has been informed and he wishes to continue," Galen stated as he removed his hand from Evan's shoulder and walked toward the gallery. "I will act as his advocate for his Ascension."

"You may wish to confer further, as I propose a slight change to our process for this Ascension, given the unique circumstances surrounding your candidate," Chance stated.

"What change?" Galen challenged.

Chance drew in a deep breath through flaring nostrils. "Advocate, candidate, and gallery," he began in a booming voice that echoed against the confines of the grotto, "never in our family's long history has any member been so careless about our cherished privacy." The giant man leveled his dark eyes down at Evan. "Your notebooks have exposed us to the world in a most unwelcome way. And further, they have attracted impostors who wish to join this group. You are the first Evan Michaels to make it this far. If you are indeed the man I knew, then I will be the first to embrace you as a brother—but any validating details from your lives that were included in your published notebooks should be forbidden during this Ascension."

Evan turned to see many nodding heads in the gallery along with murmurs of approval.

Chance turned toward Galen. "Advocate, please confer with your candidate to ensure he wishes to proceed with this solemn ceremony."

Galen turned to Evan, who kept his eyes fixed on Chance. "This will make things harder," he whispered. "There is no shame in asking for a delay for us to regroup and work to recall more points that were not in the notebooks."

Evan broke his gaze from Chance and looked up at the long spear hanging on the wall over his head. *I have come back before, I will come back again*, he thought as he focused on the rust-colored stains behind the broad point. *I can convince them.*

"I apologize for the harm I have caused us," Evan said in full voice. "My intention was to leave a record for my future self to find. It was not to expose us." He waited for the dissenting voices to fall silent and then looked up to the spear. "But I remember who I am," he declared. "I am ready to take my place here again."

Chance nodded and looked to the other judges for their approval. "Very well, let us begin. Evan, how many lives have you had?"

"This is my fourth. I remember three others."

"What is your name now, in this life?" Chance continued.

"I am called Yousef Azmah."

"And what are your parents' names?"

"My mother is Fatima, my father is Amir."

Evan noticed three white-outfitted scribes sitting at the end of the front row of the gallery, the middle one seemed to be capturing his answers in real time.

"So they are still alive? What is the address of their home? Do you have any siblings? Where did you attend school?" Chance's early questions explored his time in Syria as the other judges watched and the scribes took their notes. "What was the first memory that came to you that did not belong to Yousef Azmah?"

Galen stiffened in his seat. This was a question unasked in his preparation.

Evan smiled and reached one hand into his shirt pocket for a cigarette and the other into a pants pocket for his lighter. "It was cigarettes," he said, drawing on the flame. "One day I just remembered smoking. But it was odd, I didn't remember smoking cigarettes so much as I remembered that I smoked—like that was just part of my identity. It wasn't long after that I remembered my favorite brand." He held up the package of Lendts and caught Poppy's knowing smile. "Right after that, I remembered the old lighter that I had as Evan, and I traded for a Russian soldier's lighter that looked like my old one." Evan held up the lighter to show the judges.

"And how long ago did that happen?"

Evan looked up into the black void of the darkened ceiling while trying to recall how many months had passed. "Around eighteen months ago."

"What was the next memory that returned to you?"

Evan stroked the dragon's head and looked straight at Poppy. "I remembered her," he said, staring. "She came to me in dreams at first, then later when I was awake. I thought I was going crazy to have this woman come to me every night and then start haunting my days."

Chance looked over at her and then returned his eyes to Evan. "When were you first convinced that you were not losing your mind?"

"When I learned English in two months, and then when I learned Bulgarian just recently. That is when I knew I was different."

"How did the memory of this place return to you?" Chance asked, motioning to the hotel above the grotto.

"I remembered the outside of the hotel first—how it gleamed white in the sunshine. From there, I remembered the street and the district, then the town itself. And that is when I started my journey here."

Chance nodded and sat back in his chair.

Ramsay lifted a finger to catch Chance's attention for the next question. "Before we move on from the topic, I want to know more about the Azmah family."

"Yes," Evan said, taking another cigarette from the pack.

"Are you still in touch with your mother and father? Do they know you are here in Zurich?"

"My mother knows I am in Europe. The last time I called her was from Hungary. I have not spoken to my father in almost a year," he said as his face lit up from the glow of the lighter.

"Why have you not spoken with him for so long?"

"I wanted to—" Evan began but stopped. "I could feel myself changing then, knowing things I shouldn't know, remembering things I shouldn't be able to, feeling new things that were foreign to me," he said, looking over at Galen. "I had grown strange to them, like an alien in their midst. I stopped going to prayer with him after he demanded that I stop talking about these—" He paused again, and Galen put a hand on his shoulder. "After he demanded that I stop talking about these things that were contrary to Islam. I was his only son, and was now a stranger to him."

Ramsey looked down her straight nose at him for a few seconds as she considered his answer. "Very well," she closed and looked down the bench.

Samas took it as a cue. "Evan, I would like to start with a question, the answer to which only my friend Evan Michaels would know."

"All right," Evan agreed.

"Do you remember the first time we met?"

"I do. I was standing in the hallway of the guest rooms upstairs outside of Poppy's room."

"Inadmissible," barked Chance from the bench. "That was written in the notebooks."

"Quite correct," Samas conceded. "We left the hotel and went somewhere."

Evan nodded, remembering.

"Where did we go?" Samas asked.

Evan pulled out a fresh cigarette and lit it. "We went to a tavern not far from here. I was walking with this cane at the time," he said, tapping it against the black stone floor.

"What did you have to drink with me that night?"

Low murmurs echoed from the gallery at what they thought might be a conclusive point in the trial. Evan tumbled the lighter in his fingers as he tried to recall the detail from that emotional night. "I had a bourbon and a beer."

"Inadmissible," Chance protested again.

Evan felt a cold pressure build in his chest with each bellowed challenge.

"Again, quite right," Samas said with a sly smile. "Candidate, what was the color of the vest I wore that night?"

Galen stiffened along with the low voices from the gallery.

Evan closed his eyes and tried to find this image on the wall of the memory room he created with Galen. "Your vest was—" he started with his eyes still closed. "You didn't wear a vest that night," he said, opening his eyes. "You wore a green velvet jacket and black pants."

Samas smiled quickly at the other three judges, then turned to the gallery and addressed the seated scribes. "I would like the record to state that his answer is accurate. Perfectly accurate."

Galen let out a long exhale beside him. "This is very good," the physician whispered. "What Samas did for you there was very compelling."

Samas turned his attention back to Evan. "Thank you. Now let us get to some of the details of your life as Evan Michaels. Where was Evan Michaels born? What were his parents' names? What was his first job?"

"Inadmissible."

Evan shook off the objection and answered question after question, pacing his progress by the count of crushed cigarette butts in the clear ashtray in front of him. He let his mind drift as he answered inquiries about this somehow distant, yet ever-present *other* man. The memories were native to his mind but still felt alien to this new body, like being an adult and remembering who you had been as a child, or who you would have been before you moved to that new town to start that new life. Is that what this series of lives would always be like—an endless treadmill of new starts, undiscovered, unrequested, unreturnable?

He recognized a few faces in the gallery in the flickering torchlight— Kress, Jens, and the impish Mr. Ing. He studied what detail he could see of their faces and tried, for the first time, to see them not for their current veneer, but for the layers of lives beneath. He imagined each of them sitting in his defendant's chair, recalling the facts and dates from their own half-remembered stranger-selves. Their collections of successes and failures, loves and losses, triumphs and defeats all dumped out as a scattered assortment of irregular stones that you are forced to build a new life from.

"What was your prison time in Tunisia like?" Samas asked.

The question jolted Evan back into focus. He was surprised that Samas, of all people, would be the one to bring it up. "It was dark. It left me utterly defeated, without hope for redemption or relief. It was the hardest thing I have ever done in any life—until I could do it no longer."

Samas did not reply and the tension of his silence compelled Evan to continue. "And when I could endure it no longer, I took a leap of faith that what you and others in this room told me was true: once you come back and remember a past life, you will continue to do so. That was my only solace. And one day, when I could take it no longer, I chose to become that new person, this person before you. I sit here now as a vindication of that faith."

Deep furrows formed on Samas's face. "I am sorry, Evan, for what I put you through," he said, turning to watch the main scribe as he captured his confession. "It was wrong to tempt you as I did." Samas stared at Evan with a look that seemed to want forgiveness. "That concludes my questions for the candidate."

The four judges paused after Samas concluded. Then Ramsay moved forward in her seat and spoke directly to Evan in a foreign language. The strange language stunned the other judges. The scribes looked up from their pages, unsure of what to write. Galen turned to look at Evan.

Evan looked at her for what seemed like a full minute. Ramsay repeated the line, her steel-gray eyes locked on his.

He sat up straight in his chair and replied, "Tova, koeto se nauchava v'mladostta, y izdulbano v'kamuk."[12]

Ramsay smiled. "Let it be known the candidate speaks another foreign language," she said to the chroniclers as they wrote, "his native Bulgarian." She stepped down from the bench and paced in front of it as she began her series of questions. "Let us discuss your life in Bulgaria, your first life

12. Research with a native speaker identified this as a traditional Bulgarian saying—"What is learned in youth is carved in stone."

that was *not* in your writing. What school did you attend? Who was your commanding officer in the army? What did your unit's insignia look like?"

Evan lit another cigarette and took his mind into the virtual room he and Galen had created for Vasili Blagavich Arda as he found and delivered the answers for her.

Her questions took them into the night as judge and candidate reviewed the major parts of an entire life. After Evan's last answer, Chance, Samas, and Ramsay looked at each other as if taking a silent poll. Chance's purposeful cough finally caught the attention of a distracted Poppy.

"What?" she asked, shooting them a strange look. "I told you hours ago that I was a yes."

Chance scowled at her. "Please ask the candidate some questions," he said, gesturing toward the scribes, "for the record."

Poppy sighed and resigned herself to the redundant task of proving the identity of the lover she had welcomed back into her bed. She stood gracefully and stepped down from the bench. Her elegant shoes clicked a cadence on the floor as she walked up to Evan. She extended her delicate hand out to him as all eyes followed her. He took her hand in his, and she gently pulled him to his feet. "Do you remember who introduced us?"

Evan stood next to her and thought back to their first encounter, not sure how to answer. She led him to one of the tall, free-standing silver braziers that supported a small leaping flame. Evan, unable to fight the attraction, turned his head to the orange flickering as Poppy began. "Tell us all what you see here. Tell us what the flame is to you." She turned to the crowd in the gallery. "You see, this is what brought us together. This is what brought Evan Michaels to us last time."

Evan looked down into her eyes and knew at that moment that he would always belong to her. With this simple act, she had touched and opened his soul to the others in an intimacy beyond the power of a mere lover. They would see him now as she saw him, and they would have their choice to accept him in the same way she had.

Chance straightened in his chair, intrigued by Poppy's direction.

Evan kept his hand in hers. "I remember fire," he started, "in all its benevolent and malevolent forms. I remember it killing me as a boy, I remember it saving me from the cold as a soldier, I remember becoming its master as an arsonist. The thing about fire is that it is always the same whenever I summon it—a constant through lives where I have been different. When I see it, I recognize it, and it sees me too, reacts to me, validates that unseen part of me that recognizes it across time. Fire is what puts me back together from the scattered pieces of what I have seen through different eyes. It burns off the superficial and leaves behind what is lasting. It is my judge in the same way you are," he said, looking at each in turn.

Poppy smiled and turned back to Chance. "For the record."

Evan stood with her in silence, awaiting judgment.

Galen rose and spoke first. "I think that is enough for tonight. I would like to close this evening with a preliminary vote of the judges. Are each of you four judges convinced that this candidate is our returning brother?"

"You have my vote," Poppy said, not pulling away from Evan.

"We have one affirmation," Galen repeated.

"I am a yes. It is the Evan Michaels I knew," declared Samas.

"Two," Galen shouted.

Ramsay rose from her seat. "Before I cast my vote, I want to take a moment to remind the candidate of the oath of secrecy we all take when we first enter the Cognomina. We keep each other's secrets, and we keep our home a secret," she said, looking sternly into Evan's eyes. "The person you claim to be violated that oath by carelessly leaving an account that has escaped. That misguided act has drawn us into the light of the world."

Evan and Galen looked nervously at the gallery as a few voices rose in agreement with Ramsay's indictment.

"That said, I did know that man briefly and I know now that this person before me is one of us. I vote yes."

Galen sighed through pursed lips and turned to his giant friend. "And you, my friend, what say you to conclude us?"

Chance looked back at him and raised his voice for all to hear. "I will give you my vote, but know that I do not conclude this proceeding," he objected. "You will remember that the candidate must appear before a fifth judge."

"Yes, but he is confirmed back into the Cognomina with four affirmations," Galen countered.

Chance sighed and tilted his massive head back. "True. A no vote from me today means that the candidate still has a chance with Clovis's verdict. A yes vote from me today and we all see what treats our good doctor has in store for us beyond that divider," Chance said, opening a massive hand toward the heavy curtain, "as technically we can celebrate his Ascension tonight. But I want to be clear to all that whatever my vote is, the candidate *will* travel to Yemen as soon as possible to present himself to the fifth judge, agreed?"

"Agreed," Galen said before looking over to his candidate, urging him to reply to Chance.

Evan reached his right arm out to embrace Poppy. "Yes, I am eager to see him again."

"Then I have a single question for the candidate," Chance stated, leaning forward with his wide forearms covering the bench. "You claim that you flew with me to Yemen to visit our friend."

Evan nodded as Poppy squeezed her arms around him.

"What color are the seats on my jet?" the giant man asked with a tilt of his head.

Evan smiled as he held Chance's stare. "They are white leather," he answered. "And very comfortable."

Chance sat motionless as if testing the candidate's confidence. "Yes, they are comfortable," the large man said with pride. "I am a yes then," he shouted. "Let's get this party started."

"*Ibi semper est Victoria ubi Concordia est!*"[13] Galen exclaimed as he rushed toward Evan and Poppy.

Evan's knees buckled for a moment, and Poppy tightened her embrace on him as the gallery broke into applause and moved toward them. Galen's arms encircled them both, followed by others until all arms embraced Evan.

---

13. Latin—Where there is concord there is always victory, Publilius Syrus

9

Chance untied the thick rope knotted to the cleat on the wall, and the heavy black curtain crept back, revealing the rest of the grotto. The clattering noise of the curtain's ancient mechanism echoed about the cavernous room and drowned the jubilant conversations into stilled silence. Galen grabbed a burning torch from a wall sconce and walked toward the darkness of the larger half of the grotto, lighting additional braziers to show four more colonnades stretching back into the blackness beyond.

"Welcome home, Evan," Chance said, parting the crowd gathered around Evan and Poppy. "There are some old and some new family members for you to meet tonight, and we are all very excited to meet you. Let us advance to the celebration phase of Evan's Ascension," he said, directing everyone to follow Galen. "Our good doctor has organized the festivities for this evening, so at least there will be enough wine."

"Enough for me anyway," Galen shouted back. "Come, I have a mind-expanding night in store for each of you. Come, come."

Chance led them past the line where the curtain hung. One long table stretched into the darkness toward a rectangular pool of shimmering water. Dozens and dozens of wine bottles ran down the spine of the table—some clean and new, others dust-covered and oddly shaped like relics. Six tall wine glasses surrounded each place setting and chair. The first revelers looked beyond the table toward the edge of the pool to see leather chairs from the upstairs study arrayed in groups of four atop luxurious hand-woven carpets. Stainless-steel medical IV holders stood above each comfortable chair with bags of clear liquid twinkling in the growing firelight.

Galen finished lighting the last of the illuminating fires. "Mr. Pianosa, can you please have our staff bring down the menu we planned?" he shouted and heard footsteps start up the stairs.

"Brothers and sisters," Galen bellowed into the cavern, "please grab a glass of wine and line up beside me. Tonight, some of you will see a lost brother again, and some of you will meet our newest member for the first time. Ladies and gentlemen of the Cognomina, I present to you, Evan Michaels."

Everyone burst into applause and organized into a long receiving line.

Galen moved to the head of the line nearest him. "I am Galen of Pergamon, physician to gladiator and emperor, king and queen, caliph and pope, and now you." Galen embraced him tightly. "You did it, Evan. I'm proud of you," he whispered before stepping back and passing him on to Chance.

The large man gave the physician a puzzled look, unprepared to give such a florid biography. "I am Chance, speculator on everything from money to man, diviner of probabilities and outcomes, master of the games of risk and reward, and know, my young friend, that everything in this world is a game."

Ramsay was next in line. "I am Ramsay, warrior, defender, an agent of change."

"I am Samas, as you well know. So good to have you back. Remind me that we have something to show you later."

Cy, the young man with curly black hair he had seen in the dining room before was next. "Hello, Evan. I am Rafic of Los Angeles, California, by choice and Jerusalem by birth. I study history and its patterns to expose the dark and forgotten corners where many of these characters around you have left their fingerprints."

"That's why we call him Cipher," a voice shouted from behind him.

"Or Cy for short," Rafic corrected. "Nice to meet you."

"Hello, I am Etyma," said a slender black woman dressed in an elegant purple silk dress. "My passion is music in all its forms. Welcome back to us."

"I'm Jens. I handle most of the investments for our collected funds. I have a nice surprise for you later."

Auda was next in line. "I am Auda, one of the old ones. I protect our family above all things."

Nestor, Kress, Dilmun, Steen, Kerr, Mr. Ing, Castor—the names and backgrounds came to him through warm and welcoming faces. Poppy stood at the end of the line, waiting patiently. The first platters of food were arriving behind the line as he stepped down to her.

"I am Poppy," she said softly.

"I know you are. Thank you for what you did back there," Evan said, nodding back to the empty bench.

"Collected members of the Cognomina," Galen shouted over scattered conversations. "We are ready to dine. Please come and take your seats. Evan, please sit in the place of honor this evening." He directed Evan to the higher-backed chair in the middle of the table and placed Poppy opposite him. "In addition to a returning family member, we have also set a place of honor for our retiring innkeeper of the last fifty years. Please welcome to our table Mr. Leopold Diltz," Galen said, breaking into a clap that started the whole grotto into thunderous applause.

An emotional Mr. Diltz took his seat between Auda and Samas as the white-uniformed staff of young women set plate after plate on the long banquet table.

"Tonight we have prepared a sixteen-course menu for you, each with a wine pairing of my choosing. First up is a fillet of skate in browned butter with a Grüner Veltliner wine to pair. But first, I propose a toast," Galen said, raising a glass of the white wine. "A warm welcome to our returning brother and a fond farewell to our faithful friend. *Familia supra omnia*."[14]

"Familia supra omnia," they all repeated in unison.

14. Latin—Family over everything

"Am I going to have to learn Latin to spend time with all of you?" Evan asked Poppy.

"To spend time with him you will. The rest of us have pretty much learned just to nod and repeat his phrases and assume that what he is saying is wise and appropriate."

"Because no one ever questions him, he thinks we all learned Latin in our past lives as he did," Rafic said, laughing. "We don't have the heart to tell him that we have no idea what he is saying most of the time."

The staff brought down course after exotic course: smoked bison tongue with Châteauneuf-du-Pape, stuffed sweetbreads with Ribera del Duero, candied plums with an 1864 Madeira, raw fennel with champagne. They ate and drank into the night as black tattooed hands worked with a headlong hedonism.

Samas approached blond-haired Jens seated next to Evan. "Did you show him yet?" Samas asked.

Jens set down his wine glass and reached inside a jacket pocket. "No, but I have it here." He leaned over and tapped Evan on the arm. "Evan, I asked Mr. Pianosa to pull yesterday's balance from your account."

"My account?" Evan asked.

"Yes, your account," Jens answered. "The gentleman behind me deposited a rather large sum of money for you almost two decades ago."

"An increased sum negotiated by your agent," Samas said, glancing at a smirking Poppy.

"Yes," Jens continued, "we keep funds in our trust from our departed members and we like to keep it working while those members are, shall we say, *away* from us. Anyway, now that you have officially passed your Ascension, the account is yours. I will have Mr. Pianosa transfer the account to your current identity in the morning. Here is the balance," he said, placing the printout on the table next to his plate.

Evan looked over at the paper and then leaned in closer to look at the number circled in red ink at the lower left of the page—37,931,843.29 SFr. "I don't understand, what does SFr stand for?"

"Sorry, Swiss Francs. They currently trade at parity with the US dollar."

Evan looked at the number again and then at Poppy, who simply nodded with a sly smile. "Am I reading this right? That's a big number."

"It is, Evan," Samas said, "and thirty-seven million that was well earned." He clapped a fat hand on Evan's shoulder before walking back to his seat.

"Coming back to yourself and remembering who you were is always a very difficult time. We all suffer it, but looking at a surprise balance always takes a bit of the sting out of it for me," Jens said, smiling at Evan over his wine glass.

Evan's eyes fell back to the statement with its circled number. Just days ago he didn't even have enough money to buy a single piece of the fruit that he carried. He hadn't thought about money on the trek to Zurich—just about the driving desire to get to this place and these people. He raised his wine glass and drank deeply. He remembered when he first entered this group that he had felt like a second-class citizen, unable to match their budgets and appetites for life. The feeling of finding his home but not quite fitting in drove him to accept Samas's dangerous offer. Now he would join them as a true peer, able to keep up with them.

Evan began to let his mind explore what that kind of freedom would mean, but the thought was interrupted by a reveler farther down the table, eager to accelerate the evening. "Say, Doc, are the IVs for us later?"

Poppy gave Evan a knowing smile. "Our Dr. Feelgood always has the best party favors for us."

"That, my friends, is a surprise," Galen announced. "Let's call it the *after-party*."

"I hope it's not part of your medical research," Jens joked. "I don't want to be part of any experiment."

"What research is that?" asked Kerr, turning his head toward Jens so that Evan could see the long scarlet scar that ran from his eyebrow to his jawline and cleft a neat line into his short red beard.

"Oh, he plans to make it possible for humans to live forever," Auda chimed in.

"Not forever," Galen corrected, "just another sixty or seventy years.

And no, dear Jens, the IVs are more for consciousness expansion than physical improvement. After all, we must care for the mind as well as the body."

A stern look washed over Kerr's strong face. "Do you really think it is a good idea to extend their lives?"

Galen turned with a surprised look on his long face. "Sure it is. This breakthrough will be celebrated. Imagine how much improved they would be if they had more time to learn and apply that wisdom."

"What wisdom?" Poppy asked before asking Evan for a cigarette.

"Well, I don't like it at all," Kerr said to everyone within earshot. "I think it is a terrible idea."

Galen continued to pour wine for the others but kept his eyes locked on Kerr. "Noted, but I don't believe you have a vote. It's happening. I announce it in a few days."

"Auda," Kerr shouted down to the elder, "what do you think Clovis would think of this?"

The older man shrugged his shoulders in reply as he slipped his arm around a passing white-uniformed staffer.

"Imagine what more they could accomplish if only they had more time as we do," Galen offered.

"So you will be the one to chain Thanatos[15] again?" Kerr asked, one red eyebrow raised.

Galen smiled at the question. "You flatter me, Brother Kerr, and with my own mythos too. Bravo!"

Kerr stared at the doctor before turning to see if anyone else at the long table shared his opinion but was met with amused indifference. The others stood up from their chairs, and Kerr dropped the argument.

"Before we move on to the after-party," Galen said in a raised voice to gather everyone's attention, "we need to attend to one piece of business. Evan, will you follow me?" He led Evan over toward the carpets and plush cushions near the pool. "Auda, will you do us the honors again this evening?"

---

15. Thanatos was the Greek god of death. The reference here by Kerr is when King Sisyphus tricked Thanatos and locked him in his own chains for a time, during which no humans could die.

The wiry man rose from the table, his worn leather pouch of primitive tattoo equipment at the ready. Several members of the family followed to watch. Auda sat first and prepared the leather sleeve template that would guide him to yet another Embe tattoo, marking Evan as a full member of the Cognomina. Auda slipped the sleeve over Evan's right hand, a void in the worn leather where the distinctive crossed black tattoo would soon live. Evan stiffened as Auda tightened the drawstrings, and he turned to Galen.

"This doesn't feel right," Evan said. "Not yet, not until Clovis has had a chance to judge me." He looked back at Auda and then at Galen again. "Is that allowed?"

Auda said, "You are entitled to this honor now. We have a four-vote majority."

Galen sensed a deeper need behind the request. "The old man's opinion means a lot to you, doesn't it?"

"It does," he stated. "But there is more than that. My time with him in Yemen was not easy for me, and I left in a hurry and without notice. I disrespected him and I want to make it right." He looked down at the sleeve, where the tattoo would be in less than an hour. "It doesn't feel right to take this honor without him affirming me."

Auda and Galen looked at each other in silent agreement.

"Don't worry, Galen, I can convince him. I spent enough time with him to win his yes. I just want it to be this way."

"I do not worry about that, Evan. This honor is yours, but if you feel you require another step to achieve it, so be it."

"Agreed," Auda replied.

"I agree as well," Chance boomed. "We will wait on this until I have taken you to Yemen and back." He rose and spoke to the group. "I will take Evan to the final part of his Ascension in the morning and return him to us in four days." He looked down at Evan again. "That should give you enough time to get to his lighthouse, spend three days with him, and return to Mocha."

Evan nodded as he loosened the laces on the tattoo sleeve.

"I will return him to us in four nights, where we will conclude this ceremony. In the meantime"—he raised his voice for all to hear—"let's start this after-party."

"Very well," Galen shouted and began walking to the quads of leather chairs. "Before we begin, I need to inform everyone that this *activity* is potentially dangerous and even deadly without careful medical attention, which I shall provide."

"Oh, this sounds like fun," Kress said, stepping forward.

"And of course, this is completely optional," Galen added.

"What is it?" Auda asked.

Galen reached between two of the leather chairs to pull out an oversized, dusty wine bottle with no label. "I have a potent ergot wine from northern Portugal."

"Nope. No way. I'm out," Chance said. "I suffered from St. Anthony's Fire once. No thank you."

"Wait, what—what does it do?" Mr. Ing asked.

Galen stepped up onto a side table between two chairs. "Hang on, hang on. Let me explain," he said, trying to get control of a divided room. "Chance is right. Ergot is dangerous."

"What is ergot?" Poppy asked.

"It is a gift from distant Eleusis,"[16] Galen proclaimed with pride.

"What in the hell is he talking about?" Rafic asked.

"It is a fungal poison actually," the physician continued, "but it does have some medical benefits and some recreational ones. Ergot is a fungus that grows on rye, wheat, and barley. It is a powerful vasoconstrictor that can help stop bleeding, but unregulated or unmonitored, it can cause complete constriction of blood vessels, leading to gangrene and death."

"Poisoning? Sounds delightful, Doctor," Rafic joked.

"It also contains powerful alkaloids that make up lysergic acid, or LSD."

"Okay, I'm back in the boat," said Jens. "Keep talking."

---

16. Galen refers to the Eleusinian Mysteries, an ancient Greek mystery cult that centered around the consumption of a drink called Kykeon. Kykeon's primary psychoactive ingredient is theorized to have been ergot. (See *The Road to Eleusis* by Gordon Wasson and Albert Hofmann, the inventor of LSD.)

"The experience is a little different than you might be used to. There is a risk in drinking this, but I mitigate the risk with two solutions that I propose to administer to you intravenously. You will be able to control the dosages of these two solutions in real time to control the intensity of your experience tonight. The IV on your left side is an antianxiety medication and liquid aspirin as a vasodilator in a saline solution, which by the way is also an excellent hangover preventer. Press the button in your left hand to come down.

"The IV on your right side is a combination of naturally occurring acetic and citric acids in a saline solution. More of this will, shall we say, *sharpen* the experience by catalyzing an amide synthesis with the lysergic acid latent in the ergot."

"Can you put that into English, Doctor," Rafic asked, "or at least into Latin?"

The drunken group erupted in laughter.

Even Galen had to laugh. "Press the right button to continue farther down the rabbit hole. Press the left to come up. Got it? Okay, who wants to be first?"

Mr. Ing pushed his small frame through the crowd around Galen. "I will be the first."

"Excellent, sir." Galen poured a small portion of cloudy red wine into a glass. "First, drink this. It might be better all at once instead of sipped. The fungus adds bitterness, and I had to mix it with Merlot."

The small Asian man downed the glass and grimaced. "Oh, that's rough."

"Now roll up your sleeves, please." Galen deftly found a vein in each arm and inserted the IVs. "Your controls, sir," he said, handing controllers with thumb-activated buttons connected to the drips. "Enjoy your flight."

Auda stepped forward. "Me, I'm next," he said, grabbing the glass from Galen.

Samas, Castor, Etyma, and most of the others stepped forward for their drink and IV drips. Poppy sat in the next open chair as Galen completed the last voyager.

"Oh no, dear," Galen said to her, "I have a special one for you." He pointed to the last IV in the group of four chairs. "Take the one with the red ribbon on it. I made it special just for you. It has *all* the things you like."

She smiled and leaned over to kiss him on the cheek. "Thanks, Doc." She sat in the chair and waited for her turn.

Galen took the syringe end to the drip and gripped a long hand around her thin arm in a makeshift tourniquet. "Now you tell me if I am as good at this as you are," he said, slipping the needle into her fair skin.

"Mmm," she moaned, "I always love the feeling of someone else spiking me."

"There we go, my dear," he said, handing her a set of controls.

Galen approached Evan, who leaned on his cane at the back of a dwindling group of decliners. "I think you should consider doing it," he said. "These experiences can sometimes cause a transformation in the way we perceive things, and that paradigm shift might help you bring all of your remaining memories together better."

"Thank you," Evan replied, "but I just got here, and I'd like to stay awhile longer this time."

"It will be safe for you," Galen said with a laugh. "I only said it was dangerous to get most of them interested."

Evan chuckled and watched a dreamy Mr. Ing, who looked to be enjoying himself as he worked his right thumb against the button. "All right, let's do it."

Galen handed him a glass of the ruddy liquid. "Drink this. It *is* better all at once."

Evan complied as the physician found a vein in his left arm.

"Right for more, left for less," Galen reminded him. "I will keep an eye on you to see how you are doing. If you feel any tightness or cramping in your extremities, hit the left button until it clears up."

"Got it." Evan reached out and took Galen's hand. "Thanks for helping me through this."

"You are very welcome, Evan. Now relax, close your eyes, take ten deep breaths, and I will see you on the other side," the physician said, reaching down and depressing the right button twice.

Evan felt something right away—a delightful lightness. Then he saw it. His eyes were closed, but he saw that he was standing by a slowly moving river just as if it were midday. He walked down the bank to the river's edge and caught a glimpse of himself in a gentle, isolated pool.

"Can you take me home?"

He was startled by the small boy's question. He turned to see young Bobby standing beside him on the bank, pointing at a canoe.

"Where is your home?"

The little boy pointed upriver.

"What is your name?"

"You know my name," Bobby said, keeping his eyes locked on the river, "but I don't know yours."

He thought about the question, but was unsure how to answer it.

The boy continued, "Only you can help me get home from here."

"But I do not know the way."

The boy pointed upriver again. "I know the way, but you must take me. I have paid you already."

He looked downriver and saw that it was calm and flowing evenly. He looked upriver and saw that strong currents coiled under its shifting surface. He reached for the boy's hand to lead him to the boat.

Bobby jerked his hand away. "We cannot touch, not ever."

Evan walked behind him down to the canoe. Bobby stepped into the canoe and sat on the front seat.

"Would you rather go downstream? It looks easier," Evan said, pushing them off into the slow current.

"I have no choice. I can only go this way," the boy said, pointing to rougher waters.

Evan complied and began paddling toward the first bend. An hour passed as he paddled, then another. The water became rougher, more chaotic. His shoulders burned as he pulled against the strengthening flow.

"It is just ahead, one more turn and you will see it," the boy cried out.

Evan's arms ached and his lungs heaved with exhaustion as he struggled against that unstoppable water. After another ten minutes of pulling, they rounded a bend, and it came into sight: a cataract of white water churning below three feeding tributaries. He paused at the dispiriting sight, but the boy urged him on.

"Come on, don't quit now. I am the middle one. I can see it. I need you to do this for me."

Evan took another deep breath and steered the nose of the canoe into the rushing rapids. Every ten strokes brought them only a boat length closer to the foot of the low waterfall.

"I can see her," Bobby cried. "Come on now, there she is!"

Evan's pounding heart pumped lactic acid into his burning muscles.

"We're almost there," the boy shouted over the roar of the falling water. "I can almost make it from here."

Evan pulled against the rushing water until his arms failed to respond. The canoe drifted into an eddy and pitched hard to the left against the powerful current. Bobby tumbled out of the boat, and Evan reached out a hand but could not touch him. He plunged his weary arms into the water where the boy should have been, but his hands found nothing. He fell out of the canoe and let his protesting body go slack in the current. The water flattened and calmed as it carried him toward the first bend.

He looked back at the three tributaries beyond the waterfall. He knew his journey now lay downriver, but it would always be driven by the force of these tributaries. He rolled his eyes to the open blue above and imagined he could feel each one of the three carrying him downstream in their own way. He savored the stillness and quiet as he floated effortlessly, and he mustered enough strength to look back at the chaos of the cataract one last time and wondered if he had gotten the boy close enough.

Evan's eyes snapped open to see Galen sitting in the leather chair opposite him swirling a full glass of red wine. He looked around, but they were the only ones left in the grotto except for the haunting echoes of Etyma's violin playing softly somewhere in the darkness. Dirty dishes and discarded wine glasses lay scattered.

Galen rose and moved toward him. "Are you finished?"

Evan nodded, unable to find his voice.

Galen took the left controller and hit the button twice. "Count to ten for me, please," he said as he removed the IVs.

Evan complied and rose, steadying himself with his cane. "Help me to the pool, please. I want to feel the water."

10

Evan awoke to the bark of the tires of Chance's jet against the patch-work tarmac of the abandoned airfield outside of Mocha, Yemen. He rubbed his eyes and looked over at the enormous man dwarfing the controls. Outside, tan sand and blue sky dominated the horizon.

"Good morning," Evan said, getting his bearings.

"Good afternoon," Chance corrected, bringing the plane to a stop.

"Looks like I missed some opportunity for conversation."

"And you missed some damn good flying too. We had to drop below a hundred meters from fifty miles offshore to avoid the new air-defense systems they put in since the shooting started here. Harrowing," he said, scanning the horizon as he wheeled the jet around for a rushed departure. "Maybe it's best that you missed it."

"I don't remember much after last night."

"Diltz dropped you off at the hangar in Zurich. You got on, asked me if I had seen Poppy, and then slept the whole way."

"Sorry I wasn't much company."

"No worries," he said, unfolding out of the seat. "Listen, Mocha is a bit different since the last time you were here. There is a lot of shooting going on, so don't go on a walkabout and stay on the roads, as there are land mines about too. I did a low-altitude pass over Clovis's lighthouse so he will be expecting a visitor. I flew up the road and saw no checkpoints between here and his place, so you are probably good." He opened the door and folded down the steps. "Do you remember how to get to Nusel and Drusel's house from here?" he shouted over the engines that he kept running.

Evan nodded.

"Go there, tell them you want to go to the lighthouse"—he caught himself mid-sentence—"ah hell, you speak Arabic now. You'll be fine. Take these and give them to Drusel and anyone else you need help from," he said, pushing a tennis-ball-sized wad of tattered currency into Evan's hand.

Evan smiled.

Chance leaned in for a swallowing hug and gave him one last look. "You know, if you have any of your old clothes in that backpack, you would blend in perfectly here. Just a thought." He surveyed the bleak landscape. "Good luck, brother. Tell him I said hello. I need you to be waiting for me on this tarmac, at this end, in four days, or I will have to leave without you. And you'll have to walk to Zurich from the Middle East again," he laughed.

Evan gave him a thumbs-up as Chance climbed back into his sleek jet. Evan looked around the derelict hangars and burned-out maintenance buildings as Chance pushed his engines to a roar and the plane accelerated down the runway. His eyes landed on the hard-packed dirt road winding toward a distant town, and he began to walk under the weight of a midday sun.

If Mocha had been a sleepy town in decline when he walked it nearly two decades ago, it was firmly in hospice now. Its lone minaret stood witness over empty and crumbling earthen buildings. Charred craters and burned-out vehicles dotted with bullet holes decorated the mostly abandoned cityscape. A few men, hardened beyond their years, looked out from open doorways at him as he walked past on his way to the home and stables of the brothers Nusel and Drusel, who looked after Clovis.

He arrived to find the roof was half gone from their livery stable. He heard no animals inside. He knocked on the door and offered the traditional Arabic greeting, wondering how his Syrian dialect would sound to Yemeni ears. A noise rattled inside before the door creaked open. It was Drusel but as a middle-aged man.

"Hello, a friend of Clovis told me you could take me to him. Do you have a wagon we could use to go to his lighthouse?" Evan said in Arabic.

Drusel narrowed his eyes at the young Syrian and took Evan's hand, looking for the Embe tattoo. "Who are you and what do you want of him?"

Evan hadn't rehearsed the lie he would need to tell this man to get him to the lighthouse. He paused and thought about what he should say as his ears replayed the man's words and adjusted to the Yemeni accent. Eventually, he landed on telling the truth as simply as possible. "You are Drusel, yes?"

The Yemeni man took a half step back into his slanting doorway.

"I know that you know Clovis. I know that you and your brother help him. I know that you know he is a special man, and I know that you help other people, special like him, visit him sometimes. Those special people have the mark that you looked for on my hand."

Drusel's eyes widened a bit.

"I am one of those people, Drusel, but I do not have the mark yet. I need to meet with Clovis to get my mark. Do you understand?"

Drusel silently studied the Syrian from head to toe. "Can you prove that you are one of them?"

Evan thought back to his first time here. "Your brother is Nusel."

"Everyone knows this." The Yemeni man rejected him with a shake of his rugged head.

Evan smiled at him. "You had a beautiful gray horse that you would ride to his tower by the sea."

"By Allah, it is true!" Drusel exclaimed. "Dead now ten years, Imran was the greatest horse on the coast." He took Evan's hand and pulled him inside into the shade. "What is your name, friend of Clovis?"

"I am Yousef from Damascus," Evan said, deciding that name would be easier for him.

"Welcome to our home, Yousef. Damascus is very far. Blessings on the Prophet for bringing you all this way. Come inside."

"Can you take me to him?"

"Yes, yes, it is no problem. But too hot now. In a while, after the sun has exhausted itself, we will go. Have some rose water to refresh yourself for the journey."

Evan blew the dust out of an offered cup before Drusel filled it with cloudy, scented water.

"No one has come in more than a year to visit Clovis. The last was the African giant. He comes still. Others no." He sipped at his tepid water. "Will you come back to visit him again?"

"Yes, I think so, Drusel. I like it here."

"Yes, the blessings of Allah are on us here," he said, looking up through his fractured roof.

"What happened to this place?"

"It is war. Very bad. Brother fights brother. Who knows how long we will suffer?"

"And where is your brother, Nusel?"

"Blessings be upon him, he moved to Aden to be with the rest of the family. I alone am here in our family home."

"And where are your animals?"

"All taken by soldiers," Drusel replied and spat on the ground, "used for transport and then for food. A curse on their house for what they have done to this town."

Evan didn't want to insult his host, but he did wonder how they would make the journey to Clovis's remote lighthouse down the coast. "How will we travel to see Clovis?"

"On the road, of course," Drusel replied, pointing beyond the edge of town.

Evan nodded. "Yes, of course, but since your Imran is gone and there are no other horses or donkeys, how will we go?"

Drusel finished his hazy glass and set it on his chair as he rose with pride. "I have a car, Yousef. It is just outside."

Evan looked around, not remembering any serviceable vehicles among the ruins. "That's good."

"Finish your water for the journey and you can help me prepare it for our travel."

Evan looked at the murky prospect in his hand and knew better than to spurn any Arab hospitality. The precious rose scent covered the bitterness, but not the grit. "Excellent, Drusel," he lied. "Thank you for the water, and thank you for agreeing to take me. Now let's see this car of yours."

An excited Drusel grabbed a key off a ring by the door and stepped into the street next to the shot-up wreck of a car Evan had seen on the way in. The Yemeni unlocked the trunk to reveal the two missing wheels and a battery. Evan watched in amazement as Drusel reassembled the derelict hulk into a drivable vehicle in minutes. His camouflage of wreckage worked perfectly. "Help me grab some wood from inside the barn. Honorable Clovis likes it when I bring him wood for his cooking fires."

Murderous intent had shot out all the glass from the small car, and Evan felt uneasy sitting on the bloodstained upholstery as Drusel opened the door for him to enter. Drusel pushed the car to get it rolling down the main street that sloped toward the Red Sea in the distance. "It saves the battery if I clutch start it," he said in a thin wheeze as he jumped in.

The car barked to life, and they drove through the ruins of the injured and dying town, the peppering howl from the broken exhaust pipe startling villagers toward the safety of their mud homes. Hot wind blasted their faces through the missing windshield as they roared past the last of the abandoned houses and onto the hard-packed wagon tracks that passed for a coastal road.

Evan squinted over at the Yemeni man and could see the toll the last twenty years had taken on Drusel's weathered and creased face. Hardness and determination lay on him like a mask fashioned from loss. He thought about offering him a cigarette, but the hot gale whipping about their heads made that impossible. Evan looked to the right and let his eyes trace the line where the light-colored sand dropped below the white foam of the crashing waves. He pulled his shirt up to cover his mouth and nose as he looked over to the sight of the surf and imagined he could hear the waves' repetitive roar over the incessant din of the car's broken exhaust. He strained his eyes down the coast until he saw the lone spire of Clovis's ancient stone lighthouse come into view.

Evan had imagined he would have a long wagon ride out here to think about what to say when he first saw Clovis again, but now he would be there in minutes, standing in front of him. Just like the approach to the St. Germain days ago, Evan had approached this tower hundreds of times in his mind. Hundreds of times he had spoken the right words and been embraced by the old man. And now, as the car rattled to a stop at the base of the lighthouse marking the boundary between blue sea and brown sand, his throat tightened with road dust and anxiety.

Drusel left his car running at a loping idle as he hopped out and grabbed an armload of wood from the trunk. "I cannot stop the car for fear I could not start it again out here. I must leave in minutes, as fuel is very precious here." He dropped the wood next to the sparse garden, where a low line of stones held back determined sand from the struggling green stalks within the perimeter. The weathered wooden door of the lighthouse creaked open against stiff hinges, and Clovis appeared.

He looked older, but he still had a vibrancy about him of an aged warrior still standing at a post. His back stooped more than Evan remembered, and his white hair and beard framed a face peppered with age spots. Drusel embraced him, but Clovis kept his sharp eyes focused on Evan.

"I bring you Yousef from Damascus," Drusel said, turning to introduce Evan.

Clovis stood like a statue, waiting for Evan to speak first.

"It is good to see you, again," Evan said in English.

Clovis tilted his head slightly but said nothing.

"I met you before. Here, and in Zurich. I am Evan Michaels."

The old warrior stared unblinking for what seemed like minutes, then reached down and took Evan's right hand in his, turning it to expose where a tattooed mark might have been. "We will see about that," he said in English. "You came here with Chance, yes?"

"Yes, he flew me here from Zurich, where I met with the others."

Clovis nodded. "Give Drusel half of the money Chance gave you. And tell him it is a gift."

Evan spoke the Arabic of his youth to the Yemeni man. "Drusel, take this as a gift from me, and please come back here in three days.

Blessings be upon you for what you have done for me today and for what you continue to do for this man."

Drusel hugged him and took the notes. "Three days." He ran back to his car and started the noisy return back up the coastal trail.

Evan turned back to Clovis, smiled, and looked over at the old man's miserable garden. "Have your gardening journals from distant Diocletian still taught you nothing of gardening here?"

Clovis put his hand on Evan's shoulder. "Come in out of the sun, young man. We have much to discuss."

Evan followed him inside and sat opposite him at his rustic wooden table. Clovis poured water into two clay cups. "I think you should start. Why did you come here—or come back, if indeed you remember my lighthouse?"

Evan considered where to begin the story. "After I left here, I flew to Tunis to meet Samas to do a job for him—a dangerous job. That job cost me my life, that life," he corrected. "And then almost a year ago, as a teenager in Damascus, I began to remember who I was. After I had put enough of it together to know what I needed to do, I started the long and hard trek to Zurich. I arrived at the hotel, and they received me and agreed to hear my story and judge me."

"So your Ascension is done?"

"Almost," Evan said. "I would not let them complete it with the tattoo until I saw you."

"Who was your advocate?"

"Galen."

Clovis nodded. "Who judged you?"

"Samas, Ramsay, Auda, and Poppy."

"And what was their judgment of you?"

"They unanimously affirmed me."

"All four? Who was your fifth judge?" he asked, and then checked himself as he discerned the reason for the visit. "Aah, I see. Well, if it is you, you were not with us very long, and you had interactions with only a few of us, me being one of the last." Clovis took a drink of water. "But why come all this way? You have your majority of four."

"I wanted to be judged by you. I needed to know that you recognized me too." Evan took a drink to match his and tried to muster some needed courage. "And I wanted to come and apologize for the way I left last time."

Clovis looked deeply into Evan's eyes, then waved a weathered, dismissive hand. "We can get to such matters later. Tell me what work you and I have remaining for your Ascension."

"You are to judge me as you would if you were in Zurich, then write your opinion down and I'll take it back for them to announce. And one other thing: for security reasons, Ramsay asked that you write your verdict and any notes in a language that you and she understand but that I or others would not."

"Aramaic."

"Exactly. So are you ready to begin?"

The older man sensed the urgency within the younger. "When does Chance return to pick you up?"

"Three days from today, at noon. I am to meet him at the airstrip again."

Clovis nodded. "It is dangerous for him to come here now," he said, looking out the open door to the contested land outside. "That jet draws a lot of attention. It would be safer if he started coming by boat." He motioned a thumb over his shoulder to the calm blue expanse. "Where are my manners? You must be hungry after your journey here, and if I have you for three more days, we will need something for dinner. Please get some of the wood you brought and start a fire in the hearth. I will prepare us something to eat."

Evan returned with his arms full of wood and set about stacking them for a small fire.

The old warrior looked over from his work on two salted fish in the basic kitchen. "The Diocletian reference is a good start, but you will have to do better than that to convince me."

"Yes, I know," Evan replied. "I'm ready."

"We will soon know," Clovis mused. "Tell me, how many lives do you remember?"

Evan looked back at him from his preparations and knew they were beginning. "Three. I remember three. They were Vasili, Bobby, Evan, and now Yousef."

"Tell me, what was the name of the camp commandant where you were detained as Vasili?"

"Dukchov. Hristo Dukchov."

"What was the name of your commanding officer in the army?"

"Captain Hoxa."

"What were the names of the other men in your company? What was the number of Hoxa's company? What was the name of your village?" Clovis peppered him with rapid-fire questions as he worked on their dinner, recalling minute details from Evan's first Ascension nearly two decades before.

Evan looked into the small fire and tended to its needs as he answered.

"How did Vasili escape to Turkey after the second war? Where did he live in Istanbul? How did you meet Poppy for the first time? Why did you leave here without saying goodbye?"

The question jolted Evan's concentration away from the warmth of the fire. He paused for a long moment before turning to Clovis, still at work on their dinner. "I wanted the golden tower that everyone else had."

"I seem to remember discussing that with someone before."

Evan stared into the fire and reminded himself that he had practiced this explanation many times. "Clovis, I cannot explain the joy I felt meeting Poppy, understanding what she was, and through that, learning what I was. I was overwhelmed at learning that there were others like me and then getting to join them, but envy tempered that joy. I envied what the others had accumulated over their lives and how they used that treasure to enjoy life in a way I could not. Being accepted into the Cognomina validated me, but their peerage is a hard one to match. I belonged with them, but I couldn't keep up with them," Evan said as he turned to the old master. "Samas offered me an opportunity to get there quickly, and I left to take it."

Clovis nodded solemnly.

Evan took a deep breath. "But that's not all. I found your calligraphy—all of it."

"I thought so. I knew you found them, but I was unsure why it might drive you to leave."

"I was leaving anyway, but finding the sheets to be the same did alarm me." Evan walked over to the crude kitchen where Clovis was wrapping up. "I had a long time to think about that and why I reacted the way I did. It was the repetition, day after day, it seemed like you had sequestered yourself here alone, trying to reach perfection on that task. It spoke to me of a solitude and isolation that was too close to the life I led before I found the Cognomina. I couldn't accept that this new path might lead me back to the same dark place."

"It is not daily," Clovis corrected. "It is weekly. I write it once a week. I can understand how you felt."

"I was not ready for that feeling, trying to imagine your life here doing that. I was looking for exactly the opposite of that, and I ran toward Samas's offer. I think that is why I left as I did." Evan stood up to face him. "I've been a prisoner twice now, and I—"

"Is that what I seem to you? A prisoner in this tower?" Clovis interrupted in a thin voice, this time turning his unyielding eyes to meet Evan's.

Evan froze in his gaze, trapped. "What is it? What does it say, this same thing you write once a week?"

Clovis lowered his eyes back to the cutting board. "It is an apology to old friends for what I allowed to happen to them. I write it once a week to them in their native language to remind me of my failing, to remind me of my flaws and the corrections I wish I could have made then. I write it every week, and every week I find some new error in the execution of the work, and I correct those flaws as a meditation on the flaws in the character of the man I once was. But that is a story for another day." He motioned for Evan to sit. "We are trying to discern who you are, young man, and I have one final question for you."

Evan sat as the old man placed the two fish onto a rack in the roaring hearth.

"How did it feel to light that fire?" Clovis asked, looking into the flames.

Evan watched the old man hunched over his work on their dinner. "It felt like seeing an old friend."

Clovis turned to meet Evan's gaze. "Ironic. I was just feeling the same thing. Welcome back, Evan."

11

Evan woke to find a hand-carved wooden bowl filled with freshly picked figs sitting on the rustic kitchen table. *Eat and join me outside when ready*, read the handwritten note in delicate calligraphy. He stepped through the lighthouse's main door into the bright morning. He walked around the curve of the stone tower and stopped when he caught sight of Clovis on the beach, sword in hand, facing the sun as if in meditation. His first step and aggressive swing of the weapon surprised Evan. He watched the old man begin his exercise and flashed back briefly to when he saw this man work with his sword once before. Evan felt welcome as he watched him this time, like some remembered rift had been repaired.

The curved sword flashed in the sunlight and seemed to summon grace and power into Clovis's old frame with each well-practiced swing and stepping thrust. Evan watched from the edge of the lighthouse until he had finished his exercise, and then walked slowly down to meet him. "Good morning."

Clovis turned quickly, his weapon at the ready. His stance gave Evan a chill under the strengthening sun. The old man looked radiant with the light sheen of sweat on his tanned brow. "Do you not know to announce yourself well away from an armed opponent?"

"I haven't had much swordplay training or dueling etiquette so far," Evan joked.

Clovis raised his blade and plunged it into the sand next to a second sword. "Well, I can remedy that. I found my second sword this morning, and I took the liberty of bringing it out in case you wanted a first lesson."

The offer intrigued Evan.

"Go ahead, pick it up," Clovis encouraged him.

"This isn't some mortal challenge like the spear in the grotto, is it?"

Thin lips parted to show age-yellowed teeth. "No, nothing like that. I just thought it would be a great way for you and me to spend the next three days together."

Evan walked over to the two swords stuck blade first into the sand. He wrapped his hand around the second one and pulled it free. It felt light in his hand and responsive to his moves. "Is this some part of the test?" he asked, confused. "I thought you would want to question me and discern whether I belong in the Cognomina."

"Indeed," Clovis said, grabbing his blade again. "And what shall we do after that is completed?"

Evan had not thought beyond the test.

"You are done, my boy." Clovis stood still and looked at him. "You are who you claim to be. I knew it last night. I wrote the letter to Ramsay this morning. It is in my room waiting for you when you leave. It is complete."

"Really? Just like that?"

"Yes. You were right to pick me as a judge. Our previous interaction was enough for me to validate your claim, Evan, but only that," Clovis said. "Now I wish to use our remaining time to get to know each other better. Let me start by showing you something about myself."

"Are you going to show me how to sword fight?"

"Evan, the last time you were here, you left to follow an opportunity you felt could make you a peer of the others. Now I give you an opportunity to be a peer of mine," he said, turning to face the sun and resuming his starting position. "Hold your sword like this and place your feet shoulder-width apart. Now follow my steps and motions with the blade. The primary task is the steps. A good swordsman is like a good dancer, he always leads the action and puts the other person where he wants him."

Evan took a deep breath and followed the steps and motions as he listened to Clovis's direction and stories on how specific moves had worked on long-vanquished foes. Hour after hour passed until Evan could complete the first routine on his own, and then Clovis stepped through a more difficult series. Evan watched intently until he saw a large white yacht speeding up the coast a hundred meters offshore, its hull cutting a white V into the blue expanse.

"Are you expecting company today?" Evan asked, pointing out to sea.

Clovis turned to look. "No, and it is very rare these days to see pleasure craft here." He strained his watery eyes to get a better look as the yacht slowed when it came even with the lighthouse. "I used to see them ply these waters, and they would sometimes stop to photograph the lighthouse. Can your young eyes see anyone on deck?"

Evan shielded his eyes with cupped hands. "I see men in black loading a smaller boat."

"We should head back," Clovis stated. "Give me your sword." He held both swords in front of his wiry frame out of sight to the boat as they walked quickly up the beach. "Please look back and tell me what you see, Evan."

"There are two inflatable boats. Men are getting into the first one. They just launched it and are turning this way."

"How many men in the first boat?"

"I count five."

"Let us retreat to the lighthouse to receive our guests," Clovis said, increasing his pace.

"Who do you think they are?"

"In that luxury craft, they are likely not from either side in our little war here in Yemen. They could be Somali pirates with a new catch, but they only come ashore in friendly ports they know. Hurry, come inside."

Evan stopped at the curve of the lighthouse wall and looked back. "The first boat landed, and the second inflatable just launched with five more men and someone dressed in white."

"Come inside, Evan. Let us put some coffee on for them." Clovis dragged him in and bolted the door closed. "Go to the window in the kitchen and tell me what you see. I will be by the door."

"They are running now. They will be here in seconds," Evan shouted. "What do you want me to do?"

"You do nothing," Clovis said calmly, backing away from the door and swinging both swords in small circles to limber up his stiff shoulders. "Stay back away from any combat, please. I will do my best to handle this."

"But I want to help you," Evan pleaded.

"You *are* helping. Tell me what the men look like. Are they Arab or African? Do they have guns?"

"They look European to me. One is Asian and carries a bag. Only one soldier has a pistol."

"Can you see the person in white yet? That is probably their commander."

"The second boat just landed. I think the person in white is a woman. They are here," Evan said solemnly.

"Keep watching the other party and describe her to me." Clovis stepped into a ready stance, left sword held low and right sword held high over his head until the two curves formed the continuous arc of a long crescent. An unseen hand worked the outside door handle but found it bolted closed. Clovis adjusted his stance forward and waited.

The unseen hand knocked on the door. "Hello inside. Our boss would like a word with you. Can you open the door, please?" a man asked in English with a Slavic accent.

"She is tall, wearing white—everything is white. Maybe they are not hostile," Evan whispered just loud enough for Clovis to hear by the door.

"They did not come here for tea."

The Slav knocked on the door, louder this time. "We know you are in there. Please let us in so we can discuss this like friends."

"The tall woman is with the Asian man. They are walking behind the second group."

"Tell me the name of your boss. Who is she?" Clovis shouted through the wooden door.

"Oh, hello, mister sir. So you are home?" the lead soldier said, his other men laughing behind him. "Boss would like to speak to you in private, now open up." The man hit the door hard with his shoulder, rattling the bolt.

"Yes, just a minute." Clovis drew in a deep breath as he reached the tip of a sword to open the latch. "Speak only Arabic to them," he said softly over his shoulder to Evan. "If they think you are a servant, they might leave you alone. If not . . ." He let the word hang for a moment. "If not, then I will see you at the St. Germain, when we will be young together."

"Oh, come on!" Evan cried out in frustration. "I just got back."

"Stay well back, Evan." Clovis looked back to the door and thought about the last time he swung a sword in anger at another man, at other men. He smiled as he put the point of the sword under the latch, silently flipped it up, and positioned his body to be partially shielded behind the door when it opened. He listened to their low murmurs outside and readied himself for their next move.

The lead guard ran at the door again, flying off balance into the room when the door burst open without resistance. He sprawled fifteen feet clear of the pending melee, and Clovis turned his hard eyes to the narrow gap at the door's hinges to see the man's comrades advancing. He leaped around the door and brought his right sword down across the second man's chest, cleaving him open on a crimson diagonal. He thrust his left sword around the falling man, and the tip eased effortlessly into the third man's yielding abdomen.

Evan watched awestruck as the accumulation of years fell off the old man with each flashing sword movement and precise step. He looked twenty years younger with anger flaring in his eyes.

Clovis held the right sword high overhead before plunging the steel tip into the exposed neck of the terrified fourth man, which erupted in a spray of red when the swordsman withdrew his blade and turned it back to the leader, now up on one knee.

"Easy, dedushka," the first soldier pleaded, holding up two open hands and glancing over at his leaking and croaking men. "Deep breaths, papa."

Clovis looked down to notice which leg the man was kneeling on. He lunged at the lead guard with his right blade, but the man rolled in the opposite direction and popped onto his feet just in time to see that Clovis had anticipated his move, and to see the left blade already embedded deep into his heaving chest.

"Clovis, behind you!" Evan shouted in English.

Clovis yanked his blade from the lead soldier's slumping body and turned to the door just as thin wire leads hit his blood-soaked tunic. His eyes followed the delicate curling wires back to the black plastic gun in the mercenary's hand. The crackling voltage jolted the confused warrior to the floor in a heap of clanking steel.

Two more men raced to the convulsing Clovis and bound his arms behind his back with black handcuffs. Evan kept his eyes on his fallen hero as they handcuffed him as well.

"Secured!" the first man shouted over his shoulder as he holstered his Taser pistol. Two men grabbed Evan, took everything from his pockets, and sat him on one of the simple chairs before stepping away to attend to their two comrades who were still moving.

Evan, suddenly remembering Clovis's instruction to act as his servant, called out in Arabic, "Master, are you okay?"

"I know that accent," came a commanding female voice from outside, "and it does not belong this far south into Arabia Felix."[17]

A woman dipped slightly to step her height under the doorframe. She looked to be in her midforties and wore bright white pants, a white shirt, and a gleaming white cape that radiated light from the sunlight that bathed the doorway. Evan's eyes ached against the brightness as he strained to look at her, and they found little relief when they focused, taking in the sharpness of her Scandinavian features—all chin and cheekbones under a shock of pure black hair tied tight into a flowering knot at the top of her lofty head. A slight, round-shouldered Asian man stepped into the tower behind her, a stethoscope hung around his neck.

---

17. Arabia Felix is a Roman term to describe the southernmost lands of the Arabian Peninsula, including current day Yemen.

She pointed a slender finger toward Clovis in a heap on the floor. "Check his vitals," she barked and then looked over the chaos of the bloodied bodies on the floor. She stepped carefully around the growing pool of blood under the motionless body of the leader. "Idiots!" she snapped at the surviving men. "I told you this man was dangerous."

The doctor monitored Clovis's vital signs and looked up from his new patient. "He'll be fine."

She spun on one heel to face her demoralized men. "Put the old man in a chair next to this one."

"What about our wounded?" one of the men in the second group asked.

She craned her long neck to examine the two men still breathing in wheezing gasps. "Look where he placed his blades." She jutted her sharp chin at the far one. "Liver. He's got five minutes left." She turned to the other. "That looks like an opened artery, eight minutes." She pointed back to Clovis, whose unconscious head lolled wildly as they dropped him onto a chair next to Evan. "He's already killed them." She chuckled as she grabbed a handful of his white hair and pulled it back to examine his motionless face. "It doesn't look like he has lost any steps. There is nothing Dr. Ling can do for them now. Say your goodbyes and get this mess cleaned up. I want this place *spotless*—like we were never here."

The doctor checked Clovis's vital signs again. "He is well enough to get the shot now if you want."

"Oh no," she countered in an icy tone. "He and I have much unfinished business before that. Keep him stable and let him wake up of his own accord while I have a look around and decide what I want to do with this one." She glanced at Evan.

The two mercenaries died in their predicted turns as she went through Clovis's sparse rooms. Her surviving men dragged the dead down to the beach as she returned to the main room, carrying three large sheets of paper. Evan recognized the same Japanese calligraphy on two of the sheets as she rolled them up, clasped one tightly in her hand, and handed the other to Dr. Ling.

"Tuck this into the old man's belt," she instructed, then turned quickly on her heels and stepped in front of a silent Evan, who kept his eyes on the floor. "And you, young man. What of you?" She observed him for some minutes to see if he would waver. "I suspect you are not what you seem. I would say from your accent that you are Syrian or Lebanese. Either way, you are a long way from home and should be nowhere near this man's quiet corner of the world."

She turned Clovis's weathered right hand to show the faded Embe tattoo, then turned Evan's hand and saw nothing but tanned skin. "Am I supposed to believe you are his servant? Was that the idea?" she asked, walking around to face him again. She nodded to a mercenary, and he presented Evan's flip phone, cigarettes, Russian lighter, and roll of Yemeni money. The soldier flipped open the phone and showed the Arabic symbols to her as she examined each item. "What was it he said, Dr. Ling—'Clovis, behind you'?"

"In perfect American English," the doctor added, putting away his stethoscope and glancing knowingly at Evan.

"Yes, that's right," she continued. "So a young Syrian in the wrong part of Arabia also speaks fluent English *and* knows this man's true name. Interesting indeed. And then there is this," she said, holding up the third paper with two short lines of strange characters written by hand. "Do you know how many people in this world can still write and read old Aramaic?" she asked a stoic Evan. "I would guess no more than a handful." She gripped his chin and raised his face to meet her dominating gaze, finally getting a reaction as he recoiled from her. "It is a shame that two of them are in the room with you right now."

Evan's will and expression faltered under her scrutiny.

"Shall I read it to you?"

Evan shook with fear and rage, struggling to remain emotionless, but he did want to know what Clovis had written.

She looked down at the strange text in her hand. "'I have spoken with this man. He is who he claims to be.'" She rolled up the paper again, leaned in next to his ear, and whispered, "So who is it you claim to be?" She pulled back and looked into his eyes. "I suspect there's more than one of you in there, isn't there"—she leaned in to whisper again—"*Evan?*"

Evan's eyes snapped up to look at her.

"Aah, there it is," she laughed. She turned to the doctor with a bright smile on her sharp face. "Fortune smiles on us today, old friend. This is another one of theirs—the young one, I suspect." She finished a deep laugh before losing the smile on her stern face and locking her coal-black eyes back onto Evan's. "I look forward to speaking with you. We have much to discuss, young one."

She turned to one of her remaining men standing near the door. "You," she barked at him. "You're the new squad leader now. Take these two *guests* to the yacht and put them below."

The woman and Dr. Ling boarded the brilliant white yacht first, every inch of its surface spotlessly clean and gleaming. The doctor went belowdecks, and she stood at the railing of the luxurious craft as it bobbed in the blue swells, supervising what remained of her men.

Clovis's eyes flickered open, and he felt his arms restrained behind him. He shook his head to clear the remnants of electric shock and scanned his surroundings until he saw her standing at the polished railing, looking down at him. She shouted a short phrase at him in Japanese, a command. Clovis stiffened. She shouted the command at him again, and Clovis lowered his head as the squad leader tied the inflatable boat to the landing at the back of the yacht.

"Put them below," she ordered her men. "Our good doctor has prepared their places."

Two of her men led Clovis and Evan aboard and then began to grab the bloodied, lifeless bodies of their comrades.

"What are you doing?" she roared. "They're a mess. Give them to the sharks and clean those boats completely." She turned to the attentive helmsman on the deck above and signaled him to depart. The yacht's twin engines rumbled to life, and they turned away from the ancient lighthouse, leaving dusty Yemen drifting into the distance.

The guards took Clovis and Evan belowdecks into an opulent dining galley and tied them to chairs fixed to the floor. Both men stayed silent as the guards secured their restraints.

Evan spoke first after the guards went above. "Do you know who they are?"

Clovis drew a deep breath, his thin eyelids closed. "I know her. She is a longtime f—" The final word caught in his throat, unsure whether to say *friend* or *foe*. "I have a lot of history with her."

"Is she one of us?"

Eyes still closed, Clovis continued, "Yes, she is one of us. But she is not with us. Not for a long time."

"I heard about her and the excommunication. Is that—"

"Brevicepts," Clovis sighed before Evan could utter her name. "Yes, it is her. There is no mistaking it. She is Brevicepts."

"What does she want with us? Who are those men? How did they know where to find us?"

Clovis opened his eyes to get some bearing from the limited view out of the portholes in the long galley. "The first question is, where is she taking us? I can tell from the way the sea smells that we are out at sea and no longer next to the coast, and from our orientation we are headed south. The craft is not large enough to go more than one thousand miles. So I would say we are headed toward Somalia.

"I think I am her prize," Clovis continued, "not you, Evan. As I said, I have history with her. Good and bad. The French have a saying, *La vengeance est un plat qui se mange froid.*[18] Do you know it?"

"I think I get the idea. You were the deciding vote in her excommunication all those years ago."

"Centuries ago," Clovis corrected as he strained against the ropes.

Evan watched him. The killing of Brevicepts's men had breathed new life into the aged man.

"Yes, but there is more to it than just expelling her from the Cognomina," he said, looking down at the taut ropes across his bloodstained tunic and then over to Evan's. "It seems we are to be here for a while."

18. French—Revenge is a dish that must be eaten cold

Clovis sighed as he began to recall the story. "This all started in Japan a long time ago. My calligraphy, the apology you found, is from that time as well.

"But the story really starts at the Giza pyramids in Egypt at our old Sumerfest gathering on the longest day of the year, as was our Cognomina tradition before we moved to Zurich. Brevicepts was a young nobleman named Masakato,"[19] he said, narrowing his eyes in an attempt to bring the detail back into focus. "He was from an important clan in eastern Japan then.

"It was his second arduous journey from the east. Brevicepts wore a disguise of linen bandages over his distinctive Asian eyes and he walked with a blind man's long cane to fit into the dense crowd of Egyptians around Giza. I didn't notice him until he was right next to me and then he stabbed the top of my sandaled foot with his cane. I dropped to one knee from the pain, and he kneeled next to me and said, 'I am so sorry, sir. Perhaps you can help me. I am looking for a very old man who is not very bright but is good with a blade. His name is Clovis.'

"I turned and pulled the blind man's face close to mine, moving the bandaged disguise up enough to expose Brevicepts's Eastern eyes. I slapped the long cane out of his hand and lifted him off the ground in a crushing embrace. 'Welcome back, you scoundrel,' I said and held him for a long time."

"So you were friends?" Evan asked.

"Yes." Clovis craned his neck to peek up the stairs. "Yes, we were as close as brothers then. We knew each other from one life before where he joined me in the Roman Legion, so he knew I could fight and lead men into battle. That is why he came back. He made the trip from the east again for me.

"We camped in the shadow of the Great Pyramid, as was our custom

---

19. It could be that Clovis is referring to Masakado, not Masakato. Taira Masakado was a tenth-century Japanese nobleman from the eastern provinces of feudal Japan. His story was captured contemporaneously by Shōmonki and translated by Rabinovitch (and others). History professor Karl Friday has an excellent biography of Masakado, titled *The First Samurai*.

then—me, Brevicepts, Galen, Auda, Chance, and Ramsay. Brevicepts told us of his new land, an island beyond China and even Silla.[20] He said he was born into a powerful and noble family, that his family's land was good and rich and civilized. He told us that his people were good and obedient subjects. And then he invited all of us to join him in this land.

"Brevicepts's idea, even back then, is that he would create a special homeland for the Cognomina, a place that would always be ours. It would be 'a permanent place for a permanent people,' he said to us. It sounded beautiful, like an enticing new shape drawn on a blank map. We drank Galen's wine, and Brevicepts pitched us into the evening. 'Come with him,' he asked of us, 'and help create a new homeland.' I listened. We listened to his utopian vision well into the cooling night and it was then that I decided to join him and see this new place. Little did I know under those Egyptian stars that night that his journey would take me deep into his dark, dystopian heart."

Clovis smiled as he recalled the next part of the story. "What a pair we were—me a tall, blond Viking and him a young Japanese noble. The journey to Asia was long and dangerous, and the only travelers who knew the whole route were the Radhanites. They forged trade routes from Spain to China on the backs of the abandoned roads of Alexander and Caesar. This was centuries before the Polos walked it or the Venetians set their sails to the east. As Jewish traders, they could travel freely in Christian, Muslim, and pagan lands. They would take eunuchs and Slavic slave girls to Eastern harems and would haul back silks and spices to Western kings. They took the Spanish stallion to the Mohammedans and even brought an elephant to Charlemagne. They spoke every language on the long route and were happy to have two experienced swordsmen in their company.

"I can still remember the powerful aroma of their wagons. Even when empty, their wagons smelled of the exotic spice cargoes from China and India. A man could not spend more than a few hours at a

20. Silla is another antiquated term to describe the land on what is now the Korean peninsula.

time in them before he would be overcome and have to ride in fresher air at the front of the caravan.

"To combat the boredom on the long journey, Brevicepts and I would spar every time the caravan stopped. He taught me new sword techniques he had learned from Japan, and I showed him those from my northern kinsmen. He taught me his language and how to write it so that I would be able to issue simple commands to his men as their new general. And that is when Brevicepts told me more of what our true mission would be.

"He said he had been fighting with powerful relatives and neighbors for over a year and he was convinced he could prevail over them with some help—with my help," Clovis said, his eyes locked on Evan's. "He had the political moves mapped out, but he needed a field commander to form his small group of followers into an army and then grow it."

"And you did it for him?" Evan asked.

"At first, yes. I was the right man for the job, and I still had the appetite for it then. I had led Roman Legionaries, Brevicepts among them. Our first task after we had sailed from Ningbo to Shimōsa was to drill his men into shape and stand up his main rival in the neighboring village.

"I trained them well, and they became good soldiers. Those men were moral and honest, and I grew to admire them, which made their corruption more than I could stand. I remember the rage that would come over Brevicepts when he spoke about his vengeance against those who had wronged him," Clovis said, nodding his head one time to her above on deck. "That was my first clue as to how dark she was. Later, that darkness would blind Brevicepts and make me wish myself blind instead of a witness to her cruelty.

"When we arrived in Japan, *I* was now the one who had to disguise my alien features and Brevicepts had it all planned for me. He sneaked me into his fortified family compound and hid me in a room at the back of his home. Inside that modest room, I saw, for the first time, my military uniform—the armor of the samurai. It provided complete coverage—from feet and shin with lacquered metal splints to head and face with an ornate black helmet and menacing red face guard. I was to be a commander behind a mask."

"Like a samurai?"

"No, I was a shogun, which is more like a general or field commander, but I wore the armor that would later be popularized by the samurai. But none of it fit me. I must have been one of the largest men in the country. He had his armorer remake everything but the face mask. I waited in my room for a week until it was done, and by then I was anxious to start building an army. I was anxious to do anything.

"I would open the sliding door a few inches every morning and sit inside, well out of sight, and watch my small sliver of that new world outside. The people of Masakato's village moved about their cold tasks under a gray sky filled with the first falling flakes of that bitter winter . . ."

12

. . . the people of Masakato's village moved about their cold tasks under a gray sky filled with the first falling flakes of winter. Clovis watched the villagers through the crack in the sliding door to his secret room and tried to see what Brevicepts saw in them. If they were obedient subjects and a docile, productive people as Brevicepts had described them during their long journey, then he would need to spark them into flame in order to forge them into a fighting force for his friend.

He watched the women first. They were always up the earliest, fetching water from the well in the same sequence each morning. The youngest wives arrived first and filled their wooden buckets, carrying them at the ends of green bamboo poles that arced over their supporting backs. By the time the older wives were at the well, the younger ones were already feeding chickens and collecting eggs.

The older men emerged next, their lean and sinewy bodies wrapped tightly in strips of brown cloth to combat the cold. He watched two men meet at the well where they spoke for a while before moving to light the forge at the far end of the village. The raging fire beckoned younger men from their beds, and they gathered and rotated around its warmth before moving off to yoke animals and tend distant fields. The old men who tended the forge fire poured tea freely from a giant iron kettle cradled above the red flames.

Clovis studied the men as they drank their tea and planned their days. They were farmers with a few tradesmen mixed in. He looked at their physical condition. Their bodies were fit from their labors and would mold well into soldiers. He studied their interactions: who stood closest to the fire, who had smaller circles of men around them, who started and led a conversation, who bowed to whom. Clovis watched day after day until he had identified possible captains and lieutenants. He noticed the weak ones who would need more training time, and he singled out the unyielding personalities he might need to tame or break. He saw the comradery between them as the first men said their goodbyes before moving away to start their tasks. Eventually, only four younger men remained at the forge. Thicker in arm and shoulder than the others, they sorted out their hammers and tongs as the fire settled into working embers.

Clovis could see the working motions of the smiths but could not see the shape of the thing they forged—a sword, a plow, perhaps a new suit of armor for an impossibly large man. The high-pitched pinging of their rhythmic hammers carried down to his ears as three of the muscled men swung in a tight, repeating sequence at an orange square atop the round anvil that a fourth smith rotated with his tongs.

He watched their labors and envisioned the training he would soon put these men through—physical training to ensure calloused hands could swing a weapon for hours on end, tactical training to teach them how to move as squads of men, combat training against human-shaped sandbags dressed like their enemies to show where on the body to strike, and finally kill training to find and harness that darkness inside all men that allows them to end one another. Kill training was the hardest and always last in the sequence. Like the careful tempering of a blade after many hours of hot, hammering work, it imparts a hardness that is at the core of every fighting man. Clovis knew how to stoke that emotion, how to hammer and shape that menacing aboriginal remnant. And he knew how to cool it carefully so that it would keep its shape and could be controlled.

Clovis heard footsteps behind him and turned from his observations to see Brevicepts slide open an ornately painted screen at the back of the room where it joined his main house.

"Hello, brother," Clovis said.

"I brought you some things," Brevicepts said, placing a bundle of Japanese clothing on the floor next to the ornate black-and-red painted mask.

"I do suppose I should start dressing the part," Clovis replied.

"And acting it," Brevicepts added, "but I will get to that in a bit. Take these and dress behind the screens there. I will have my staff prepare the room for us. Please stay out of sight behind the screen until I return."

Clovis rounded the painted screen to see the low heating brazier filled with coals and plates of food set out on low tables. When Brevicepts returned, he admired his friend dressed in his own family-crested official white robes. Clovis ran a finger over the maroon embroidered crest.

"It's a butterfly,[21] the symbol of the family I was born into here. Perhaps one day, it will be the symbol of what we hope to achieve here," Brevicepts said. "Sit with me."

Clovis dropped to the floor opposite his kneeling friend and crossed his legs in front of him.

Brevicepts shook his head. "Sit like I am sitting. Kneel with your legs underneath you," he directed. "The mask will attach to the helmet we are refitting and will shield your strange face to them, but your actions and behaviors need to be in line with ours, or they will notice you are not like us and they will reject you."

Clovis picked up the mask and placed it over his face. "How do I look?"

Brevicepts considered his friend for a moment. "Tuck in the beard and the excess hair and you will look the part," he said with a smile.

Clovis lowered the mask and looked at it as he folded his long legs under his large frame. "How is this going to work? How am I going to train and lead your men from behind a mask? Can I not just be a foreign general you brought in?"

---

21. This butterfly reference is another powerful clue to the veracity of Clovis's recollection, as the Taira clan had an ornate butterfly as their family symbol.

Brevicepts poured a cup of tea and handed it to Clovis, who fidgeted uncomfortably in this new posture. "It is not the way in this place. These people have a long-bred distrust of foreigners and outsiders—they even dislike those from other parts of their nation. This distrust is one of the tools we will exploit to rally them to our ends." Brevicepts sipped the hot tea. "The mask is a great honor and is only allowed to be worn by the most accomplished warriors. They will revere you and obey your every command. Use some of those basic commands I taught you on the journey—the more complicated ones you will whisper to me and I will relay them to the men for you. And you can always use the whistle commands we used in the Legion."

Clovis smiled at the shared Roman memory. "Truly, is there no other way?" Clovis pleaded.

"If you walked out there now, they would run in panic from you. It would be as though a god or a devil had been set loose from this house." Brevicepts reached over and adjusted the overlap of lapels on his friend's robe. "These are good people, Clovis. They are obedient and hardworking, but they are stubborn, superstitious, and hopelessly set in their ways. After we have built a fighting force and they have some victory banners to ride beneath, then perhaps they would be open to accepting you, even embracing you, but until then, there is no other way."

"I have been watching them," Clovis said, grabbing pieces of fish with his fingers. "I see what you see in them. I think it should be easy to train and lead them."

"Use these. Here, let me show you." Brevicepts handed his general a pair of red lacquered chopsticks. "I am glad you see their potential. What do you need to start training the men?"

"Besides the refitted armor to hide this hideousness," he said, motioning to his bearded face, "the men will need swords. Do they have swords or other bladed weapons?"

"Most do," Brevicepts answered, "but they do not know how to use them well."

"I can see to that. Have the smiths begin making swords so that every man has one and then make extras. Others will want to join after the first victories, and our ranks will swell. Every man will need a wooden sword for practice. Have your carpenters fashion some right away. Do they have horses and saddles?"

"Most have a mount."

"How many men can you summon to start?"

"I am preparing that list now," Brevicepts said over his cup of tea, "but I estimate it will be over five hundred men."

Clovis looked up from his clumsy labors with the chopsticks. "That is a good start, and winter is always the best time to raise an army from farmers."

"Your armor will be ready tomorrow."

"Then let us begin tomorrow. I have an idea of how I want to start with them," Clovis said. "You know, if we are to be an army, we will need an insignia to identify and honor the men. I like this one," he said, pointing to the maroon butterfly. "Have your seamstresses make five hundred headbands for our new soldiers."

"Right away, General," Brevicepts said, lowering into an exaggerated bow that coaxed Clovis to bend at the waist. "Starting tomorrow, watch the way the people bow and act toward me in public. You will need to do the same, Clovis. After all, I am a lord here in this land."

CLOVIS AROSE BEFORE DAWN THE NEXT MORNING and practiced four sword exercises in the silence of the paneled room. He then cracked the exterior panel door open and sat back on kneeled knees to watch the village come to life under a pink-and-orange sunrise.

The young wives' routine at the well was disturbed by the first arrivals of young men from the nearby villages. Masakato had sent messengers with his decree summoning all fighting-age men to Shimōsa, and they came on foot and horseback, in talking groups and alone in silence. Clovis listened at the gap and strained his new Japanese ears to catch their conversations and their attitudes at this imposition. He heard less complaining and more reverence than he expected, but there were complainers; there were always complainers at a muster.

One of Masakato's administrators greeted the men and assembled them in the open courtyard around the center well. Clovis donned his resized armor as the men kneeled in anticipation of their leader's arrival. Clovis heard the shuffling of numerous feet near his room and saw the procession as it moved toward a low platform at the far side of the square; his friend Brevicepts was at its center.

All eyes followed Brevicepts as he walked gracefully with his entourage dressed in ornamental white-and-yellow robes with the red butterfly symbol covering the left breast of their garments. The regal group stepped onto the platform and kneeled in curved ranks around a low desk at the front. Brevicepts walked to the center of the short stage and bowed deeply to the assembled men, showing his black-knotted hair atop his head. All bent forward and prostrated themselves flat against the packed earth. Brevicepts then kneeled at the low desk and began reading from a text that was handwritten across a long roll of paper delicately folded onto itself like a primitive, pleated book.

"Your presence here honors me," Brevicepts began in a voice loud enough to carry to every man. "I have summoned you here to help us achieve a common goal. But for me to help you, I need each of you to help me. We all understand the same threat we face. I speak of course of the most recent tax increases and property confiscations decreed by Kyoto at the end of the last harvest. While we all honor the emperor and revere his name, his bureaucrats in the capital and the provinces place a heavy thumb on the scales when factoring our share that goes to them." Brevicepts turned a page, and a few men murmured some agreement. "This last increase was too much for us to endure. Some of you here today were even forced to surrender your lands to the regional governor. I have personally accepted five of these displaced families into this compound after the Hitachi governor seized their lands. And do you remember what that criminal from Hitachi did with those lands? He gave them to his relatives, who sleep under those stolen roofs to this day. This is a disrespect to us and to our emperor, who would never permit this to happen if only he could know about it."

A few men shouted approval from the anonymity of their numbers.

"This is how I propose to combat this insufferable injustice. We must let the emperor know by sending a message to his local leaders that we are strong and must be offered the respect we deserve. That respect will not be given by them freely. It must be demanded of them, and that demand can only come from a position of strength and power. That strength we shall have, if you will join me." Brevicepts paused to measure the building resentment in the assembled men. "I have summoned a famous warrior, a general from the other side of the kingdom. If you will join me in forming a force of our families, this warrior will train and strengthen us into an army that can demand respect from our neighbors. So I ask you now as your lord, but also as your brother, will you join me in this effort? Will you join our new army? Will you be trained by our new general?"

"I will join," shouted a voice from the front row.

"I will fight with you, my lord," shouted another.

Brevicepts looked out on the assembled men while a frenzy of agreement rolled through them like a wave. He held up his hand to quiet them and pushed his folded paper to the edge of the desk. "Please step forward and leave your mark on this paper to show your commitment to make a better life for ourselves."

One of Masakato's administrators moved forward and placed his short knife on the table next to the paper. Clovis watched in fascination as each man stepped forward in an ordered, unspoken turn and silently ran his left thumb against the edge of the administrator's blade before placing a bloodied thumbprint on the paper. The administrator turned page after page of red circles as every man stepped up and left his sanguine signature before returning to his kneeling position in the crowd.

Clovis knew his friend was about to introduce him as their general. He adjusted the metal sleeves on his blacked metal suit and picked up the full face mask. He turned it over in his hand and admired the white eyebrows and beard that framed the large nose in the middle of a red lacquered menacing face. *Not a bad likeness*, he thought, tying it in place against the metal helmet and sliding open the panel door.

He exited his secret room and started a carefully stepped path through the dotted pattern of kneeling farmers, laborers, and tradesmen in the large courtyard. A full head and shoulders taller than almost every man assembled, Clovis towered over them as he stepped in long, clinking strides. He scanned the men's faces from behind his mask, looking for four specific men. Brevicepts rose from his kneeling position to receive Clovis onto the platform and bowed to him as he stepped up. Clovis returned his bow and then bowed toward the five hundred awestruck faces staring up at him.

Brevicepts cleared his throat and addressed his new force. "I present to you Shogo Korubisu. Korubisu-san has fought and won many battles. He has countless heads to his credit, and it is an honor to have him here with us to train us, to lead us, to fight with us if need be. Korubisu-san was injured," Brevicepts said, motioning to his own throat as an example, "so his speech is limited now, and he will communicate through me most of the time and can command by whistling. Korubisu-san wishes to start our work with a demonstration of what you will soon be able to do yourselves."

Clovis walked over to one of the prepared racks of wooden practice swords. He grabbed four hand-carved training blades and scanned the faces of the men below him. His first quarry was the easiest to spot— the largest of the men he had studied from behind his cracked panel. He was the tallest man in the village, one of the muscular smiths from the forge. Clovis thought he looked strong as an ox and likely as smart.

Clovis bowed and handed a wooden sword to the confused man. Next to the smith was the natural leader of the village—young but unmistakable in his charisma. This young man attracted people and knew how to keep them close. He smiled as Clovis bowed and handed him a wooden sword. The next man was the first Clovis identified days ago—the other leader in the village, but a negative one. This man also attracted men to him, but through commiserating complaint, and his eyes did not look up as Clovis bowed and handed him a wooden sword.

Clovis rose from his bow and scanned the faces of the crowd in hopes of finding his last man. He did not yet have this man identified, but he knew what he was looking for: a man who by now had figured out what was about to happen and was skilled enough, fearless enough, or crazy enough to want to be the fourth man in this upcoming exercise. Most faces lay pressed against hard earth; some dared to look up but then quickly looked away. And then he saw him.

The fourth man was smaller than Clovis had expected. He remained in a respectful kneel but craned his thin neck high to meet a menacing, masked gaze. His unblinking black eyes showed absolutely no fear. Clovis stopped in front of him and motioned for the short man to rise. He sprang to his feet and received the wooden sword in a deep, respectful bow. Clovis returned the short man's bow, whistled loudly, and motioned the other three men to follow him to the cleared practice area to the right of Brevicepts's regal stage.

Clovis removed his strange Viking sword, placed it in the rack, and inspected a wooden one before slipping it into the leather waistband of his armor. He stood in the middle of the practice area and directed the four men to surround him as points on a compass, then nodded to Brevicepts, who spoke to the four men in a voice loud enough to carry to all ears.

"Shogo Korubisu instructs you to ready yourselves to attack him in unison on his command." Brevicepts looked at each of the four men in turn. "Are you prepared?"

The small brave one nodded first, and the others followed.

Clovis barked a command for *go* in his best Japanese, and the small man lunged at him like a flailing lunatic. He parried the smaller man's surprisingly good sword thrusts and then stepped deep inside his unbalanced stance, hip-checking him to the ground. Clovis raised his wooden sword to meet the blow he had expected from the young leader, steered his blocking move to the right, and swung his leg behind his opponent's lead leg, bringing him down in an uncontrolled heap.

The small man was already up and running at his new instructor again. Clovis stepped back and to the side, just missing the whistling downward swing from the village strongman. He grabbed the smith's waist sash and spun him into the oncoming smaller man, sending them both crashing to the perimeter. The negative man rushed last, as Clovis anticipated he would, and swung wildly at the master's head. Clovis toyed with this man until the other men got back to their feet. He dueled all four at once in a blinding display of speed and precision footwork that always circled a primary assailant and kept the other two or three just out of striking distance behind him.

He could have gone on longer, but he saw his chance when a circling step to the left brought the negative man front and center. Clovis dug his right foot into some loose dirt and kicked it up into the fierce, unyielding eyes of the small man, blinding the most difficult of his opponents. Clovis kept his target man in front of him but allowed a gap for the strong smith to charge at him. Clovis circled again to the left, but this time he buried the blunt wooden sword handle into the large man's ribs as he passed. He heard the air escape him in a groaning wheeze as the blacksmith fell to one knee.

Clovis watched the complaining leader and let his eyes follow the outline of the sword in his dominant right hand. He traced the arc of his arm up to the shoulder, where his gaze fixed on the thin collarbone jutting beneath tight skin. He waited for the fourth man to move, which he finally did after some hesitation. The master deflected the negative man's blow, and in a stroke too quick for most to follow, he brought his wooden sword tip down on the target man's right collarbone with just enough force to yield the telltale click of a fracture. The man dropped his weapon and fell to his knees in pain. Clovis smiled in satisfaction that he had accomplished an important first step in isolating this nuisance from the other men.

Clovis brought his hard wooden blade across the back of the young leader's hand, and it sprang open in pain, dropping his sword. Clovis stooped to pick it up and then stood between the two remaining men, a wooden sword extended to each of their necks. He bowed to each of them, and the lesson was over.

"Why did they fail?" Brevicepts asked in a booming voice. "Because they did not work as a unit," he replied, not waiting for an answer. "Think of the fingers—what a marvel they are and what they can do. Think of their power when curled into a fist. And now think of that fist holding a weapon. This is the power of the fingers multiplied. This has been

Master Korubisu's first lesson to us. Let us thank our master and begin with his exercises that will turn us into a unified fist holding a weapon."

Every man, save the injured fourth, rose to his feet and brought his hands together in synchronized sets of three claps.

Proof they are capable of acting as a unit, Clovis thought.

CLOVIS STARTED THEM ON CALISTHENICS and worked them until they could barely climb into their saddles at the end of the day. The following days brought basic weapons training. Clovis stood on the platform and stepped through swordplay practice routines while looking out from behind his mask at the hundreds of wooden sword tips tracking his as the men mimicked his moves. After several days, Clovis saw how their minds were structured by their society and were ordered in a way he had not seen before. The men would follow any order and would make sure everyone else in the squad would too. This is what Brevicepts saw in them.

By the end of the first week, they had learned all the basic sword and footwork techniques and could use them in one-on-one sparring. Clovis learned the names of four men: Katsutaka, the young natural leader whom all the men looked to for guidance; Kasuno, the strong smith who was smarter than he appeared; Tsuneaki, the small man with the fierceness of ten warriors; and finally there was Haruaki,[22] the wounded fourth man whom Clovis had intended to marginalize.

The next week brought kill testing with real swords against sand-filled dummies. Clovis watched them one by one as they practiced pushing sharp steel into yielding flesh. He noted the ones who showed the most ease in the task, and he formed them into command groups for extra leadership training and consultations with Brevicepts, who spent long hours with them alone.

He sent the more timid ones through the drill over and over—until their swords swung heavily in their aching arms, until they shouted in

---

22. Of all the Masakado lieutenants Clovis mentions in his account, only Haruaki is mentioned by name as the man for whom an arrest warrant was issued by the local governor. (See the Shōmonki translation.)

hatred at the mocking, undying man-shapes that hung before them, until he knew even the weakest ones would be able to find that fiery blood-lust and follow one of their new leaders into a fray. They were now hot metal ready to be forged into the shape of a weapon.

Clovis identified new leaders at each step: those who helped a slower student master a movement, those who demanded more of those around them, and those whom the others looked to when lost on something new. These were like finding precious nuggets in shovel after shovel of mined earth, and Clovis marveled at their order and discipline before sending them to Brevicepts for his long one-on-one meetings.

The next week brought marching and unit movement training, and Clovis watched them move and even think like a larger group. He learned about their use of the whistling Kabura arrows that the Shinto priests would shoot ahead of a battle to ward off evil spirits. In addition to a set command of loud mouth whistles he could deliver behind his mask, Clovis developed a signaling system of shooting the whistling arrows in sequences of one, two, three, and five to direct Brevicepts's men at distances of up to a kilometer away.

The next week Clovis drilled them in fighting and archery from horseback. Katsutaka, the young leader, brought an enormous draft horse from the countryside for Clovis to use, but no man could find a saddle large enough to accommodate their general.

The farmers and tradesmen amazed Clovis with their bow-and-arrow accuracy on horseback. Each day finished with more kill training against sand-filled practice dummies—first on horseback, then on foot. Every man embraced it now and anticipated the feeling of arrow and sword penetrating real men. They finished each day by bragging about their new abilities, spoiling for a fight with their hated neighbors. They were now hot-forged into the shape of a fighting force and only needed a cooling-off period to temper their stoked bloodlust into a controllable, disciplined rage.

Clovis waited past sunset for Brevicepts to finish his daily walk with each of Clovis's newly identified leaders. It was not unusual for him to be late. Clovis kneeled in front of a low bench and practiced crude calligraphy with a brush stylus and black ink.

Brevicepts knocked and entered, carrying cold fish and rice. "I see you are keeping up with our studies from the long journey here," he said, looking over his general's shoulder at his work. "Pretty good. Correct this part," Brevicepts said, placing his tattooed right hand over the top of Clovis's on the brush and deftly stroking an improved character beside the flawed one. "The men seem ready for use."

"They are trained, but they are not ready yet. I want to send the men home for a week," Clovis said, studying the differences between the characters to find his flaw. "They are ready for battle, but they need time at home with their families to cool off and internalize their new skills. They are too hot, too dangerous to use just yet."

Brevicepts knelt beside Clovis and bowed in his direction so that the general could see the distinctive topknot of black hair on his head. "Clovis, there has been a development. The regional governor has issued an arrest warrant for Haruaki-san."

"Let them take him," Clovis spat in contempt. "The man is trouble, which is why I injured him and exempted him from the training."

"He is also the favorite of my uncle, whose forces we will need later. I must keep this man. And that is not all. My advisors believe the governor has learned of your training and that the arrest warrant for Haruaki-san is meant as an insult to me. My spies tell me that he plans to march here in force in two days to make the arrest in my village. This cannot happen. We must ride to Hitachi and confront the governor and his general with my new army." Brevicepts bowed again in respect to his friend.

Clovis shook his head. "The men are too hot, too raw with emotion to be controlled well right now. They need to cool off and temper the hatred I have put in their hearts."

"That hatred is what I must harness now," Brevicepts countered. "Let me worry about controlling them."

"I cannot guarantee that I, or even you, could control them as they are now." Clovis turned away from his calligraphy and adjusted his feet underneath him as he faced his friend. "I have made this mistake with freshly trained men before. If you let them taste blood too soon, they will be like wild animals—not easily controlled. But if you give me just three days to send them home to the comfort of their wives and the embraces of their children, their blood will cool and they will be the army you want. Trust me on this, brother. I have built forces like this before, and this rest, like the cooling water that makes the blade hard, is the most critical part of building a force that stays together in hardship. Three days is all I ask."

Brevicepts shook his head slowly. "No, we march tomorrow on Hitachi. It will only be a show of force to let them know we can defend ourselves. I will hold them back, and we can give them their rest after tomorrow."

"We cannot let them fight tomorrow. Agreed?"

Brevicepts extended his hand to his general. "Agreed."

THE MEN ASSEMBLED IN THE VILLAGE square at dawn.

Brevicepts stood with his retinue of advisers on the low platform. He kneeled, and the multitude followed. "Today is the day you have been working toward. Through your hard work and Shogo Korubisu's training, you are like a newly made weapon—hard, sharp, and deadly. I admire your effort and your accomplishment as men of Shimōsa." Brevicepts paused and bowed to them. "Now we are ready to become an army." He reached down to the mat in front of him, raised a clean white strip of cloth with the red Taira family butterfly symbol on it, and tied it around his head. The other advisers did the same. "Leaders, please step forward, take your place as part of our larger clan, and bring your men."

Clovis's leaders clambered forward as Brevicepts distributed a pile of cloth headbands. Tsuneaki, the small man, was the first of the officers in line. The men buzzed with energy as they admired each other's hand-embroidered insignia.

"Men," Brevicepts shouted to refocus their attention, "today has brought us our first challenge. Our provincial governor in Hitachi intends to arrest one of you. My messengers tell me his army will ride here tomorrow to take one of you away." Growls of disagreement grew from the men. "But they will not be expecting *us* when we march to see him in Hitachi *today*."

The men rose to their feet, roaring and shaking their swords. "To Hitachi!"

CLOVIS RODE WITH BREVICEPTS at the head of their column of men until the lantern lights of the provincial capital came into view just as the disappearing sun sent streaks of color across the sky. War drums summoned a scurry of local men to arms, and the first group of around two hundred men fell into ranks across the well-worn road into the provincial capital of Hitachi. Four swordsmen from the capital stepped forward to meet Brevicepts, Clovis, fierce Tsuneaki, and the young Katsutaka.

"What is the meaning of this?" the senior-most military leader demanded without bowing.

Brevicepts stepped forward and bowed to the men, which took them aback. "I am here to see the governor about the warrant he issued for one of my clan. Will you please let me see him so that we can make our protest known?"

"The governor is not taking appointments this evening," the leader laughed. "Besides, he has plans to visit your dusty village the day after tomorrow. You should run back home and wait for us to visit you then," he said, giving a deep, mocking bow.

"I will see him tonight. Please show us the way or step aside," Masakato said as Tsuneaki lowered into a combat-ready stance.

Over the heads of the swordsmen, Clovis watched large numbers of Hitachi men still falling into ranks at the back. "There are a lot of men mustering back there," he whispered to Brevicepts.

"And who will lead you against us? This little one?" their leader said, looking down into two burning eyes. "I think a fight might serve us better. What do you think, boys?" He turned to his three silent comrades. "Should we escort them to the governor or should we crush them?"

"Crush them," said their youngest leader, standing opposite Tsuneaki. "Let's start with their little pet here," he laughed, looking over to his leader, and he never saw the small man's blow that killed him.

Tsuneaki drew his sword, stepped forward, and thrust the tip of his blade deep into the man's chest just as it heaved with a hearty laugh.

Clovis froze and watched his pupil's efficient movements: the unsheathing and step were perfectly timed, the stance and position of the arm were well practiced, and the sword tip penetrated exactly where the red-painted dot had been on the practice dummies. The opponent slumped and slid back off Tsuneaki's red-stained blade.

Clovis sprang to action with a spinning move that pushed Brevicepts back into the protection of the first two ranks of Shimōsa men, who were already advancing. He drew his straight sword and swung it behind him at the position he anticipated the enemy leader would be, and Clovis felt the familiar resistance of flesh to his blade. With his back still to the Hitachi men, he sounded off three piercing whistles that commanded their mounted riders to charge. In seconds, two tight columns of mounted men charged past a fighting Clovis, Tsuneaki, and Katsutaka, scattering the ranks of Hitachi men into disarray.

Clovis stepped back two paces and gave two loud whistles that sent soldiers on foot into their ranks behind the horses. In minutes, the enemy force was in full flight and retreated into the assumed safety of their city. Katsutaka, Tsuneaki, and Brevicepts's other mentored leaders led the charge against their retreating foes.

Brevicepts grabbed Clovis by the arm. "Let's find the governor before he can regroup his men. The palace is this way."

Clovis nodded. "Let's end this quickly and limit the damage."

In the mere minutes it took for Clovis and Brevicepts to capture the sobbing governor, the fight had moved deep into the city. Clovis could still see most of the mounted Shimōsa men swinging down from their saddles. He raced forward to catch up but slowed his strides when he began to see old men and boys littered among the motionless dead defenders in the streets. The combat lay in front of him, marked by a line of orange flames that leaped from the wood and paper houses.

Is it too late to stop the fighting? Clovis wondered as he heard screams ahead of him. *Has their anger already flared out of control?* Clovis picked up his pace again, finding two of the whistler-arrow messengers to bring with him. He passed some of his men who were collecting valuable vases and silks from the homes and swords from fallen soldiers. The looting had started.

At the front, there were still small pockets of Hitachi defenders swinging out from shrinking circles of safety. Clovis caught up to a group of his men and leaped into the fray ahead of them. He struck down the leaderless defenders and sounded three short whistles, signaling the men to stop and hold their position. The men obeyed and bent at the waist to catch their breath in the swirls of smoke that danced about the burning homes. The arrow messengers shot volleys of three whistler arrows, but their piercing sounds were drowned out by the wails and lamentations of loss as the men pressed on.

Clovis peered through his mask at the hardening faces of the men around him. Only minutes before, they had done nothing more than practice stabbing and slashing at target bodies. And now they had practiced that ultimate power over man: they had killed. He could see in their faces now that they felt their new power but were not yet comfortable with it, that they knew they could take whatever, or whomever, they wanted, that it was now their choice.

Clovis yearned to warn these men that they stood at the edge of a precipice that would fall into a moral abyss. He yearned to tell them that the difference between being a soldier and being a savage was so small at a moment like this. But like a debt, it would compound on them in their later years into a burden they would be unable to forgive. He wanted to save them from that, but the menacing mask he wore was an embodiment, a totem, of that power.

They watched him as he struggled to communicate, then looked toward their comrades still fighting in the distance, their leader's grunting sounds of combat slowly changing to cheers and shouts. A few at the back turned and ran ahead into the melee, and Clovis knew he could not caution them, much less control them. His only chance now was to outdo them and try to bring the fight to an early end.

Clovis whistled the charge command at the men around him and raced to the front line of combat, striking down dozens. Brevicepts's leaders were in full plunder now, allowing Clovis and his cadre of men to dispatch the remainder of the opposing soldiers.

At the end of their bloody labor, Clovis turned to see the city now almost completely in flames. The mounted riders stood in a semicircle around a group of burning houses. He whistled to his men to follow as he regrouped with the rest of the force, Brevicepts's distinctive topknot of hair among the mounted riders who watched and cheered some spectacle just out of sight.

Clovis pushed his way through the crowd of men to see a group of archers shooting arrows at victims as they escaped from their burning homes. A cheer rose from the men each time an arrow found flesh, and they jeered in well-practiced unison when a victim retreated into the flames and certain death. A few of Clovis's cadre pushed their way toward the front of the circle with him. Clovis scanned to see the faces of the men who directed this carnage. Each familiar face had been a virtuous, disciplined man whom he had identified and trained before sending to Brevicepts for some instruction that had led to this.

A sharp, unanimous roar went up as two arrows simultaneously hit a woman carrying an infant, the second shaft permanently pinning the child to her silent breast. Clovis turned and looked up at Brevicepts who cheered loudest of all and shouted direction and encouragement in Japanese to each evil apprentice. His black eyes glowed red in the reflection of the fire, and Clovis thought back to all of those sequestered conversations Brevicepts had with his leaders. *Had he intended this? Had his friend conditioned and instructed them in this contest in butchery? Was the story of the arrest warrant even true?*

Clovis turned away and saw dozens of men, soldiers an hour ago, farmers and fishermen a month ago, grinding on top of wailing women. Some women were still moving; others were motionless. Half of Clovis's cadre were already stripping off their clothes, rubbing themselves in anticipation.

Had they made their choice or had their choice been orchestrated for them by Brevicepts, Clovis wondered as he looked back up at his friend. He took a bottle of sake from one of his soldiers, raised the ceramic bottle to his mouth to drink, where it clanked against the metal mask. He tore the mask from his face in anger and threw it into the burning pyre before him. He drank and watched his new warriors turn toward their darkened leaders like a hot blade warping to scrap under the hand of the unskilled smith.

He walked the streets for hours, nursing a second bottle and then a third against the cold of that long night. When he found a fallen soldier wearing the Taira butterfly headband, he respectfully moved him to the side and covered him with a section of fine silk from one of the plundered bolts that littered the streets before laying the embroidered red butterfly on the top.

He retreated from the action, retracing his steps back to the governor's palace. It was well behind the main front and lay unmolested except for the scuffle in arresting Brevicepts's fabricated foe. The evening lamps still burned brightly in the vacant office. Clovis kneeled at the deposed governor's desk, grabbed sheets of parchment, and began to mark them with an inked brush. He spent ten minutes on the first page, admired it, and then started another. He worked into the night, alternating between the sake bottle and the next copy. Brevicepts arrived just before dawn.

Clovis finished the final strokes on his page as Brevicepts stepped into the room. "Can I have a look?" he asked, announcing himself cautiously to his distracted general.

Clovis shook his head and rolled the copies and tied each one with an imperial string seal on the governor's desk. "Not this one, Brevicepts. It is for me."

"I see you have lost your mask."

"I know what you did. I can only imagine what you promised your leaders to turn them into the monsters they became tonight. But I have just one question for you." Clovis looked up to ensure he caught his friend's eyes. "Did you bring me here to help conquer this land—or empty it?"

"What? That?" Brevicepts motioned to the approaching sound of the continuing carnage audible in the distance. "Where is your taste for it, man? I remember you counting the heads of our enemies with me more than once."

"Enemies," Clovis interjected. "Not women and children. We were soldiers, not butchers," Clovis countered as he looked up to meet his friend's stony glare. "You *wanted* the men hot-tempered and raw from their training, didn't you? And you carefully prepared your leaders to execute this slaughter. I can see it now, but for the life of me, Brevicepts, I cannot see why. Why this way? What are you trying to accomplish with this savagery?"

Brevicepts smiled in a combination of concession and condescension. "You are a good soldier, Clovis, and you believe you are a good leader of men. But your shortcoming is that you are naive to what truly motivates men in this world. They want the power we have as Reincarnationists, as immortals, but they can never have it. They can never be like us—or even have a fraction of what we achieve with our lifetimes of knowledge and skill. But what they can have and will work for, even kill for or butcher for, is the promise that they *could* have that power over other men. That is true motivation, and that is how *I* lead men: by showing them what they are truly capable of. Those men out there," Brevicepts said, motioning to the noise outside, "they feel a power now that they couldn't have dreamed of when they woke this morning. Now they are capable of carrying me to Kyoto."

"Well, they will have to now," Clovis spat the words back at him. "You cannot do this any other way after this night."

"Precisely," Brevicepts replied with a satisfied smile. "You ask if our goal is to conquer this land or empty it for us. I say the mission is twofold. If we are to have a home for ourselves, we will need to conquer it. This you know in your heart," he said, placing his smooth hand over the embroidered butterfly on his chest. "But ask yourself this, my friend—once conquered, do you want to live next to their crying children and stinking hovels? No!" he bellowed, shaking his head so that the twisted topknot danced as he shouted down to a still seated Clovis. "We are to live as princes, not peasants. This land will be for us. This land where green fields meet the bounty of the sea will be ours forever. And these people, radically fewer of them, will remain only in an appropriate number to serve *us*. Part of their service to us now, as distasteful as it may be, is to clear the surplus of them from this new Eden."

"No, I cannot be part of this," Clovis said, raising his bearded chin in defiance. "Had you told me this was your way, I would have stayed in the West. I cannot do it, brother, not like this. I cannot live in a land stained with the blood of innocents."

"You must stay until we are finished," Brevicepts pleaded, raising his voice over the shouts of his men now at the door. "Think about the future, our future. I need you to do this for all of us in the Cognomina. Your help will provide us with a homeland for centuries."

"You have your monsters now. I hope they serve you well," Clovis said, patting the bundle of rolled messages tucked into his waistband.

"What are you doing?" Brevicepts demanded.

"I have explained myself and apologized to the men I gave you," Clovis said, facing Brevicepts, but keeping his back to the panel that shielded them from the marauding soldiers in the next room. "They are now your men."

"Stay back and do not enter!" Brevicepts shouted the Japanese command past Clovis.

Clovis smiled at his enraged friend, then curled his lips between his teeth and blew the whistle to charge. Eight of Brevicepts's leaders broke the screen and burst into the room. Clovis turned his unmasked face, now red with drink and framed in blond hair and beard, and glared down his long nose at them. Drunk on liquor and bloodlust, they stood stunned and then fell to their knees in unison.

"Sarutahiko,"[23] Tsuneaki whispered, his proud head pinned to the floor with the others.

Brevicepts stepped toward them. "He is not a god. He is just a—"

Clovis spun on one foot and planted a forceful kick squarely into Brevicepts's stomach, folding him in half and leaving him in a gasping heap on the floor. Clovis faced the leaders, who were shaking with fright, removed his roll of parchments, and handed a calligraphed page to each man in turn. He handed the last one to Tsuneaki and patted his obedient head as he stepped out into the light of dawn.

---

23. Sarutahiko was a Shinto deity known as a kami. Interestingly, he is portrayed in Japanese prints and woodcuts of the period as very tall, with a full white beard and hair that surrounded a red face with an oversized nose.

Clovis untied and dropped sections of his armor as he walked toward the fresher air near the sea. He knew he would find a boat there—a boat large enough to get back to the continent, a boat whose owner would no longer miss it. Piece by piece, he left sections of his discarded defenses in his wake as he walked down to the water until he found it. The boat bobbed and gently tugged at its mooring line in a beckoning motion that promised of home . . .

13

"... the boat bobbed and gently tugged at its mooring line in a beckoning motion that promised of home," Clovis concluded just as the engines stopped and the *tick tick* of Brevicepts's white leather boots clicked as she descended the stairs from the deck above.

"That kick did hurt," she said, stepping into the cabin and moving to the side of them so that both could turn to face her. "And that is the one true part of that heartwarming story."

Brevicepts leaned in to inspect Clovis's aged face. "I remember us winning," she continued in a low voice. "I remember us defeating our rivals and being well on our way to meeting our goal."

"Your goal," Clovis interrupted.

She walked a circle around both seated men, inspecting their rope restraints. "No, no, no. You were *with* me. You were excited about the mission. I remember it. I remember us driving our enemies before us. I remember them cowering and begging for their lives. I remember you competing for heads along with the rest of us." She bent over to look straight into his face. "And I remember you abandoning me." She spat the words at him.

Clovis swallowed hard. "I did not abandon you. I abandoned what you became: a mad and cruel corruption of the person I loved and followed. That is what you were then." He leveled his stern eyes back at hers. "Perhaps you still are."

She moved closer to Evan and let out a low laugh as she motioned to Clovis. "He may seem old and frail to you now, but make no mistake—he's killed more than cholera. He was the best trainer of killers since Pompey, a bit slow-witted at times, but he was the best." She looked down into Evan's dark eyes. "Truly, he was the best. Why do you think I traveled from Asia to get him?" She walked around to the side again to view them both. "I asked him to do what he had done countless times before. Was there violence that night?" she asked rhetorically. "Yes. But he, more than anyone, knows that plunder follows victory like the night that darkens the end of each day. I cannot say exactly what did it, but he lost his nerve and cracked that night," she said, motioning a long accusatory finger at the old man. "And it was *that* night he became this shell of the man I once knew. It is a shame it was on my watch. I did not break him, but make no mistake that his failure broke our dream of a permanent home," she said, looking at a slumping Clovis.

"Imagine it, Evan," she said, turning back to face him. "We could be moored off the coast of Japan right now, off the coast of our homeland where we would be together as a large family. We could be a united people, leading and administering a healthy and sustainable planet. But no," she said, shaking her head so that her topknot twisted atop her head, "because of him and what he did, we are a scattered and fractured people drifting in an ever-darkening world on the brink of destruction for the lack of leadership *we* could have provided."

She turned back to her old friend. "We could have been living in peace for a thousand years since then. We could have preserved this world as the Eden it once was. Clovis, I know you blame me for what you have become, but know this, old man"—she drew her face right up to his—"I blame you for what this world has become because we had a chance to change it for the better, and you poisoned that. You set back my efforts to save this world by ten centuries."

"I saw you that night," Clovis shouted, no longer able to contain his swelling emotion. "You would have burned the whole world to achieve your vision."

She leaned in until her face was inches from his. "Well, I will have to now, won't I?"

She rose, reached her slender hand behind her back, and produced an ornate, bejeweled dagger. She leaned her lips to Evan's ear as she slipped the blade between his restrained hands, cutting him free with one quick stroke. "Dinner is being served on deck. Please come up and join me." She turned and ascended the stairs without looking back, without any worry for her safety.

Evan rubbed his wrists and looked back at Clovis.

"Don't worry about him," she called. "I'll have something sent down."

"Don't trust her," Clovis shouted as Evan followed her.

He climbed the steps to the main deck and squinted against the setting sun. The yacht rocked gently in an expanse of dark blue. Brevicepts walked over to a table set for two on the front deck. She took a seat and marveled at the sunset while her hand dropped down and found the head of an attentive spaniel at her feet.

Evan stood and thought about the consequences of sitting in that chair opposite her. *Where would the journey take him if he did? What would happen to him and Clovis if he did not?* He walked over and took the chair opposite her. "Where are we?"

"Somewhere private," she answered, her eyes still locked on the last rays of the sun as it touched the water at the horizon. "I value privacy above all things, Evan. We are in the Red Sea somewhere. I hope you like what my chef has prepared. I'm a strict vegetarian. Some wine?" she offered politely, as though she had not been his captor an hour earlier.

"What do you want with us?"

Brevicepts poured wine for them both. "It's a lovely Barolo. Please do let me know what you think of it." She adjusted the bottle on the table and began. "In case you were wondering, it was him I was after. We have old and unfinished business, as you heard." She raised her glass to toast him, prompting him to follow reluctantly. "You were a bonus, and I must say that I am excited to meet you. I do apologize that it had to be like this," she said, motioning below. "But we will get to you. I am sure you are curious about me, are you not? Besides that fiction he told you, have you heard about me?"

Evan stared at her. "How did you know about me, what I am, and my name?"

"Please eat," she implored him. "As I told you, I read it from his note written in the Aramaic of our youth—intended for Ramsay or Auda or Galen, I presume. It would have to be addressed to an old one that I would have known." She stopped and took a drink from her glass, letting the liquid linger for a moment in her mouth. "Speaking English and knowing his name were giveaways, but I would have known anyway, Evan. I can spot us easily enough. There is something unmistakable and easily recognizable about us, wouldn't you agree?"

Evan ran through dozens of scenarios of how he should interact with her to win their release. "What you are going to do with me and Clovis?"

"You are easy. You are my guest and are free to go anytime you want," she said, motioning a long arm beyond the polished railing of the yacht to the infinite sea beyond. "Though you may want to wait until we make landfall—and you may want to stay a bit longer once you learn a bit more about me. But as I said, that choice is yours."

"And Clovis?"

"And Clovis." She sighed. "What to do about Clovis?"

"I must say your intent, with your mercenaries at the lighthouse, was obvious."

Brevicepts set down her fork. "Think back, Evan. Those men were unarmed and had only nonlethal devices. Clovis was never in any danger, save falling on his own sword. I knew he would likely resist my invitation, but I wanted to speak with him about options for a reconciliation with the Cognomina. But now that I think about it, you might be a better emissary." She poured more wine for them both. "As for him, I need to spend some time with him alone, but I promise you I will not kill him and that no physical harm will come to him. Does that satisfy you?"

"What choice do I have?"

"As it relates to me and Clovis, you have none," she stated matter-of-factly and took a bite of roasted eggplant. "We are going to sort out our old business and then see about new business. But between us," she said, looking into his eyes, "you are free, Evan. You are an equal. You are someone I wish to know and make myself known to. The best way to do that is by offering and not by taking. So I offer to talk about myself first."

Evan weighed his options again. He didn't trust her, but he wanted to gain as much of her trust as he could to gain any advantage for Clovis. "A few of them mentioned you, but it seemed like a topic no one really wanted to talk about. Some of them mentioned a rebellion you led, where you tried to consolidate regional power for the Cognomina."

"Is that all?"

"No. They told me about the excommunication and that Clovis was the deciding vote against you."

She picked at her plate with the silver fork. "That is true. But it is also true that many of the Cognomina supported me and supported another attempt for us to"—she paused as she searched for the right words—"take a more active role in this world."

"Some of them seemed to feel sorry for you—banished, exiled, estranged," Evan continued.

She finished a bite of asparagus and looked out over the darkening sea. "I was angry at first, very angry. I was angry that the decision went against me, angry that friends turned their backs on me. For a while, in successive incarnations, I would return to the Cognomina gatherings and watch them from a distance just to see their faces and look at the black tattoos on the backs of their hands. That anger eventually turned to longing as I wandered alone in this world." She turned back to Evan. "You must still remember that feeling of being alone in the world, don't you?"

Evan set his fork down and watched her. *She knew the pain he felt— the pain that had driven him from Syria, that had driven him almost to madness. She knew his pain because she had been living it for centuries.* He kept his eyes on her for a long time and tried to fathom the depths of despair that must be there. "I do remember it."

"*He* read the judgment to me," she said, pointing to the stairs that led belowdecks. "And he condemned me for having appetites for power, which others in the Cognomina did not share. I was angered by that, but not for the reasons you might imagine. It was not that I had appetites or ambition that they did not have, it was that I saw something—something that was already happening back then—that many of them did not see. That is what angered and frustrated me.

"It's funny," she continued, reaching down to stroke the head of her dog. "I imagine there is no one in the Cognomina who would fail to see it now, which is why I am eager to talk of reconciliation. But we will have time enough to talk about that later."

Evan let her sentence linger for a moment before finding the courage to dig deeper with her. "I thought of something else to ask you."

"Yes?" She perked up in interest.

"What have you been doing all this time?"

She paused for a minute and looked down into the eyes of her dog. "I suppose I have been finding my true purpose in this world." She looked up at Evan and leaned forward to capture his attention. "It's rare to find true meaning and purpose in this world, is it not, Evan? I think finding meaning and purpose is paramount for us—I mean, beings like us. We have a longer timeline to take on larger projects, and this is precisely where I found my purpose. I believe I have found that thing that gives all of us who remember a purpose in this wider world." She swept her arms wide as if to embrace the expanse of sea and night sky surrounding the rocking yacht.

"Evan, we are the court of the world. We are the witnesses for the earth across time." She closed her arms tight around her torso and continued, "Think about us and think about them. We are special in what we are, in what we remember. The rest of the world—they are common, transitory, disposable. They are only here for an hour, and then their glass is empty of sand and they are gone. But we return, we are constant, we are vigilant throughout their ages." She poured more wine. "Have you ever stayed in a nice hotel, even if only for a single night?"

Evan nodded and sipped the Barolo.

"It's wonderful, isn't it? You arrive at a nice place, and they welcome you. They provide a nice room and a comfortable bed for you, and you enjoy it, even relish it. Have you done that, Evan?"

"Yes," he replied, "in a past life."

"Did you clean that room before you departed?"

Evan looked at her for a moment and then caught the message of her question.

"Of course you did not. The thought didn't even occur to you because you were only there for a day. Only the hoteliers, who are constant, can give witness to the long-term condition of those rooms and the devastating actions of their temporary occupants." She took her glass and swirled it. "In their hour here, they destroy, befoul, and degrade their environment without concern for those who follow, without concern for us, without concern for the earth itself." She leveled her dark eyes at Evan, anchoring him to his chair. "But for us, we see their behavior, we see these crimes as we live on and on in an ever-ravaged world. You may not appreciate it as I do, for how old are you truly, Evan?"

Evan recalled the math from his memory work with Galen and his Ascension. "One hundred and twenty years, but four lives, including this one."

"Ah, I see. Just a youth, no offense intended to you, Evan. But when you have lived as long as I have—some eighteen hundred and ninety years and forty-two lives lived—you easily see their corruptions and crimes amassed before you. I will give you an example."

She looked up at the amazing array of stars visible in the clear sky above a darkened sea. She extended her arm and index finger to a first star and then got her bearings by finding a reference second star. She connected the two with a graceful motion and then lowered her finger to the horizon, pointing back over Evan's right shoulder.

"Just beyond the horizon, there, lies Puntland, or Somalia today. Did you know that, as recently as two hundred years ago, magnificent lions roamed that land? Now they are gone forever. The humans don't care. They remember those beasts only as quaint memories and will never miss them." She looked around her elegant craft. "I used to sail this route all the time and I used to watch the lionesses come right down to the sea and play in the surf. *I* miss them, and *I* know why they are no longer here. I assure you, it was through no fault of their own that those majestic creatures are gone.

"Did you know there used to be tigers in Kazakhstan? They were beautiful to behold, held up in their high mountain passes, stalking Caucasian ibex that are now gone as well. These ghosts haunt me and drive me to my purpose to save this world. My work, these past lifetimes, has been to gain some control in this world to correct the downward trajectory we are on as a society and as a planet.

"I believe this is why we are here. This is why we keep coming back. We are a force that can offer a unique and unfailing perspective over the centuries. This world is ours, really," she said, refilling their glasses. "It is ours to protect, to preserve, to guard over, to provide balance. *That* is why we keep coming back."

She let her comment land on Evan as she looked out from the yacht, now floating in a sphere of darkness as the night sky and black sea blended together. Evan looked at her in the low glow of the deck lights and thought about what she must have witnessed in all that time here, alone.

She took a long drink of her wine. "That may be more detail than you anticipated, but *that* is what I have been doing 'all of this time,' as you say." She shifted in her chair and looked over at him again. "But what about you? What drives you? What is it that makes you want to come back?"

The question struck Evan like a blow. In his previous life in Los Angeles, his only goal was to discover what he was and why he remembered the lives of Vasili and Bobby. In his search, he had found Poppy, and through her, he had found a family. In this life, his only goal had been to get back to that family, and he had done that. The closest thing Evan could find to a purpose now was saving the old man tied up belowdecks.

Evan looked over at her and wondered if telling her the truth could somehow advance an opportunity for their freedom or if his confession would only entangle them further. His mind flashed back to Poppy, who comforted him as he faced the trial of his first Ascension and who told him to just tell the truth.

"My story is a little different," Evan started. "I am on my fourth life, but I did not live long enough in my second life for the memories to come back to me. I only began to remember in the life before this one. In that life, I lived in Los Angeles. I was alone, and I lived a lie to the rest of the normal world while I searched for an answer to what I was. By chance, I found it and, in doing so, found the Cognomina. After I found that there were others like me, my only purpose was to join them, and I did. After I joined them, my only purpose was to be an equal with them."

"And are you their equal?" she asked.

Another blow. *Was she striking at a discovered vulnerability or was she helping him find some deeper truth about himself?* "If we are talking about money, then yes, now I am their equal."

She shook her head dismissively. "Money is just a tool, Evan. It solves problems and builds things. If you have as much money as they do, then you are equally tooled for your task, but what task is that? What overarching goal do you plan to leave for yourself that some struggling and confused teenager in the future will remember and embrace to help bring you back to who you are? What task drives you now and will drive your future lives?"

Yet another blow. In this life, Evan had thought only of returning to the Cognomina and rejoining the only family that mattered to him. *But would that be enough to sustain him in future lives?* He remembered Samas and his collection, Chance and his probabilities, Ramsay and her good fight, Galen and his healing, Poppy and her glass, and he was still not an equal in their peerage.

"I don't know," he confessed. "I don't know what mine is."

"An honest answer," she said softly into the surrounding night, "and a fair one." She looked up at the stars. "I know you don't trust me. I can see it all over you. But I know the answer you just gave me is a true one. You do not have to trust me now—you do not have to trust me ever—but please believe what I am about to tell you, as one who has many more lives than you." She looked back across the table at him. "You need to find your purpose for living. It is the most important thing you will ever do. You must find your reason to *want* to come back."

She sat in silence as she looked down at her sleeping dog. "I don't think Clovis wants to come back," she mused. "I think he wishes it could all be over. And in a way, I wish I could help him with that. Time can be a cruel master to a person with no purpose."

She sank back into her chair, the wine soothing her toward slumber. "I yearn to come back. Each time I cannot wait to return to continue my labors left unfinished."

Evan sat up in his chair, wanting to throw a blow of his own. "And this conservation work is how you coped all this time being isolated from the rest of us, being alone?"

"Oh, I'm not alone," she countered. "I have found many of us— many more than are in the Cognomina, I should think." She stood and clipped a silver leash on her dog. "Evan, you have a whole other family to meet. Join me and another of our group for breakfast if you wish to learn more."

14

A guard escorted Evan to a cabin belowdecks. Clovis was no longer tied to the chair that was still fixed to the floor in the galley. A second guard stood in front of a cabin door next to his, and Evan assumed Clovis was there. He listened for him until the engines roared to life and they were underway again.

Evan barely slept as his mind raced with the thoughts of another group of Reincarnationists, potentially larger than the Cognomina. *Would he get to meet them? How would the other members of the Cognomina react to this revelation? How would they react to the news that he had met and spoken with Brevicepts—the first time any of them had done so in centuries?*

He was still awake when a note was slipped under his cabin door: coffee and breakfast were ready on deck. Evan did not see the guard outside the next cabin door in the morning. The yacht's engines droned, and they were still moving at speed. He climbed the polished wooden steps to the deck and found a young woman sitting in the morning sun on an upholstered bank of cushions on the foredeck.

The woman did not see him yet and he took a moment to look at her. She was young, about his age, perhaps a year or two older. She was fit and looked like an athlete. She wore white shorts that showed off tanned legs. He couldn't see her face behind her blond hair that glowed in the sunshine. She held a book in her elegant hands. She turned a page and looked up to catch him staring at her. Her lovely face broke into a warm and welcoming smile of perfect white teeth.

Evan froze and studied each detail of her face. Nervous energy surged through him as she held his stare.

She rose to greet him. "I take it you are Evan and not Clovis," she said, extending one hand. "I'm Elsa. Please sit with me. She told me a bit about you this morning. She said I should speak to you and get to know you."

"Is *she* joining us?"

"She's in a meeting and will join us after she finishes," Elsa said with a warm smile. "She takes a lot of meetings."

Evan looked around the front part of the yacht that he could see. They were gliding through calm blue waters. "Is she meeting with my friend?" Evan asked.

"I don't think so. She's on a conference call with the World Wildlife Conservancy. She works with a lot of charitable organizations. It was the Global Resources Foundation yesterday. I wasn't invited to join her." Her eyes were the color of jade and stayed locked on his as they spoke.

"Are you with her?" Evan asked, then struggled nervously under her stare to clarify his question. "I mean, are you part of her group, someone like me? What did she tell you about me?" he finally asked.

She flashed a disarming, innocent smile. "She did. And yes, I'm one of her group. And yes, I am like you, Evan. I'm one hundred and thirty years old, and this is my third incarnation. It is so exciting to meet you. Some coffee?"

Evan was simultaneously stunned and excited by her openness about herself. "Yes for coffee," he said as she poured a cup for him from the setup at the end of the seating bank. "I have one hundred and twenty years, but this is my fourth time."

"Wow, we're almost the same age. She told me you and your friend are part of a different group, a group she used to belong to before she started ours. Is that true?"

Evan thought about the implications of her question. *Had Brevicepts never told her group about the Cognomina? If she had, what would she have told them? About how they had rejected her?*

Elsa looked at him like he was the only other person on the planet. Her warm eyes and smile made Evan want to open up and talk about himself. "Yes, my friend and I are members of another group." He checked himself before giving any details about the Cognomina but then remembered that Brevicepts already knew everything about them.

"That's fascinating." She paused and sipped her black coffee. "I've heard her speak in the last two years about reaching out to these others she once belonged to. I'd like that."

"Did she find you? I mean, did she discover what you are and bring you into her group?" Evan fumbled his question again.

"She did find me. She finds most of us." She paused and rolled her eyes up into the sunshine for a moment as if trying to remember. "I was in an institution when she found me." She locked her intense eyes back on his. "I'm still so grateful she found me and pulled me out of that horrible place. I'm sure you remember how troubling it can be for us as we begin to remember who we are. She finds many of us that way. She makes a habit of keeping in touch with many institutions and prominent psychologists and then takes a special interest when someone displays a truly profound past-life recall. Some of them end up joining us," she said, narrowing her eyes at him, "and some are just lunatics apparently. How did your group find you?"

Evan thought back to his burning times in Los Angeles. "I was being a lunatic."

She laughed, and it touched him and disarmed him in a way that made him want to keep hearing her laughter. She looked him up and down in a way that felt welcoming to him. "I can't see that in you."

"How many are in Brevicepts's group?"

"Who?" Elsa asked, genuinely confused.

"Brevicepts," he repeated and pointed a thumb over his shoulder at where he imagined she was on her call. "The woman we were just talking about."

"Was that her name in your group?" Elsa asked, tilting her blond head to one side. "That's an odd one."

"What is her name now?"

Elsa looked over his shoulder at that moment and stood to greet her leader with a short bow of respect. "Good morning, Lesannées."

Brevicepts strode into the sun of the foredeck. "My apologies for being late, but our work rarely rests along with us. How did you sleep, Evan? I sleep better at sea, I always have."

"Where is Clovis?" he asked abruptly.

"He is below, ruminating on his transgressions, I imagine." She wore a flowing white silk angelic-looking cape that covered her long arms.

"I want to see him," Evan said, trying not to stare at the black sprout of hair that rose above her head in another fashioned topknot.

"Surely," she said, taking a coffee from Elsa. "You can see him this afternoon when we make landfall. I trust you two got to know each other a bit in my absence."

Elsa nodded. "Yes, we are about the same age. He is from the other group you told us about, the group you said we might get to meet."

Evan noticed the excitement and anticipation in her comment.

"Yes, we might yet achieve that goal," Brevicepts said, looking at Evan over the rim of her cup. "I think part of that duty could soon land on Evan's shoulders."

"My shoulders?" Evan stammered.

"Yes, why not? We are always looking for capable captains," she answered, glancing at Elsa. "I thought about this last night, and you could be the perfect candidate for this, Evan. You know the Cognomina and now you know me. You are the first member of the Cognomina to speak with me in a very long time. I imagine all of your friends in Zurich know of me, and some of the older ones will even remember me. Surely they must know that I still exist, that I have continued my work, and that I have found others like us—many others." She set her cup down in front of Elsa, who instinctively topped it off.

"After Japan, the rebellion, and the excommunication"—Brevicepts pointed below to where Clovis must have been—"I resolved to find as many new Reincarnationists as I could, Evan. I knew there had to be more of us out there, so I started searching, and through that searching, I found the pattern. And that pattern was like a key to unlock a new treasure trove of us. The pattern," she continued, after taking the coffee from Elsa, "was in how the world views us and our differences. As I think back, the world's reaction to us has not changed over time."

Brevicepts sipped her coffee. "In medieval Europe, some young person who began to remember other lives or speak in strange languages would be turned over to an inquisitor. So back then, I befriended and co-opted inquisitors and exorcists as agents for me. Today, that same person would most likely land in a psychiatric ward instead of an inquisitor's dungeon, so I put hundreds of psychiatrists around the world on a private payroll. And in this manner, I have found a new family," Brevicepts said, placing a parental hand on Elsa's bare knee. "The Cognomina found you by accident, did they not?"

Evan nodded.

"I assure you I would have found you in time, languishing in a mental institution or some other warehouse they have for people like us who don't fit neatly into their world. But unlike the Cognomina, I do not leave things to chance, Evan. I promise I would have found you. I will find us all eventually," Brevicepts asserted.

"How many have you found?" Evan asked.

"Evan, I will give you the chance to count them yourself if you desire to meet them, but I have an assignment I want you to do for me, for us." She patted Elsa on the knee again. "Elsa is right. I have spoken to her and a few others in our group about the Cognomina and the possibility of reaching out to them after all this time. I desire it, Evan. I long for reconciliation with long-lost members of my family. I long to meet new ones like you." Brevicepts paused and looked at Evan. "And that goal of family and belonging is one I believe we both share."

Evan shuddered at the request he knew would come. *How many does she have?* he wondered. *How many of us are there in the world? Us,* he thought. *Had he already started thinking about the two factions as one family? Could he be the one to unite them? Could his cooperation now help her forgive Clovis and free him?*

"I'm listening," Evan said flatly, trying to calm his racing emotions.

"Think of yourself as an emissary of sorts. In a way, you are already an emissary to me from the Cognomina—and a good one so far, as you have done far more listening than speaking and have betrayed precious little information about your side." She took another long sip from her cup. "As my emissary, I would send you back to them with a message and an invitation from me. I would like you to tell them about my work, my purpose. I believe that if you explain what Elsa and I and the others are doing now, many of them would like to hear more. And if they are interested, I would very much like to meet them and tell them about it."

She turned in her seat on the cushion and squared her shoulders. "Evan, if you do this for us, I will invite you into our inner sanctum to meet each Reincarnationist from our group. If you deliver my message, I will bring you into our side—regardless of the reception you receive from the Cognomina." She leaned forward. "Will you do this for us? Will you do this for the possibility of uniting our groups into a single family?"

Evan sat paralyzed, his mind racing between risks and rewards, consequences and opportunities. *Could he be the catalyst that merged the groups? Could that be his purpose? Would she turn a new union toward her darker ends? Would saying no right now increase or decrease his chance of getting Clovis back?* He thought about the other risks of saying no to her. He didn't know anyone else in her group. He didn't know their real names or their locations. He would have no way of contacting them again if he didn't agree to do this now. It was a ship he could catch only once before it sailed beyond the horizon forever.

Evan thought about his options until only one remained. "I'll do it."

Brevicepts sat still for a second, thinking through something, before breaking into a smile. "Excellent, Evan. Let me tell you in some additional detail what I would like for you to communicate to them."

"The endangered animal protection work?" Evan prompted.

"Yes, but it is more than that. Do you know what we are, Evan?" she asked, motioning to all three of them.

Evan leaned back with the impact of the question. It was *the* question—the only question, really. *Has she cracked it?* he wondered. *Is this the message I can carry back to the Cognomina?*

"Please tell me," he said, not daring to offer his own opinion.

"Do you know what *monarch* means?" Brevicepts asked as she leaned back into the cushion. "It means a person who reigns over a place with authority and responsibility for that place. And *reign* is the key word here—for a king or a queen will reign only as long as they live, and when they are gone, their heirs then reign. But what happens if the king or queen doesn't die? How long would their reign be? Would their reign be a better one for the wisdom they could accrue in an unending life?"

She swept her arms wide again toward the wet horizons. "We are meant to reign over this world, Evan, not because of what our ambitions might be, but based on the very nature of what we are. We are royalty here—designed to reign, destined to reign, and now determined to reign."

"So is the message that we all get a region or principality to rule over as part of a combined collective?"

She shook her head. "Nothing so draconian as that. Besides, that would never work. Japan taught me that. No, our principalities are over people, not places. You see, I have learned in my long work at this that people are much easier to conquer than places. They are easier to hold too. Japan taught me that as well.

"People are the real power in this world," Brevicepts continued. "From people comes policy, and from policy comes progress. My team and I are not rulers over lands, we are more like farmers who plant ideas and cultivate people. We focus on people in power, of course—people who will effect the change that we desire—and we direct them from the perspective of our longer timelines. We recruit, we organize, we coach, we educate, and we motivate."

Evan looked from Brevicepts to Elsa, who stared at her feet.

"We pay for passage for a religious radical and his followers and he later conserves the forests of his new land,[24] which King Charles II

---

24. Brevicepts is likely referring here to William Penn, founder of the colony of Pennsylvania. William Penn instituted a policy of conserving one acre of natural forest for every five acres cleared for planting. The state takes its name from Penn and *sylvania*, Latin for *forests* or *woods*, and remains one of the most densely forested states in the US.

changed to Pennsylvania in honor of the elder Penn. We place a fresh thinker in his first professorship on population and politics, who pens essays that educate while they inflame.[25] These are our agents in this world, and they do our work for us. We are looking for more help in this work, and I am interested to see if the members of the Cognomina see the root of the problem and its solution as I do."

"Which is?" Evan asked, a small measure of confidence building within him, sufficient enough to probe a bit deeper.

She moved forward on the bench as if to lean into his question. "Take any problem we face as a planet today: the extinction of species that we discussed last night, the plastic in our oceans, the rising temperatures, or the rising seas against our shores. These all have one thing in common, don't they?" Her stern eyes fell on him and stayed there, waiting for him to speak it.

"It's people," Evan said flatly. "Too many people."

"Too many people," she echoed in agreement.

"So are we to kill them off?" Evan challenged.

Brevicepts sighed as she understood where she would need to start with him. "Well, for the record, the proper word would be *cull*, but you are missing the subtlety of this, Evan. I have not been averse to pitting one camp against another toward our ends and have done so in the past. But after 1945, even we have nowhere to hide from the consequence of their weapons. Evan, I wish for us to live in an Eden, not an ashbin."

She crossed her long legs and leaned back against her cushion. "No, Evan, that is no longer my style. Now we are like a guiding hand behind the scenes that directs the actors and action from offstage. More like forming a group of like-minded intellectuals in Italy and then slipping their findings to a friend like Tse-Tung[26] and now the result is that there

---

25. It is not clear from the clues in the text, but Brevicepts could be referring to Thomas Robert Malthus, a clergyman, professor, and inflammatory essayist on demographics and population control.

26. This is a very interesting reference to Mao Tse-Tung in that Brevicepts refers to him in the very familiar form of Tse-Tung, indicating she was a close friend and confidant to the man. She is no doubt alluding to his controversial one-child policy. The like-minded intellectuals in Italy could be a reference to Aurelio Peccei and the Club of Rome.

are half a billion less of them in this world." She stopped and casually sipped her coffee. "There was no wailing or gnashing of teeth at this loss, but rather it is hailed as a victory. That is how we work now, Evan."

"What do you call yourselves?" Evan asked.

Brevicepts brightened with pride. "We call ourselves La Mutuelle,[27] and our work is about bringing back a golden age when we lived in harmony with the world."

Evan was about to ask another question when a woman from the uniformed yacht crew stepped onto the deck and coughed loudly enough to catch Brevicepts's attention.

She turned. "Yes?"

The small crew member bowed. "The news conference feed you wished to see is beginning shortly. I have it ready on the monitor."

"Excellent. Please call Dr. Ling to join us," Brevicepts said. "Come, Elsa, there will likely be a small assignment for you in this."

They both rose and walked to the center of the yacht.

Evan reached over on the cushion for the book that Elsa had been reading. He turned it over to see the title, *Die Leiden des jungen Werther.*[28]

"Evan," Brevicepts called back to him. "Please join us. We will be watching one of your friends."

Evan shuddered for a moment with thoughts of who from the Cognomina it could be. *Had they already coaxed a confession out of Clovis and made it public?* Evan followed them below and took a seat next to them in front of a large television. The screen showed an unmanned podium with microphones. The shaky footage seemed to be streamed from a handheld phone.

"What are we watching?" Evan asked, trying to keep his anxiety in check.

Brevicepts did not reply, keeping her eyes focused on the live feed. Evan felt immediate relief when Galen stepped to the podium and adjusted the microphones up to match his height. He wore a white lab

27. French—La Mutuelle is *The Mutual* in English.
28. German—*The Sorrows of Young Werther* by Johann Wolfgang von Goethe

coat over a pale blue dress shirt, the black Embe tattoo visible on his hand as he began to speak.

"I would like to thank the citizens and the press of Davos for welcoming me today for this historic announcement. I wish to thank and recognize my collaborators and patrons at the Swiss Academy and Afuqua Labs, who have made this groundbreaking work possible. Together, we are pleased to present and make public the finding of our decades-long work and research into human life extension. The previous report and conclusions we presented three years ago confirmed that through stem cell therapy, along with our experimental senescence and mitosis cell drug therapy, we can extend the normal lifespan in laboratory rats by eighty percent. Our report today shows we performed a double-blind test with simian specimens during that same time. For this ape study, we needed a longer term to prove the results, but I am pleased to announce that this report shows the same age-related disease retardation and restoration of cellular health at the DNA level. This simian breakthrough has afforded us approval for limited human trials here in Europe."

Galen looked up from his prepared notes at the crowd and the cameras. "Imagine what this could mean if we could extend human life expectancy from seventy-five years to a hundred and thirty or a hundred and forty—or longer. And that those could be healthy and productive years we would add. Imagine how much richer our existence could be, how much more fulfilled we could be as individuals. Imagine a whole new demographic—the super senior. Imagine a world where information and application forms would need a completely new category, ages eighty to a hundred and thirty. Imagine how—"

Brevicepts thumbed the remote, turning off the feed as she let out a long exhale. She sat for a moment, looking at the black screen. "A setback," she said somberly, turning to Dr. Ling, who stood near the open door. "He's further along than we thought. Good doctor, please call Mr. Banks and prepare Operation Botis. Get it ready and have them meet us at the airstrip."

Ling nodded curtly and left the room.

"Elsa, please go with him and leave us for a moment."

Elsa gave Evan a long look before leaving—a look that felt to Evan like a combination of attraction and sadness.

"Do you like Venice?" Brevicepts asked Evan, changing the subject.

Evan noticed her mood brighten with the question. "I've never been there, but I hear it's marvelous."

She looked at him with genuine surprise. "Yes, the city is marvelous," she replied. "I hope you can one day join me in my palazzo. Venice is sort of a special project of mine. It is indeed a marvel, but it wasn't always so. Venice is an example of the positive results of our work. There are about sixty thousand people that live there today. And that has been the population of the city for the last three centuries or so, and that size feels about right—comfortable and sustainable. But only three hundred and fifty years ago, there were over a quarter of a million people in that tiny island city. It was a disgusting slum, apart from a few nice palazzos on the Grand Canal, like the one I still own. It was fetid, wretched, and foul," she said, pursing her lips as though recalling a distasteful memory.

"But with sixty thousand, it is a fantastic place." Brevicepts faced him with an odd expression of pride. "I did that."

A puzzled look came over Evan's face. "What do you mean you did that? You did what?"

"I solved the problem. I fixed Venice," she said with no more emotion than if she had fixed a bicycle. "It is an old story and involves two of my oldest captains. I remember our voyage like it was yesterday. I was an accomplished sea captain then. I remember that we rode a sirocco[29] up the Adriatic. I picked up the men and their ship in the port of Siracusa in Sicily. I heard that the sickness was there and the city was under quarantine. With blackening fingers they pulled at both oar and sail . . ."

---

29. The sirocco is a strong wind that blows north from Africa to southern Europe. Venetians use that name to describe the wind that blows northwest up the length of the Adriatic Sea. This wind can cause sea levels to rise at the northern end of the Adriatic near Venice in a flooding phenomenon called *acqua alta* (high waters).

15

. . . With blackening fingers they pulled at both oar and sail in the hopes of a promised Venetian cure. Their captain urged them on through aching joints and exhausting fevers as the strong sirocco wind blew them north into the narrowing Adriatic. Their flagging spirits were lifted with stories of medical advances that had been made in the capital of the republic, and by midnight they would arrive at their destination.

Just sixteen days earlier, the captain, the doctor, and the magistrate sat in an abandoned tavern in the quarantined city of Siracusa. The tall magistrate leaned his thin frame over the empty bar to grab bottles and glasses and pour for the three.

"Do you have the item?" asked the captain.

The short doctor nodded and took a cup of wine from his colleague.

"How are we to use it?"

"I mixed it with lard to preserve it. Just smear it on surfaces that people will touch, and most will contract the illness," the doctor said, looking into his cup. "It will take a week for them to show the first symptoms. A few days after that, they will get very ill, and about half will die."

"So it is agreed then?" the captain asked.

Both men nodded.

The captain shook his head. "No, I need to hear it from you."

The doctor and the magistrate looked at each other. "We will take Milan."

"And I will take Venice," said the captain, raising his cup in a toast. "To our mission."

"To our mission."

"Grab the rest of the bottles behind the bar—as many as you can carry. We will need them to get us off this stinking island tonight," the captain said, standing. "Now let's go find a ship and crew."

They exited the tavern with their liquid bounty and started the long downhill walk to the blockaded harbor, their trio of footfalls the only sound above the plaintive moaning and vomiting behind closed doors. The captain walked the piers, looking for a ship large enough for the journey, small enough to get through a secret passage in the barrier islands of the Venetian lagoon, and already sick enough for the crew to want to leave.

"Do you have the fever aboard your ship?" the captain asked. "I have a doctor with me who can treat you."

"Come aboard. Save us," they pleaded. "Our captain is sickest."

The captain turned to the magistrate. "I will take half the wine. You take the other half and smuggle it onto that warship at anchor in the harbor. Take a skiff. Come straight back when you are done. It will not take me long to win them over. We sail tonight."

The captain poured wine and inspected both the men and the craft while the doctor tended fevers and examined men for swollen glands and blackening toes. He filled and refilled their glasses until their eyes were wide with the story of the Venetian doctor who could cure strong men who reached him in time. And at less than a fortnight's sail, the captain assured them that most of them could survive if they desired to leave that night and save themselves.

A drunkard's decision is not a difficult one, and by the time the magistrate had returned from his errand, the doctor had poured enough wine to secure the voyage. The captain waited at his mooring until he heard shouting and loud laughter from the menacing warship as the drink took hold. The captain and the doctor smiled at the magistrate as they raised a single foresail and drifted silently past the blockade to the mouth of the harbor. In an hour, they were even with it; in two, they were past it; in three, they were out of sight of it and underway.

The captain stood on the polished boards of the foredeck and looked up at the stars. He reached a pointing finger to a star in the heavens, traced a line to its neighbor, and continued that line to the horizon before shouting back to his helmsman, "To port!"

THEY CAUGHT A STRONG WIND at their stern that pushed them quickly toward their destination. The men got worse, and the rats got more brazen as the days wore on. The captain counted the remaining wine and biscuits and factored them against the decreasing number of active mouths to consume them. They lost one or two men a night—always at night and always after the rats had been at them. The captain, the doctor, and the magistrate all manned rudder and ropes on those last two days when the water turned from clear blue to a cloudy green.

"This is our last day, men. You will be in Venice tonight and in the care of the doctor with the tattooed hand who can save you. Pull on your lines, men," the captain commanded.

At sunset, they saw the outline of the Lido barrier island, her three inlets, and the six large warships that protected them. The captain ordered the sails lowered until nightfall to keep their smaller ship out of sight. He stood on the foredeck and welcomed the wind at his back—a wind that would bring the acqua alta and high tide. This would be the wind and tide he would need to get through his passage, to get through this night. They raised the foresail at midnight and worked their way along the coast of the main barrier island between the two menacing flotillas that protected the inlets at either end.

The captain lowered himself flat against the foredeck to reach a hand into the water. He tasted the water as they went, spitting and directing the remaining crew to port or starboard in the dark.

"What are you doing?" asked the magistrate.

"I am trying to find the Sila River. It has a small canal that joins it, and that is our only way into Venice without facing the cannon of those frigates tonight. The sea tastes of brine, but the river will taste of dust and fish guts," the captain said, spitting again. "To port."

He tasted into the night until his tongue found the small river in the darkness. "There," he commanded. "Raise all sails and row. Row for your lives, men!"

The ship's mast strained with the strong wind that pushed the small ship into the mouth of a narrow river whose banks were just beyond the tips of the churning oars on both sides. The captain leaped to the bow and strained his eyes in the dark for the small canal he knew lay off to the left. Unable to turn the ship around in such a narrow waterway, he would only have one chance.

"Strain, damn you!" he screamed back at the remaining men. "Be ready to turn," he bellowed to the two men on the rudder at the stern. And then he saw the canal inlet, just ahead and to the left and mercifully filled to the tops of its narrow banks. "Hard to port now!"

The ship steered left, and the deck rolled down to the right as the rudder bit into the water. "Brace!" came the command from amidships. The ship made the turn, shuddered, and jerked hard as its keel briefly touched earth at the bottom of the shallow canal. The ship then broke free and found its buoyancy again as the wind pushed it against the right bank of the canal, snapping oars on that side as they scraped hard against the rocky bank. The captain jumped back to the mast and adjusted the sail trim to force the ship forward once again.

They were free. He had done it. They were in the canal and, in minutes, would be in the open lagoon headed toward Venice.

"We're taking on water, sir," came the word from belowdecks, but the captain could already feel it under his feet. They were listing to starboard. He was through the blockade and in the lagoon, but he still faced two hours of tricky navigation in the dark around hundreds of smaller islands to get to Venice itself. He looked at the magistrate, who jumped belowdecks and into action to preserve their mission. The captain stood at the bow of the ship, shouting directions to his sickened helmsman. The captain ordered the remaining men to stand at the port railing as ballast to even out their lean.

"There is Venice, boys," the captain pointed and called out to all hands. "We're going to make it."

The magistrate emerged from his wet efforts below, soaked and shivering. As they neared the empty docks on the north shores of the Cannaregio district, the ship slowed to a painful crawl from the weight of the water inside its fractured hull.

"Remember, men, ask for the plague doctor—the one with the tattoo on his hand," the captain shouted as he turned the sinking ship alongside the dock. "His name is Galen."

The men jumped onto the dock in unison, hobbling and limping on blackened and gangrenous feet into the vulnerable city in search of their salvation.

The captain motioned his colleagues off the craft and he took one last look at the ship as the starboard rail began to dip below the water. Rats by the dozens clambered up onto the last dry portions of the deck. The captain took two ropes and threw the ends onto the dock, providing a functional footbridge for the infected rodents before he stepped onto the dock himself. He turned to the freezing magistrate and the doctor with his leather pouch. "I will take mine now," the captain demanded, motioning to the doctor's bag.

The diminutive doctor pulled out a fist-sized clay jar sealed with red wax and handed it to his captain.

"Remind me again, how long did you say it will take to work?" the captain asked.

"A week. Maybe less."

The captain nodded solemnly and looked down the dock to the rowboats tied up at the end. "The port of Mestre is there," he said, pointing to the dark horizon. "And Milan beyond it. Take a boat and go now before their commotion stirs up the city."

"This is it then," the doctor said, a tone of finality in his voice.

"It is," the captain said, turning to face them both.

"I will see you at our meeting place," the shivering magistrate said, "in the next life, if not this one."

The captain took a deep breath and addressed both men in their familiar salute. "I am my own servant," he said, extending a hand to each of them in turn.

"And I serve a just master," they said back to him in unison and then turned to go.

The captain watched them row until they had disappeared into that long night. He rolled the jar in his hand and measured the weight of its deadly contents as he thought about his mission and theirs. He dug his sharp fingernails into the red wax seal until it gave way and revealed a snow-white paste streaked with veins of black flecks.[30]

The captain turned away from the dock and started down the maze of narrow, trash-filled alleys toward central Venice. He paused at the first arching footbridge crossing a canal and looked at the stone handrail, worn smooth from centuries of use. The air stank with human filth and rotting garbage that floated in the water, and he felt a hatred well up inside him—a familiar enmity he had felt and harnessed before. Without even realizing it, he had pressed two fingers deep into the black-and-white grease until they touched the bottom of the clay jar. Then the captain removed his slick fingers, placed them on the worn handrail of the footbridge, and started walking toward his home.

The captain walked a route through the city that crossed most of its bridges, going back and forth over the Rialto to cover each of the different handrails on its walkways. He greased doorknobs and boat oars and he greased the tips of drinking fountains and the rims of the wooden buckets in each well he could find.

---

30. If Brevicepts's account is accurate, there is an astounding correlation to events in Milan in 1630 related to a plague outbreak there. Two men named Piazza (a health commissioner) and Mora (a barber) were arrested, tried, tortured, and executed for the crime of being "bringers," intent on spreading a disease and infecting others via "poisoned anointings." (See historian Carlo Torre's account of these events in his History of Milan published in 1674.) Mora's home was torn down after his execution, and a "Column of Infamy" was erected in its place to mark the deadly deed they had done in the city.

He paused at the last well, the one closest to his palazzo, and he tossed the empty jar into its welcoming black mouth. He listened for the splash and imagined the last remnants of the contagion dissolving into the water. He then raised the communal bucket from the depths and drank deeply from it. He let the bucket fall back down into the shaft until it splashed, and then he drew it up once more. The captain lifted the bucket to his lips again, and again he drank.

He drank in anger that this is what they had forced him to do. He gulped and swallowed in a rage against them in their masses. He drank with a determined fury to infect them all. He drank until he gagged and choked and felt the familiar revulsion they elicited in him. He drank until his stomach ached and he could take no more and then he fumbled for the large brass key in his coat pocket and walked toward a simple doorway set into the wall of a tan, four-story building. He rotated the key inside the stiff corroded lock and leaned his weight into the heavy door until it began to move.

The simple exterior of the back of the building downplayed the opulent facade and interior of the spectacular palazzo that faced the Grand Canal. He pushed the door closed against its groaning hinges and turned to see two servants wiping the sleep from their eyes.

"Master, we were not expecting you," the older of the two men said, stepping forward to take the captain's hat.

"Bring my favorite chair up to the balcony. I do not wish to be disturbed. And do not fetch your water from the well outside—go to the next one."

The servants nodded as the captain turned and climbed the long stone staircase to his rooms on the second floor.

THE CAPTAIN SAT ON THE BALCONY of his palazzo every day and stroked the head of the dog in his lap as he watched the gondola and barge traffic on the Grand Canal. In the afternoons he would turn his chair to face the Rialto Bridge and watch the vendors put away their goods and wares for the day.

The first sounds of coughing and moaning came on the third day.

By the fourth day, the fever hit him, but he remained at his post on his balcony. By the sixth day, the boat traffic on the Grand Canal slowed to only a few brave gondoliers. By the eighth day, the bargemen were pressed into service to carry away the stiffened bodies of the dead.

The captain's fever had broken, but his fingers and toes were now black as ink and his breathing was irregular and strained. On the morning of the ninth day, the captain was delirious and drew breaths only in short gasps. Out of fear and concern, the servants summoned a passing barge and offered gold ducats if the oarsman would take their beloved captain to the plague doctor on the quarantine island Lazzaretto. The veiled oarsman nodded and took the coins as the servants lowered their beloved master into the crowd of the dying in the bow of the dirty barge.

The small island of Lazzaretto lay well away from the bustle of Venice. The governing Council of Ten had ordered that all remaining infected persons be evacuated there and enticed the citizenry into compliance by moving their best doctors there. The stench of pestilence soiled the air on the island, and buzzing flies swarmed at the eyes and mouths of those still living but too weak to move. The convicted prisoners who had been forced to the island to serve as orderlies carried the captain to an empty rectangle on the stone floor of the island's lone building, an abandoned palazzo that now served as an impromptu medical ward.

The captain came to and focused his eyes on the startling sight of the doctor in the distance. He wore a black leather cloak that covered him from his neck to his feet, a black tri-corner hat, and a grotesque white mask with oversized spectacles and an elongated bird beak.[31] The doctor was examining patients halfway down the hall, working his way toward the captain, who struggled to lift his head and get a better view of his new surroundings.

The woman to his right was dead, her lifeless, blackened fingers lay frozen against her face in a final ignoble action of wiping dried vomit from her open mouth. The man to his left convulsed with each breath

31. Brevicepts's description is accurate, and many physicians wore this protective attire at the time. (See *Daily Life during the Black Death* by Joseph Patrick Byrne.)

and constantly crossed himself with a rosary. The captain chuckled to himself with grim satisfaction. Every moan, every weep, every sound of a stomach's contents splattering onto the stone floor made him laugh all the harder. He laughed until his breath escaped him and would not return, prompting the costumed doctor to rush down the row to attend to him.

The plague doctor's cloak was wet and smelled of vinegar as he reached his right hand out to grab the captain's belt, lifting his waist into the air to help his exhausted diaphragm recover. The captain caught his breath and reached a tar-black hand around the doctor's, turning it to expose the black Embe tattoo on the back. The captain kept his grip and drew another long breath before saying in a thin voice, "So good to see you, Doctor."

"I am a physician. I will save you," he said from behind that hideous mask.

"You could barely save a drowning dog. Do you even remember swimming the Tyrrhenian Sea with me, you fool?" the captain said, falling into coughing laughter again.

The doctor froze, snapped off his hood and mask, and stared into the captain's dark eyes for some additional clue.

The captain smiled with a sinister grin, and his final laugh drew a discharge of blood. "You're too late," the captain whispered. "*Acta exterior indicant interior secreta*,[32] my dear Galen." The captain spat the name as his vision blurred and narrowed into darkness . . .

---

32. Latin—Exterior acts indicate interior secrets

16

". . . The captain spat the name as his vision blurred and narrowed into darkness." Brevicepts sat up in her chair. "I expired right there. Venice had its fever but was eventually saved and became the gem it still is today," she said, wrapping up her story.

Evan gaped at her for several seconds before replying. "So that's it? That's how you fixed Venice—by killing everyone?"

Her topknot danced back and forth as she shook her head in disbelief. "Nobody misses those people today, Evan," she said matter-of-factly. "They are a footnote in history, occupants of *our* hotel that got kicked out of their rooms nearly four hundred years ago. They do not matter now, do they?" she challenged. "*We* are what matters. We are the ones who are still here."

"So is it just about us then?"

"No, it also benefits others. Think of the dozen generations that have lived in Venice after the plague or future generations that will appreciate that we protected things now. Once you live long enough, Evan, you begin to adjust your timelines."

"Why didn't you wear a glove and protect yourself while infecting the city? Why infect yourself?"

She watched her young companion for some seconds before

answering. "Evan, this work requires commitment, and we demand that from each other. Commitment is the difference between effort and accomplishment." She looked out at a brown coastline coming into view on the starboard side. "You would do well to remember that as our emissary back to my old friends in the Cognomina."

Evan thought about the kind of mind that could infect a city and justify it. *Was it justified, in hindsight?* Her voice sounded far away as he replayed her words in his head: *"Venice had its fever." Was that all it was to her? If she was capable of that action four hundred years ago, what could she be capable of today?*

Clovis's warning rang in his ears: *"Don't trust her."*

"And what are my old friends doing now?" she asked as she reached for her coffee again. "I know now what the healer Galen is up to," she said, motioning to the black monitor on the bulkhead. "Did Chance ever solve the equations to explain the phantoms of randomness and luck that haunt him? Is Ramsay still bloodying his knuckles against the injustices of the world? And what of young Jens—not so young anymore, I imagine—is he still counting his farthings and trying to build a mountain out of them?"

Evan looked at her but remained silent.

Elsa walked up to Brevicepts and bowed. "Lesannées, the pilot is on the ground and waiting for us, and security will be in place in five minutes."

"Excellent," Brevicepts replied.

Evan watched Elsa as the same anxious feeling washed over him. *Does she feel it too?* he wondered.

Elsa did not move from her spot.

"Is there something else?"

"The captain is nervous about pulling into port," Elsa said. "He says he cannot raise a harbormaster and has no charts for this area."

"There has not been a harbormaster in this port for decades," Brevicepts said, rising to her full height. "I will deal with this."

Evan and Elsa followed as she strode onto the captain's deck and immediately raised her hand to cut off his protests. "Stand aside. I

have been sailing these waters for a very long time. I will take us in."
The captain stepped out of the way as she moved toward the controls,
took the chrome-plated wheel in her hands, and shoved the throttle
to maximum. "It's best not to move too slowly in these waters these
days," she shouted over the roar of the engines as all hands gripped a
polished rail.

Evan watched the horizon in front of them as the narrow opening
of an old port came into view below a sprawling mass of decaying and
crumbling buildings that formed the remnants of a coastal city. The
captain shouted his concern at their speed, but Brevicepts ignored him
and raced at full speed past the rock-lined breakwater, surprising the
groups of hard-looking men resting next to their battered assault rifles.

Evan looked up at a derelict cargo crane that lay askew on its rusty
platform. Barely visible amid the peppering of bullet holes and sun-faded
paint was a sign that read Port of Mogadishu.

Brevicepts steered the boat inside the small port, sending rough wake
toward the open boats now filling with armed men. She spotted her La
Mutuelle security team at the far end of the abandoned harbor. Their
black assault rifles peeked out from a perimeter around four gleaming
black SUVs that looked out of place in this backwater. She turned the
yacht toward her uniformed men and slammed the engines into reverse.
The yacht shuddered and trembled under their feet but slowed to what
seemed an impossible stop right next to her team on the dock.

"Let us not tarry here," Brevicepts commanded, scooping her spaniel up in her arms as her men moored the yacht to the dirty concrete
of the dock.

Pops of distant gunfire crackled at the far end of the harbor as two
uniformed guards took Clovis off first. Evan pushed ahead of Elsa on
the walkway to get to him. "Clovis," Evan shouted as he put his hand
on the old man's shoulder to turn him. "Are you all right, Clovis?"

The old man's mouth was gagged, but his lively gray eyes brightened at the sight of Evan.

"I'm going to get you out of this," Evan whispered into his friend's
ear. "I need to do a task for her that I think could help win your release."

Clovis shook his head vigorously but could only vocalize a muted objection as the guards broke them up and pushed them toward the caravan of black SUVs. Bullets buzzed in the air around them as two of the mercenaries pushed Clovis into the second vehicle with Brevicepts and then pushed Evan into the third next to Elsa. One of Brevicepts's armed men aimed and returned fire on an approaching boat as two distant rounds thudded into the metal of the SUV.

"Drive! Drive!" Elsa shouted to the driver as he raced with the other trucks away from the harbor and into the ruins of Mogadishu. Evan turned to look back at the dock and saw dozens of armed young men shooting their assault rifles into the air in celebration from the decks of Brevicepts's luxury yacht.

Evan took deep breaths to calm his nerves as he took in the strange scene passing beyond the tinted windows. The streets they raced through were devoid of cars, save a few burned-out hulls that had been pushed to the sides to allow military trucks and animal-drawn carts to pass. Thousands of blue tarpaulin-covered handcrafted huts lined the sidewalks and dotted ornate Arabic arched entryways to abandoned mansions. Larger clusters of huts gathered under the eaves of bombed-out modernist architectural masterpieces from the city's 1960s heyday. At every turn in the ancient labyrinthine city, shocked faces looked out, aghast at the gleaming marvel of the passing black luxury vehicles.

"This is precisely what Lesannées aims to prevent with our work," Elsa said, placing a hand on Evan's arm. He savored her touch, but his eyes kept scanning from behind tinted glass, locking with each pair that searched back through the dark glass for the faces they somehow knew must be responsible for their misery.

"Is it worth it?" Evan asked, thinking back to Brevicepts's Venice story and imagining that her presence here must somehow be tied to what he saw outside. "Is it worth the pain they go through?"

"The way she explains it, it is," Elsa said over the roar of the engine. "She says you must weigh the quality of the experiences of those generations that will follow against the suffering of the now—like her example of Venice or of neighboring Ethiopia a generation ago. Those places had their contractions and now are better for it. As she says, it is our responsibility to have the long-term vision for what is best for this world."

"Do you believe that?"

Elsa looked out at the decay and destruction. "I believe that something must be done to save this planet."

Evan turned his head forward to the bomb-cratered main street ahead of them. Elsa saw the boy at the same time Evan did. "No, no, no," Elsa shouted to the driver as a Somali boy darted into the street after a goat that was startled by Brevicepts's lead SUV in the caravan.

The driver swerved sharply to the left, missing the boy but not the goat. The impact of the carcass under the wheels sent the heavy truck farther left and into the edge of a water-filled mortar crater. The SUV bucked hard on the way in but harder on the way out, throwing Elsa across the back seat and squarely on top of Evan. Evan caught and held her tightly until the driver regained control. Her blond hair draped into his eyes. She kept her eyes fixed on him as they breathed in unison until the driver regained control.

"Are you all right?" Evan asked, breaking the tension between them.

Elsa kept her eyes on his as she pulled herself away from him and back to her side of the bench seat. "At least we didn't hit the boy."

"And we know what they are having for dinner tonight," the burly driver shouted back to them in a Russian accent.

Elsa ignored his crude comment and put her hand on Evan's. "I probably shouldn't do this, but I don't want to see anything happen to you. There is something I need to tell you," she said in a low voice as she slid closer to him. "We are headed to the airport where there is a jet waiting for us. Once we are there, she will give you the assignment she mentioned."

Evan looked deep into her eyes and nodded. "Yes, I thought so." He turned his hand over to receive hers. "I have been thinking about this assignment and the possibility of bringing our groups, our families together. If I do this for her, perhaps she will leave Clovis alone."

Elsa squeezed his hand tight. "Evan, be careful with her." She paused in search of the right words to prepare him for what she imagined might lay ahead. "She's complicated and unorthodox in her method," she said in a low voice, glancing at the mercenary driver. "And sometimes she is unpredictable. But what I do know is when she makes a commitment, she keeps it."

"What are you saying?"

"No matter what happens," she started, "if you do as she asks, she *will* let you meet everyone in La Mutuelle. And perhaps we could have a chance to see each other again."

"Do you know something you're not telling me?" Evan asked, his eyes narrowing.

Elsa turned away from him. "I don't know. She doesn't share much. I've said too much already, Evan." She pulled her hand away from his as the idle airport came into view. "We're here."

Evan reached over to touch her arm. "Will you help me by talking to her about releasing my friend?"

"I think you should follow through on her assignment. That is your best chance to save your friend. You have seen what she is capable of."

Evan nodded. "If anything should happen, there is a hotel in Zurich where you can find me or get a message to me. It's called the Hotel St. Germain."

"Zurich sure seems better than here," she said.

Their SUV screeched to a stop with the rest of the caravan next to a perimeter of armed men surrounding a pristine white corporate jet with its engines running and stairs extended to the tarmac. Elsa jumped out on her side and motioned for Evan to follow her as she joined Brevicepts watching her guards escort a bound and gagged Clovis from her vehicle.

The circle of black-clad armed men parted as Brevicepts and her doctor walked toward the jet. Two guards grabbed Clovis by his shoulders and led him behind her. Elsa led Evan toward her leader. The perimeter of men retreated into a tightening circle behind them, their trained eyes and muzzles scanning for movement at the edges of the airstrip.

Brevicepts stopped five meters from the bottom of the stairs while her dog ran ahead of her up the steps and sat at the open jet door. She barked a command in Russian to the guard she had made squad leader after the deaths at the lighthouse. He handed her a smartphone and stepped back, turning his head toward the harbor. Brevicepts keyed a code into the phone, hovering one long, elegant finger over the keypad as she looked up. She kept her gaze on the horizon and touched the phone lightly. They all saw it before they heard it. A giant fireball rose like a red-orange flower over the coast. It grew for several seconds before the sound and distant shock wave hit them.

"Did you just blow up that beautiful yacht?" Evan fixated on the rising blossom of flame that bloomed into a clear blue sky above the city.

"Leave no trace," Brevicepts replied with a grin. "I like to leave a very light footprint when I travel."

"But those men."

"Pirate scum," she spat the words as she turned to face him. "They are a symptom of why this place is getting a correction." She handed the smartphone back to the lead mercenary. "Evan, this is your time to shine as our emissary. One might say that the fate of both our groups now lies in your hands. Return to the Cognomina as soon as you can and convey my offer to them. Those who are interested in learning more should come to our office at Montparnasse Tower in Paris."

"I will travel straight to Zurich after we land."

"I am afraid you will not be joining us on this flight," Brevicepts corrected.

"What do you mean?"

"Evan, listen carefully. I need you to take one final message to them," she commanded before spinning and kicking a defenseless Clovis square in his midsection. Clovis wheezed and collapsed in a writhing heap on the airstrip as he fought to get breath back into his lungs. An unfazed Dr. Ling bent over to inspect him. Evan attempted to rush to Clovis, but a muscular guard grabbed him and lifted him off the ground, being careful to keep him facing their leader.

Brevicepts straightened and smoothed the white folds of her pants. "Pay attention, Evan," she continued over the barking of her panicked spaniel. "Tell your friends they are free to choose. But they need to know that their choices will have consequences, just as Clovis's choices long ago will have their consequences now." She nodded to her doctor, who produced a syringe and small medical vial of liquid that glittered silver in the bright Somali sunlight.

"What are you doing?" Evan shouted, struggling against the restraint of the larger man. "What are you injecting him with? Stop—there has to be another way," Evan pleaded.

The doctor filled the syringe and stretched tight a patch of aged skin on Clovis's arm. The needle entered effortlessly, and the doctor pushed the silver solution into his victim. Clovis's eyes shot open and he immediately stopped struggling to catch his breath. His whole body shuddered twice and then fell into a series of fast convulsions for five seconds.

Evan looked on in horror as the convulsions calmed and Clovis's body became rigid and stiffened into a perfect prone position. He lay motionless except for his alert eyes that darted wildly as if searching for an answer as to why his locked body had betrayed him.

The doctor put a stethoscope to the old man's chest that rose ever so slightly in a slow rhythm. "He's in there," the doctor said to Brevicepts. "He has stabilized and should be fully aware of his surroundings. He'll make it."

"Excellent." She turned back to Evan, still in the grip of his captor. "You have your assignment. Both of our houses are counting on you. This is where our paths must part for now."

Two of her men picked up Clovis's rigid body and loaded him onto the plane.

"Where are you taking him?" Evan demanded in a thin breath compressed by the guard's grasp.

"He owes me a lot of time," she answered coolly. "I will now get it back."

She motioned Elsa and half of her guards onto the plane with her as she climbed the steps and raised them from the tarmac. The guard holding Evan released him, and the remaining mercenaries jogged over to the caravan of SUVs, leaving a gasping Evan alone on the airstrip.

"You can't just leave me here," Evan pleaded above the increasing engine noise.

"Remember our talk of tools. Use your tools to get yourself out of this," she shouted from the door of the jet. "Consider it your first test," she laughed, "as a potential captain in our organization."

"At least give me my phone back," Evan shouted.

Brevicepts nodded to the lead mercenary, who handed her Evan's cheap flip phone. She stared oddly at the simple phone before flipping it open and looking at the tiny screen. "Good luck finding service here," she said, tossing the phone to him before pulling the door closed.

Evan caught the phone and bent over to draw a few welcomed deep breaths. The engines roared to full throttle. Elsa looked out at him from a window in the middle of the plane, and Evan locked eyes with her and smiled through the pain and shock as the jet began to move.

Brevicepts looked out the window at Evan to see his attention focused two windows back. She turned to see Elsa pressed against her window. Brevicepts turned to catch a last glimpse of Evan and she caught his glance right as he took a photo of her face with his flip phone. She snapped the privacy shade closed as Evan quickly photographed the jet's tail number and the numbers of the blue-and-white United Nations license plates on the SUVs. He stood on the runway and watched the jet rise out of sight, then opened the grainy photo of Brevicepts, her topknot barely visible on her head. He closed the photo and looked down to see no bars of reception.

He felt the menace of the city circling him like a stalking animal. Evan flashed back to his conversation with Elsa and her warning to him. He thought he knew the risks in dealing with Brevicepts—or at least imagined that he could negotiate them to a better ending than this. *He had lost Clovis, and the only chance he had of saving him now was to follow through with her assignment, but how many more might that endanger?*

He walked to what looked like an abandoned passenger terminal at the far end of the runway. *Think, Evan*, he thought as he walked. "*Use your tools*," Brevicepts had said.

He pried open the battery cover on the cheap phone and removed an additional hidden SIM card inside, this one with Arabic writing from his trek from Syria. He swapped in the new chip and powered on the phone to see three bars—three miraculous bars.

Evan took a chance and hit the zero key. "Marhabaan, marhabaan," he shouted hello in Arabic until a local operator answered. "International operator, please. Yes, connect to an operator in Switzerland, please. Zurich prefix code. I will give you the number. Yes, I will hold the line.

"Mr. Pianosa, it is so nice to hear a friendly voice. I need your assistance with a travel matter. I need a charter flight out of Mogadishu as soon as possible, and I don't care what it costs. Get me back to Zurich as quickly as you can, and please gather the members of the Cognomina. I have an urgent update that affects all of us."

17

Evan stared out the window of the Mercedes limousine as it passed through the rainy streets of Zurich on its route to the Hotel St. Germain. He had two long days of hopping UN aid flights, waiting for private jet charters, and this limousine ride to prepare, but now that he was only a few blocks away, he still struggled with how to tell them about everything that had happened.

His pulse quickened as the driver pulled into the curved driveway of the hotel. He exited the car and instinctively walked to the golden corded doorbell chime. Evan ran his hand over the cord and thought about the consequences of pulling it. *Would they be disappointed in him that he hadn't been able to save Clovis? How would they react to the news of another group? Would they be as excited as he was initially? How many would be interested in meeting Brevicepts and learning about her mission? How many would reject her offer and face her unknown consequences?*

His vision blurred from fatigue and burden and then Poppy's words came back to him—words she had spoken to him inside this building a lifetime ago: *"Just tell them the truth."* Her words soothed him as he thought about what would happen in the next few hours. There was no turning back from the course Brevicepts had put him on. Evan pulled the cord and heard the bell inside, but the feeling in his hand was of putting a complex series of events into motion—events he could not predict nor control.

The young Mr. Pianosa answered the door and escorted him inside. "Good afternoon, sir. I took the liberty of having the staff set out a change of clothes for you. I was sure you would need to refresh yourself from your trying journey."

"Are they all here?" Evan asked.

"Yes, I can have them ready in the grotto in one hour."

"We can't afford that much time. I will be down in twenty minutes to address them."

"Very well, sir."

EVAN SHOWERED AND DRESSED QUICKLY before grabbing the cane that rested against the foot of the bed. He stared into the faceted blue of the dragon's sapphire eyes and took a long calming breath. "Let's tell them together, shall we?" he said aloud.

He walked to the last room on the ground floor and stood at the false bathroom door that led to the secret grotto below. Cracking the door open, Evan could hear their collected voices floating up the stone stairs to him. He stepped down, counting the torches as he passed until he was at the opening to the grotto. All eyes turned to him in silence when he walked into the room and approached Galen, who stood next to the table that faced the judges' panel.

"How are you, Evan?" Galen asked as he opened his arms to embrace him.

"I am tired, but all right," Evan answered. "Why is everyone staring at me?"

"Well, they want to hear about your time with Clovis, but your message to Pianosa about assembling everyone for a message has started some rumors. Is there anything you want to share with me as your advocate before we continue?" Galen asked in a low voice as the four judges walked to their chairs.

"No. You need to hear this along with the others," Evan said, reaching for a cigarette.

"I'll have one of those," Poppy demanded, pointing to the pack as she walked up and kissed him passionately without warning. "Thanks," she prompted, snapping him out of his stunned state to light hers.

"Ha! And thanks for saving me from a dangerous flight back to Yemen," Chance said, passing them on his way to his seat on the judges' bench. "I don't like to push my luck."

"Evan Michaels," Ramsay said in a voice loud enough to carry to the filled gallery. "I do hope your time with brother Clovis was enjoyable and productive. Do you have the letter from him that you can present to me?"

Evan clasped his hands around his cane to keep them from trembling as he scanned the gallery and judges' panel to take in every face that looked back at him. "I do not," Evan stated and then fumbled nervously over his words. "I mean, I did have it, but I don't have it now. I no longer possess it. It was taken from me."

"Taken from you?" Ramsay repeated. "Please explain."

"Much has happened in the past three days that potentially changes our secret world." Evan looked down at the dragon cane. "I have reviewed these events over and over, trying to discern if I could have done anything differently that would have caused a different outcome. But I don't think I had much control over anything that happened."

"The letter, Evan. You said the letter was taken from you—taken by whom?" Ramsay asked.

"I was in Yemen with Clovis. I met him and spoke with him until he was convinced of who I am." Evan looked up to the opaque expanse of the grotto's dark ceiling. "I suspect he knew right away—by the first night anyway. The next day we were on the beach when I noticed a luxury yacht approaching at high speed. I mean, I knew there was a conflict in the area so—" Evan struggled against the rising emotion.

Galen put a hand on the shoulder of the younger man. "It's all right. Just tell us what happened."

Evan closed his eyes and took two deep breaths. "There was a woman. She was tall, nearly two meters, and she wore all white. She led a group of mercenaries who attacked us. I believe her target was Clovis because she seemed surprised that I was there. She read Clovis's confirmation letter about me in Aramaic and discovered my name."

"She read Aramaic?" Ramsay asked in disbelief.

"Yes, and she seemed to know Clovis. They took us onto the yacht, where Clovis and I were tied up belowdecks. It was there that he told me how he knew her, how they had fought together in feudal Japan, and then he told me her name." He paused when he heard the name whispered by half a dozen low voices in the gallery and on the judges' panel.

"Yes, it was Brevicepts," Evan stated loud enough for all to hear. "She separated us once onboard, and I didn't see Clovis again until we reached Somalia. During our voyage, Brevicepts spoke to me several times. And during those conversations, she told me about herself and what she has been doing for these many centuries. She also told me about her group of other Reincarnationists that she has found and collected since she was forced out of the Cognomina."

The gallery erupted with shouted questions. "*She* has a group?"

"There are more of us?"

"How many more?"

"Where are they?"

"Can we meet them?"

"We must meet them, right?"

"The group," came the loudest interjection. "Tell us about her group."

"They call themselves La Mutuelle," Evan replied over their rising voices. "And though she didn't tell me their numbers, she was confident her group was larger than ours."

"Larger than ours? How could that be possible?" Auda demanded from the judges' bench.

Evan turned to face the questioner. "I met another member of her group, a young woman named Elsa, who confided in me that Brevicepts found her in an asylum. Later, Brevicepts described her process of finding new Reincarnationists. She keeps psychologists from all over the world on her payroll, and these experts actively search through cases of schizophrenia and psychoses to look for clues of highly detailed past-life recall." Evan scanned the stunned faces in the gallery. "She's actively recruiting—*that's* how it's possible."

The gallery buzzed with conversation and speculation until Ramsay gaveled the chaotic room back to order. "Why did she want Clovis? What has she done with him?" the judge asked.

"I believe her motive in capturing him was revenge. Brevicepts spoke about her time and her friendship with Clovis and how he turned on her in Japan in her quest to establish a permanent home for the Cognomina. She said his betrayal set her back by centuries in her plans for us, for all of us."

Ramsay tapped the gavel lightly on the bench to quiet the murmuring from the gallery. "Please tell us what happened to Clovis."

Evan lit another cigarette and drew deeply enough to steady his nerves. "I believe she planned to kidnap Clovis in advance, and that it happened during my visit was pure coincidence. Had I not been there, she would have taken him, and we would not have known." Evan paused and let his eyes wander to focus on the flickering flames in the closest burning brazier. "I think that she plans on punishing him and that she may have devised a way to harm him, or potentially harm any of us."

Ramsay hushed the rising voices again. "What happened?"

Evan snapped his eyes back to the judge. "There was a doctor with her who injected Clovis with something that sent him into convulsions and paralyzed him in seconds. His body shuddered hard, and then he stiffened from a fetal position into a perfectly prone one, legs stretched out, arms at his sides, head resting on the ground. His motionless body appeared perfectly at peace, except for his eyes. I remember his eyes remained open and alert. They darted around wildly until they found mine, and they communicated a type of trapped horror, as though he were completely awake, alert, and aware inside an inert and unresponsive body.

"I rushed to him, of course," he continued, "but her guards restrained me and held me back. I could do nothing but watch as the doctor examined the stiff body for a pulse and eye movement. I remember the doctor saying that Clovis was still in there, and I took that to mean he was still conscious inside that trapped body. Her guards grabbed him like a piece of lumber and carried him into the jet."

"So that's it? She just flew away with him?" Chance asked from the bench.

"Yes, and she left me there on the airstrip in Mogadishu with instructions to deliver a message to all of you about her mission and how it affects the Cognomina."

"What mission?" Auda challenged.

"Her mission is to stop the destruction of this planet by ignorant humans who have no long-term appreciation of the damage they are doing. She believes that we remember our lives for a reason, and that reason is to act as a witness, judge, and jury for an out-of-control human race that is too short-sighted to see the impending doom that imperils us as well." Several members of the gallery nodded in subtle agreement. Evan remembered that Brevicepts had anticipated that this message would resonate with many people in this room. "Her group works behind the scenes of global politics and economics to effect the change she wants to see."

"That sounds very organized," Ramsay said.

"It seemed that way to me," Evan agreed. "From the conversations I had with her and Elsa, I think their La Mutuelle organization runs and controls a network of well-placed politicians, business leaders, and celebrities around the globe that do their bidding."

"It sounds like an influence network," Rafic said from the front row of the gallery.

"They made it sound as if they can affect politics, economics, even culture from behind the scenes through this network. I got the impression they recruit and place these allies, or agents, into positions of power. It's like they groom them and place them into careers in politics, business, and media in return for their allegiance to her mission and agreement that they will carry out her plans."

"Now that sounds more like a secret society," Samas offered in Rafic's direction.

Another question came from the gallery. "Do you have any more detail about her plans?"

"Yes, you said her plans included or affected us," came another voice. "Please explain."

"I will," Evan said, turning toward the gallery again. "I believe the only reason she released me was to bring this message to all of you as her emissary."

"What do you mean when you say *her emissary*, Evan?" Auda asked from the bench. "I'm not sure I like the way that sounds."

Evan paused to steady his nerves. "After she captured us, she separated us and all I could think about was what I could do to free us both. When she invited me to speak with her, I took that opportunity to learn all I could about her in the hope that I could somehow win Clovis's release." Evan choked on the words and struggled to continue. "I obviously failed. But while I was trying to get information about her and La Mutuelle that would be valuable to us, she made an interesting offer to introduce me to the rest of her group if I carried out a single task for her."

"And what is that task?" Auda asked with hard suspicion in his raspy voice.

All eyes narrowed toward Evan, and the room fell into complete silence, save the crackle of the small illuminating fires. "She asked me to tell you that she wants to reconcile our two groups and that she wants members of the Cognomina to help her accomplish the mission that she has started with La Mutuelle. She said that she will welcome any member who wants to meet with her and understand more about her mission and how you can help."

"She extended an invitation for any of us to meet with her?" came a loud voice from the gallery. "And we can meet her others like us?"

"Why would we not meet with her if it gives us a chance to expand our numbers? This is amazing, Evan," shouted another voice from the crowd.

Auda shouted above the rising voices, "This is the same Brevicepts we shunned centuries ago, and it sounds as though her hubris to rule has only grown."

Evan held up his hand to quiet the numerous voices. "There's still more," he said, trying to suppress the anxiety rising in his throat. "She seemed so open to me about herself, her group, and what they are doing. I was just trying to help Clovis in any way I could, so I agreed to deliver this message and offer to you before she told me the conditions"— Evan paused to calm his quavering voice—"and the consequences of our choice."

The grotto erupted into a tumult of voices and questions again. "What conditions? What consequences?"

Ramsay gaveled the group into silence once again, and Evan continued, "She asked me to tell you that each of you should decide now, tonight, if you want to meet her and learn more. For those who decide to meet her, you should present yourselves at Montparnasse Tower in Paris and she will receive you."

"This sounds like a trap, especially after what she did to Clovis," Auda shouted.

Evan looked up at him and mustered the courage to answer. "Don't think I haven't considered that, but at the time I thought agreeing to carry this message for her would be my *only* link to her and her group. If I had refused her, then none of us would have the opportunity to learn more about her group, be they friends or foes." Evan paused and drew in a deep breath. "And most importantly, I was trying to preserve any link, any lifeline back to Clovis."

Ramsay tapped the gavel lightly on the bench. "Evan, I can appreciate the extraordinary challenges and decisions you faced while with her. I cannot imagine myself choosing any differently than you." She glared at Auda. "None of us fault you for your actions, but we do need to hear everything in its entirety. Specifically, I want to know what she told you about the consequences."

"She said we should discuss her offer to reconcile and help her, and each of us, myself included, were free to make their own choice. But that our choices would have consequences." Evan stiffened as he recalled the scene on the tarmac. "That was right before she instructed her doctor to inject and trap Clovis in the paralysis I described." Evan turned to look at all the faces that stared back at him. "I believe what she did to Clovis is what she meant by the consequences of our choices."

Silence filled the grotto as each member contemplated what terrors might await them if they declined her invitation.

"Galen, what do you think they did to him and what danger is he in?" Chance asked from the bench.

Galen rose from his seat next to Evan and paced the distance between the bench and the gallery. "I have been contemplating that since Evan first described the events. Her doctor injected him with something that paralyzed his muscles and motor skills but did not affect his breathing or heart rate, given that her doctor checked those after Clovis had stabilized. There are a few ways to do that to the human body, but the curious part for me is that his eyes were open, moving, and apparently tracking what was around him with an awareness that suggests complete consciousness." He stopped pacing and focused his attention back on Chance. "That is what concerns me most. You see, if she had killed him or put him into a subconscious state like a coma, then his body would age and die and we would simply await his return to us in a new body." Galen paused for a moment to complete his next thought. "But on the other hand, if he was completely conscious and trapped in a body he could no longer control, that would be a danger to the psyche that none of us has ever contemplated, much less experienced." He began his pacing again as his mind raced with potential consequences.

"Like a lifetime of solitary confinement," Evan offered.

"An apt analogy," Galen said in agreement.

"That could be a fate worse than death for us," Poppy said, leaning forward in her chair.

"Yes, it could be that dark," Galen conceded. "If only I had a sample of what they injected him with, or any additional detail."

"There was something else, Galen. She watched your press conference on your life-extension research. She knew who you were and appeared to know what you were working on. She seemed simultaneously interested and upset as she watched. She turned off the feed when you mentioned the possibility of living to one hundred and forty and limiting clinical trials in humans." Evan looked up at the black ceiling, trying to recall what she said to Elsa. "She told Elsa to get the jet ready in Mogadishu and start something she called Operation Botis, whatever that means."

"Botis, you said?" Rafic asked from the front row of the gallery.

"Do you know it?" Ramsay asked him.

"Yes, I found a reference to it in some research I was doing on the Illuminati last year," Rafic answered. "Botis is a demon, described in a centuries-old spellbook called the Lesser Key of Solomon.[33] Botis supposedly has the power to recount the past and divine the future."

"He sounds charming," scoffed Auda.

"Interestingly, Botis is also the unifier of friend and foe," Rafic concluded.

"Well, that's impressive. What don't you know?" asked Poppy with a smirk.

"I don't know what is going to happen next," Rafic answered. "Evan, are there any other details that you can recall that would help us identify who Brevicepts is in this life? I mean, if she controls a group larger than ours and if that group interacts and controls hundreds or even thousands of prominent and influential normal humans, perhaps I could identify her from a description or another name."

"Elsa called Brevicepts by another name: Lesannées, with the accent on the last syllable," Evan offered.

"'The years'?" Ramsay asked with an inquisitive look on her face.

"In French, one could interpret the name that way," Rafic answered.

"Perhaps she has found a sense of humor after all this time," Ramsay quipped.

"We still don't know who she is today," Auda said. "The only one here who even knows what she looks like is Evan."

"Wait a minute." Evan shouted as he felt for the lump of the old flip phone in his pocket. "I took a photograph of her as the jet was taking off."

---

33. This is a work of collected spells and manuscripts from Hebrew, Latin, and French sources that date back centuries. A few researchers have undertaken scholarly attempts to translate and compile them all in a single treatise—most notably (and first) was Aleister Crowley.

"Excellent. I can use that," Rafic said as he reached into an olive drab military rucksack for a laptop. "Bring me the phone, please," he said, motioning for Evan to sit next to him in the first row of the gallery.

Ramsay tapped the gavel lightly. "I recommend we let our intrepid Rafic see what details he can find on Brevicepts. Let us pick this up again after a short recess."

18

The members of the Cognomina burst into boisterous debate as Evan walked over to Rafic. He eavesdropped on them in their groups of three or four.

"I can't believe there are more of us. I don't care about the risks. I'm going."

"Her side attacked one of ours. I don't care if she and Clovis have a history together—that's a shot across the bow to me."

"At least they stand for something and have a mission, and a damned good one at that."

"What is *our* purpose?"

Evan sat between Rafic and Mr. Diltz and watched in amazement as Rafic pulled out an oversized, chrome-plated laptop with a clear glass screen. Rafic flipped open the glass top that acted like a see-through heads-up display. His hands flew over the keyboard as applications sprang onto the large pane of scrolling information.

"What is *that*?" Evan asked, pointing to the futuristic device.

"Oh, this old thing?" Rafic smiled. "One of my friends in British Intelligence lent this to me. It took me nearly a week to get all of their spyware off it, but I *was* able to keep their access links," he said, stroking the machine like a new pet, "and add a few new ones of my own that they don't have. I feed MI6 enough information that they like to keep me outfitted with great hardware. Now let's see that phone, Evan."

Evan pulled the scuffed-up flip phone from his pocket and handed it to Rafic.

Rafic stared at it like an ancient artifact. "Geez, technology much? Just because you remember past lives doesn't mean you have to use their tech."

"Hey, this workhorse picked up every cell tower between here and Damascus," Evan said defensively. "And it has a picture of her as well as the tail number of her jet and the license plates of her team's SUVs in Mogadishu."

Rafic took the device with the care of an archaeologist and gently flipped open the cover to reveal a postage-stamp-sized screen with tiny Arabic writing barely visible through cracked glass. He looked up, confused. "Can you just text it to me?"

Evan took the phone back and worked on the keypad.

"Wait a second," Rafic interjected. "I just remembered I have been wanting to try something." He pulled out a sleek chrome smartphone that looked to be the smaller sister to the laptop. "Another gift from my English spy friends. They told me it has a near-field data-sniffing capability that will pair with unknown phones by posing as the nearest active cell tower. It even has a stealth mode that steals data when it's powered down. Put your phone back in your pocket please and sit next to me," Rafic instructed as he keyed at his phone and laid it on the bench between them. "Let's see if my spook friends are as good as they think they are." Rafic watched as small icons emerged and then disappeared into the mirrored finish on his phone.

Evan watched the futuristic phone and listened to the intensifying conversations around him, picking up the most emphatic points being made by the others.

"The normal humans *are* destroying this planet, and someone has to save it. You told me yourself you had to move out of India due to the pollution."

"Don't accuse me of not caring about Clovis. I just think this too important an opportunity to pass up."

"I just want to meet her. All those old-timers think about is their past with her. I want to explore what she is doing right *now*."

"Perhaps she has information on our origins."

"Maybe she discovered why we remember."

"Is there some calling for us that we have been missing this whole time?"

Evan's chest tightened with the tension rising in the room as he could hear the members of the Cognomina divide into two camps. *He was supposed to join two families, not fracture his own.*

"What do you normally do with these things?" Evan asked Rafic in an attempt to quiet the conflict building around him.

Rafic kept his eyes glued to his phone. "Do you remember me telling you at your Ascension party that I study history and some of its darker corners?"

"Rafic is our resident conspiracy theorist," interjected Jens without bothering to turn around from his active debate on Brevicepts with two others.

"Conspiracy analyst," Rafic corrected without looking up. "When the conspiracies are proven to be real, we are no longer dealing with theories, are we?" He directed the last question to Evan. "I am a data hound and use it to add to my research."

"What do you research?" Evan asked.

"Everything," Jens and Poppy answered in unison.

Rafic glanced up from his phone at Evan with a pained look of a misunderstood genius. "I have believed for a while now that there is something not quite right with this world and the decisions we make politically and culturally. It's hard to explain to others because we can't see it, and yet we can see its effects over time."

"I'm not sure I follow," Evan conceded.

"It's a bit like dark matter. We can't see it or touch it, yet we can see its effects in our universe—enough to know that it exists and affects everything around it. That's what my research is pointing me toward—there is something out there driving our history in directions that it shouldn't normally take."

"Your account of Brevicepts and La Mutuelle will no doubt throw him down another rabbit hole," Jens said, turning his blond head to face them now. "Is that phone really able to capture data?"

"Yes, but it can do more than that. It also has a bilocation ability, which can look like it is calling from a different location and phone number. The Brits jokingly call this the Padre Pio[34] feature, but I haven't used it yet."

"Sounds like a nice party trick," Poppy mused.

"Well, it could be the right rabbit hole this time," Rafic sneered back at Jens before turning to Evan again. "Part of this research is in history, and often many of us have been a witness or party to those historical events. All of us would do well to recognize that history is also what is happening around us right now. The longer I work on this problem, the more I end up working in the present day. Ah, it worked," he said, picking up the sleek phone. "I hope you don't have anything too embarrassing in there, Evan." Rafic's fingers popped open and manipulated files before sending them to his laptop screen by holding and flicking the file toward the larger machine.

"Nice trick," Jens said, pulling away from his conversation to take a seat next to Rafic.

The grainy photo of Brevicepts caught in the window of the private jet popped up on the laptop screen as a facial recognition scan program began to run through millions of potential matches. "Now let's see who you really are." Rafic threw the photos of the jet's identifying tail number and the United Nations license plates from the mercenaries' SUVs into separate search windows on the laptop. "Are there any other details you remember about her?" Rafic asked Evan.

"She was a vegetarian, and I'm pretty sure she was left-handed. And she was quite tall, over six feet."

---

34. Padre Pio was a twentieth-century Italian priest who reportedly had the supernatural gift of bilocation, or the ability to appear in two places at once. He was made a Catholic Saint in 2002 by Pope John Paul II.

"And she always liked animals," Ramsay offered. "Did she have a pet with her, Evan?"

"Yes, a dog. A spaniel, I think. And she wore her hair up in a topknot."

"See, she has not changed," Auda shouted as he walked back to the judges' bench.

Rafic's fingers danced across the shiny chrome-plated keys and entered their comments as additional search terms.

"She was an excellent sailor," Galen said, taking a seat in the gallery behind them to get a view over Rafic's shoulder.

"I saw her in action, navigating a luxury yacht," Evan added. "She seemed to know what she was doing."

"I have a hit on the tail number of the plane," Rafic shouted as more members took seats around him. "A6 prefix is UAE, United Arab Emirates. The jet is owned by Demantius Capital, a reinsurance firm based in Paris. Flight records show it hasn't left Dubai in months, so she might be operating it without a transponder to stay off the grid. That would likely mean she is flying out of smaller airports or she's pulling some serious strings to land that luxury sled at major airports with no identification for the aircraft." Rafic's eyes darted to the third search window as more members of the Cognomina broke off their debates and circled him. "The SUVs are registered to the United Nations, last used in Nairobi two weeks ago."

"UN-registered vehicles for mercenary work tells me she is connected politically," Ramsay said.

"Or she could be simply bribing or blackmailing people to get what she needs," Jens added.

"Is there anything on her yet?" Poppy asked as she sat behind Evan and put her hands on his shoulders.

"Gotcha," Rafic whispered as he pulled up a small series of photographs matched by the software.

"That's her all right," Evan confirmed.

"Do you have a name yet?" Jens asked, leaning in to study the face.

"Yes, there it is," Rafic said with satisfaction. "Her name is Beatrix

Thorvald. She sits on the board of half a dozen eco-charities and, oddly, two defense contractors. There are only seven pictures of her that the software was able to match and only the one that crossmatched to her name. Take a look at these while I start a deeper search on the other six images." Rafic enlarged the photos into a slideshow.

"Stop," Evan shouted. "That picture, the fourth one. Enlarge it to show the woman beside her."

Rafic enlarged the photo to show a young blond woman walking behind Brevicepts and four other men.

"That's her," Evan said as he noticed the same rush he had felt when they were together. "That's Elsa—the one I met from her team, who cautioned me about dealing with Brevicepts."

"That was good advice," Auda shouted from his lonely seat on the bench.

"Can you search for her too?" Evan asked.

"I will search for all the other people in these photos. It's weird that I only get seven matches for Brevicepts. That is an unbelievably low result set."

"Are you searching only MI6 data?" Jens asked.

"No, I hacked this machine to pull from everywhere—Langley, Tel Aviv, Moscow, Beijing." Rafic pulled up another program on the laptop and started another search on three of the photos. This time the algorithm scanned the background of the photos. "This is another feature they asked me to test out. See how these three photos all have snow on the ground? This program searches backgrounds and geographies in photographs and matches them against billions of archived photos that have location data. It's like the ultimate crowdsourcing hack that leverages social media platforms."

"I can tell you where those were taken," Galen said, leaning in. "That's Davos, Switzerland. And since it is winter, those were most likely taken at the World Economic Forum that takes place every January. It is a gathering of the world's political, economic, and cultural elites."

"He's right," Rafic said as he looked down at the search results. "It's Davos."

"What about Elsa? What name did you find for her?" Evan asked, unable to take his eyes off her grainy, enlarged image.

"I can't find any name for her, but the other four men in her picture are all Italian—the deputy finance minister, the chief of staff to the prime minister, and I know the third man. He is head of AISI, the Italian secret service."

"Perhaps Elsa has some responsibility for Italy within La Mutuelle?" Jens offered.

"Perhaps," Rafic said. "The matches for the others in the photos turn up other senior-level political figures, except for this fourth man." Rafic pulled up a second photograph with Brevicepts that showed the fourth unidentified man again. "This man shows up twice with Thorvald, but there are no other photos on record for him . . . anywhere," Rafic said, lingering ominously on the final word.

"A henchman perhaps," Poppy said.

"Do you recognize him from the yacht or the jet?" Galen asked Evan.

Evan leaned in and studied the man's sharp South Asian facial features and long black beard. "No, I didn't see him."

"What's she like?" Rafic asked Evan in a low whisper.

"Brevicepts?"

"No, Elsa," Rafic clarified. "The others might not notice, but you smile every time you see her picture on my screen."

"She's nice," Evan whispered back, still looking at the grainy image of her. "She has a good heart and somehow landed in the wrong spot. She tried to warn me."

"Do you think you can trust her?" Rafic challenged without looking away from his searches.

Evan thought about this question as he replayed their conversations. *Could he trust anything he felt right now?*

"Come on, Rafic," came a voice from behind. "What are you finding?"

"I must confess, guys, this is a bit eerie for me," Rafic said, turning around to face what now was the entire group of the Cognomina around him, save Auda. "If I did a photo and name search on a nomadic Bedouin shepherd boy, I would find more data than I can find on Beatrix Thorvald."

"So she's, what, like a ghost?" Jens asked.

"No, you don't understand the depth of these searches," Rafic corrected. "She is like a ghost of a ghost."

"I don't understand," Poppy said.

"These data sources I'm searching have access to every part of our lives, every day, for every one of us. What I am saying is that these three—Brevicepts, Elsa, and the mystery man—have never lived anywhere, traveled anywhere, or purchased anything—ever. Statistically, it is not possible. No one is this clean. If your Elsa were not snapped casually with these officials, she would not exist."

"And yet there she is," Galen countered. "Like some dark matter we cannot see."

"But that affects everything," Rafic murmured.

"What are we going to do about Clovis?" Auda shouted from across the grotto, clearly annoyed at the attention spent on Brevicepts. "You do remember our captured brother, Clovis?"

"We just want to know who we are dealing with," Kress said. "Don't you think we should get as much information as possible before making a decision?"

Auda leaned forward in his judge's chair. "You want to get as much information as possible to know who you are dealing with?" Auda asked rhetorically. "Let me give you some information to help you decide. She is a maniacal psychopath who is bent on ruling the world, with the sole goal of burning most of it down. That's how she was in the third century, the eighth century, the eleventh and the fourteenth centuries. This is who she is. She will not have changed. She will not have softened. I have seen her disregard and hatred for mankind. I have witnessed her willingness to turn on her brothers and sisters—some of whom are in this room now and know I speak the truth about her." Auda straightened his tall, lean frame as he rose from his chair to address them. "I warn you. Do not believe her. Do not seek her. Do not trust her, lest you fall into a trap as Evan has."

Evan snapped his head up from Rafic's search results, but Ramsay spoke first. "That's not fair, Auda."

"Of course it's not fair," Auda countered. "That is why she did it.

She saw she could exploit him because that is what she does. Even her own lieutenant warned Evan not to trust her."

Evan's hand shook on the cane, and he clasped the other hand over it to keep it still.

"He did his best," Ramsay said stepping in front of Evan on her way back over to the bench.

"Yes, and look at what is happening now. This meeting right now is probably going exactly to her plan. Look at us," Auda bellowed, his patriarchal arms spread wide. "She has already begun to divide our house. If she would attack one of our elders and then invite you into her group only under threat, does that sound like she thinks of you as her equal? She is seeking servants, not associates. And I, for one, will have nothing to do with her."

The room fell silent as Ramsay took her central seat on the bench beside Auda.

Kress broke the silence from her seat behind Rafic. "I wish to meet her, and I will go on record as such."

"Why?" asked Ramsay.

"I want to meet her and the others. I see them as our estranged relatives. I do not care about her terms—the opportunity is too precious, too unique in my mind," Kress said, looking around the grotto for any sympathetic faces. "Judge or condemn me if you want, but I intend to go to Paris to meet with her."

"I'm going too," said the tall, grizzled man with the menacing scar on the left side of his face whom Evan remembered from the Ascension party as Kerr. "I am a hunter but also a conservationist, and I want to learn how she is working to stop our environmental decline. I don't care about her methods, I want results."

Several voices mumbled in agreement.

Ramsay tapped her gavel lightly on the bench as Samas, Chance, and Poppy all returned to their seats on the bench. "You have that choice, Kerr. You are free to go—you all are. But before you make your choice, I think a few of us, especially some of us older ones, would like to share a few stories about Brevicepts."

Samas spoke first. "Like the time she got us all killed and our first Zurich home burned to the ground by forcing the citizens of this canton into violent revolt against her tyrannical rule."

"Or the time," Galen started, "when she was a Japanese nobleman and wanted to turn her family lands into a permanent home for the Cognomina but could not stop herself after her first victories and declared herself emperor before burning down the eastern part of Japan."

"And becoming a legendary demon in the process,"[35] Rafic added.

"Yes, that is true," Galen concluded.

Evan stood from his seat in the gallery and walked back to his chair at the table in front of the judges. "Auda, perhaps you are right about me. Perhaps I was naive in my enthusiasm at learning there are more of us and perhaps she did exploit me in order to plant doubt and derision in our house. But if I have brought this into our house, then I must also bring another story of her—one she told me personally."

"Go on," Auda prompted.

"Her group executed a plan to infect Venice and Milan with the black plague. It killed hundreds of thousands, and she did it for the primary reason that she thought her city was overcrowded. She takes pride in that even today," he said, taking his seat next to Galen.

"Do you want to know who you are dealing with?" Auda asked sharply. "*That* is who you are dealing with."

"How do we know those events even happened?" came a voice from the back.

"We have made a practice of not discussing her as she was excommunicated from this order after the Zurich revolt and fire. You can look it up in the archive if you don't believe us. We have detailed it for our record," Ramsay said, pointing to the open leather tome in front of the scribe. "I'm sure we can direct you to the exact codex in the library."

"You say you want to know who you are dealing with. I also would like to know who I am dealing with," Auda said, looking around the

---

35. Taira Masakado was revered and worshiped after his death. His severed head is still interred in the Kanda Shrine in Tokyo.

room at the faces on both sides. "I plan to free my captured brother, and I need to know who in this room I can depend on to help me with that task—a task that cannot abide divided loyalties," he concluded ominously.

Kerr stood up straight with determination. "So you're putting us to a test? Stay with you and abandon any outreach or communication with her, or sacrifice our place in the Cognomina?"

"I'm not sure I like your ultimatum," came another voice.

"I am saying you cannot have it both ways, not after she attacked one of ours," Auda countered. "She simply cannot be trusted."

"There is a high likelihood that the invitation is a trap," Rafic said.

"You can't be serious that you want us all not to engage with them?" Kress said in protest.

Kerr looked around and saw several faces in the group nodding gently. "I'm sorry, my friends, but the opportunity to meet another family is too great for me to pass up. I am going to meet her in the hopes I can meet others like us. Her business with Clovis is between them. If anyone else wants to do that, you are welcome to come with me."

Kerr put his hand on Evan's shoulder. "You did the right thing, Evan," the hardened man said, looking down through eyes wet with emotion. "Thank you for bringing us this opportunity. This might be remembered as a great day—equal perhaps to the day your notebooks were released," he said and then marched out of the grotto.

Half the members in the gallery slowly rose and followed Kerr toward the exit.

Kress followed last. She turned back to Auda, who looked utterly defeated. "I am sorry, but I must meet them. I promise I will try to find Clovis and free him. I hope you will keep the door open for us," she said over the sounds of shuffling feet ascending the stairs, "but I am going to Paris."

"Make sure you and the others take your things from this house," Auda shouted in anger after them, his voice cracking. "You two," he commanded the second and third scribes, "please ensure our departing friends find their way out of the hotel."

Evan and the remaining members of the Cognomina sat in the grow-ing silence as the defectors' footfalls faded into the world above. "This is my fault," Evan conceded, his eyes locked on the polished black of the stone floor. "I thought I could be the one who brought a message that could unite us with a new family, and instead we have this."

"It is not your fault," Ramsay countered after a few seconds.

"I agree," Auda said. "It might have worked out differently had you killed Clovis before they took him on the jet. But that would have been a nearly impossible decision for any of us to make."

"But one we may have to face now," Ramsay said.

Evan looked up, confused. "Kill Clovis?"

Galen nodded solemnly. "If our theories about him being trapped are accurate, that might be better for him than where his mind is now."

"She orchestrated this perfectly," Auda continued, "as expected."

"And like you said," Galen said, "it was my research that likely started this operation. What did she call it, Rafic?"

"Botis, the uniter of friend and foe."

"I hate to lose those members for now, but it is good we have this many left," Ramsay said, looking at the dozen faces in a room that now felt quite empty. "Who knows, perhaps we will have to rescue more than just Clovis before this is through."

"Sure," said Poppy as she sat on the table next to Evan. "If those who just walked out on us eventually decide they don't like what Brevicepts offers them, what do you think she will do to them?"

"She certainly would not let them return home to us," Samas said.

"They could be injected the same way Clovis was," Jens mused. "She gets the help she needs, and she takes out those among us who could work to stop her."

"Exactly," Ramsay agreed. "Which is why we should be thinking about saving more than just Clovis when the time comes. Surely they won't all join her."

"Well, she will know soon that we refused her—again," Chance said, looking at the remaining faces in the room. "We should anticipate that she will come for us."

Ramsay nodded toward Auda. "We're going to need a way to find out what she is planning for us and how to counter it."

"And how to get our people back," Auda concluded. "Let us put our heads together and teach this witch a lesson."

19

"Here's something interesting," Rafic said, breaking the silence from a lack of ideas for where to begin. "The Montparnasse Tower is the lone skyscraper in central Paris."

"Yes, and a generally hated eyesore," Jens interrupted.

"Indeed," Rafic agreed. "It has also been in receivership for the past eighteen months because the previous owning consortium could not afford the asbestos abatement."

"When does this get interesting?" Poppy asked.

"The company that lost the building was called Woland Capital Group, and the building was insured by Grantham."

"I like where this is going," said Jens. "Follow the money and find the players."

"Money always has a trail," Auda added.

"Well, it does until it doesn't," Jens countered. "But that is my area, and I might be able to help."

"Anyway," Rafic interrupted to get back to his point. "The chain doesn't stop at Grantham. Bankruptcy court records from Paris show Grantham should have taken a complete loss when the building was condemned for asbestos removal and all the tenants kicked out, but they didn't. They had something called reinsurance."

"What is that and where is this going?" Poppy asked.

"Reinsurance is insurance for insurance companies," Jens interjected. "It's like super insurance that pays out for only the worst of the worst-case scenarios like earthquakes or hurricanes. Companies like Grantham would use reinsurance to offset their risk from a single big loss that could wipe them out."

"Want to guess who their reinsurer was?" Rafic asked, letting the question hang in the air of the grotto. "A company called La Communauté Mutuelle was on the contract. They eventually took control of the building in the receivership proceedings."

"Wait, La Communauté Mutuelle as in *her* La Mutuelle? You think they are the same?" Ramsay asked.

"The global headquarters for La Communauté Mutuelle is in the top three floors of the Montparnasse Tower in Paris."

"No way," Poppy blurted out. "She's running a global influence network through an insurance company?"

"It's perfect," said Jens, the financier, as he rose to his feet and began to pace in front of the bench. "It's more than perfect. Think about it. Everything of importance or value in this world is insured, and every insurance company is insured by a giant reinsurer. This would allow her to be involved in anything, in everything!" he exclaimed. "I don't think La Communauté Mutuelle is a listed company, is it?"

Rafic tapped a few keys. "It is a private company and does not post its earnings or its holdings."

"My God, it's genius," Jens said. "She's hiding in plain sight. It's the perfect cover. She would have access to anyone through a giant like that. Every major business would need her, governments would need her. She could ostensibly touch anyone she wanted. It would be like weaponized capitalism."

"Is Beatrix Thorvald listed as the president?" Poppy asked.

"No," Rafic replied as he scanned the data streaming across his screen. "There are no officers listed in any public record, and they have no web presence at all. The only thing I find is the name, the address, and the logo."

"What does the logo look like?" Poppy asked.

"Oh, you'd like it," Rafic answered. "It looks like it came right off one of your tattoos. It's a Japanese-style butterfly."

"Wait, let me see," Evan shouted as he sprang over to look at the image on Rafic's screen. "It's her. It has to be. On the boat, Clovis told me about his time with her in Japan, and he mentioned her family crest was a butterfly."

Jens walked over to Rafic and Evan. "Nice job. It's not much, but it is a start."

"So do we assume that Clovis is in Paris with her?" Samas asked.

"I think we can assume that Brevicepts is in Paris, but we should confirm that," Ramsay said.

"Damn, I just lost my connection," Rafic complained. "Let me cut over to my hot spot."

"If her building in Paris is empty, it's all the more reason to think the others are walking into a trap," Poppy offered. "I think we should call them."

"Great idea," Ramsay said, turning toward the gallery seats. "Mr. Pianosa, can you send out a message to those who left? Tell them her building in Paris is empty and might be a trap."

All eyes turned to Pianosa's seat, which was now empty.

Ramsay turned to the attentive scribe. "Did you see him leave?"

The young chronicler shook his head and kept at his writing.

"Well, where the hell did he go?" Ramsay asked.

Galen rose to answer but was cut off by the sound of an intermittent wail of a siren that echoed down the grotto stairs. "What is that?"

"It's a fire alarm," Evan said, looking over at the wall torch at the base of the stairs and noticing the excited flame licking upward and to the left toward the fresher air above. Evan snatched up the cane and strode over to the stairway to investigate. "I think our hotel is burning."

"Damn that woman, not again," Auda shouted and followed the others toward the stairwell.

All of the torches were dancing in a rapid burn as the fresh air from the grotto was being sucked up the stairs in a noticeable draft. Evan led the way, leaping two and three stone stairs at a time to get to the top.

Ramsay kept up with him stride for stride, with the others falling back and Chance helping a winded Samas make his climb.

"Can't we just wait it out down in the grotto?" Ramsay asked between gasping breaths.

Evan shook his head and pointed to the first torch. "Look at the torches. They are an indicator that all of the oxygen is being drawn up and into the fire beyond this door. We would suffocate down there. Our only way out is through here," he said, placing his hand on the warm doorknob to feel for how intense the flames might be on the other side. He turned the knob and pushed open the door to reveal a room already filled with dark red flames crawling across the ceiling and down the exterior wall around the window.

Evan stepped into the bedroom of the hotel suite and had to stoop down to distance himself from the heat. He scurried to the closed door leading to the hallway, wrapped his hand with the bottom of his shirt, and turned the hot brass doorknob. The air between the hall and the room equalized, sending a shock wave of brighter orange through the flames on the ceiling as they fed on the fresher air. He dropped to his knees and pulled the door open with the hooked handle of the cane. He poked his head around the corner to look down the orange hallway.

The entire hotel was aflame, but the fire in the hallway kept to the ceiling and undulated in waves of fresh fuel as it snaked its way toward the hotel's entrance. It was not on the walls yet, and Evan felt that the hallway to the front door was their best chance of escape as a group. He crawled back to Ramsay, who stood on the third step down the stone stairway to the grotto, just as Auda and Jens had reached the steps just below her.

"I've only spent a handful of nights in this place. Where are the exits aside from the front door?" Evan asked his three colleagues.

"There is a service entrance at the back of the kitchen," Auda said.

"What about the window in this room?" Ramsay asked.

Evan shook his head. "It would open an air source that would fuel the fire and draw more of it this way before we could get everyone out. When that glass goes, this room will explode into a fireball."

"Auda, Jens," Evan commanded as he stripped the sheets and blankets off the unused bed, "take these down and soak them in the pool. They can help protect us on our way out." He then returned to address Diltz, the young scribe, and the remaining members of the Cognomina who huddled in the stairwell. "We can't stay here or in the grotto because we would suffocate. This fire looks bad, but trust me, it is just coming to life and we will get out of this if we stay low and protect ourselves. I know how this beast behaves. If you follow me, you will survive this," he said, hoping it was true.

Evan looked up at the flames on the ceiling and thought back to all the times he had summoned this familiar foe. And he remembered all the times he had beaten it at its deadly game—though this would be the first time in all their heated encounters he would have to help others escape those fiery fingers.

Auda and Jens panted hard as they returned with the wet bedding and distributed it.

Evan might have been the returning youth of this group, but he could see the panic in their faces. "Remove any synthetic clothing, get on your knees, cover your mouth with a piece of clothing, and take shallow breaths," he directed in a voice loud enough to carry over the hissing and crackling of the menacing fire in the hallway. "Crawl behind me two at a time, side by side. I will lead us out. Mr. Diltz, please take the scribe and follow right behind Poppy and me. Chance," he said, locking eyes with the giant, "I need to come up the back with Ramsay. Don't stop. Carry people if you have to." He looked at each face in turn and measured the fear in each one. "Poppy, you're in the front with me. This will feel hot—hot enough to make you want to stop. But don't stop. Whatever happens, don't stop," Evan said, making eye contact with each one to ensure they received his message. "Take a sheet or a blanket to cover yourselves and don't throw it off unless it is on fire. Chance, you and Ramsay cover yourselves with the bare mattress. Are you all ready?"

Evan watched each face stiffen into the resolve he wanted to see. "Let's go." He grabbed Poppy, pulled her to the floor, and threw a blanket over both of them. He crawled down the center of the hallway, pulling her as he advanced toward the brighter flames at the end of the hallway.

"I've never died in a fire before," she said, crawling beside him. "I imagine it makes an impression."

"And you won't today. I've done this many times. Come on, keep up with me." Evan felt the familiar heat pressing down and scratching its devil-red nails down his back as they crawled on their hands and knees past what he imagined to be the halfway point.

"This bitch is really getting on my last nerve," Poppy said in a choke of smoke as she scurried next to him.

"Did I ever tell you about the time when I burned a warehouse in Los Angeles and was nearly shot by this crazy-hot tattooed woman after my getaway?" Evan said to her in short gasping breaths.

He heard her choked chuckle and knew she would make it. He peered through the smoke and noticed the billowing clouds start to swirl under the promise of a new fresh air source, likely the front door. Not much to go. He could see orange flames ahead, which meant hotter flames.

"Hurry through this part," he shouted loud enough for the others to hear. "We're almost there!" Evan strained his searing eyes through the smoke and dancing sparks to see the wood-paneled hallway open into the high-ceilinged stone foyer.

"I want to come back, I want to come back," the young chronicler screamed out in pain and terror.

Diltz tugged at the young scribe's robe to move him forward. Evan reached back and extended the handle of the cane to the caretaker, who gripped it for leverage as he pulled on the scribe's robe.

"It's too hot!" Poppy screamed. "It's like a furnace."

Evan could feel the strength and resolve fade in her as he clasped his left arm around her to help her along. His memory flashed back to young Bobby watching his mother screaming and thrashing on the floor as the flames engulfed her. "I've got you," he shouted to Poppy. "Just five more meters and we're safe."

He dragged her the last few paces to the thick wooden front door, which the other two scribes pushed open before pulling them both out onto the open driveway. He took two deep breaths to steady himself before running back in to show the next two to safety. The flames leaped at the new air as it rushed into the building, but the high ceiling and stone walls of the front receiving room dissipated the life-threatening heat.

Evan ran back into the heat of the hallway and guided the others to safety two by two. He took inventory of them as he went: Diltz, Jens, Galen, Auda, Castor, Dilmun, Rafic, Etyma, Samas. Evan focused his stinging eyes on what was quickly becoming a wall of flame, looking for the movement of the last two. He called out but heard nothing except the crackle and roar of the monster around him.

He was about to call out again, when Chance emerged from the smoke, one hand holding the burning mattress over his bald head for protection and the other massive arm cradling a barely conscious Ramsay, who cradled ten large leather volumes in her arms. The mammoth man dropped the flaming mattress and scooped up Evan without missing a stride until all three were outside in the safety of a clear Zurich night.

Chance dropped Evan, then gently placed Ramsay and her books on the cool cobblestones of the driveway. Galen and two of the scribes rushed to her, and the doctor raised and lowered Ramsay's arms to accelerate her breathing.

"She insisted on saving the records," Chance said, worriedly watching Galen stabilize her.

Ramsay coughed and choked with every forced breath as Galen extended her arms to work her exhausted diaphragm back into action.

"That's it," Galen said. "More breaths like that."

Evan checked everyone else for burns or smoke inhalation before returning to Ramsay. The sharp sirens of approaching fire trucks wailed in the distance, and Evan had to fight his remembered instinct to run from this burning scene that he felt in his core he had somehow started. Ramsay finally breathed without Galen's help, and her eyes blinked open to take in the complete catastrophe that lay burning before her.

Evan wanted to turn and watch the familiar flames as they devoured that gleaming white vision that had beckoned him to walk from Syria, that had welcomed him twice, and that was now dying before him. He looked at Ramsay breathing and imagined how many nights she had spent in the comfort of that inn. She raised her blue-gray eyes to take in the lovely old St. Germain one last time before it was completely gone. Galen and the others turned their focus from their friend to the flames as though saying a silent goodbye to the one member of the Cognomina they could not save.

"There was twenty million euro in there," Chance said as he smoothed the scorched fabric on his sleeves to extinguish a few embers.

"There were two Titian masterpieces in my suite." Samas sighed as he watched the flames leap into the night sky.

Etyma wiped her eyes. "My instruments."

Poppy reached over and tapped her hand on Evan's cane. "At least this old friend made it out."

Evan clutched the cane in both hands as he listened to Galen, Etyma, Rafic, and even Auda begin to cry as the Hotel St. Germain's wooden roof beams cracked and surrendered, sending a shower of sparkling red embers high into the darkness over Zurich.

Evan could not bring himself to look upon the destruction he had wrought on their house. *He had brought the message that fractured their ranks, only to finish by bringing their house down on their heads. Where would they go after this night? Would they all be scattered to the wind like the rising ash from their home?* Evan held the cane and embraced it as a symbol, a talisman for a new mission to undo this.

Galen leaned over and put his arm around Evan and drew him in close next to Ramsay.

"I'm so sorry," Evan choked out between breaths. "I'm so sorry I have done this to us."

Ramsay looked at him and drew several deep breaths before speaking. "What are you talking about? You saved us." She shifted her eyes over to the scribes who scanned the treasured volumes for any traces of damage. "You helped us save our history." Ramsay looked at the collected faces bathed in hot orange firelight. "She would have won in a single stroke tonight if not for you. Look around you, Evan," she whispered between wheezes. "We have this core group. And if we can keep it together, we have a chance against her."

Evan wiped at the smoke and fresh tears in his eyes and looked at each member as Ramsay had instructed. He watched, and his spirits rose slightly as he saw each face stiffen from sobbing loss to hardened resolve with each new part of the hotel that collapsed into the fury of flames. He hoped she was right about them being a team, about them having a chance. But most of all he hoped she was right that they didn't blame him for this destruction.

"So this must be Operation Botis," Rafic said, cradling his rucksack and inspecting his precious laptop for damage.

"I think it's just a start," Auda added.

"I thought we were all going to die," Poppy said, patting a hand over Evan's pants pockets in search of his pack of cigarettes.

"But we didn't," Ramsay said, looking around at the entire group. "Please help me up, Chance. It's not safe here. We need to find a place to recover for a bit. A public place with security would be best."

"I know just the place, and it's within walking distance," Chance said, helping Ramsay to her unsteady feet. "Follow me, everyone."

Chance held most of Ramsay's weight as the refugees walked down the driveway, past the approaching fire engines, and into the welcoming anonymity of the night.

THE GROUP ROUNDED A CORNER and watched Chance and a staggering Ramsay walk past two large guards in Italian suits and into a sleek modern building covered in a blanket of glimmering gold lights. The sign above the door read Swiss Casinos—Zurich.

"Welcome to my office," Chance bellowed when all were inside the gleaming white stone and chrome-accented lobby. The escalator transported the guests to the second floor through an ethereal bath of warm white light. "This place has better security than the airport. We will be safe for as long as we wish to stay here," Chance said, speaking to all on the escalator with him. He strode to the front desk, where all three staff members brightened at his approach.

"Good evening, sir, welcome back," the concierge said warmly, taking in the blackened and burnt clothing on the disheveled group. "It looks like you have some guests tonight."

"Indeed, Marcel. We are literally in need of refuge this evening." Chance reached into his pocket and placed a black metal credit card with no text or bank logo on the white marble counter. "Can you send someone out to find some clothing to get us by for a few days? I'd also like for you to open the Montagu room for me, and please alert the usual suspects that the black whale is here and that there is blood in the water this Friday night."

"Of course, sir. Right away, sir," the concierge said, motioning four staff members into action. "Would your guests like to freshen up, sir?"

"Yes, can I please have your largest suite for the evening?"

"Of course, sir," the concierge said, running the card, pausing, then sliding it through again. "Ah, there seems to be some problem here, sir."

"Well, run it again," Chance commanded.

"I have, sir," the man answered sheepishly.

"Having credit issues?" Samas joked at Chance's expense as he placed his card on the counter. "Try this one," Samas said confidently.

The concierge ran the second card and then ran it again. "I'm so sorry, sir. This one is not working either."

Poppy, Jens, and Rafic frantically pulled out their phones.

"My phone has no service. Can anyone else get service in here?" Poppy asked.

"I'm on Wi-Fi," Jens answered, his voice cracking into a panic. "No, no, no. It can't be. My account is empty."

"Mine too," Rafic said flatly. "They're all empty."

"We're broke?" Evan asked.

"How can this be?" Chance asked.

"I'm going to fucking kill this bitch," Poppy growled.

Chance coughed loudly enough to refocus the concierge's attention as he fished for a key in his trouser pocket. "Marcel, in my locker you will find ten gold bars, twenty black house chips, and an unopened bottle of twenty-five-year-old scotch." He placed a gold key with the letter *Z* etched into the handle into the concierge's hand. "Please bring them all to me. We will be in the Montagu lounge."

"Of course, sir," Marcel answered before scurrying off to the cashier's cage on the nearby casino floor.

Auda looked up from his phone screen. "We're wiped out. But how?"

"Who is missing from this scene?" Ramsay asked the group.

"Pianosa," Diltz answered. "He had access to everything. This could be bad."

"How bad is bad?" Jens asked, wrinkling up his face as if preparing for the worst.

"I'm so sorry," Mr. Diltz started. "Pianosa passed all of our security screenings. I accept full responsibility for this catastrophe."

"Well, you will just have to stay with us now, won't you?" Poppy said as she placed a hand on the old man's arm.

"She must have gotten to him," Rafic said.

"Do we have any assets that were not under his control?" Auda asked Jens.

"Only things that are tangible," Jens answered. "Things like Chance's safety deposit box or Samas's art collection. Everything else—anything with an electronic record like a bank account, stocks, even home or business ownership—is likely gone or transferred to a new owner."

"Like a giant reinsurance company, perchance?" Rafic quipped.

"Save for what things of value we can get our hands on and sell," Jens continued ominously, "we're probably penniless."

"Quite right, Jens," Chance said, trying to calm everyone down. "Listen, Marcel is bringing me over a hundred and fifty thousand dollars, along with a very nice bottle of scotch. I can give each of you ten thousand dollars in the next sixty seconds."

"But it won't be enough," Ramsay countered. "That won't be enough to keep us safe, much less keep us together long enough to come up with a plan."

"And it won't be enough to get our friends back," Auda added.

"You all know well what I can do in a place like this," Chance said, raising his voice. "I will give any of you your share of what I have left right now, but if you trust me, it could be ten or twenty times that by dawn. Marcel is calling in the biggest gamblers from all over the region. Take a chance on me, and I will get us back on our financial feet."

"I'm in," Evan shouted.

"Me too."

"Same here."

"Let's do it, Chance."

The giant man beamed as eventually all heads nodded as one. "All right, it's settled then. Come with me and see how a professor conducts his class," Chance said, striding into the din and excitement of the casino floor.

20

"What game would you like to start with, sir?" the casino manager asked as he swung open the doors to reveal a luxurious private room equipped with a variety of empty gambling tables. Velvet upholstered spectator chairs ran along the sides toward an opulent cocktail bar at the back of the salon.

"I'll start with baccarat until the other players arrive, then send in a poker dealer," Chance directed.

"Very good, sir," said the manager.

"And can you bring in some telephones for my friends to use? They have some business to conduct while I play."

The manager nodded and left.

"Make yourselves at home," Chance said to the group, motioning them toward the chairs and the bar. "They are opening up a hotel suite for us, and I have asked them to get us a change of clothes. We can stay here for as long as we need to rest and recover and to plan."

A uniformed waiter approached as each sank into a plush chair. "Can I get you anything?"

"I'll have two bottles of your finest French wine and two glasses," said Galen, reaching for a house telephone on the table. "Do you guys want anything?"

"Water."

"Champagne, please."

"Vodka rocks, no fruit."

"Water."

"Cognac."

"Cold beer," Evan said, looking over at Jens. "I can't believe I had thirty-seven million dollars an hour ago, and now I have just enough to pay for this drink."

Jens looked down at his phone. "I'm sorry, everyone. I've checked all the accounts that are online, and our losses are complete. Pianosa's treachery has ruined us."

"Do you have any idea where your apprentice might have gone?" Auda asked, looking over at Diltz, who shook his gray head.

Ramsay turned to Rafic, who was booting up his laptop. "Start looking for him *now*. Brevicepts might be clever enough to travel off the grid and cover all her tracks, but our young Pianosa may not be."

Rafic nodded and took a sip of his drink.

Marcel the concierge returned, cradling the gold bars with ten black poker chips on top and a bottle of scotch under his arm. He placed the collection—the entire remaining assets of the Cognomina—on the red felt of the table in front of Chance.

Galen signaled the confused waiter to open both bottles at once as he spoke into the receiver. "Please repeat that, Manuel. Calm down. So long as you are all right, everything will be fine. Start again, from the beginning."

Poppy sat two tables down and spoke into the next available phone. "Are you all right, Ruben?"

Samas placed a call from the telephone at the bar. "Yes, my love, I am fine. Do what the men say, but do not let them into the art vault. I am on my way to you. I will meet you at your sister's home."

Ramsay took in the conversations around her and kept her eyes focused on the gold bars and chips in front of Chance as she ran through plan after plan in her clearing head.

"The city of Los Angeles building code department just condemned my church and kicked out my butler," said Poppy. "And my shares in the glass company were sold today and moved into cryptocurrency. I have nothing."

Samas spoke next. "My wife is being evicted from our home by the Rabat police right now. They are taking the artworks off the walls, but they will not be able to enter my art vault—at least not until they can figure out the combination."

"They raided my lab," Galen stated. "My lab manager said a squad of armed men that looked like mercenaries came with an Asian-looking doctor. They took all of the life-extension trial serum we had produced for our upcoming human trials." He sniffed one glass and then drank from it. "Those were my real assets, my life's work."

"Wait, we're broke? Like, really broke?" Dilmun shouted into the phone, slipping into a panic. "Oh no. Hell no. I'm not broke. I am *not* poor again. I can't be poor again. Maybe I can go to Paris to meet Brevicepts and get my money back. Do you think she will give it back if we join?"

Chance ran his fingers over the gold bars, relishing their cool, silken surface as his oversized hands pulled in the first won pot of new black chips. "I have lost and won many fortunes," he said loud enough for all to hear, "and the first is always the hardest. After that, you realize that money is just a tool to accomplish your goals."

"Chance is right," Evan said. "She hasn't killed us. She has just taken one of our tools away from us. That's all money is—a tool for getting things done, right?"

"That is right," Ramsay agreed. "We need to rally around our other tools and add one or two new ones if we are to stay ahead of her. And the first one we need is secure communications between us. Rafic, do you think your English friends could get us more of those special phones?"

Rafic shook his head, his eyes still glued to the multiple search windows on his laptop screen. "I thought about that already," he said dismissively. "It would take me a week or more to get them, and the better part of another week to scrub them clean of their spyware and GPS tracking features. Besides, given that the Italian secret service was with her, I don't think we can be sure that other government agencies are not compromised—even the English."

Evan sat up in his chair. "So what we need are new phones that don't have spyware, that have no GPS tracking, that can't be traced to us, *and* that can be used anonymously?"

"Sure," Rafic goaded, looking up. "And they should be cheap and available in the middle of the night too."

"I don't know technology much, but I think this meets our requirements. Catch," Evan said, tossing his beaten and worn flip phone to Rafic.

Rafic caught the simple phone and laughed. "He's right. It's perfect."

"I can buy these for forty euros each at any convenience store that caters to immigrants," Evan continued. "I can get us twelve working phones for cash in one hour."

Chance picked up a yellow chip from his stack and tossed it to Evan. "Cash this out at the cage. It should be enough." He then summoned the concierge with a loud snap of his fingers. "Marcel, my friend here needs to run an errand, but I want to make sure nothing happens to him. Can you send two guards with him? Two of the larger ones, please, and take him in one of the casino sedans if you can."

EVAN RETURNED AN HOUR LATER to find the placid Montagu lounge a near riot of energetic shouting, emotion, and currency exchange as eight new players sat at the red felt table with Chance, whose chip stack had grown many times over.

Evan took a seat at the larger side table and dumped the simple, black flip phones into a pile. "I took the liberty of mixing up the countries of origin for these basic text-and-call-only SIM cards. Syria for you, Somalia for you, Turkey for you, Nigeria for you," Evan said, handing them out one at a time. "I taped your new phone number on the back, along with everyone else's numbers too. You will note that the batteries are not in these phones now. If you take them out, then you are truly off the grid and no cell tower can ping you or find you. This is as dark as you can go and still stay in contact when you want."

Ramsay smiled approvingly. "Perhaps I have some tricks to learn from our returning son."

"The life of a refugee is a life off the grid."

"Noted," said Rafic, examining his state-of-the-art phone with suspicion. "Maybe I should leave this somewhere now."

"Or use your bilocation feature to place the phone in Paris. That might be a fun trick to play on her," Evan countered. "On my trek from Syria, authorities in Hungary were tracking us to our secret sleeping spots by the Danube, so we hid the leader's phone on the other side of the river and watched them swarm the place. You can't be too careful with something you cannot completely power off."

"Good thought in getting SIM cards from different countries," Jens said, taking an Algerian formatted phone.

"Jens, I keep thinking of your comment about La Mutuelle hiding in plain sight," said Evan. "There are tens of millions of immigrants in Europe, and now we can hide among them."

"Yes, now it's our turn to be the ghosts," said Ramsay. "Let's only power them on when we are away from Zurich on our first tasks. This is what I am thinking." She motioned them all in closer. "Rafic, you have all of the other members' cell phone information on your phone, right? Send out a warning text that her building in Paris is empty and might be a trap. Tell them she burned down the St. Germain and took all of our funds. Tell them she is potentially hostile now and that her offer might be a trick.

"Next thing is money. Chance is winning like I have never seen before, but that still might not be enough," she said, turning to Samas. "You're one of our bankers now. If you can get into your home, gather your art collection and try to sell it. We need those works on an auction block in London as soon as possible."

Samas sighed and shrugged his wide shoulders. "Well, it is a good thing I will live long enough to buy them all back again."

"As we have seen with the fire," Ramsay continued, "battle lines have been drawn, and we should assume that Brevicepts and La Mutuelle will be hunting us. We should travel in twos or threes for safety.

"Samas, I want you to take Poppy with you. Poppy, you should take a chance that your corporate pilot has not been informed that you are no longer on the board of your company. Get the casino guards to take you right up to the jet. If the pilot won't let you on, come straight back. If you can get on, fly to Samas's home for the art and get to London.

"Jens, stay with Chance and set us up with cryptocurrency wallets. We need them to be secure, anonymous, and available for deposit from here and from auction galleries in London."

She looked at Galen next. "We have to find out what they injected Clovis with and try to get an antidote. We have to assume at least some of the others who left will befall the same fate. Can you set up a new lab in a safe location—perhaps one that is off the grid, somewhere no one would suspect?"

Galen smiled. "I know a place I can go back to. I can be ready in twenty-four hours."

"When I find Pianosa, Brevicepts, or her doctor, I will try to find what they used on him and get it to you," Ramsay promised. "Auda, I think you should go with our good doctor. Rafic—"

"I know what you are going to ask, and I just found him," said Rafic, his eyes glued to his laptop screen. "Evan's phones gave me the idea. Pianosa's phone just pinged two cell towers south of Milan at a speed that would indicate he's on an express train."

"Where is it headed?" Ramsay asked.

"Rome. He's headed for Rome."

Ramsay sat back and rubbed her tired eyes. "If they are in Rome, I know exactly where to plug us in," Ramsay said, smiling. "I just hope he is still alive after all these years."

"You hope who is still alive?" Evan asked.

"An old friend, someone I helped a long time ago," Ramsay said, trying to remember his face. "We're going to need a car, something that can't be traced to us."

"Oh, Marcel," Chance shouted, and the uniformed man came at a trot. "Marcel, what kind of car do you drive?"

"Is this to settle a wager, sir?" the twenty-something attendant stammered as he looked around at the imposing table of hardened gamblers.

"No, but as you can see, I am on quite a run tonight, and I am thinking about showing you some gratitude in a way that might help my friends over there. You see, they need a car."

"My car?" Marcel asked, stunned. "But I drive a used Škoda."

"Ha! As it turns out, a used Škoda is exactly what my friends want," he said, picking up a black chip off the top of his mountainous stacks. "Would this cover your trouble for lending it to us?"

Marcel swapped his car keys for the chip with the speed of a magician. "Always happy to be of service, sir. Keep it as long as you want."

Chance tossed one brown poker chip to Ramsay, one to Galen, and another to Samas before he handed the car keys to Evan. "You had better get going if you're going to catch that traitorous bastard."

"He's right," Ramsay said, turning to Evan. "You're with me. We're going on a road trip to Rome. There is someone I need to find."

"WHO ARE YOU LOOKING FOR IN ROME?" Evan asked as they walked to the casino's parking garage.

"It's a long story, but it will help fill our time on the drive. I am looking for a man named Perez, who would be about eighty now if he is still alive. I heard he was in Rome a few years ago, but the first time I saw Perez was as a boy in the fall of 1943. I was Jack McKean then, a young captain in His Majesty's Fifth corps of the Eighth British Army. I was assigned to something called Wigforce," she said with a laugh. "That was our nickname for Major Lionel Wigram's idea of seeing if his classroom lessons worked in the field. He fancied himself a guerrilla warfare expert who had taught tactics at Sandhurst or someplace like that. I spoke Italian, though with a distinctive Pre-Raphaelite accent I might add, so I was 'volunteered' to join him and get him started with the partisan Italian anti-fascist resistance called La Brigada Maiella.[36] I had been serving in a commando unit until I

36. The Maiella Brigade was indeed an Italian resistance force that worked closely with a Major Wigram of the British Army. They organized sometime in the fall of 1943 in the Abruzzo region and fought bravely alongside the Allies until the end of the war in Italy. (See *The History of the Maiella Brigade* by Nicola Troilo.)

received a mysterious transfer order to Wigram. I will never forget the first time I saw him. Major Lionel Wigram sat behind a ridiculously ornate desk that had belonged to the mayor of the town of Termoli, Italy, until the Allies arrived . . ."

21

Major Lionel Wigram sat behind a ridiculously ornate desk that had belonged to the mayor of the town of Termoli, Italy, until the Allies arrived.

"Captain McKean, reporting as ordered, sir," Ramsay said, snapping a crisp salute.

Major Wigram rose from his desk and returned the young captain's salute. "Your file says you volunteered to train as a commando, is that accurate?"

"Yes sir."

"How did you find the training?"

"It was good. I rather enjoyed it, sir."

"Enjoyed it?" the major asked as he walked around the opulent mass of his commandeered desk. "I've heard it's the hardest training in the army."

"It was tough, but I enjoyed it. I enjoy military training—always have, sir."

"We can knock off the formalities, McKean," he said, reaching out for a handshake. "Say now, what's that?" Wigram turned the captain's hand for a closer look at the black Embe tattoo. "That's a bit of an odd one."

"Oh, this old thing," the captain said, sheepishly pulling his hand back. "All the lads in our village get it when they leave for secondary."

"Hmm," the major mused before getting back to the point. "Your file says you speak Italian."

"Yes, I do."

"Dove hai studiato?"[37] the major demanded in well-practiced Italian.

The captain cocked his head and smiled before answering with a rapid recount of his Italian abilities in his remembered tongue.

"All right, all right," interrupted Wigram. "You've made your point, captain. Your Italian is certainly better than mine and better than anyone else's in our division, but that accent. I can't quite place it. Veneto?"

"Good guess, Major. It's Lombardy," the captain lied. "We had a governess from the lakes region, up north."

"Do you know why you are here?" asked the major.

"I confess that I do not," replied the captain.

"We have been hearing reports of insurrections and revolts by Italian citizens in the German-occupied areas of southern Italy. These are happening everywhere from Torricella to Lanciano,[38] here and here," the major said, pulling McKean over the map on his desk and pointing out the two towns. "The Germans are brutal occupiers—stealing, raping, and killing indiscriminately. While the Italians might have been Axis allies with them, the Teds[39] have certainly worn out their welcome here in Abruzzo. Your assignment is to use your commando training and your rather odd-sounding Italian to find and befriend these agitators to our side as partisans."

"I sound like just the right man for that."

"Indeed," Wigram brightened. "If we can get the Teds watching their backsides instead of watching our boys, then we can focus on giving them a proper dusting. We've arranged for transport to our closest airbase tomorrow morning. You'll parachute in here," he said, pointing to an *X* next to a larger blank spot on his marked-up map.

37. Italian—Where did you study?

38. Major Wigram's reference to a revolt in Lanciano, Italy, is memorialized in the town's Monumento ai Caduti di Lanciano, which details the events and victims of an uprising on October 5, 1943, and matches Ramsay's account.

39. Teds seems to be a nickname for the German soldiers. The word for Germans in Italian is *Tedeshci*.

"I don't think that will be necessary, Major. Just have the transport take me to that little town on our side of the line. I can make my way from there."

The major eyed him skeptically. "Very well. What will you need, Captain? We have submachine guns, grenades, sapper mines, field radios."

"I will need cigarettes, cartons of them. Whatever hard liquor you can give me and hard candies," the captain detailed. "Oh, and I will need a donkey and Italian lire, lots of it."

"But what about armaments, provisions, communications?" Wigram protested, not quite sure that the captain understood the scope of the engagement. "You could be gone for weeks, how will you defend yourself and communicate back to us?"

"I will defend myself with this," McKean said, slapping the holstered revolver on his hip. "If I need a bigger gun than this, then I will shoot the man holding it. I will be able to get what I need if you give me the pack animal, cigarettes, booze, candy, and money. Anything more would just draw attention to myself."

"And how will you let us know if you find men who want to become partisans?" the major challenged.

"Well, I'll bring them back to you."

CAPTAIN JACK MCKEAN REMOVED A HANDFUL OF LIRE and purchased one of the scruffiest donkeys in the small village where the Eighth Army transport had dropped him. He found a stable boy that was about his size and paid him in lire for his tattered clothing and work boots, leaving the poor boy smiling but nearly naked except for polished new-issue British commando boots and paratrooper pants. He stopped at the baker and the butcher and tucked their provisions away inside his military jacket that he wore under the stable boy's grimy overcoat. Jack was about to mount the donkey, but thought better of it and instead led the poor animal by the rope as he wandered north on the dirt road toward German-controlled territory.

He wandered from village to village for the first week, never speaking but always being seen by the local Italians. The normally lively and bois-terous Italians were subdued on the north side of the no-man's-land that served to buffer the two armies, and the vibrant Italian landscape seemed painted in German Army grayscale in these fearful oppressed hamlets.

Captain McKean slept in abandoned and bombed-out barns and houses, steering clear of buildings still occupied by the unburied dead. He took mental notes of which villages the German soldiers frequented and on what days and in what numbers. He noted the bars and tavernas the Italian men visited, and he noted the homes that doubled as broth-els for drunken soldiers after sundown.

He watched the boys of each village pick up sticks that looked like rifles and pistols and act out the scenes of military atrocity their young eyes had seen. The older boys placed their younger brothers against the wall and pretended to gun them down. A boy placed his stick pistol next to the head of a playmate and shouted the sound of a shot before making his friend play dead in the street.

Camouflaged perfectly as a wandering refugee, Captain McKean spent his days edging closer to the playing boys in each village, pretend-ing to shoot at them through the legs of his donkey and then falling dead under their fusillade of return fire and laughter. As he got closer to them, he kept hearing them pretend to be the same heroes in each village: L'Avvocato and Re Zingaro.[40]

McKean focused on the largest village in the area, the one with the most men of fighting age. He followed his ears to the sound of boys play-ing and fell into their familiar game. Only this time when he pretended to be shot and mortally wounded, he groaned, held in his guts with his hands, and then with a sleight-of-hand trick, he spilled brightly colored candies onto the cobblestones toward the boys. Each budding partisan dropped his stick and raced to grab the scattered sweets. The bravest boys rushed forward to inspect his hands for more treats.

"Aah, you got me," the captain shouted in his formal, centuries-old Italian. "Don't stab me, or I might leak some more." The brave boys

40. Italian—The Lawyer and Gypsy King

pretended to stab him, and he slyly threw more treats to the scrambling mob. "Tell me," he groaned, "who is it that has killed me?"

"Re Zingaro," shouted the oldest boy with pride. "He is the one who kills the Tedeschi in the night."

"And I am L'Avvocato," his mate shouted as he pretended to stab the captain. "I make the plans for the attacks."

"And where do these heroes live?" McKean asked, spilling a few more candies onto the street. All of the boys pointed to the same forested hills at the western edge of the village. "And who are the other brave men that the Tedeschi fear?"

"My father is brave. He is the tailor, and he sews the patches for the men."

"My father is braver than yours," said a smaller boy with blond hair. "He knows L'Avvocato."

"And what does your father do?" the captain asked in a pretended last gasp.

The boy's small chest swelled with pride. "My father is the mayor."

AFTERNOONS AND EVENINGS TOOK THE CAPTAIN to the bars in the smaller villages that served as gathering places for subdued Italian men. Some opened their doors to the occupying Germans; others radiated an unseen hostility toward their occupiers. A dirty and disheveled Captain McKean drank and handed out cigarettes only in the latter ones. He broke the ice and entertained them with deft sleight-of-hand tricks with cigarettes he had learned in the evenings at the remote commando training in Scotland and perfected on the transport ship to Sicily.

He told them he was a socialist and refugee from the north who now smuggled things like English cigarettes and Scotch whisky in from the liberated areas. They smoked his cigarettes, tolerated his smoky scotch, and laughed at his strange accent. They always asked about life below the line.

"Was there food and produce there?"

"Were the people happy?"

"Did the sun still shine there the way it used to shine here? The sun never seems to shine here anymore."

"Did the women dress up down there like they used to here?"

And finally, after two or three drinks, they would always land on the same questions. "What are the Americans and the English like? Do they plunder and retaliate the way the German soldiers do?"

McKean's answers would give them hope but would inevitably lead to retellings of the reprisal rapes and executions he had seen their children reenact in the streets. He sensed the fear the German soldiers instilled in them, but he also sensed the deep hatred in their proud hearts, and he hoped he could tap into that and nurture it into rebellion.

"The English tell me they are looking for men willing to strike back against the Tedeschi," he would tell them, but any spark of revenge in their eyes at the mentions of L'Avvocato and Re Zingaro would immediately dim with yet another story of brutal German reprisal on a village that dared to shoot an officer or set fire to an occupied building. They were a defeated people.

He visited the taverna in the largest village last, convinced now that he must provide some example, some catalyst, to give them confidence that they could strike back at their oppressors. He felt for the comfort of his service revolver tucked deep in his waistband as he walked with his donkey up the long hill to the bar that sat at the main crossroads of the ancient village of small stone buildings. He tied his animal to a post and stepped inside out of the biting November cold.

A woman watched him as he entered. He stopped at the bar and lit a cigarette. He ordered a drink and paid with a lire bill large enough to need change to buy at least three more drinks.

"Will you give me a cigarette?" she asked as she took the seat next to him.

"But you already have one," the captain answered. "Should I show you?"

She narrowed her dark eyes at him as she replayed his strange response and stranger way of speaking. He slowly moved his empty hand up to her ear and touched it gracefully as he magically produced a clean white English cigarette as though pulling it straight out of her head. She gasped and stood still with shock before breaking into a loud laugh that turned every head in the bar.

"Do it again, do it again," she pleaded, taking the cigarette from his fingers and putting it in her delicate mouth.

"Finish that one first, and we'll see if you are hiding any others. Perhaps you can offer some to the others. Would you like a drink?" He left the question hanging in the air as an invitation for her to offer her name.

She nodded and savored the warm smoke of the cigarette. "I'm called Tatiana. Where are you from? You have a very strange way of speaking, like a professor or a cardinal."

McKean studied her before answering. She had dark olive skin and looked a few years older than him. She dressed like a student or young professional, not like the peasant women he had seen in the smaller villages. She had confidence, but there was also a hardness about her that hinted at tragedy.

"I am from the north, Lombardy—a socialist refugee who fled south. Now I cross the line in the night and bring back things."

"Aah, I heard about you," she interrupted and pointed with her cigarette. "You're the one they call Dante."

"Dante? I have not heard this. That is not my name. Why do you think I am a man called Dante?" McKean asked defensively.

She took a long sip out of her glass, finishing half of the drink. "Because you sound strange when you speak, like what it sounded like when we all studied Dante Alighieri in school. And because you know of the paradiso on the other side of the war and the inferno on this side. And because you dream of some divine comedy of us rising up against the Tedeschi."

She kept her eyes locked on his as she drew deeply on her cigarette. McKean's blood ran cold with the realization that he might have been so careless and clumsy in his efforts.

"It is okay," she continued. "Others share this dream and long to see the paradiso, but there is fear—always there is fear. Perhaps someone can show them what their fear has done to them."

"What do you think their fear has done to them?" the captain asked.

"Their fear is like a prison, a prison of German creation. And once the Germans put us inside that prison, they don't have to watch us anymore. We have become our own jailers."

Two young men who looked like farm laborers got up from a table at the corner of the room and walked to the bar next to McKean and Tatiana. "Can we have cigarettes?"

The captain reached his empty hand up to the shorter man's ear, miraculously pulled out a fresh white cigarette, and handed it to him. He then reached out to brush the nose of the taller worker to perform the same trick, but the hard-looking man grabbed the commando's hand in a move too quick to react to. The lanky laborer turned over the captain's hand to reveal a white cigarette hidden between two dirty fingers. All three laughed as loud as Tatiana had at first.

"Please do it again," the tall man asked as McKean motioned to the bartender for two more drinks.

Captain McKean nursed his first drink slowly as the group started on their second round. They encouraged him to do the cigarette trick slowly enough for them to see how he did it, and they marveled at his mastery of it. He heard the rare sound of an automobile come to a stop in the street in front of the taverna, and he noticed all three sets of eyes that had watched his hands now turned with an animal focus to the front window.

McKean turned to see a shiny black Mercedes come to a stop across the street. A German soldier exited the driver's door and walked around to open the rear passenger door. A well-dressed officer, imposing in his black SS uniform, emerged and surveyed his surroundings before entering the home opposite the taverna. The driver followed him inside.

Captain McKean could feel the enmity radiating off the three. "Who is he?"

"He is a colonel," Tatiana replied coolly, her eyes still focused on the front door the men had entered. "He is the commanding officer of a camp near here. He stops here every Friday after paying his men."

"He stops here *every* Friday in the afternoon?"

All three sets of eyes narrowed back to the captain in an unspoken understanding.

"What kind of camp?"

"A detention camp," she answered in a voice wavering with emotion. "For political prisoners."

"He and his driver visit two sisters who live in that house," the stout, barrel-chested man said. "Both of them now widowed by his countrymen."

"And now they open their legs to their late husbands' murderers. It is shameful," said the lean worker.

"It is fear that makes them do it, not desire. They want only to keep on living," Tatiana said, reaching for her drink. "They are not to blame."

The captain took a look at the car and turned back to them. "It doesn't have to be this way."

"Sure, Dante. Guide us on that journey to the inferno," she challenged. "If someone were to kill him, we would all be dead by dark. They would kill the whole town to prove a point."

"Agreed. To attack them outright would be foolish." McKean stood up from his stool at the bar. "The Germans are a proud people who avenge their dead, but that pride is also their weakness, and they will recoil from shame and embarrassment every time." He took his glass and drained it as he reminded himself of his mission. He had to encourage and rally these defeated people if they were ever to fight alongside him. "I'll be right back."

The three Italians watched in stunned silence as their new friend exited the bar and walked across the road to the beautiful black staff car. The disheveled captain transformed before their unbelieving eyes as his stooped refugee posture straightened into an alert combat readiness that betrayed his commando training. They watched as he scanned the windows of the home and then turned to look downhill in both directions to study the roads below for traffic and playing children.

The three moved toward the window as he deftly produced a military knife and sliced an opening in the smooth black leather of the convertible top of the luxurious car. He ran his arm through the slit until it found the door handle inside, which popped the car door open in silence. In an instant, he was inside and slipping the gear selector into neutral. All three vocalized their alarm, murmurs at first and then louder in a chorus as the captain stepped out and pushed the car forward until gravity began to take over. The captain gave the wheel one last correction to send the driverless car straight down the road below him.

He ran back across the road to the taverna and studied the shocked expressions on the three faces in the window. Their heads turned to the left in unison as their eyes tracked the runaway car on a loud, slow-motion journey of crunching metal and breaking glass as it bounced between stone houses on its way toward flipping over into a twisted heap in front of the stone bridge at the river.

In seconds, the entire village emerged onto the street and stood in stunned silence as they surveyed the smoking wreck at the bottom of the hill. Their eyes led them up the hill, through shattered glass and scattered stones knocked free from the corners of impacted homes, to the confused and disheveled SS colonel, who tucked his shirt into his unzipped pants as he stood in the spot where his car should have been. The shirtless driver emerged right behind him.

The entire village watched like a nervous audience, unsure of how to respond and waiting in silence for the action to begin. The colonel turned and slapped his incompetent driver in the back of the head, shouting in German, and with that, every mouth in the village erupted with uncontrollable laughter. Captain McKean jumped at the outburst of spontaneous laughter of the three next to him at the window.

The SS officer froze in the middle of the next insulting slap at his half-naked driver with the awareness that every member of the village was laughing at them. He pulled the younger man by his unfastened belt back into the makeshift brothel, and the howls of delight from the street grew even louder as they closed the door behind them.

"A divine comedy indeed, Dante," Tatiana said, wiping tears of laughter from her dark eyes.

The captain stepped back into a street now filled with bright faces already retelling the story and children retracing the path of the ruined car.

A tall man with golden blond hair put an embracing arm around the cheery captain. "I think it is time we met," he said, pulling the English soldier tight to him. "I'm the mayor of this village."

McKean spun out of his embrace and grabbed the mayor's hand.

"Come with me," the mayor continued. "I have someone who wants to meet you." McKean followed the mayor back into the taverna along with dozens of other happy villagers. The blond man placed the captain at a table in the back corner. "Wait here, please."

The captain obeyed and watched the gathering crowd as drinks flowed and smiles spread and songs were sung. The mayor reappeared through the back door of the taverna and motioned two men in behind him. The first was a serious-looking man with a small, academic build who wore a black beret at an angle on his head of jet-black hair. The second was bigger than McKean and in his midforties. The sturdy and confident man looked like a tanned, retired athlete and moved with the grace of one. McKean rose to greet them, but the mayor signaled him to stay seated as the three men took the other seats at the table.

"Thank you for joining me. It is a pleasure to meet you," the captain started in Italian.

The short, serious man laughed. "My God, it's true. You sound like you stepped out of the fifteenth century. Where in heaven's name did you learn our language, Dante?" he asked through a warm, sly smile.

"Lombardy."

"If you say so," the big man interrupted. "My name is Ruslon, and this is Ettore."[41]

"But you might know them by other names," the mayor stated over the growing celebration in the bar.

"You are L'Avvocato and Re Zingaro," McKean offered.

The smaller Ettore nodded once. "Yes. I am the lawyer. And who exactly are you, Dante? And don't give me that Lombardy crap."

The captain swallowed hard, removed the stable boy's coat, and unbuttoned the dirty shirt to show the Union Jack on his uniform

---

41. Ettore Troilo was indeed a trained attorney turned resistance partisan fighter. He was instrumental in forming the famous Maiella Brigade in the fall of 1943. Ettore survived the war and returned to practicing law.

underneath. "I am Captain Jack McKean, British Commando of His Majesty's Eighth Army."

"And what is your mission here?" asked Ruslon.

"I am here to find men who will rise up and fight back against the Germans."

"And you think we could be effective fighters against their army?" Ettore asked.

"Yes, I do. My commanding officer and I believe that with the right training and armaments—"

"So you want us to fight together as a team?" Ruslon interjected.

"Yes, exactly," McKean said, trying to contain his excitement. "We would start by bringing you back across the lines for a few weeks of training and then—"

"No," Ruslon said, cutting him off. "We are not going anywhere. Our fight is here."

"Yes, of course it is," Captain McKean confirmed with delight that he had achieved the first contact. "But with only a short—"

"And more importantly," the lawyer Ettore interrupted again, "our fight is *now*. Right now."

The mayor leaned in to take control of the conversation. "Mission accomplished on finding us, but your little stunt today has already jeopardized our next attack."

Ruslon reached out his wide hand, moved the mayor back into his chair, and pointed a thick finger at the group of women surrounding the front door of the house across the street. "That officer shitting his perfect black pants right now runs a camp, a prison camp near here. That camp is filled with members of my family and many men who will fight against the Germans. We planned to attack and free them next Friday," the large man said, leveling murderous eyes at McKean. "But now, thanks to you, we must attack this Friday, today. So if you want to fight with us, then you join us and show us English courage today. Otherwise, we do it ourselves." He turned his regal face to the window.

The captain thought about his mission and the berating he would get from Wigram for going on a raid with no intelligence, no training, and no idea of Ruslon's weapons or abilities. But he did know two things: this would be his only chance to bond with these brave men and he *had* wrecked their plans as thoroughly as he'd wrecked the SS colonel's car.

"I will come across the line with you for more training," Ettore said. "But only after we save his family tonight."

"I am with you," stated the captain. "We start together today."

Ruslon turned back to McKean and smiled. "We leave in ten minutes. The mayor will show you the way. Bring the candies and cigarettes, Dante."

MCKEAN FELL IN WITH THE COLUMN of twenty men and three women as they marched into the forest at the south edge of the village. Tatiana and her two laborer friends from the bar were among the fighting force.

The captain walked beside Ettore, the planner, to get as much information as he could. The attack had to be on a Friday, L'Avvocato explained, because it was a payday for the soldiers, who always took their money into the village for drinking, leaving the old convent[42] that now served as a prison largely unguarded. If they attacked today with the commanding colonel besieged, their odds of success improved even further. The captain handed out cigarettes to each soldier via his magic hands, taking the opportunity at each encounter to inspect their captured German guns and ammunition counts. He thought at first about asking to lead the force, but there was no doubt that Ruslon, the Gypsy King, was in command.

The white-painted convent stood on a hill at the edge of the village just as Ettore described it. A view from the lawyer's antique spyglass showed only one unhappy soldier manning the gate. Tatiana returned from the village to confirm the bars were full of soldiers, already drunk.

---

42. Research seems to identify this as the convent of San Bernardino in Agnone, 120 kilometers east of Rome. During fascist rule, it served as a detention compound for Roma prisoners. Sadly, most of the Italian fascist collaboration with Nazi eugenics policies has been poorly researched. The best source of information on the Italian participation in the Porrajmos, which means *the Devouring* in the Roma language and what the Romani people call their "Forgotten Holocaust," is available at porrajmos.it (in Italian).

Ruslon whispered in her ear, and she chuckled and moved toward the edge of the trees nearest the gate.

"Can you cut more than convertibles with your soldier's blade, Dante?" Ruslon asked, and McKean nodded. "Go with her then."

"Use knives once inside. If you have to shoot, then shoot any soldier you see," Ettore commanded.

McKean caught up to Tatiana just as she began her first moan. The lone German soldier squinted his eyes against the setting sun and took two steps forward as she grew louder. She kept her eyes on the soldier as her moans of faked delight drew him ever closer. She saw the man shoulder his rifle and smile as she increased her rhythm. "Più forte, più forte," she panted until the lone guard was at the edge of the woods.

The captain sprang from behind a tree and dispatched the soldier quietly with his commando knife. Ruslon kept his men still for ten minutes until another guard came to the gate. Tatiana started her siren call of desire again, and this time the soldier came running with shouts to his departed counterpart who he was sure was enjoying himself instead of standing at his post. Again, the captain killed him silently.

After another fifteen minutes by McKean's watch, Ruslon moved his squad into the courtyard of the makeshift prison and expertly directed his men into twos and threes with hand signals as they fanned out into the buildings. The captain stayed with Tatiana, and they moved to help secure the near end of the largest building, the main block of cells.

He thought their plan of attacking on a payday was working perfectly as he heard a few short screams but no shots as they reached their target door. Tatiana opened the security latch on the outside of the door and pushed it open to reveal a blond SS officer standing in the main hallway of the barracks. He held a small boy with his left arm and a pistol at the boy's head with his right hand.

The captain raised his pistol, but Tatiana jumped in front of him and shouted, "Perez!" as she ran in. The officer turned the gun toward her, and the captain squeezed off a shot that snapped the soldier's head back as he landed in a heap with the crying boy. Three more shots rang out into the night from other buildings in the convent and then all was silent again except for the sobbing of frightened children, Perez loudest of all. Tatiana held her son and tried to comfort him as Ruslon entered the barracks and took an inventory of his Romani clan.

The captain walked next to the gypsy leader and noted the inverted black triangles[43] stitched onto the dingy prisoner stripes the adults wore. The children who were too young to fit in the smallest uniforms had the brown triangle sewn onto their shirts. "The other soldiers will have heard those shots," McKean said to Ruslon.

"My men will be ready for them, and they will enjoy this night. Please keep the children quiet, Dante," the Gypsy King said softly as he turned to the English captain. "There will be a lot of violence yet this evening, and their little eyes have seen enough already. Children," the Gypsy King bellowed in their comforting Roma tongue. "Come and see the magic man. He can do tricks and has candies for you."

The captain took his cue from their leader as he reached over and magically drew a cigarette out of a sobbing Perez's ear, and the children rushed to him. He dropped to one knee and held out a tattooed hand that trembled with the emotion he saw in those small faces around him as he offered the multicolored treats to the crying and hungry children. The captain looked up from the crowd of small faces to see Ruslon snap a sharp military salute to him before running toward the sound of his squad's crackling rifle fire below the gate of the convent . . .

43. Ramsay refers to the colored symbols the Nazi SS placed on prisoner uniforms to classify them: yellow triangles for Jews, pink triangles for homosexuals, red triangles for communists, and black or brown triangles for Roma. An excellent explanation of the code (with examples) can be found online at the United States Holocaust Memorial Museum.

22

"I looked up to see Ruslon snap a sharp military salute to me before running toward the sound of his squad's crackling rifle fire below the gate of the convent," Ramsay said, finishing the story as she turned the casino concierge's borrowed car through the chaotic streets of Rome.

"Whatever happened to Wigram, Ettore, and Ruslon?" Evan asked.

"Ettore and his team came back with me and joined up with Wigram's unit just as he had promised. Major Wigram got himself shot through the heart on his first mission with his forces.[44] I led them for a while after that, and Ettore's partisans chased the Germans all the way to the Swiss border," Ramsay said as she turned into an alley behind a row of abandoned, graffiti-covered buildings.

"And Ruslon?" asked Evan.

"He quit the fight after he saved his clan. He, Tatiana, and Perez came to Rome. And I am hoping we will find Perez right around the corner here." Ramsay steered the car around piles of trash and rusted cars as the narrow alley turned to follow the Tiber River before opening into an open field dotted with rows of modern tow-behind campers.

44. Indeed, Major Lionel Wigram was killed in action on a night mission against German forces in the Abruzzo village of Pizzoferrato. Sir Denis Forman, his second in command, detailed the major's fatal raid in his war memoir titled *To Reason Why*.

"What is this place?"

"The Romans today call it the Ex-Mattatoio, or the old slaughter-house. It has been abandoned since the 1970s. Now it is the home of the Roma, and our best hope of getting information on Pianosa and Brevicepts, if they are here."

"The Roma? Do you mean the Gypsies?" Evan asked, looking at faces turning to stare at them.

"Don't use that word," Ramsay corrected. "They despise that term and prefer Roma or Romani. No one knows this city and what happens in it better than they do. And they are loyal to those who help them. I just hope Perez is still alive and that I can call in a favor for us."

"How old would he be now?"

"He'd be in his eighties, but I heard he was alive just a few years ago. He is the Re Zingaro now."

"But he won't recognize you now," Evan said.

"That's right. Hopefully, I can help him remember what I did for them as Captain Jack McKean and then try to get their help. Let's walk from here," Ramsay said, stopping the car. "Give me your pack of cigarettes. We're going to need to make friends if we are to find him. The Roma are a friendly people, but they do like to keep to themselves," she said, walking into the irregular rows of parked camping trailers with colorful cryptic symbols painted next to their doors. Small hand-painted totems of playing cards, downward pointed hands, raised fists, dollar signs, horse heads, and dead rabbits deco-rated the campers and told each Roma person's story and rank to all who knew the meaning of the codes. Ramsay studied the symbols as she and Evan walked, while a curious group of Romani men started to form behind them.

Evan followed her, but his thoughts kept going back to what Samas and Poppy must be doing just then. He envisioned Samas pulling his precious paintings off the walls of a house he no longer owned. He wondered if Poppy could forgive Samas and if this hardship and the necessity to work together might thaw the centuries-old ice between them. Evan watched Ramsay as she continued her study of the symbols painted around the doors of the aging camper vans that stood as the modern equivalent of their brightly painted wagons of the past.

"What are you looking for?" Evan asked as he thought about how the ornate cane in his hand might be used as a weapon as he eyed the hard faces of the men who followed them.

"I don't know exactly, but I'll recognize it if it is here." Her close examination of every doorway drew more unwelcome attention, and the group of men now followed them more closely.

"Ah, here it is," she exclaimed, pointing to an inverted brown triangle with a crown painted above it. She knocked on the door and ignored the shouts from the semicircle of young Romani men that surrounded them. She answered one of the men in crisp, antique Italian. "I am looking for a friend named Perez. Does he live here?"

"Yes, I live here," an old man answered in Balkan-accented English from behind the narrow screen door of his caravan.

Ramsay recognized the same crying boy that had clung to his mother all those decades ago. "Mr. Perez, my father told me to find you if I ever needed help."

The old man remained skeptical behind his screen door. "Who was your father and what is he to me?"

"My father was in the British Army. He said that he saved your life and helped free your clan during the war." She held out her hand, palm slightly downward so that Perez could see the Embe tattoo. "His name was Jack McKean, but you might remember him as Dante. I am his daughter, Ramsay, and I need your help."

The crowd of men stepped in closer as angry accusations rose from the back.

"Silence!" the old man shouted them down as he carefully stepped down out of the caravan. He looked at her tattooed hand as if he recognized it but did not reach out to take it. "Everyone knows I was part of the family that was rescued that night. How do I know that I owe anything to your father?"

Ramsay reached her left hand up and magically pulled a cigarette out of Perez's ear and presented it to him. Perez gasped and held his weathered hand to his mouth as tears formed in the corners of his weary eyes. His face cracked into a smile as he grasped her hand and pulled her into a full embrace.

"What do you need, child?" He freed her and held his arms wide. "Name it and you shall have it. The Roma are at your service this night."

"Thank you. My father, God rest him, said I could trust you. Mr. Perez, first we need rest and a safe place to stay. Second, we are looking for two people who we think intend to harm us and we believe they are in Rome."

Perez barked a command in his native Romani language, and eight men stepped forward. He turned to an athletic midthirties man and nodded before he returned his eyes to Ramsay. "Lucca here will help you. Please tell us about these people so that we may find them for you."

Ramsay described Brevicepts and Pianosa to Lucca as he led them to a vacant caravan at the end of Perez's row.

"If they are in Rome, we'll find them," Lucca said, showing them inside the humble camper.

"My father was right to direct me to you for help," Ramsay said.

"Did your father really rescue the family in the war?" Lucca asked.

"Yes. We fought—he fought," Ramsay corrected, "with Ruslon when he was the Re Zingaro. They didn't lose a single fighter or a single prisoner."

"Did these people we are searching for injure your friend?" Lucca asked, pointing to Evan who walked behind them with his cane.

Ramsay looked back at her newest colleague and smiled. "I think the cane is a souvenir for him. A token from another time."

"Can you give me a cigarette?" Lucca asked. "With the trick?"

Ramsay pulled the cigarette out of his nose this time and offered it to him as he chuckled.

"I want you to teach me, but tomorrow," said Lucca as he stepped out of the caravan. "I'll get you what you need, and we'll talk then."

Evan flopped onto the small couch, exhausted. "Do you think they will find any trace of them?"

Ramsay sat on the edge of the bed and took her shoes off. "If they are in Rome, Lucca and friends will find them. They have a network that even Rafic's intelligence friends would envy."

"Thanks for telling me the story about you and Wigram," Evan said, surveying their temporary home. "I am glad Perez is still alive to recall your fight for them."

"Me too," Ramsay sighed, leaning back on the thin bed. "It seems I'm always in the fight. It's what I do. It is my mission—my purpose, I think you called it back in Zurich. The secret, Evan, is to always fight on the side of the angels as I did with Ruslon. That way everyone involved is always happy to see you again," she said with a slight smile of satisfaction.

"What are we up against here?"

"Evan," Ramsay started again with a serious tone, "we're likely in a fight for our very survival against Brevicepts and La Mutuelle."

"Did you know her well?"

Ramsay looked around at the worn interior of the camper as she considered her answer. "I knew her, but not as well as Galen or Auda."

"Auda seems to really hate her."

Ramsay let out a long sigh. "He does hate her—he always has. I'm not sure what happened between them, but I know he would do anything to keep her away from the Cognomina."

"What was she like?" Evan asked, draping his arm across the back of the narrow couch.

"She was cruel," Ramsay said flatly. "She was a merciless ship's captain who often used her power to toy with people." She eased up onto her elbows and looked over at Evan. "She once wagered me five gold coins that she could make two friends fight to the death on the foredeck of her ship, and then she did it."

Evan considered her description of Brevicepts as he replayed his conversations with her. "Did I make a mistake?" Evan asked as he clutched his hand around the head of the cane. "Did I make the wrong choice in agreeing to deliver her message?"

Ramsay held his unwavering gaze. "I don't think you had a choice, Evan. She orchestrated it so that your only choice was the one she wanted. That was always her gift. And that was always the darkness that surrounded her."

Evan looked away from her stare as he absorbed her words.

"Whatever happens from here," Ramsay continued, "however dark it gets, you need to know I will always keep us on the right side to defend those innocents who need our protection. It might get ugly, but we're always the good guys here."

LUCCA'S SUNRISE KNOCK AT THE DOOR woke them out of a needed rest. "We found them—in Vatican City."

"Like inside the Vatican?" Ramsay asked.

"Yes, they are in the Ethiopian College within the walls of the Vatican. The lady you described with the hair knot left this morning, but last night she was seen at a fundraising event hosted by the city of Rome. We believe the man, the accountant you spoke of, is still here in Rome. There is also an injured man with them and an Asian doctor who comes sometimes. The doctor always goes to the top floor. We also believe they are under the protection of a powerful cardinal named Forpo."

"Excellent work. Do your men know a way inside?" Ramsay asked, hoping for some miracle or idea on how to get inside one of the most secure places in the world.

"Sure," Lucca smiled as he held out a temporary worker's badge. "We encouraged one of the regular cleaning ladies at this building to take the rest of the week off while you fill in for her. Her shift starts in two hours. Here is her uniform," Lucca said, presenting Ramsay with a pale blue smock.

Evan turned to Ramsay with an astonished look on his face.

"I told you they would find them," she said with a satisfied smile.

Lucca loitered for a moment after she took the uniform and badge from him. "I am ready now," he said like a boy trying to get his mother's attention. "Show me the cigarette trick again."

RAMSAY WALKED UP TO THE imposing tan brick walls that protected the Vatican and held her breath as she scanned the stolen badge at the Porta del Perugino service entrance with a gloved hand and walked past the armed guards and into the secret sanctuary of Catholicism. She strode quickly toward the service entrance of the four-story Ethiopian College administrative building tucked into the garden greenery in the exclusive protected grounds behind St. Peter's Basilica. She held her breath again as she scanned the badge at the rear service door and then quickly stepped inside after hearing the metallic click of the lock opening.

"You're not Nora," said the old cleaning woman, her back stooped from a lifetime of labor.

Ramsay was caught off guard by the short woman's question. "No, I'm Rana," Ramsay said, grabbing a blue cleaning glove and snapping it onto her tattooed right hand before offering it to her new coworker. "I'm filling in for a few days. Nice to meet you. Can you help me get started?"

"Sure. I'm Rosa. Do you mind taking the top floor?" she asked as she handed a master key to Ramsay. "There are some new faces up there I do not like, and the cardinal is a difficult man."

"It would be my pleasure to take it," Ramsay answered politely in Italian.

"That accent," Rosa said. "It sounds different. Where are you from?"

"Lombardy," Ramsay said with a smile.

THE ELEVATOR OPENED AT THE TOP FLOOR to reveal a long hallway lined with office doors stretching in each direction. Two muscular men in black suits stood in front of the double doors at the far end. Ramsay pushed her cleaning cart to the opposite end of the hall and began a dutiful cleaning sweep, along with her reconnaissance of the floor plan and the stairway exits. She worked her way down the hallway, cleaning what seemed to be mainly unused offices. Imitating the stoop of the older woman, Ramsay sheepishly pushed her cart toward the two imposing guards.

"Stop," shouted a guard. "That is close enough. Just wait there while we get the trash." The older of the two guards checked his hidden earpiece and stepped inside to bring out a white plastic refuse bag, tied at the top and held at full arm's length from his expensive suit. "Here," he said, handing it to her. "That will be all. Please move along."

Ramsay took the bag from him but kept her eyes fixed on the room beyond the double doors where she saw the scarlet red vestments of a cardinal standing at the end of a hospital bed. The telltale beeping of medical equipment echoed through the gap in the doors.

The heavyset clergyman looked out and locked eyes with Ramsay, who quickly turned away with the garbage bag just as the cardinal threw open the door and berated the two guards for their clumsiness in letting a lowly cleaning lady so close to their operation.

"Very sorry, Your Immenseness," the older guard struggled to say in Italian with a thick Russian accent.

"Idioti!" the cardinal bellowed at them before turning to walk toward Ramsay's cleaning cart.

Ramsay kept her head down as she stuffed the valuable trash bag deep into the protective confines of the cart.

"Come here, cleaning woman," he demanded in Italian. "Give us the trash bag."

Ramsay reached for an earlier trash bag and extended it toward the cardinal's open right hand, which was adorned with a large gold ecclesiastical ring.

"Give it to the guards, you moron," he said, raising his right hand away as though he might strike her. "Burina!"[45]

Ramsay slinked away and handed a regular trash bag to the guard before retreating to the elevator on her way to the basement. She retreated to a secluded corner where she carefully unpacked the contents of the stolen trash bag and sorted out the only items of value: discarded needles, vials, test tubes, and two soiled adult diapers. She packed the contents into a clean garbage bag and tucked it into the bottom of her purse before returning to a full day's worth of cleaning duties on the other floors.

RAMSAY RETURNED TO THE ROMA CAMP after her shift and found Evan still sitting in their borrowed caravan, his eyes glued to the small television.

"I got some things today that could be useful," she said to Evan, but he kept his eyes locked on the screen. She sensed that something was wrong. "What is it?"

45. Italian slang—a female yokel or bumpkin

"Poppy called me an hour ago," Evan said in a flat monotone. "They have Samas."

"What? How?"

"It's all over the news. They kidnapped him right out of Leetsdale's Auction House." Evan's voice sounded deflated, defeated.

"They kidnapped him?"

"Well, that's not what the news is reporting. They are reporting that someone popped a smoke grenade in the auction room and that a Moroccan art magnate suffered a heart attack and had to be removed by ambulance."

"But it was another attack like Clovis?" Ramsay asked.

Evan nodded, unable to turn away from the television, in the hopes the network would replay the footage. "Poppy saw an Asian man inject Samas in the commotion from the smoke. Samas dropped and convulsed and lay motionless with his eyes wide open. There was an ambulance crew there already. Poppy said they looked and moved like professionals and had earpieces."

"And Poppy, did she escape?"

"She got away and managed to follow the ambulance. They didn't go to a hospital, but straight to Gatwick Airport. She got the tail number on the private jet, a different one from the one I saw in Somalia. Perez helped me find a laptop in the camp. I ran the tail number for the flight plan. It is headed for Rome."

"Great work by her. How is she feeling?"

"She is very shaken up." Evan turned finally to look at Ramsay, still dressed in her cleaning uniform. "I was waiting for you to get back and tell you before I left."

"Left for where?"

Evan cocked his head at her question. "To London, of course, to get Poppy."

Ramsay sat next to him on the small couch in the caravan. "Evan, I know where Clovis is, and I believe he is alive."

"You saw him?"

"I think so, but I can't be sure. I did get some other items that could help verify that Clovis is in the Vatican. I need you to deliver them to Galen tonight in Venice."

"But I am going to London to get Poppy."

Ramsay put her hand on Evan's knee to comfort him. "I know you are close with her, but I need you to deliver this to Galen. I have to return to the Vatican tomorrow and work my shift again," she said, flashing her badge. "I have to stay close to Clovis, and I will be able to tell if they bring Samas there."

"But I told her I would leave right after I spoke to you," Evan protested. "We can't leave her alone."

"Evan, I will call Poppy and explain. She'll be fine. You must go to Galen tonight with these items. Don't bother opening them—trust me on that," she directed, indicating the bundle of artifacts. "Take the car. You need to drive to Venice tonight." She wrote an address on a slip of paper and handed it to him. "Go to a bar in Venice called Il Santo and wait for your contact. Remove your phone battery now, and don't use it from Galen's location. We can't be too careful at this point," she said and took his hand in hers. "First Clovis, then the St. Germain, and now Samas—it's war now."

Evan sighed and took the white bundle and address from her.

"Evan, you need to leave now in order to be at the bar before it closes tonight," Ramsay urged him. "We're counting on you. You have just enough time. Go now."

23

Evan drove into the night and kept himself alert by trying to imagine what the other members of the Cognomina would be doing: Galen setting up a makeshift lab somewhere near Venice, Chance sitting at a gambling table behind a growing mountain of needed chips, Poppy alone and hunted in London, Clovis and Samas trapped like prisoners in their own inert bodies with nothing to occupy them save the echoes of their own thoughts from a permanent solitary confinement. Evan looked over at the stinking refuse bag on the seat next to him and wondered if this was the best help he could provide, given that he still felt some responsibility for setting all of this in motion.

Evan pulled the borrowed car into the giant island parking garage at the edge of Venice, grabbed his cane and Ramsay's captured trash bag, and walked through the ancient city toward the small bar in Cannaregio where Ramsay told him he would meet his contact. For Evan, traveling this light and meeting an unknown contact felt like Los Angeles a lifetime ago. It felt exciting and he felt more alive, more like his old self than he had in this body so far. He entered the nearly full Il Santo, stood at the bar, and ordered a beer in English.

Halfway through his drink, a leathery-looking man dressed like a fisherman walked up to the bar next to him to pay his bill. "Are you Mr. Evan?" he said in a thick Spanish accent, still looking straight ahead.

"Yes," Evan said.

"I am Gonzalo. I will take you to see Mr. Galen. Are you ready to go?"

Evan looked over at the man's hardened face and drank the last of his beer. "After you."

Gonzalo walked out of the bar and directly into a small fisherman's boat moored in the canal. Evan thought he could detect the outline of a pistol underneath Gonzalo's jacket. Evan climbed in, and Gonzalo started the sputtering motor. They glided through smaller waterways until they arrived at the busier Grand Canal. Gonzalo navigated the evening gondola and boat traffic in silence while Evan marveled at the elegant palazzos as they passed, wondering which one was Brevicepts's.

Evan broke the silence when they picked up speed at the end of the canal. "Do you work for Mr. Galen?" he asked.

Gonzalo thought for some time. "Not important who I work for. It is important that I am here to help Mr. Evan."

Evan kept his eyes on Gonzalo as he piloted them away from Venice and deeper into the lagoon. "How do I know that you aren't going to shoot me with your pistol?" Evan asked in a dangerous probe to get more information.

Gonzalo showed no emotion and stuck to his piloting, "The pistol is for our protection. All is fine, Mr. Evan. Mr. Galen is there," he said, pointing a weathered hand toward a set of abandoned brick buildings that appeared to float on the dark waters of the tranquil lagoon. Gonzalo killed the motor and drifted the last fifty meters to a small, weather-beaten dock at the back of the largest derelict building.

Evan sat uneasy, weighing his options for escape and not liking any of them. Evan turned at the sound of a seagull behind him and caught the Spanish boatman making the call with hands cupped to his mouth. A call returned from the dock, and Gonzalo turned the coasting craft toward a mooring.

Two men dressed in black with submachine guns in hand emerged from behind a low, vine-covered wall, and one threw a line to Evan at the front of the boat. Evan held the line as it went slack with the boat's forward momentum, and the gunman pulled on his end to steer the craft in.

Gonzalo took the line and tied off the boat. "This way, Mr. Evan," he said, stepping onto the neglected dock.

Evan followed and noticed that the two guards went back to their station instead of falling in behind him as Gonzalo disappeared into the first large, dilapidated building. The inside, however, was filled with incredible state-of-the-art medical and research lab equipment.

Galen sat perched at a large microscope and turned when Gonzalo and Evan walked in. He rose and strode over to embrace a relieved Evan. "Good to see you, my friend. Welcome to Lazzaretto,[46] my erstwhile home of sorts. I understand you have some things for me."

"Yes, here is what Ramsay gave me," Evan said, handing over the white plastic bag as he took in the surreal scene.

"Let's see what we have here. Did you get a look at Clovis?"

"No, but Ramsay did—sort of," Evan replied. "She saw a hospital bed and equipment in a guarded office, so we know the building and the floor."

"Where are they being held?"

"In the Ethiopian College," Evan answered.

Galen looked up from his work. "They're in the Vatican?" he asked with a confused look on his face.

"Yes."

"That's one of the most secure places in the world. This will be harder than we thought. It speaks volumes to the power of Brevicepts's influence network that she can hide them under the pope's nose," Galen mused.

"It appears they have Samas."

"I heard," Galen confirmed. "It's war then."

Evan nodded.

"Have you had anything to eat?

"No."

---

46. Lazzaretto Vecchio is a small, now abandoned island in the Venetian lagoon that once served as the quarantine station for disease victims.

"Follow me," Galen said, walking into the adjoining abandoned room, where Auda sat at a wooden dinner table in front of a wine bottle and Rafic sat with his face glued to the transparent screen.

"How are you?" Auda asked, drinking red wine from a laboratory beaker that had been pressed into service as a makeshift wine glass.

"I'm all right," Evan answered. "I'm more worried about Clovis and Samas."

"As am I," Auda replied.

"Did you find Pianosa?" Rafic asked without lifting his head from his work.

"We found where he's been," Evan answered. "Ramsay's Romani contacts think they were inside Vatican City."

Rafic slowly turned to Evan. "They must have a patron that could set that up."

"Try searching for Cardinal Forpo. They saw Brevicepts with him."

"Sit and rest a bit," Galen said to Evan as he pointed to the tray of cheese and salami beside the wine bottles on the table.

Galen laid out the contents of the bag on a stainless-steel medical table. "This is interesting," he said, holding up an empty vial of medicine. He turned the vial in his hand to read the small print on the label. "Zagreb. This comes from a compounding pharmacy in Zagreb, custom made no doubt." He shook the vial to coalesce a few droplets of remaining content. "This is likely what they shot Clovis with. Does the color look right?" he asked as he held up the vial for Evan, who nodded. "Whatever could you be?" Galen studied the scant droplets that remained. "We'll find out soon enough."

Galen set the vial aside and grabbed another vial from the assortment of spent gauze. "This one, unfortunately, is mine—the life-extension research I told you about in Zurich. They took it in the raid on my lab, but I am surprised that they used it. Perhaps they are just analyzing it."

He reached for the last remaining item, a rolled-up adult diaper. He carefully unraveled the coil to expose matted excrement. "From our brother Clovis, no doubt. Inelegant," he said, closing the bundle against the foul smell, "but valuable to be sure. This will contain his DNA, which

I can run through the analyzer. I don't have a direct sample from him, but I have looked at enough mitochondrial DNA in the last two lives to know an eighty-year-old's sample when I see it. It was rather sloppy of the security team to let this fall into Ramsay's hands."

"What are you looking for?" Auda asked.

"Clues, my old friend. Anytime you take something into your body, like, say, some mystery injection from Croatia, it can affect all sorts of things in the digestive tract." Galen paused to focus on Evan. "You and Ramsay did great work in getting this."

He walked back through the wide-open passageway into his makeshift lab room and put a long needle syringe into the unknown vial. Working carefully, he manipulated the needle around the bottom edge to get the last remaining droplets of the solution. "Gotcha. Now let's see what you are." He put two drops onto a glass slide, covered it with another slide, and slid it into a computerized spectrum analyzer. "This isn't much to work with, but it can at least get me started. It would be better if Ramsay could somehow get her hands on more of this."

"I got some hits on Forpo," Rafic said, keeping his eyes on his screen. "Your cardinal has been a naughty boy. He was censured early in his career as a bishop for a scandal with Vatican Bank funds, and he was once disciplined for slapping a woman—a nun to be precise."

"He sounds delightful," Auda said. "What is his tie to all of this?"

"Ramsay's sources said that Pianosa and Brevicepts were seen with him," Evan answered as he looked down the two rows of blinking and beeping equipment surrounding the doctor. "Galen, how did you get all this here?"

"We moved it, of course," he said, motioning outside to where the two armed men would be standing guard.

"Do those men work for you?"

"Yes, they do, Evan. Those and a few others." Galen smiled. "I imagine I am near the top of Brevicepts's target list, because if I can find what kind of drug cocktail she used to paralyze and subdue Clovis, then I could possibly counteract it or even cure it."

"How long would that take?" Auda asked in a voice loud enough to carry over to Galen.

"My research affords me the best equipment in the world," the physician said, giving an expensive machine a loving pat. "I should have some first results in the next hour or two."

"And then what?" Auda pressed impatiently.

"Well, my plan is first to find out what her doctor injected Clovis with so I can know what we are dealing with. Second, I need to replicate it so I can test it on animal subjects that would eventually receive my first antidote tests to see if we can even counteract what they have done to him."

"So are we just supposed to sit here and wait until this machine is done?" Auda challenged.

"Perhaps I can offer some assistance," Rafic said in Galen's direction. "What is the name of the custom pharmacy in Croatia?"

"Iva Labs. See what you can find. They make special medicines or compounds to doctors' or researchers' specifications. There is a serial number on the bottle," Galen said, handing the empty glass vial to Rafic. "If you can hack in, I would be interested to see if there are any compounding notes or even get a peek at their supply chain records to see what things their pharmacists have been ordering over the past six months."

"I'm on it," Rafic shouted. "Do you have some more wine stashed around here?"

Galen captured Evan's attention and pointed to a stainless-steel cabinet sitting on the floor. "Can you open the two Spanish ones on the top, please?"

Evan opened the cabinet to find two dozen bottles and two more empty beakers. He grabbed a bottle and held it out toward the doctor.

Galen glanced away from his work to examine the bottle. "No, not that one. Fetch another, please."

Evan returned with another bottle, which Galen snatched out of his hand. "That's better. This will do nicely." He produced a corkscrew out of his white lab coat. "Unfortunately, in my haste setting up here,

I forgot glasses. So we've made do with beakers, I'm afraid." Galen half filled each beaker and handed one to Evan. "Here's to us. *Dimidium facti qui coepit habet.*[47]

"What are you talking about? We are not even close to half done," Auda growled as he reached over and picked up the used vial.

"Iva's cybersecurity is good—a little too good," Rafic said, rubbing his hands together as if to answer a challenge. "I bet you weren't expecting this," he said as he stabbed the return key with a sure finger. "I'm in! They always overlook the proxy users."

Auda rolled the vial across the table until it clinked against the hacker's custom laptop. "See if there is anything in their records about an antidote to this monster."

"Nice idea," Galen countered, "but I doubt her doctor commissioned one." He squinted his eyes toward the findings popping up on his monitor. "Their goal is to torture Clovis until he breaks, not until he repents. This beast was designed for a one-way trip to madness. They probably never planned on needing a way to counteract it."

"Do you think she would kill us—or end us all, if she had a way?" Evan asked as he spun the cane in his hand.

"Oh, I have no doubt," Auda interjected. "I imagine she plans to kill a lot of humanity too. It wouldn't be the first time for her. One might say she has an enmity with man," he said, spitting the final words.

"When she told me about Venice and the plague, she said it made Venice a better place in the end. Do you think that's true?" Evan asked Galen.

Galen swirled his wine and considered the statement as he craned his long neck to try to see the distant lights of Venice beyond the expanse of tall grass that hinted at the muted multitudes below. "I suppose she's right in a way. It is nicer now than it used to be, and I would know. Did she tell you that I was here when it happened?"

"She did. She said she met you right before she died."

"Yes, I remember. Brevicepts found my Embe tattoo and mentioned

---

47. Latin—He who has begun has the work half done, Horace

a memory we shared from a happier time." Galen sipped from his beaker and looked up at a patch of stars visible through a hole in the derelict roof. "They buried Brevicepts on this island—and me next to him about a week later," he said, pointing a thumb toward the burdened earth beyond the broken window.

"It's easy to see her points, especially from our unique and timeless point of view. But at what cost, Evan? A global graveyard?" Galen asked, shaking his head. "Not for me, thank you. For me, humanity—even ugly, out of control, running riot—is what makes the world tolerable, beautiful, and fascinating. Those people, even in their masses, are vessels for the ideas that improve our world." He lifted his glass toward the younger man. "And, brother, we're going to be here for a while. I'd rather be humanity's helper than their undertaker."

"I don't find anything about an antidote," Rafic reported as his eyes scanned his screen. "But I did find the name of the pharmacist tied to the serial number: Marko Tajani. He seems legit, at least by Eastern European standards, medical school in the old Yugoslavia. He's been at Iva for five years."

"Any notes on the formula?" Galen asked.

"It says: See pharmacist for details."

"It's an off-the-books job then," Galen sighed. "Try searching for what Iva has ordered. Look back six months. No, make that a year."

"That could be a long list," Rafic warned.

"I'll know what I am looking for, and then we can get our hands on the same items from their sources."

"Well technically, I am in their system now and I could just reorder them and have them sent to"—he looked up from his laptop and smiled at Evan—"the Ethiopian College in Vatican City, where Ramsay could intercept them?"

"How about we just find the precursor chemicals first, and then we can get them in Milan or Vienna or wherever their source is," Galen said, trying to downplay Rafic's joke.

Evan leaned forward against the edge of the table. "Speaking of their source, why can't we go directly to the source?"

Auda leaned in next to him. "I like where you are going here."

"What are you proposing?" Galen asked as he reached for the wine in his beaker.

"One of the things I learned on the trek from Syria to Switzerland was always going to the source of your need," Evan started. "Need a ride? Go to a truck stop. Need food? Go through restaurant trash bins."

"Need a custom inoculation? Contact a compounding pharmacy," Auda answered.

"So, what, we call in our own custom formula with the same ingredients?" Rafic asked before downing the last of his wine.

"No," Evan interjected. "We call from Paris on your magic phone and reorder it *for* La Mutuelle. Zagreb is only a few hours from here. We could call in the morning and pick it up tomorrow from Marko what's-his-name."

"That sounds like the wine talking," Rafic said on his way over to Galen's stash of bottles.

"It seems risky, but it could save days or even a week's worth of work," Evan insisted.

"I agree. I would argue there is a greater risk to Clovis and Samas if we have to wait," Auda said, holding out his beaker to Rafic. "Those days or even a week might be time we cannot afford to lose."

"So I call and just say, 'This is Dr. . . .'" Rafic paused as he tried to recall the name.

"Ling. Dr. Ling," Evan added.

"Just call from a central Paris number and the pharmacy will think it is La Mutuelle calling. Pretend to be an assistant, then just bluff your way through," Auda said with a flip of his bony hand. "It's worth it if it saves us time. Besides, what's the worst that can happen—they capture us when we pick it up? They're likely going to get us eventually anyway. I say we take the action to them, starting tomorrow."

"We call in the morning and then pick it up tomorrow?" Rafic asked. "That's the plan?"

"No," Evan said, cutting off Galen. "*You* call tomorrow, and the new guy without the trademark tattoo they will be looking for goes and picks it up tomorrow," he said, rolling his unmarked right hand over to make his point.

All three sets of eyes around the table turned in unison toward the silent Galen, who stared at his monitor as the results slowly trickled in. The doctor sighed and looked down at his beaker of wine before turning to them. "*Audentes fortuna juvat.*"[48]

"That's the spirit," Auda snapped, slapping Evan on the back.

"What he said," Rafic quipped in Evan's direction.

"It's bold enough that it might just work," Galen said, walking over to them. "It's settled then. We call in the morning."

"To boldness," Auda said, holding his beaker up for all to toast with him.

"And luck," Evan added as they clinked lab glasses and drank together.

"Pull up a map of Zagreb for me," Auda said as he pulled his chair next to Rafic's.

Evan took his chair and followed Galen back to his workstation. "What was Brevicepts like back then, in that happier time with her?" Evan asked the doctor as he went about checking his findings.

Galen turned back to him. "Sorry, can you repeat that?"

"Earlier, you said in Venice that she mentioned something from a happier time."

"Yes, quite right." He pointed to the stainless-steel wine cabinet. "Grab me another bottle, and I will tell you about it. Stregua was an excellent sailor. She just had a knack for knowing what she could ask of a boat and how to position it. One of my favorite stories about her involved her sailing skill."

"What did you call her—Stregua?" Evan asked.

"Sorry," Galen said, catching himself. "Stregua was my nickname for her, it was shorthand for *water witch*. I called her that as a joke because of her ability in a boat, any boat. She was a woman then. We were traveling

---

48. Latin—Fortune favors the bold. These were reportedly the last words of Roman historian Pliny the Elder when he sailed toward an erupting Mt. Vesuvius.

together from Sicily up to Rome and had to catch a boat across the Strait of Messina. She had a dog with her, a small Saluki named Bocchi. The boat was overcrowded, and Brevicepts didn't like the look of it from the beginning. She said it was too old and broken down." Galen poured some more wine for them. "I remember her asking the ship's captain if he had purchased it in Phoenicia. I also remember that she didn't like the look of the clouds on the western horizon.

"Anyway, we paid our fare and set off for Calabria. And about half-way into the voyage, the storm hit us. First, heavy seas, then rough seas, then downright dangerous seas. After about an hour of choppy water, the passengers started to get seasick. It was just a few at first, and they instinctively tried to vomit overboard, but after a while, they lost their strength and just started emptying themselves into the floor of the sloop. Poor Bocchi couldn't help herself, and she started lapping at several small pools of vomit that ebbed and flowed with the tossing of the creaking boat. I can't be certain if the dog was truly to blame for escalating it, but watching the animal lick up pooling vomit started a wider wave of sickness in earnest. It is a medical fact that if a person sees and smells vomit, they are more likely to vomit themselves, and pretty soon all the passengers had given back their breakfasts into the bottom of the boat. The dog had a field day, and Brevicepts got angrier with each new wave that crested over the side of the open boat.

"'Steer into the waves, you dullard, or you will end us all,' she shouted at the captain.

"'That way lies Sardinia,' the captain countered as he shielded his eyes against the wind and spray. 'We are headed toward Ostia, ma'am.'

"She turned to me and asked me to keep an eye on the dog. 'You're headed straight for Hades, you damned fool,' she shouted back at him.

"'I don't need sailing lessons from a woman,' said the captain, and those were his final words in this world."

Galen looked over at Evan. "I think that was the first time I had seen Brevicepts at her full anger. She calmly slipped a sandaled foot into the sloshing slurry at the bottom of the boat until her foot found the center beam, then she placed a hand on the near edge of the hull and started making her way back to the captain at the rudder. When she got to the back, she shook the sick off her foot and promptly kicked him hard in his midsection, sending him sprawling face down into the swirling stench. She quickly took the rudder and corrected course, and the ship calmed down a bit.

"The captain got to his feet, seething with rage as he wiped the collective vomit from his face, and the first thing his stinging eyes saw was her Bocchi still lapping away happily. The captain grabbed her dog and tossed it overboard into the enormous swells.

"She shouted at me, 'Keep your eyes on that dog and don't lose sight of her.'

"I remember looking at those towering waves and thinking, 'What in the hell are you talking about? That dog is gone, just as I would be if I went in.'

"Without missing a beat, Brevicepts grabbed a coil of rope at her feet, tossed it right at the captain, and shouted 'Catch!' And he did, right as she slackened the sail line and leaned her body weight into the rudder to bring the boat around. She ducked her head just in time and missed the heavy wooden beam at the bottom of the sail. But the captain didn't, and the beam caught him right on the jaw, lifting him clear over the railing of his boat and into the angry, thrashing arms of the Tyrrhenian Sea.

"'Get ready to jump in,' she commanded me. 'We should be coming up on her soon.'

"And I remembered thinking she's completely cracked, but I saw the murderous focus in her eyes and knew I had to do it."

Galen took a long sip and looked over at Evan. "I know we have confidence we will come back again, but even that confidence is not enough to overcome the fear of something like that raging sea that would certainly mean your death. You likely remember this feeling of dread from when you chose your end in Tunisia last time," Galen said, raising a glass.

"Well, I had that feeling as I looked into those wind-whipped waves. Then I looked back into her menacing eyes and I chose to jump in after that damned dog. To this day, Evan, it was the hardest swimming I have ever done, but I found Bocchi. She struggled to keep her sleek head up as the waves capped over her. She was happy to see me, as was Brevicepts to see us both bobbing in the distance.

"It seemed like a magic trick at the time. She brought that broken-down old boat right up to us and seemed to stop it there against the relentless wind until we could climb back aboard. To this day, it was the best sailing I've ever seen." Galen finished the story and saw that Evan, exhausted from the drive, could barely keep his eyes open.

He leaned over and nudged the younger man toward a row of cots in the next room. "Go to sleep, Evan, you need some rest. You can use my bunk in the next room. Your company has reinvigorated me, my friend. I will continue our work here."

24

Evan awoke and rose in the early light to find Galen still working at his equipment, a half-full beaker of wine sitting next to two more empty bottles. "Are you okay?" Evan asked him in wonder as he rubbed his hands over his throbbing head.

"Sound as the pound," Galen replied.

"Have you been working all night?" Evan asked in a voice low enough to avoid waking Rafic, who slept on the end cot.

"Indeed," a bright Galen answered, still full of energy. "I have some exciting news, some good news, and some really bad news," he said, assembling his notes and turning to meet his guest at the table. "I was able to process all of the samples overnight, and I still cannot believe some of the results."

"Like what?"

"Well, I know now why they raided my lab. The test results show that they have used my life-extension serum on Clovis. I am 100 percent sure of it. This is amazing," he said, still not quite able to believe it. "I mean, this will sound selfish and self-serving, but Brevicepts using it on Clovis in the doses her doctor is administering is five years ahead of schedule for me, maybe even ten. That is what kept me up all night."

"Does it work the way you thought it would?"

"I think so, but it's too soon to tell for sure. That's the good news. As a researcher, I was hoping for positive results but would have been happy not to introduce negative results or side effects with my first trials, but his samples show some positive results even after only a few days in his system. His samples already show some mitochondrial lengthening for a man of his age."

Evan leveled his bloodshot eyes at the physician and stared, hoping for a layman's explanation.

"He's getting younger, at a cellular level. It is working, Evan. I can't believe it's working already!" he shouted and took another sip of wine from the beaker. "I can't be exact in my analysis of his single sample, but I believe they are giving him a full dose. I wasn't going to get to that for nearly a decade. Evan, if they continue administering the same dosages, his cellular structures should improve even further. Within a month, I would say that his cellular age should regress by ten years—in another six months, twenty years."

"And then?"

"Well, the effects will plateau. Continuing the treatment will not make him a teenager again. But for a man of his age, we should expect him to live another twenty to thirty years."

"So what's the bad news?"

"Aah yes, the bad news. I think I have found out what the chemist in Zagreb cooked up."

"What is it?"

"It's a poison basically, but the compound is unlike anything I have ever seen before. It's a cocktail, really. One part is a venom that paralyzes all voluntary muscle activity—cone snail or krait snake is my guess until I can get a full sample to test. I am running a second analysis now on the trace amount. The second part is a stimulant that, as far as I can tell, is meant to shorten the sleep cycle and keep all vital signs just slightly above normal."

"What would that combination do to Clovis?" Auda asked, walking in from the weathered dock.

Galen thought for a few seconds and swallowed hard. "It would be like a waking coma. I think their intent with this combination would be something neurologists call Locked-In Syndrome."[49]

"What is that?" Evan asked.

"Well, it is about as bad as we imagined it could be. You are completely paralyzed, but also completely aware of everything around you. You can hear people speaking, but you can't respond. You feel heat, cold, pain, but you can't react. If you add to that a stimulant that deprives you of sleep over time, that could lead to incremental brain damage, psychosis, schizophrenia, total mental breakdown, and eventually, incurable insanity."

"That *is* bad," said Evan as he felt the guilt and anxiety rise in him again.

"It gets worse," the physician continued. "First, imagine you are trapped in this hell in your own body, and then imagine, thanks to my serum, that you are in that condition for a very, very long time."

Evan closed his eyes and saw himself back on the yacht with her, replaying her poisonous words in his head, *Clovis owes me a lot of time, and I am about to get it back.*

Galen continued, "Moreover, I believe there is a good chance, as some of the others feared, that such a condition might very well transcend our incarnations. Think of Samas and his sleep disorder, or your affinity toward the flame, or mine with the grape." He held up a beaker as if to toast. "These things stay with us, Evan."

"Do you think that's what she meant when she said she had figured out a way to end us?"

"I do," Galen said with a nod. "I think her end for us, for Clovis and now Samas, is locking us into dormant bodies until our minds crack."

"And stay cracked in all future incarnations," Auda added.

"Can you imagine anything worse? That's dark," Evan said, lighting his first cigarette of the day.

"Dark indeed," the physician conceded.

---

49. Locked-In Syndrome is a rare but real medical condition in which the afflicted is paralyzed except for eye movements and the ability to blink. (See "The locked-in syndrome: a syndrome looking for a therapy" by José León-Carrión et al.)

"One way to mitigate the danger could be to end the threat," Auda said matter-of-factly. "Sure, it would be best to save Clovis and Samas. But if we cannot save them, then it would be better to kill them and ease their suffering in the knowledge that they would return to us again."

"That's a play I know all too well," Evan sighed behind a cloud of cigarette smoke.

Galen took a drink and gave a long look at his troubled young companion before he changed the subject. "How are you holding up, Evan?"

Evan turned his eyes toward the glow of the sunrise. "I keep replaying my time with her over and over in my head. I try to imagine making a different decision about her, and things happening differently."

Galen put a hand on his shoulder. "I think her actions are more about me and my research than they are about you."

"What do you mean?" Evan countered. "You weren't there on the yacht with me."

"Wasn't I?" Galen challenged. "Think about it, Evan. She was on a yacht in the middle of the Red Sea and she had my press announcement on a direct feed? That announcement wasn't even supposed to be televised. How could she have known about that announcement unless she was tracking me and my research the whole time? Given what she told you, I think she would have some objection to my helping humanity live to one hundred and forty. I've been thinking about this too, Evan. For all I know, La Mutuelle might be funding part of my research through some front corporation or foundation just to keep eyes on me until my research got to this point."

"When she could steal it?" Auda interrupted.

Galen nodded solemnly. "There had to be an insider besides Pianosa—someone from La Mutuelle on my research team. Did you know that my lab wasn't broken into? Someone had a key for that raid when they took my research and my serum."

"But she started this war against us only after I was with her," Evan replied.

"We don't know that," the doctor challenged, shaking his head.

"We don't know when Pianosa turned. She plays a long game, Evan. Ask Clovis about that once we get him back. We have to assume that this was in the works for years, and that my life-extension break-through was the key she needed to break us permanently and get us out of her way for good. You were just a convenient messenger who dropped into her lap when she grabbed Clovis." Galen paused until Evan looked up at him. "You're not the only one who is look-ing back for clues as to how this could have played out differently. I likely caused this, not you."

Evan looked at the physician and felt some relief as he absorbed the truth in his words.

"But I want you to know that I would do it again, in the exact same way," Galen stated.

"Really?"

"Of course I would. I want to help humanity. That's why I do this," Galen said, motioning dramatically to the ridiculous scene of his state-of-the-art medical equipment filling derelict buildings on an abandoned island. "I have seen Rome at its glorious height, and I saw her fall. I carried the light of medicine for man through a dark age and into a sparking renaissance that has carried us to the medical miracles of today. Evan, there was a time when a toothache was a death sentence and an infection in a fingertip could cause the amputation of an arm. Those days are behind us—in part, I like to think, due to my tireless efforts." Galen refilled his beaker and extended the bottle toward Evan, who winced and shook his head gingerly.

"And I'm not the only one. Evan, you are still new to us and know us primarily by our excesses and parties we have lavished on you, but the others in the Cognomina have their passions as well. Jens's innovative finance work sparked the commerce that gave rise to the Medici and the Sforzas, and their patronage rekindled the rise of our civilization. The same for Etyma and her music, Dilmun and archi-tecture, and who knows how many human conflicts were resolved by Ramsay or Clovis in their day? Our collective efforts have enriched humanity as we have lived with those innovators among them who bring new ideas into the world. Enabling them to live longer will help them even further."

"But what about the consequences?" Evan countered.

"There are always consequences to advancements, and people who are fearful always focus on those first." Galen looked away for a moment, and his eye caught the white silhouette of a passing plane. "Some people hate flying because they fear dying in a plane crash. That's a potential consequence of that wonderful advancement that has brought such benefit. Living longer will be the same. There will be some disruptions, but the benefits will outweigh them—they always do."

"How can you be so sure?" Auda asked, pouring a small splash of wine into his beaker from the night before.

Galen looked at his old friend and then back at Evan. "I helped you recall your memories. You have been a young man whose young blood burned with the fever of war, and you have been an old man who stood on the cool firmaments that only the wisdom of age can bring. The difference there is age—only age." He stopped to take a sip of wine. "Brevicepts believes that a longer age would allow humans a longer course of destruction. I believe that a longer lifespan would give humans what they most desperately need: wisdom—or more specifically it would give them the gift of additional time to become better people, better leaders, better residents here. This is the new Promethean gift."

"Do you think they deserve such a gift?" Evan asked and immediately imagined that the question could have easily come from Brevicepts herself.

Galen ran a long finger over the tattoo on the back of his right hand. "Did we deserve it?"

Evan reflected on the experiences of the three lives he'd lived before as the physician's question rang in his ears.

"I am wiser now than I was just ten lives ago, wiser than even two lives ago, and I am certainly wiser than I was when I would injure a pet just to prove a point." Galen swung the beaker in a tight circle to spin the red wine into motion. "They'll be better with more time, just like we are. I'm just trying to get them a little closer to us. That's why I help them. And that is why I wouldn't change a thing. I'm on their side."

"All of us might be now," Auda said gravely. "Should we wake our friend and get started?"

THE FOUR MEN PLACED THE CHROME CELL PHONE in the center of the small table and looked at one another as Rafic configured it to call from central Paris.

"It's ready," Rafic said finally.

"Well, it will work or it will not," Auda declared as he reached out to hit dial.

"Wait!" Rafic interjected as he grabbed Auda's hand. "Who's doing the talking?"

"You are," Galen said. "Just say that you are Dr. Ling's assistant and that you are reordering for him."

"Okay," Rafic sighed. "But why me?"

Galen smiled at him and poured an ample portion of wine into his beaker. "Who could do this better than you?"

Rafic opened his mouth to protest but paused. "Okay. Here goes." He touched the smooth glass, and the phone's screen jumped to life.

"Iva Labs, good morning, guten tag, bonjour."

"English, please. May I speak to Marko Tajani about my order?"

"Hold the line."

Rafic muted the phone and took two deep breaths.

"Hello, this is Tajani."

"Good morning, Marko," Rafic began with cool confidence. "I am calling from our friends in Paris, for Dr. Ling."

"Yes, yes," answered the voice. "How is it working? I hope everything is to the doctor's satisfaction." The voice sounded young and eager to please. "And I hope everyone in the organization is pleased with my small contribution."

Galen raised his dark eyebrows and looked at a surprised Rafic. "Yes, your contribution has been well noted. I am calling you for more of the compound," Rafic stated and looked over at Auda, who raised a long finger in the air twice as though encouraging him to press harder. "I trust we can count on you again, Marko."

"Yes, of course, I can make more. When do you need it?"

"We need it today, Marko. We need it by the end of the day," Rafic said as he stared hard into the phone screen. The phone was silent for two seconds, then four, then six. "I am sure you would not want to disappoint Dr. Ling," Rafic said, pausing for effect, ". . . or *her*."

"All right," the voice answered with a tone of compliance. "Does he want additional doses of metocin and phenamine too?"

Galen nodded his head vigorously.

Rafic smiled. "Yes, please. Your extra efforts here will not go unnoticed."

"I'll have it ready for Bruno to pick up after lunch."

Rafic's eyes widened for a moment as Evan pointed at himself. "Ling is sending a new man to pick it up. His name is Yousef."

The line was silent again. "How will I know him?"

Rafic looked across the table at Evan and smiled. "He's easy to spot. He'll be using a cane."

"A cane, got it," Marko said quickly but lingered on the line. "Please put in a good word for me with Dr. Ling—and with her, if you can."

"I will, Marko," Rafic said, hovering his finger over the End Call icon as he smiled at the others in celebration.

"I am my own servant . . ." Marko said, startling a stunned and unprepared Rafic, who muted the line.

"What do I say?" Rafic pleaded.

"I am my own servant . . ." Marko repeated with a greater sense of expectation.

Panic washed over the faces of Galen and Rafic as Evan leaned forward. "I remember it from her story on the yacht. It's their code," Evan hissed at Rafic. "Answer him with: 'and I serve a just master.'"

Rafic unmuted the line. "And I serve a just master."

All four men moved to the edge of their seats as the line was silent for a few seconds and then went dead.

"What the fuck?" Rafic shouted as he ran his hands over his mop of black hair. "What the fuck was that?"

"I heard Brevicepts mention that phrase when she told me about delivering the plague to Venice," Evan said defensively. "It was how they said goodbye to one another."

"Yes, in 1630," Galen countered doubtfully.

"Do you think they are using the same code four hundred years later?" Auda asked.

"It's all I could think of," Evan answered. "I'm pretty sure we said it right."

"Do you think he hung up because we countersigned correctly or because we just got made?" Rafic asked between deep breaths.

"I guess we'll soon know," Auda offered as he clapped a reassuring hand on Rafic's heaving back. "Do you want to drive?" he asked Evan.

"It will be faster than walking," Evan said with a wry smile.

GALEN LOOKED UP FROM HIS MONITOR and rubbed at his tired eyes as the low sun marked a full day of work intermingled with worry about how the other three had done in Zagreb. *They should have been back an hour ago*, he thought as he glanced down at his watch. His heart jumped when he heard the low putter of Gonzalo's outboard engine idle to a stop alongside the battered wooden dock. He stepped away from his equipment and walked through the open double entrance doors that hung half off their rusted hinges. He squinted against the orange glare of the sunset and was relieved to see all three of them in the boat with Gonzalo. He studied the expression on their faces for any clue that they had been successful.

Auda stepped out first, followed by Rafic, and finally Evan. They walked up the dock together toward the doctor.

"We got it," Rafic said with pride as Auda held up two full vials of silver fluid that glinted in the remaining sunlight.

Galen smiled in relief as he held his arms open to hug Rafic. "Well done," he said, pulling him close. "Well done, all of you. This will accelerate us by days or even weeks."

"It was easy," Evan said, tapping his cane against the wooden boards of the old dock. "Marko was positively effusive to Ling's new man."

"It did feel good to do something—to strike at her, even if in a small way like this," Auda said, throwing his arm around Galen as they walked back toward his makeshift lab.

"What are these other two drugs for?" Evan asked, handing two larger vials to Galen.

"I heard Tajani mention them on the call this morning, and I did some research," the doctor said, reading the labels. "Phenamine sulfate is a generic term for a mild stimulant to treat narcolepsy—it keeps people awake. Psilocin is the interesting one," Galen said, gauging the weight of the liquid in the vial as he held it. "It is a hallucinogenic alkaloid that is very difficult to synthesize."

"Why do you think they would be pairing this with the original solution?" asked Auda.

"I imagine that they are using them after the original shot puts the subject into the Locked-In state. The stimulant would disrupt the natural sleep cycle, and the psychedelic would ostensibly allow easier access to darker parts of the mind. I imagine that prolonged exposure to these in a paralyzed state would be quite terrifying. But we will eventually get to that part after I do the first experiments on some animal subjects. Can I have the vials?" Galen asked, holding out his hand to Auda.

"How long are you talking about?" Auda countered, keeping the serum in his hand.

"Testing on rats would be first, and I can do that here for the rest of the week. After that would be monkeys and I would need a proper lab infrastructure for that."

"Would a live human trial accelerate the process?" Auda asked.

"It would accelerate things," Galen conceded as he led them back into the lab. "And if we could get Clovis or Samas back, I would experiment directly on them, of course."

"Who are you thinking about?" Rafic asked with a laugh. "Pianosa?"

"No," Auda answered calmly. "I was thinking about me."

"No. No," the doctor repeated. "Absolutely not."

"We don't have time," Auda said, keeping his grip on the vials. "You don't even know enough about this thing to know how quickly it is attacking and permanently breaking down our brothers. If you inject me now, I could give you immediate feedback on antidotes via eye signals."

"That is not the way medical research works. It's unethical and dangerous."

"We don't have time for ethics. We need results," Auda said, straightening his back, trying to match Galen's height. "And to get them, you need a test subject."

"I won't do it, Auda. I won't willingly subject you to whatever terror this is."

"Then I will inject myself," Auda said, walking over to pick up a syringe from one of his makeshift lab tables. "And you will be forced to do it."

"No," Galen shouted and reached for the syringe as Auda pulled it away.

Auda took two steps back and faced Galen again. "This is happening, tonight," he said, setting his lean jaw in firm resolution. "I understand your conflict, and I respect it. I do. But I also know that if they had injected me in Zagreb today, you would work directly on me for an antidote. I know it, and so do you, Galen."

Galen gritted his teeth at the truth of the statement.

"All I am asking you to do is what you have done from the beginning—heal your patient," Auda pleaded. "I will inject myself if I have to, but this is happening now."

"How would you even communicate with us?" Galen asked, trying to find another way out of his ultimatum.

"I've got it," Rafic interjected as he turned to Auda. "Do you remember Francis Bacon's cipher that we used in our work against the Habsburgs?"

"The two-letter code.[50] Yes, I remember it."

---

50. Sir Francis Bacon developed an early cryptographic code in 1605 using only the letters *A* and *B* in unique combinations of five in what today would be called a five-bit binary cypher.

"We can use that. Left for *A* and Right for *B*. This would allow for communication with complete words, even short sentences," Rafic said.

The doctor looked down at the cracked tiles that had witnessed his previous work here.

"This sacrifice is what our situation requires," Auda said in a softening voice. "All I am asking from you is to bring me back."

Galen shut his eyes tight and sighed through clenched teeth. "Come this way," he said with a tone of defeat. "Let's get you comfortable."

Auda nodded as Galen grabbed a cot and dragged it in front of the row of medical equipment. "Let's get this over with," he said as though fearing that he or Galen would lose his resolve.

Rafic took a knee next to him and kept his attention as the doctor readied a syringe. "Look up for yes, down for no, and use left or right to build the code that spells the words."

Auda grabbed his hand and forced a tense smile. "I remember."

Galen turned and looked toward Evan, who watched from a distance. "Do you remember how much of this compound Ling used on Clovis?" he asked as he started filling the needle with liquid silver.

"That looks about right," Evan said, keeping his eyes on the syringe and knowing what was coming.

Auda touched Galen's trembling arm as he readied the shot. "If you feel like you are losing me or if I am not able to communicate or help you, you can always euthanize me. I promise I won't hold a grudge."

The doctor looked down at his patient as tears welled in his eyes. "*Calamitas virtutis occasio est,*"[51] Galen said as he quickly inserted the needle into Auda's leather-brown skin and depressed the plunger.

Auda took one normal breath and kept his eyes locked with Rafic's until the first shudder hit him. His lean body bucked against the frame of the cot as violent convulsions crashed over him. Rafic released his twitching hand in horror and fell to the floor at the shock of the unnatural movements. Galen grabbed his stethoscope and clapped a small blood pressure cuff around Auda's thrashing arm.

---

51. Latin—Disaster is the opportunity for bravery, Seneca

Evan kept his eyes on Auda's face. He knew what to expect, and he saw the same look of shock and terror on Auda's face that had been on Clovis's. The tremors faded, and an eerie calm fell over him as he slowly stiffened and became rigid on the cot.

Galen listened to his heart and monitored his vitals for nearly a minute before turning to Evan. "Is that what happened to Clovis?"

"Yes," Evan said gravely. "It was the exact same reaction. Dr. Ling monitored him for a bit to ensure he had survived it."

Galen double-checked Auda's vital signs. "He is stable now," he said to Rafic and Evan before turning back to Auda. "You made it. You're alive," the doctor said with a tense smile. "Can you hear me?"

Rafic scrambled back to his feet and looked down into Auda's wide-open eyes and saw him look in an upward direction. "That's a yes," Rafic said, placing a reassuring hand on Auda's chest as it rose and fell in long, slow motions. "What else should we ask him?" Rafic asked Galen.

Galen took a step back and blinked as a lone tear fell to his tanned cheek. "Ask him if he is in any pain," he whispered in a cracking voice as he held his trembling hand over his mouth before turning and walking quickly through the open doors to the dock where Evan heard him being sick.

Evan's cane tapped on the wooden boards of the dock behind Galen as he pulled himself together. "I can't believe I just did that," he said, wiping at his brown eyes.

"You did what was needed," Evan said, reassuring him.

"I hope you're right, my friend," Galen said, still not able to look back into the building. He paced on the dock as he collected his thoughts. "All right, I have induced him successfully. He can communicate. I have a plan for my first antidote," he said to himself as he counted the steps to his plan on his fingers. "What I don't have is data or samples on what Ling is doing to them with the other two drugs after the first shot."

"Rome," Evan stated.

"Yes, I think so. Ramsay is still gathering information and evidence inside the Vatican. I need you to return to Rome and then bring her new samples back to me."

Evan thought about the mundane task of courier as he looked inside the building at the catatonic Auda on his cot. "That's it? I just drive the car?"

"The first samples you brought me were enough to get me started on my hypotheses for how to counteract the shot, but I suspect that Ling is still injecting them with boosters of those other two drugs. That presents an unknown, a moving target for me," Galen said as the plans solidified in his head. "I have to get new samples, or I am flying blind here."

Evan dipped his head twice in acknowledgment as he lit a cigarette. "What is our plan after that?"

Galen looked around as if the surrounding ruins were all they had. "With the attack on Samas—and now Etyma is missing as well—there is too much risk for us out there in the world. I think after you return to Rome to check on Ramsay and get my samples, both of you should bring the remainder of the Cognomina back here to Lazzaretto. We can't afford to lose any more of us. This place is secure," the physician said, looking at the distant lights of Venice beyond the neglected buildings. "After all, the best place to hide is not a secret place, but a place that has been forgotten."

25

Evan's thoughts kept flashing back to Auda convulsing on the cot as he drove south toward Rome. He replayed the courage Auda showed to sacrifice himself so that Galen's work could accelerate. He replayed the doctor's words in his mind about how his life-extension research *was* more to blame for triggering Brevicepts than his chance visit to Clovis. He could see it, but he could not stop replaying his time with her and thinking about how she had played him to create and foment this chaos in the Cognomina.

He didn't listen to the news or music to pass the kilometers but kept company only with the drone of the economy car's laboring engine as he thought about ways to undo this. *Perhaps there was a way he could bring back those who had gone to her. Perhaps he could win over some on her side like Elsa into the Cognomina.* He replayed his new memories of Elsa—there was goodness in her that overshadowed whatever her duties might be in La Mutuelle. He also found himself still feeling that spark between them he had felt in the SUV in Somalia.

Evan turned the car down the last dark alley after the abandoned pens of the old slaughterhouse next to the river and could hear the boisterous music coming from the Roma camp as he turned off the ignition.

Fires burned in open metal barrels around the edge of the center camp and provided some heat against the February night.

He could see people dancing in the firelight in couples and groups of men with their arms locked together. They swayed and kicked in a centuries-old choreography that every Roma knew since they could walk. Their dance steps followed the wailing clarinet and frenetic violin that drove songs of slavery, of wandering, of escape, of living outside the world.

Ramsay sat with Lucca as Perez danced with half a dozen men crouched below him, snapping their fingers in time with accelerating music and their gray-haired Re Zingaro's quickening steps. Evan put a hand on her shoulder to get her attention.

She turned her head to see him, and Lucca stood and opened his arms to embrace Evan. "Hello, my friend," the man shouted as he took him into his arms. Lucca was drunk; they all were.

Ramsay held out a bottle to Evan, who shook his head and said, "I don't really feel like celebrating."

"Me neither," she said before taking a drink from their bottle. "But they had a wedding today, and this is the reception."

"I have a message from Galen," Evan said. "He asks if you have more samples."

"I have several more samples from Clovis and a few from Samas. I'll get them in a bit, okay?" Ramsay kept her eyes on the smiling dancers and their colorful undulations of skirt and scarf as they stepped and stomped the ground together. "I want to enjoy this a while longer."

"Sure," Evan said as he sat beside her and watched the master musicians working feverishly at their burnished and well-worn instruments. "We were able to get more of the serum they used on Clovis and Samas."

Ramsay looked at him out of the side of her eye. "That might come in handy for us. I haven't heard from Dilmun in over a day, and I suspect they have him."

"Contact with Etyma went silent too," Evan added as he rested his cane across his lap.

Ramsay rubbed her forehead with the back of her hand and then took another drink from the bottle. "That explains why two more hospital beds arrived at their building in the Vatican. We need to find out what those injections do to them."

"Galen injected Auda with it."

"Galen did what?" Ramsay asked in surprise.

Evan nodded and turned back to watch the dancers. "Auda forced him to do it in order to accelerate Galen's efforts toward an antidote."

"I told you Auda would do anything to defeat her. Is he able to communicate?"

"He and Rafic have a code that uses eye movements," Evan said. "He was able to say that the shot was very painful at first. He communicated that he could hear everything and see things in his field of vision, but that the feeling of being trapped in his body was"—Evan paused as he recalled Rafic's translated words—"'a waking nightmare.'"

"So it's as bad as we thought for them."

"Perhaps worse," Evan countered. "We have the two other drugs they are using on them, and when Galen injected him with those, Auda's messages became odd and incoherent as if he was struggling to stay with us or even to stay together. I had to leave right after that, so I don't know how bad it has gotten for him."

"Auda is the strongest person I have ever known. It was brave of him to force Galen to treat him. We will all need to find bravery like that if we are to come back from this," Ramsay said as the song continued to build momentum. Perez stepped out of the circle of men to sit down, and Lucca hopped up to take his place as the song sped to a climax and then stopped.

Ramsay took another drink as the next song started. "Just look at them, Evan. They are oppressed and hated today, just as they were imprisoned and executed in the thousands when I fought for them a lifetime ago. Look at how beautiful they are. They don't have a care in the world and have no more concern for the provisions of tomorrow than the sparrows they follow in their wanderings. They have no land save that beneath their feet, no flag save the clothes on their backs, no anthem except this song," Ramsay said, taking another drink from the bottle. "They shun worry as they shun our labors and our expectations of them. I believe they are the freest people in the world, and that is why the world hates them. Their freedom from our expectations reflects how ridiculous most of the world is.

"If Brevicepts is collecting a powerful elite for some new utopian plan, these souls will likely be persecuted again," Ramsay continued, motioning to them with the neck of the bottle before a laughing dancer swung around and snatched it out of her hand.

"And us with them," Evan said as he watched them in their revels.

"I fought on their side once and freed the ones who had these children that laugh and dance before us. This is what I fight for, Evan," she said, looking at him out of the corner of her bloodshot eyes. "It is people like this that make this place worth living in—and worth fighting for."

"What can we do to fight now?"

Ramsay kept her gray eyes focused on the figures in front of her. "I haven't figured it out yet," she slurred, "but I have a feeling these rogues will have a part to play."

"Galen thinks we should gather everyone and regroup on his island."

"With Poppy on the run and Dilmun and Etyma likely gone, he might be right," Ramsay said, casting an eye over at Perez, who was still catching his breath. "On your drive back, you should make some stops to put in your phone battery and text message the others to go to Venice and meet at the contact point." She slowly stood up on unsteady feet as Evan rose beside her. "They have given me a car, so I can join you in a day or two after I finish some more preparation here. I'll get you those samples for Galen now so that you can get on the road."

EVAN MADE THE TRIP WITH GONZALO to Lazzaretto Island to drop off the samples, and then Galen turned both of them around to wait for the returning members of the Cognomina. Gonzalo sat at the end of the Il Santo bar and only contacted Evan at the other end when he stepped up and greeted his arriving tattooed companions. They arrived in pairs and by themselves, staggering in like refugees from a world they once owned.

Evan knew the transport routine without the boatman having to explain. Gonzalo would exit the bar first and walk to his small boat. Evan would continue the conversations but discreetly ask each returning member to present their phones and show the emptied battery before inviting them outside for a shared cigarette on their way to the boat. They would get in without a question or a fare for their ferryman as Evan watched them load and depart before returning to the bar to repeat the cycle.

They sat at opposite ends of the bar and looked up at the clock that ticked toward closing time. Jens, Chance, Dilmun, Etyma, and Poppy were still missing. Evan nursed his beer as the bartender started wiping down the tables. He stood to stretch his legs and saw that Gonzalo had switched to coffee. Evan stepped outside for a cigarette when he heard the booming bass voice of Chance echoing down the canal. He could tell that the giant was talking with someone else, and his heart jumped with the anticipation that it was Poppy. He stepped to the edge of the walkway next to the canal, leaned out to get a glimpse of them, and saw Jens's blond hair as they walked under a light. Evan walked toward them and lit a cigarette to calm the rising anxiety he felt about Poppy.

"Hello, little brother," Chance bellowed for every sleeper in the neighborhood to hear.

The sound of his warm voice comforted like an embrace. "This way," Evan responded in a voice just loud enough to carry down to them. "How did you finish at the tables?"

"You mean, do we come bearing gifts?" Jens joked.

"I only finished this afternoon when you called us back here," Chance answered with a chuckle. "I gave back a little near the end, but it was a good run. Our financier here knows the total take and how much each of us gets as a split. This is your share," he concluded, offering a black USB drive with a gold letter *Z* from his open hand.

"It's in crypto," Jens explained. "There are instructions on the drive along with the coins. Each person's share, for the ones who are still with us, is 281,365 euros—and the key phrase is *bonus content*. We're not going island shopping," the blond man mused with a shrug, "but we're not on the streets either."

"If I can get to Macau, I can get us twice this," Chance boasted.

"I haven't heard from Poppy, Dilmun, or Etyma," Evan confessed. "Ramsay thinks some of them might have been captured like Samas."

"We saw that," they said in grim unison.

"Auda is at our meeting point," Evan said. "You will see him shortly."

"Capital idea meeting at a bar, Evan," Jens said with a grin. "Do they make a decent spritz?"

"Let me see your phones," Evan interjected as he stood in the middle of the walkway. "Show me the batteries."

Chance looked down at him with a smirk.

"I'm not kidding," Evan demanded. "Did either of you hear anything from Poppy?"

Both men shook their heads as they pulled out their flip phones and showed the removed batteries. "I suppose that level of security is sound if we are all to be in the same palazzo," Jens said.

They looked ahead to see the bartender locking the door closed behind him before walking away. "Nothing so luxurious as a palazzo this time," Evan said, motioning to stoic Gonzalo at the helm of his open boat.

"Oh, charming," Jens rasped as he eyed the humble craft. "And no drink either."

Chance motioned for the smaller man to step on first before leaning down to Evan's level. "Is it Lazzaretto?" he whispered with a smile.

Evan nodded, which sent the giant into loud laughter. "Ha! It's perfect," he bellowed. "I love that doctor." The large man stepped onto the boat carefully and extended a black casino chip to Gonzalo. "An obol[52] for your trouble, sir. I am ready for my passage to the other side."

Gonzalo waited for the boat to stop rocking and then motioned for Evan to get in.

Evan stood on the walkway and shook his head. "We're missing one. I want to stay and wait for her."

---

52. An obol was the name of any number of ancient Greek coins. Chance likely alludes to the coin that dead souls would give to Charon the ferryman for passage across the river Styx.

The boatman nodded. "I will be back before dawn," Gonzalo said without emotion before starting his motor and easing down the canal.

Evan paced the length of the narrow quay that ran in front of the bar. A freshly stomped-out cigarette butt punctuated every second circuit. He stopped and listened as he lit up again, waiting for the click of her shoes against the worn stones of the causeway.

Evan started thinking about her when the nervous energy of worry was no longer enough to keep him awake. He recalled their brief time together at his Ascension and the troubling time with her during his last life. Her beauty and mystery still attracted him, but there was something else about her that held him captive. She had been the first to see him, the first to recognize him for what he was. She had been the one to call him out of his wilderness of solitude and into a family of others like him.

He sat in one of the two chairs that confined the lone patio table next to the shuttered front door of the bar. *Will she always hold this power over me?* he wondered as he blew into his cold hands and let his head rest against the stone wall behind him. *Will I ever have a choice when she calls to me?* Evan knew he couldn't trust her with his feelings, but he still wanted her now, even if it was only to know she was safe. He had received a reply from her yesterday when he first sent the text to gather, but nothing since then.

His mind drifted to the memory of their embraces and the focused look of passion in her dark eyes. *Was that passion for him, or was that fire fueled by her own appetites?* Her familiar hands had touched him in a way that had validated his clearing memory of her. He recalled the feeling of her nails drawing down the front of his thighs as she whispered to him.

"Hello, lover," she whispered, tapping him lightly on the leg with his cane to wake him. "I see you've kept my old dragon as a companion."

Evan snapped awake to see Poppy shivering visibly. He sprang to his feet and embraced her slight frame into his. "I was dreaming of you."

"Well, I was dreaming about something else," she said through chattering teeth. "I was dreaming of getting warm and getting a fix."

"How are you?" he asked, trying to warm her against him. "I was worried about you."

She stiffened at first but relaxed into the warmth of his embrace. "I don't feel well, Evan," she said in a thin voice. "I lost my kit in London after the attack. I need to score or I'll crash. Give me a cigarette. I haven't had a smoke in half a day either."

Evan gave her a cigarette and lit it. "Galen has what you need. Just stay with me, Poppy. We will be there soon."

"Do we have to walk?" Poppy asked, hoping for a rest.

"No. There is a boat. It will be back shortly. When you were late, I was worried that they had captured you," Evan said, rubbing her bare arms. "How was it? Being with Samas again and seeing him attacked? I know the history you two share. He told me—last time."

"This whole thing has been a nightmare, even before the attack," Poppy said in a low voice as she drew hard on the cigarette. "I didn't speak to him at all on that first day. But I watched him swallow his emotions as he dismantled his precious art collection, including *The Rendezvous*, and I started to feel a bit sorry for him. It felt like I was watching a sacrifice," she said with a yawn. "All of his lives were wrapped up in those paintings. It felt like a step toward redemption, at least to me."

"He was doing it for us, for all of us," Evan said.

"Yes, I saw it," she conceded as she blew a lungful of smoke into the silent night. "When the first pieces went on the block in London, he joked to me that he looked forward to buying them all back over the next few centuries. Five minutes later, he was lying on the floor amid the chaos of their attack. The way he fell and started shaking was horrible, just horrible," she said, barely holding it together through the waves of exhaustion, emotion, and withdrawal. "His eyes, Evan—the way he looked at me with those eyes. They reached out to me from some dark place that terrified him. They reached out to me for help, but I could do nothing. I saw the attackers looking at my tattoo, and I bolted. I just ran."

"I'm glad you did. You did the right thing by getting away and then following them," Evan said, turning his ear toward the low drone of Gonzalo's boat.

"Evan, I hated that man for over four hundred years. And now I just want him back. I want to get him back."

"Samas is not the only one to make a sacrifice for us," Evan said, walking her to the edge of the water where a smiling Gonzalo pulled to a stop. "We will get him back, Poppy. You did the right thing by saving yourself. We will need everyone we can get for what is to come."

"Being broke sucks," she snapped, visibly shaking. "I haven't been poor in over three hundred years. There has to be a way to get that bitch."

"Yes. I have an idea of what to do next," Evan confided as he stepped into the boat after her.

RAMSAY AND THE REMAINING MEMBERS of the Cognomina gathered around Galen's makeshift dining table and waited for the physician to emerge from his lab. Chance, Castor, Rafic, Poppy, Jens, and Mr. Diltz were in the crowd, but Ramsay noticed that some faces were missing. Galen emerged from his lab, looking like a wreck of a man. "When is the last time you slept?" Ramsay asked Galen.

"I nap between experiments while the analyses run. I get enough to keep up," the physician said, walking out to embrace each of them. "I am happy to see each of you. So long as you don't use your phones, you should be safe here on Lazzaretto. It hasn't seen visitors in decades, as you can see." He waved an animated arm like a realtor in a ruin.

"What is our plan?" Poppy asked.

Galen reached into his pocket and withdrew a handful of DNA swab test kits. "First thing is that I get a sample from each one of you," he said, handing out the kits. "I need to be able to identify you if any others fall into her hands. Ramsay has infiltrated the building in Vatican City where they are being held and can give us that update." Galen motioned to Ramsay, who stepped forward to speak.

"I need to leave today to get back to Rome for my Monday shift. I am pretty sure that Etyma and Dilmun have been taken and are now with Samas and Clovis in Rome. My information on Pianosa and Brevicepts has dried up, and my contacts think they have both left Rome."

"My sources are quiet as well," Rafic added.

"So what is our plan?" Poppy repeated.

"I've learned quite a bit in the past two days, but I wouldn't call it all progress," Galen said as emotion choked his words. "Auda has been able to communicate with Rafic, but he shut down last night after . . ."

Rafic stepped forward to complete the doctor's sentence. "He started to slow down after the second round of follow-up drugs we believe they are using on them. For the last six hours, Auda has been unresponsive except for the tears."

"It can work that quickly?" Chance said with concern.

Galen stepped to the side of Rafic to address them all. "I am continuing to work on an antidote for what she injected them with, but I need more time. I should tell you that I can confirm our worst fears. She is using an exotic poison to paralyze them, but it is combined with an amphetamine to keep them conscious and sleep-deprived, and they have added a psychedelic. I have seen the first evidence of this in the samples Ramsay has been able to get from where they are being held."

"What would the psychedelic do?" Jens asked.

"I wondered that at first too," Rafic said and turned toward the doctor.

"Some of you might remember my short ergot-induced trip we did during a happier time," Galen said, looking over at Evan. "Now imagine being trapped in that internal world with only your demons for company."

"With no relief or end in sight," Chance offered.

"Can she do that?" asked Rafic. "Can she keep them alive indefinitely while they are still conscious and locked in?"

"If she keeps feeding and hydrating them and caring for any signs of disease, their bodies will survive indefinitely."

"And in essence, trap them," Poppy added.

"Yes," Galen conceded. "From our first communications from Auda, it does not take much imagination to conclude what this Locked-In existence would do to their minds." The doctor paused as he measured his words. "The longer they are in that state, the worse it will be. Which brings me to the darkest point," he said, tears shining in his dark eyes. "She has corrupted my life-extension research and perverted it toward her own evil ends." His hands trembled from a combination of exhaustion and rage as he took a sip of wine from his beaker on the table. "We have to assume that she intends to keep them alive in that tortured state long enough to induce a psychotic break, which could be permanent. And now, thanks to my research, they could live for many more decades in that state, even Clovis. In a way, I have likely made our destruction possible."

"The stakes are real for us now," Poppy said, shaking her head. "The danger is that we could come back broken or that we might not be sane enough to remember ourselves or each other."

"It could be the end of us," Jens said.

"And the end of the Cognomina," Ramsay added.

"I've tried a few things so far to bring him back," Galen said, "but they haven't worked. I will try two novel approaches in the next hour to try to find an antidote so that if we can rescue them, hopefully I can free them from the effects of the drugs."

"That is not the only recourse here," Chance said gravely.

Ramsay stepped forward. "He's right. If we cannot undo it, then we should just kill them."

"We might need them back," Galen countered. "I can find a cure. I know I can. I just need more time. We will need their numbers added to the few we are now," he said, looking at the faces around him. "And we need what they know. As we know from Auda, they are aware of what is going on around them. Perhaps they have heard about Brevicepts's plans for us or what La Mutuelle plans for humanity and the world."

Evan spoke up. "Galen is right. We need to know more about her and her operation if we are to ever have a chance of leveling the playing field and rescuing our friends."

"Sure, but how?" asked Rafic. "We are flying blind with no way to know what's happening inside her group."

"That's right," Evan said, stepping forward. "I plan to defect to her side and join them so we can learn more."

Galen gathered himself and cut Evan off. "I have considered this, but it is too dangerous on numerous points. First, you have only the slightest idea of what she is capable of doing, or worse, what she is capable of making you do. Second, your age is a huge risk factor. Clovis might live another thirty to forty years in this condition if my calculations are correct. But you could be facing well more than a century of that torture. No, it's way too dangerous."

"There's a risk that Brevicepts could coerce you into giving information about us and our plans," Ramsay said.

"That's not going to happen," Evan replied, shaking his head. "It has to be me. Pianosa was her source of information about which of us voted back in the grotto to shun her again. That is the only way she would know who to welcome and who to hunt down." Evan turned to face the remaining faces of the Cognomina. I didn't vote, I only relayed her message to you. I expressed no opinion. It was all of you who decided in front of Pianosa. I did not. It can only be me, and *should* only be me. I was the one who underestimated her and brought this ruin on our house when I agreed to carry her poisoned offer." Evan looked into each face around him. "I do not want a vote on this. I do not want a discussion on this. I only want your support in trying to make this right for us."

They all looked at Evan and then at each other in a building acknowledgment that his plan was their only option.

Poppy stepped forward and scanned him from head to toe. "If you don't come back, I'll kill you."

Evan chuckled. "I hope that is a promise because that is our fallback plan, remember?"

All other members remained silent as Evan scanned their faces for approval.

Galen approached him. "Evan, she enjoys toying with people and finding their limits. You may have to do things to win her trust—terrible things that you will not want to remember and bring into a new room in your house of memories. Regret is one thing—memory is quite another for us. Beware of things you don't want to remember."

26

Evan exited the Parisian tailor's boutique and stopped to admire his new suit in the faint reflection of a freshly washed window. The fine blue fabric hugged his shoulders and highlighted the hard-earned tan on his face. In distant Syria, only important men wore suits, and seeing himself in this one somehow felt right.

He walked south with his tapping cane through the streets of central Paris, always aware of the menacing black glass obelisk of Brevicepts's Montparnasse Tower that grew closer with each corner he rounded. Evan felt his stomach turn every time her tower came back into view—each time taller and more imposing than the last. He focused on his feelings as the full height of the skyscraper came into view. At least he felt *something* now in place of the emptiness where his hope of bringing the two groups together had once been. This tower would be a way through or a way out.

The wide concrete plaza surrounding the foot of the building stood eerily empty, save a ring of blue construction barricades. Evan stepped through a service opening in the fence and walked toward the lobby doors that opened to a once-elegant foyer that was now a construction zone filled with empty scaffolding and dust-covered plastic wrap on the walls.

Evan jumped at the shouted question in French from the guard at his desk at the far end of the lobby.

"La Mutuelle," Evan replied.

The guard's face softened, and he motioned Evan over to a service elevator. The guard spoke too fast for Evan to follow as he guided him inside and inserted a key while pressing the button for the fifty-fifth floor. "Adieu," the guard said as the doors closed on Evan.

Evan gripped the cane to keep his balance as the elevator raced skyward. He thought about Clovis, Samas, Etyma, and Dilmun locked still in their beds, their desperate eyes darting wildly in search of help. He thought of the others in Brevicepts's group and wondered if there were good souls among them. He thought about Elsa and hoped she would be waiting.

The construction-scarred service elevator doors parted on the fifty-fifth floor to reveal a refined open floor plan, styled with exotic marble and stainless steel. An ornate Japanese butterfly logo was inlaid into the smooth marble of the empty lobby, ringed by the letters for La Mutuelle.

"Evan!" Elsa shouted behind him. "I was hoping to see you again."

The same feelings rushed over him again at the sight of her. She wore a professional-looking tan skirt and short-sleeved blouse that showed off her toned arms. He studied her bright smile and warm eyes as she walked up to him, and he could tell she was genuinely excited to see him.

"I wasn't sure there would be anyone here," Evan said. "The building looks condemned."

"Oh, we have the entire tower now. It's nice, isn't it?" Elsa asked, turning to look over at the top of the Eiffel Tower.

Evan paused for a moment to absorb the stunning panorama of Paris below them.

"You look very nice," she said, taking in the sight of him, "and a cane—very dapper. Is it from a previous life?"

Evan held it up and extended it to her. "It is actually, but it's a long story."

"I hoped I would get to see you again. I think Lesannées will be happy to see you too. She is here." She took his hand and squeezed it as she led him around two corners and into an open corner office that overlooked all of central Paris.

"What are you reading now?" Evan asked as he fell in behind her.

"I'm on the same book," Elsa confessed as they walked toward a corner office. "But I'm almost done."

Brevicepts wore a sleek white pantsuit and stood tall at a standing desk against the window, her eyes fixed on a monitor. Her spaniel ran over to greet Evan and Elsa. Brevicepts turned to see Evan and smiled for an instant of satisfaction before walking over to a group of five chairs near the window.

"Welcome, Evan," Brevicepts said. "I am pleased you are here. Please forgive the dust, but we are reinventing this place to our liking, and things will be chaotic for a while."

Evan nodded and walked past the chairs to the floor-to-ceiling windows, unable to take his eyes off the sweeping view of Paris below. Brevicepts stood next to him and looked down on the city like an attentive archangel.

"It's quite a view," Evan said.

"Yes, I rather like it," Brevicepts agreed. "But from this height, all the buildings look so small and stark—like so many vaults filling a cemetery. Some just seem larger and more celebrated than others."

Evan turned his head to see her smiling.

"Thank you for completing your task. You showed some resourcefulness in getting out of Somalia as you did," Brevicepts said, motioning for Evan to sit. "I had hoped to have a positive response from all, but they have made their choice."

"I did what you asked me to do."

"So have you come to join us?" Brevicepts asked, taking a cup of coffee from Elsa.

Evan pushed down the hatred he felt in her presence. "I have come to learn more. I am still embracing part of my role as your emissary between the two groups. The remaining members of the Cognomina trust me, and I think I just need to give them additional information to make a decision that can unify us."

"They trust you, you say?" she asked, looking out over the city again. "Do they know you are here?"

"They do," Evan answered truthfully.

"Should *I* trust you?" she asked, putting that penetrating gaze back on him.

Evan's stomach turned again. "You should trust my intention, which is to bring both groups together. I am interested in your work, if not your methods, so far."

"Do you not approve of my methods?"

"Did you have to attack Samas and the others too?"

"I gave them a choice, and you told them that their choices would have consequences. They chose, did they not?"

Her words seemed to come from far away as they echoed in Evan's head. "Can you undo the injection to give Samas a second chance?"

Brevicepts shook her head, and her topknot of hair tossed from side to side. "I'm afraid not."

Evan mustered the strength to stare back at her, hoping for an elaborated answer that might indicate whether the effect of the shot was physically permanent or if she was just unwilling.

"That man sent you to a Tunisian prison, I'm told—a place so vile that you chose to end your life rather than endure it—and now you want to lobby for his release from me?"

"He gave me an opportunity."

"And a fortune as I understand it—a fortune I am willing to return to you, as I have done for the others of the Cognomina who have joined me. But you must prove yourself to La Mutuelle."

Galen's warning shuddered through him as he found the words he needed. "I can prove myself. I just want to save my friends and give them a second chance."

"You should be focusing on those who remain," she said, shooting him an icy stare.

"I am. That is precisely why I am here now. I am open, and I want to learn more." Evan felt his heart hammering in his chest. "I still want to meet the others," he said truthfully. "I want to bring us together."

"And this has already started, thanks to you." Brevicepts kept her paralyzing eyes on him over the rim of her coffee cup. "Your little friends have gone to hide. Are you the one who will bring them in?"

Evan froze with a rage he hoped wasn't discernible. *Stay calm*, he said to himself. *She's testing you.*

A double chime from the service elevator broke the silence that was settling between them as two men walked through the lobby toward their chairs. The first man was the menacing mystery man from Rafic's image search of Brevicepts. He wore a tailored gray suit and looked Indian or Pakistani with a mass of hair pulled back into a bun atop an angular face that sprouted a long, well-trimmed black beard. The second man had a long scar running down the left side of his face—Kerr.

The spaniel raced over to the mystery man, who knelt to greet the animal. "Hello, Vasa. Hello, boy."

"Evan, this is Zao, one of our leaders. Zao and I have been together for a long time," Brevicepts said, looking fondly at her henchman.

Kerr kept his eyes locked on Evan as he spoke to Zao. "This is the one I told you about."

Zao buttoned his burgundy suit jacket and extended a strong hand collared by stiff white cuffs and ruby links. "I've heard about you. You wrote the notebooks. Lesannées said that you have introduced La Mutuelle to your side," the elegant man said, admiring Evan's fresh suit before fixating on the cane, "but she didn't say you were cool. Nice look."

Evan lifted the cane to give him a closer look. "I like your suit color."

"Yes, hate and Armani are my favorite things to wear."

"I believe you and Mr. Kerr already know each other," Brevicepts interrupted. "Mr. Kerr is starting his work with Zao. Evan, I want you to apprentice with Elsa."

Elsa perked up in her seat and looked over at Evan, who kept his eyes locked on Brevicepts.

"Elsa, take him to Milan with you. Zao, take one of the jets and drop them off in Italy on your way to Dubai." She turned her gaze briefly to Kerr and then landed on Evan. "There will be a lot of eyes on you now.

Follow Zao and Elsa and learn from them. They will show you every-thing you need to know. I will meet you and the rest in Venice."

ZAO AND KERR EXITED THE STRETCH MERCEDES limousine first and walked right onto an elegant blue-and-white jet. Evan memorized the tail number and noted that it did not match the ones he and Poppy had seen before. Evan walked next to Elsa as they approached the stairs to the private jet. "Why do I feel like you are going to leave me on the tarmac again?" Evan quipped.

She slipped her arm around him and pulled him close. "No," she laughed. "We're not going to be separated this time."

Evan and Elsa took two plush leather seats opposite Zao and Kerr. Zao reached into a cabinet for an ornate bottle of cognac and four glasses as the flight attendant closed the door and the engines roared to life.

Kerr drained half his drink in one long motion and set the half-empty glass on the armrest. "So where do we start?"

Zao savored a sip and swirled his glass. "We start," he said formally as he straightened his sleeve, "with a bit of background. She told me about your group, the Cognomina. She told me that you"—he stopped as if to measure the words for effect before speaking them—"were a frivolous people. Her words, not mine," he added defensively. "She said you were unfocused and decadent, that you had lost your way and your purpose."

"That might be a bit harsh," Kerr countered before he took another gulp of the dark brandy.

Zao looked over at Kerr's Embe tattoo. "She said you live your lives without karmic consequence for your hedonistic behaviors. We, on the other hand, believe in a type of karma where we try to improve not only ourselves but the world we leave to our future selves."

"And to future generations," Elsa added.

"Yes, she told me all of that," Kerr responded. "But how does all of this work?"

"La Mutuelle works on a territory model, with each captain, like me or Elsa, controlling one territory. A territory can be a geographic area, like northern Italy for Elsa or the Middle East for me. But a territory can also be an industry or entertainment sector, like Dr. Ling in health-care or our colleague Mr. Pandaman in Hollywood. What we do," he said, refilling Kerr's glass with less brandy, "is identify people in power or people we can bring into positions of power, and then befriend and help those people fulfill their ambition."

"How do you find them?" Evan asked.

Zao brought his glass up to his prominent nose and drew in the intoxicating vapor. "We look for ambitious people whose goals are aligned with ours or rising stars whose goals can be realigned to ours."

"Realign?" Kerr challenged. "How does that work?"

"We educate and enlighten them about what is happening to the earth."

"And if that doesn't work?" Evan interjected, eager to hear the answer.

"Then it becomes a question of motivation," the bearded man replied coolly before raising the glass to his dark lips. "We find that person's weakness and exploit it when necessary to help keep those powerful friends focused on our long-term goals."

"So it's blackmail then?" Kerr asked with a subtle excitement in his voice.

"To put it crudely, yes," Zao said, understanding the need to clarify. "But La Mutuelle is not interested in money, we earn and distribute plenty of money as a side effect of our real goals, which are to improve our living conditions on this planet through influence and long-term policy change. As our leader often says to us, 'We're going to be here for a long time, so let's get this house in order.' I like that and I think that summarizes what we do. You asked if it is blackmail—I call it leverage over the target. Some of our account management can be, at times"—he studied his delicious amber drink as he searched for the right word—"unsavory."

"And sometimes those people will need convincing," Kerr concluded.

Zao looked out the window of the jet and watched as Paris fell into the distance. "They tend to need motivation at times. Our work is making sure they stay motivated to our cause, even when the work might be distasteful to them."

"And what about the money?" Kerr asked before slurping at the expensive cognac. "She told me we get a payout."

"Think of it as profit sharing," Elsa said, crossing her legs.

"Profit of what?" Kerr countered.

"Let me put it into context for you," Zao began. "The way I understand it, your Cognomina was run very much like a trust. You put or will your assets into it in this life, and then you reclaim those assets in each successive incarnation. For us, we do things a bit differently. We run La Mutuelle as a business—a private business that specializes in insurance. And what is at the core of any insurance business? Mitigating risk and minimizing loss, and what better way to do that than by knowing, through our network of accounts, what is going to happen?"

"Because you are telling them what to do," Evan interjected.

"Precisely," answered Zao. "And that information allows us to run one of the most profitable corporations in the world. The ambitious people that we recruit, champion, or exploit are often minor shareholders, but we captains hold the preferred shares that enjoy a higher payout of La Mutuelle profits."

"So we are shareholders in a company?" Kerr asked, not seeming clear on the concept.

"No, you both are provisional shareholders until she determines that you can adopt our goals and competently run a territory," Zao said, smiling behind his black beard.

"Does it pay well?" Kerr asked.

"Last year my preferred payout was one hundred and twenty-eight million euros, but I run a large territory."

"Wow," Kerr blurted out, nearly spilling his drink. "What do you do with all that money?"

"I purchase things like priceless liquors that once belonged to my friend Napoleon Bonaparte," Zao answered, taking a carefully measured sip, "and share them with new apprentices."

"What territories do you think we'll get?" asked Kerr.

"That depends on ability and aptitude," answered Zao with a sidelong glance at his apprentice.

Elsa reached over and put her hand on Evan's forearm. "Because you come from Bulgaria, I think she will give you the Balkans. Your territory would be next to mine," she said, letting her tanned hand linger on him.

"How unsavory does the work get?" Evan asked.

"It's a fair question," Zao replied. "Sometimes it gets downright distasteful. I once sailed with our leader from Sicily to Venice with a plague-sickened crew just so we could reduce the overpopulation of our hometowns. That was quite unsavory."

"She told me about that," Evan replied. "Don't you worry about being viewed as villains?"

"Sometimes the methods may look extreme to the uninitiated," Zao conceded. "But we're the victims in this ongoing crime, not the villains."

"We have a different perspective," Elsa chimed in, trying to soften the tone.

"You know that she always has a pet," Zao asked Elsa in a bid to change the conversation. "Did she tell you why she likes spaniels?"

"I know she always names them Vasa, but I don't know why," Elsa added.

"Vasa was the family name of a Polish king with the unfortunate name of Sigismund, who our leader loved and influenced during his long reign. Today in La Mutuelle, we would call him an *asset*, which a territory owner like me would manage. Back then, at the turn of the seventeenth century, he was just part of an up-and-coming royal family that we wanted to infiltrate and use to our ends. I remember it was one of those damned red-headed Sforza women from Milan who liked the spaniels. She saw them in the court of the Bourbons and thought they looked regal so she purchased a breeding pair and brought them back to dreary Poland. As a boy, young Sigismund fell in the love with the dogs and kept them his whole life.[53] Lesannées shared his love for the breed and keeps them to this day in his honor."

---

53. Zao seems to describe Sigismund III Vasa, King of Poland and Sweden. Zao's claim that King Sigismund III kept spaniels his whole life would seem to be corroborated by two paintings (one from his youth and another two years before his death) that portrayed him with his beloved animals. The first is in the Swedish National Museum, and the second is in the Wawel Royal Castle National Art Collection (Krakow).

"I never knew that," Elsa said.

"She keeps naming them Vasa as a reminder of the success of her time with her regal lover."

"What success was that?" Kerr asked.

"She nurtured and grew an ambition in the Sigismund that started several decades-long wars, cemented a religious schism, and reduced Poland from a dominant power in central Europe to a wreck by orchestrating military misadventures that cost the country half its population."[54] Zao sniffed the antique brandy again. "And I think she really loved the king. They were a pair to be sure, like two dark stars in a tight orbit around each other."

"Is what you do—what we do," Evan corrected, "evil?"

Zao looked up from his glass, his sharp face brightening at the question. "Is it evil?" he mused. "I think evil, as you mean it in the context of what we do, is a relative term that deserves a full hearing with a jury of all the aggrieved parties potentially affected by any act deemed evil. Wouldn't you agree?"

Evan felt the moral ground underneath him shift under the ambiguity of Zao's question, but thought there might be important information here. "Yes, I suppose so."

"Excellent," Zao said, leaning forward in his leather seat. "Australia and China are roughly the same size geographically, but Australia has just over twenty million people. There are that many people living just in Shanghai right now. Australia is an Eden, a standard for what we desire, while China is an overcrowded environmental disaster."

"So what are we to do—influence them to kill over a billion of their citizens?" Evan asked.

"You're looking at it from the wrong point of view. You are quite right that over a billion people live in China today, if you can call that living. But how many people will live there over the next thousand years? Thirty-five, forty generations would be something like forty to

54. King Sigismund III did start a series of wars with Sweden, Russia, and the Ottoman Empire that lasted for nearly seventy years and devastated the Polish Commonwealth. A statue to him stands in central Warsaw.

fifty billion new people, right? Shouldn't they get a vote on what their inherited world should be? Some might say to deny them a voice in their future is evil."

Zao leaned forward in the leather seat. "Evan, do you doubt that this future majority would desire a different future for themselves than what is being planned for them? We're the only voice they will ever have in our present day. That is the same approving voice we hear from today's Venetians and Milanese for our unsavory work nearly four centuries ago. We work on a longer timeline for a leveraged future benefit that we can enjoy alongside those anticipated approvers of our present labors. It takes a genius to work on this problem on a global scale with centuries for your timeline. And that is what we have in Lesannées," he said, raising his glass in a toast that Elsa joined, followed by Kerr and Evan.

"You ask me if it is evil," Zao repeated with closed eyes after finishing another precious sip. "Sure it is. It can be as evil, as hateful, and as repugnant as you can possibly imagine. There will always be weeping and gnashing of teeth that will fill our ears as we labor, but those cries and protests do not endure." He chuckled to himself for a moment. "The surviving citizens of the plague of Milan erected a column of infamy on the ruins of my barbershop,[55] but it stood for only one hundred and fifty years and is now forgotten."

Evan nodded in agreement and then mustered the courage to probe for more information. "Why do you think she is hunting down and capturing the members of the Cognomina who do not join her?"

"She has a long memory and has talked with me for centuries about how you excommunicated her, but now it is about your doctor friend's breakthrough. There is no way she'll allow that gift to fall into the hands

---

55. In this passage Zao seems to claim that he was Gian Giacomo Mora, a barber in Milan who was tried and executed in 1630 for spreading a contagion in the city. If true, this is a stunning corroboration of Brevicepts's account of her work (with two Milanese associates) in the Venetian plague. Mora was brutally tortured for six hours before confessing to the crime. His barbershop was torn down by an outraged citizenry, and a column was erected in its place to commemorate his crimes against Milan. The column was removed in 1778, but the plaque indicting Mora can still be seen today in the Sforza Castle museum in Milan.

of humanity at large. Imagine what a cesspool the world would be if they lived twice as long. No way. That's why she's doing it."

Elsa set down her drink and spoke. "She wants to control life-extension technology as a way to hold leverage over our human assets in La Mutuelle. Dr. Ling just needs to complete his research and replication of the formula. She believes that the promise of that longer life could be the exact incentive to get our assets to agree to anything we might ask of them. She plans to announce it this week at the Conclave."

"What's a Conclave?" Kerr asked.

"Like a board meeting at a masquerade ball," Elsa answered with a mischievous grin.

"That turns into the most amazing party you've ever experienced," Zao added. "It's not to be missed."

"The next one is happening later this week," Elsa said.

"Where are they held?" Kerr asked.

"In Venice on the first night of Carnival. Lesannées finds it best to run the Conclaves during Carnival," said Zao with a smile. "The kind of people we recruit do not like to be recognized attending such a meeting, so the masks work perfectly."

"And we have a La Mutuelle team dinner with Lesannées before the real fun starts. That is where you will get to meet the rest of our family," Elsa added.

"One more thing that apprentices need to learn—we have a traditional greeting and goodbye that the leaders and Lesannées use with each other," said Zao, leaning forward. "'I am my own servant,' followed by the reply, 'and I serve a just master.'"

"What does that mean?" Kerr asked before finishing the last of his brandy.

"It means that, in our current incarnations, we act as servants and benefactors to ourselves in our future lives," Zao answered.

"And hopefully in a better world," added Elsa.

The pilot's voice broke into their conversation over the cabin loudspeaker. "We touch down in Milan in two minutes."

"My old hometown," said Zao, looking out the window at Milan coming into view. "You kids have fun now," he said with a smile before turning to a serious tone as he looked at Elsa. "I am my own servant," he said to her and extended his dark hand.

"And I serve a just master," Elsa replied before taking Evan's hand to lead him off the plane.

27

"What do you want me to do in this meeting?" Evan asked as the middle-aged Italian driver pulled the black Maserati sedan to a stop in front of the white-marbled Ministry of Defense building.

Elsa glanced over at her youthful new apprentice and took his hand to lead him out of the car. "Sometimes it's hard for the officials we work with to take younger-looking people seriously—just try to look like you are over a hundred and twenty years old," she said with a wink.

She strode confidently into the lobby and spoke perfect Italian to the female receptionist at the front desk.

"Very good," the receptionist replied. "Can I record your identification please?"

Elsa reached into her briefcase and pulled out a white card with only the blue La Mutuelle butterfly logo emblazoned on it. "Can you tell Minister Gorgone that we are here on an insurance matter?"

The receptionist spoke into the phone, returned the card, and used her badge to escort them up to the sixth-floor office of the deputy minister of defense, Oscar Gorgone.

"Buongiorno, Ministero," Elsa bellowed across the room at him as soon as the door closed behind them.

"Buongiorno, Maestra," he replied to her but kept his keen eyes on Evan.

"Minister, I would like to introduce my new associate, Mr. Evan—" Elsa paused as she realized she didn't know his last name.

"Michaels," Evan said. "Evan Michaels."

Elsa glanced over with a surprised look on her face and paused for a moment before turning back to face her target. "Evan Michaels is to be one of our new leaders. Shall we get down to business, Minister?"

The deputy minister was younger than Evan thought he would be for such a senior role in the government of a European power. "Yes, sit please," he said, motioning to two chairs in front of his wide desk.

"Let me assure you that anything you would share with me as your liaison to our organization you can share in front of Mr. Michaels," Elsa said. "We have three new tasks for you, Minister Gorgone."

A flash of anxiety washed some of the enthusiasm from the man's face as he prepared himself for what Evan imagined were three unpleasant requests.

"First, we want you to work to impede the Italian military interdictions of refugee boats departing from ports in North Africa."

The young minister began shaking his head before she had even finished. "My prime minister ordered my boss and myself to double the patrols to interdict those boats. It is a reelection campaign issue for him. We stood in front of him, and he ordered us directly."

She smiled, but her smile did not put him at ease. "Why don't you let us worry about the prime minister's reelection? Our group is interested in the continued flow of migrants and specific cargoes into Europe."

"But they will sack me for failing in my duties and I will be ruined—and then of no use to you, by the way," he protested.

"Never put down to conspiracy that which can be explained by incompetence. Find one or two disfavored underlings and blame this impending failure on them. Second," she continued, cutting him off from any further complaint, "you are in the final selection phase for the services around the Italian joint military five-year cyber defense budget."

"Yes, we are down to Cogniti and Gemini."

"Yes, we know. A man named Vittorio from a company called Syntaxos will call on you next week. His bid will be the one you choose. Do you understand?"

"But Syntaxos is terrible."

"I know," Elsa countered in a sympathetic tone, "but you will take your orders, just as I take mine."

"And who gives you those orders?" the minister asked, tilting his head back.

Elsa stiffened in her seat as her tone changed. "You know who gives the orders, Oscar."

The minister slumped in his seat and nodded.

"You may want to think about investing part of your dividend into Syntaxos." She paused. "I plan to."

"And the third item, Maestra?"

"There will be a vote on responses to Islamic extremism in the UN next week that will galvanize support for accelerating Western military action throughout Africa. We need an Italian force of at least a hundred soldiers deployed to the abandoned American bases in eastern Libya in the next thirty days."

"Bah!" the minister exclaimed in gesturing protest as he stood up from his desk. "No, I won't do it. I won't! That area is under Islamist control. It would be a suicide mission. No. This is too much."

Elsa looked over at Evan for a moment before lowering her eyes to the floor. She looked back over the desk at the young Italian minister and raised her eyebrows in a questioning way that spoke of the power she knew she had over him. "Won't? *Won't* seems like a strong word to use with the organization that guided your career to be the youngest deputy minister of defense Italy has ever had. *Won't* does not sound to my ears like the type of drive required for you to be the youngest minister of defense in Italy's history."

Evan looked at Elsa, and was stunned as she transformed into a confident power broker dictating terms to a senior government official.

The deputy minister breathed deeply and smoothed the lapels of his charcoal suit as he took his seat again. "Forgive me, what I meant to say is that I cannot do this thing you ask." He lowered his head and shook it in defeat. "I would be sending those men to their deaths. I'm sorry, what you ask of me is too much this time, Maestra."

Elsa stared at him until he picked his head up again. "Who is to know the moves of the endgame, the knight, the lowly pawn? No, Oscar. It is the queen who decides the moves, and in this time when a critical move by a knight or the sacrifice of a pawn can facilitate an unseen win, I want you to remember what you agreed to do for us and remember what we promised you."

"Yes, but things are different now," he protested.

"Do we have to do this here?" Elsa challenged as she leaned forward onto his desk.

Oscar Gorgone kept his watering eyes locked on hers. "This crosses a line, Elsa."

Her green eyes hardened as she shook her head slowly in exaggerated motions. "Oscar, Oscar, Oscar. It's me. Don't pretend you haven't crossed lines like this before." Elsa paused and let her target reflect on her message before she continued. "Your response shows me," she said before glancing over at Evan and correcting her sentence, "it shows *us* that you believe we don't know you as well as you know yourself, Oscar." She reached into her briefcase, pulled out a brown folder, and placed it carefully on the desk in front of her. "We know, Oscar." She opened the folder to show a grainy black-and-white photo of Oscar Gorgone in a hotel bed with two young-looking African men. "We know you and accept you as you are. We understand your needs and your appetites, do we not? But one wonders if your wife and daughter would be as understanding."

The deputy minister broke into sobs. "Please put them away," he choked.

"Then we are in agreement," she said, snapping the folder closed and placing it back in her briefcase. He nodded quickly. "Excellent, Oscar. Excellent." She pulled out a thin metallic plaque the size of a small book—the La Mutuelle butterfly logo engraved onto the square of shining silver. "Here is your invitation to the Conclave in Venice. Be sure to come in costume, Minister."

He nodded and wiped his eyes as he dropped the metal invitation into the top drawer of his desk.

"Once I hear of progress on your tasks, I will try to forget this moment of weakness, Minister." She gathered her briefcase and rose to leave. "Be a dear and walk us to the elevator, please."

The young deputy minister rose, wiping his eyes again.

"Take a minute to get yourself together, then meet me outside the ladies' room," she said as she left his office.

Evan rose, unsure of what to do or say as the young bureaucrat took deep breaths to regain his composure. The deputy looked away as he smoothed the front of his designer suit but kept bringing his eyes back to Evan until he finally mustered the courage to ask a question. "Are you like her? Are you one of them?"

"What do you mean? Am I in their organization? Yes, but I am new."

"No," he said, shaking his head. "Are you old like her and her boss? Do you remember other lives like them?"

Evan stood shocked in place. *Did Elsa tell him that?* His mind raced with the consequences of the minister knowing. *Do all the captains in La Mutuelle tell these people what we are?* he wondered, still unsure how to answer the young minister's earnest question.

"Is it true that the leader can help us live to one hundred and fifty?"

My God, Evan thought, *how attractive, how intoxicating, how effective would it be to tell these assets what we truly are? No wonder the deputy minister reveres her.*

ELSA LED EVAN OUT OF THE BUILDING and into the waiting black sport sedan. She sat in the back seat next to Evan and was silent for a minute. "To the train station," she directed the driver in a shaky voice now devoid of the supreme confidence she had just used to intimidate her asset. "I'm sorry you had to see that, Evan."

Evan wondered how he could comfort her, but his mind couldn't shake the impressions of how she had transformed into another person in order to control the man. There was a darkness in her somewhere that drove what he had seen her do. "It's okay, Elsa."

She kept her head turned to the scene of Milan passing by, and Evan thought he could hear her crying. "It is *not* okay," she snapped as they approached the piazza in front of the dominating white stone building of the Milano Centrale train station. "This part of the work hasn't been okay for a long time."

Evan wanted to touch her, to comfort her, but was unsure how.

"I wanted that to go differently. I didn't want you to see me like that with him."

He could sense the conflict raging within her as the car pulled to a stop.

"Come with me, Evan," she said, taking his hand in hers as she stepped out of the car. "I want to show you something."

He walked with her, hand in hand, along the shops under the high-ceilinged galleries of the train station until they opened onto a grand metal-and-glass arched roof that spanned the dozen central tracks. She led him through the bustle of travelers and arriving trains toward the end of the main platform and into a smaller side platform with six tracks. The sleek high-speed express trains of the central platform gave way to boxy, slower-moving local lines on this side platform. She led him through the crowds of office workers commuting to their suburban homes and toward the final outermost empty platform with only two tracks. An unused local commuter train sat idle on the nearest track, and on the last track at the station rested a pair of restored vintage passenger cars attached to a standard local locomotive.

Evan stopped and admired them like museum pieces. Their glossy burgundy paint was highlighted in gold-trimmed letters that spelled out *Linea Dolomiti*. Elsa dug a skeleton key on a chain out of her briefcase and inserted it into the lock on the door of the last car. They were the only two people on the platform.

"This belongs to La Mutuelle?"

"No," she replied, stepping up into the car. "This is mine, Evan. This is my home." She held out a welcoming hand to him. "Come with me."

Evan stepped inside the opulent train car. The interior looked like a 1920s-era salon with a plush sofa and leather chairs below long windows and a coffered ceiling covered in decorative tinwork. A hand-carved mahogany bulkhead framed a narrow door with stained glass windows that hinted at a bedroom in the back.

"This is like a time machine," Evan said, admiring the antique sconces and brass railings that ushered him back to memories of his first life.

"It is," she said, breaking into a smile that reminded him of the first time he saw her on the yacht in the Red Sea. She pulled on a loop of red braided cord that rang a small bell outside of the car. "It is an escape for me. Come," she said, stepping through the narrow wooden door toward the back of the train.

Evan entered to see a dimly lit sleeping cabin with vintage-looking luxury linens pulled tight across a double-sized bed. The train jolted once as the locomotive started pulling them away from the platform. He felt her hand on his shoulder and turned just in time to see her beautiful, tanned face draw close to his. She kissed him, softly at first as she put a hand on his cheek. Evan slipped his arm around her waist and pulled her close. Elsa moaned to his touch and opened her mouth to him, gently sucking and teasing at his lower lip as she slipped off her suit jacket and worked at the clasp on her skirt. Evan fumbled at the buttons on his unfamiliar new suit pants as she threw him onto the bed and climbed on top of him. She looked down at him and kept her green eyes locked on his. She seemed to drink him in with her eyes as she slowly took him. She pressed her hands onto his chest for support as she began to move and grind her weight against him. The train rolled away from the empty platform and picked up speed along with Elsa and Evan. She drew her face down closer to his and ran her gentle fingers over his temple as if to prove what she was feeling was real.

Evan opened his mouth to speak, but she placed a lone finger over his lips to protect the silence of a treasured moment. "This is who I am," she whispered. "This is me, Evan."

He concentrated on how it felt to be close to her, to feel goodness and beauty blossom from her. It felt different with her; it felt right in a way he couldn't quite capture. Elsa rocked in time with the rhythm of the accelerating train, and she looked deep into his dark eyes for as long as she could before burying her head next to his neck as she surrendered to a shuddering release.

Evan held her close, keeping silent until she was ready to speak.

Elsa rested her head on his chest and looked out the window at the passing landscape of an Italian night. "I wanted to feel something good," she eventually said between panting breaths. "Something genuine."

Evan stroked her golden hair and thought about how good it felt to just lay next to her. This moment, which he had thought about this many times since first seeing her with her book on the yacht, did feel genuine. "Elsa?" Evan asked after a long silence. "Why are we the only passengers on a hundred-year-old train?"

She laughed and transformed back into the glowing girl with the book on the boat. "It is a bit odd, isn't it?"

"Yes, Elsa, it is odd." He laughed with her.

"I suppose I should start at the beginning," she said as she stroked his chest. "In my first life, I lived in northern Italy at the foot of the Dolomite Mountains. And my first job was working on a train, this very train. I was a maid and cook's assistant. I loved it. I loved seeing the scenery and meeting new people. I was the coolest girl in our village after I got that job."

"I can imagine that."

Her voice turned serious. "I was so happy then, before all of this," she said as if indicting her current circumstances. "Everything was new and bright and good in the world. Do you remember feeling new?"

Evan thought back to his first life in Bulgaria as Vasili, and it seemed like a fantasy to him that life could have ever been so simple. "Yes, I do."

"When I came back this time, I resolved to get back on this train somehow. So I took my first annual dividend from La Mutuelle, found the train abandoned in Verona, and purchased it. It took two years to restore, but now it is back—my little time machine," Elsa said, caressing the polished wooden trim.

Evan held her and thought about how fire was his touchstone back to a past he could never catch. He sensed the movement of the train carrying them along the tracks, and he felt like he saw her for who she really was: a lost girl on a familiar train, forever traveling forward, in the wrong direction.

"I can travel all over Italy with it for my work for La Mutuelle," she continued, "and it keeps a very low profile. Lesannées likes us to live and work off the grid."

"Yes, I assumed that," he said, remembering how little information Rafic was able to find on her.

"I have everything I need on my train. Are you hungry?"

"Sure," Evan answered, but a bit confused, "but how?"

Elsa rolled off of him and pulled three times on the loop of red cord to ring a bell that was barely audible over the sound of the moving train. "Oh, I bought the dining car too."

THEY DRESSED, AND SHE LED HIM PAST a second sleeping cabin into the elegantly appointed dining car. A long mahogany table ran down the middle of the car with twelve linen-covered chairs surrounding it. The white velvet curtains on the panoramic windows opened to expose the moonlit mansions and estates of the Italian lake country. Elsa took the seat at the end and directed Evan to the seat beside her, just as a young, blond, white-uniformed woman emerged from a swinging door with a bottle of wine and two glasses.

"Evan, this is Silvia. She works for me on the train and is an excellent chef."

The chef smiled and nodded as she poured wine for them.

"Thank you, Silvia. Please bring out the meal as soon as you are ready." Elsa waited until the chef was beyond the swinging door to the galley, then raised a glass to Evan. "What do we toast to?"

A dozen thoughts ran through Evan's head as topics to toast: *Did she share the same feelings for him? Was there a core of goodness in her he could find? Was this work getting any closer to his goal of saving his friends?*

"To my apprenticeship," he said, and immediately her smile hardened as she clicked her glass and drank. "I'm sorry. I didn't mean to jump back to work so soon."

"Well, you see what it is now," she stated flatly, all joy now gone from her face. "What you saw in Milan is life in La Mutuelle. This is how it is with her."

"Why do you do it, Elsa? It's obvious that you don't like it, and I know what I saw today is not who you really are."

She stared at him for nearly a minute before turning her face away to the window to quell her emotions enough to respond. "Evan, this is all I know. This is the only life I have ever been offered. After I came back from my first life on this train, everyone thought I was crazy for speaking a strange language and wanting to return to a homeland I could not have known. I was locked up, sequestered away from the world. She freed me. She saw me for what I am and brought me out of that prison and into her family."

Evan remembered that feeling.

"At the beginning with them, I was so grateful to meet others like me who understood what we go through. But then the work came, and then the work got worse, and eventually, it became what you saw today," she said, looking into Evan's eyes. "You may not like some members of your family or what they do, but you have no place else to go. What are we supposed to do, try to live in the normal world with normal people?" she asked but didn't expect an answer. "I have to live in a world with people who know what I am and know what this kind of existence is. So when I began to remember who I was, I had to come back to La Mutuelle, back to the headquarters in Paris. Does your group use a special place as a gathering point or home base?"

"We did. It was a hotel in Zurich, the Hotel St. Germain. It is gone now, burned down by your leader, *our* leader," Evan corrected, "a few nights ago."

"Zao told me there was an event that caused some new faces like you and Kerr to show up but he didn't tell me or the others any details. Was anyone hurt?"

Evan thought back to the familiar fire and pain of that night. "No, I got everyone out."

"Will you rebuild the hotel?"

Evan thought about how to answer the question when he had already presented himself as an apprentice to Brevicepts. *Could she be asking as part of a plan to visit a different family in her next life? Could this be a test of his loyalty to her group?* He kept thinking about his first goal of being able to join both families together. *Would some members of La Mutuelle want to escape Brevicepts as Elsa did? Would some come over to the Cognomina in their next lives?*

"I never dreamed there was another group like ours," Elsa said.

"I never knew either. I mean, we knew about her because our group had kicked her out, but we didn't know there was another group. That is why I agreed to her demands to try to bring the groups together."

"If you don't rebuild the hotel, how would your returning family members find the Cognomina?"

"I don't know if they will rebuild. I hope they do," Evan said, turning his eyes to the window to remember a happier time.

"What are you doing here?" Elsa asked as she reached out to touch his face.

Her blunt question triggered a nervous rush through his arms and legs. "What do you mean?"

"You have a family, a group who knows what you are and who you are. Why did you come to Paris? You saw in Milan what our side is now."

"Well—"

"No," she interrupted. "What you saw is life in La Mutuelle. It is vile labor that only works by intimidating and destroying people. Evan, I do this because I never imagined that my life could be any other way. But you can. Which is why I ask you, is that what you want? Could you do this dark work, Evan?"

Evan thought about her question, but his mind kept landing on a larger question of whether or not he could trust her. *Was she probing and working at his weaknesses at Brevicepts's direction or was she really just that lost girl trying to get back home on the train?*

Evan reached for her hand. "I think I can see you for what you truly are."

She took his hand in hers. "I think I can see you too, Evan. And you don't belong here with this group. What do you hope to accomplish?"

Evan let out a long sigh that signaled his decision. "You saw in Somalia what she did to my friend. Well, in addition to burning the hotel, she has also captured more of my Cognomina family members and is torturing them as well. I"—he stopped and struggled for the next words—"I want to get them back, and the only possibility of that is to get closer to her and La Mutuelle." He pulled his hand back and placed it under his leg to keep it from shaking.

"She would torture you alongside them if she knew," Elsa said.

Evan looked down at the red ripples in his wine glass as the train rumbled along toward an uncertain destination. "I know."

"You must love them to risk so much," Elsa said.

Evan thought about Clovis, trapped with only his violent memories and regrets for company. He thought about Auda, lying frozen on a cot as a flood of faces from the Cognomina ran through his mind. Some he barely knew, others he felt he knew, but every one of them had heard his stories and all had accepted him as one of their own. "I don't know if it is love, but I feel it is a duty. I need to do this for them."

Elsa took her glass in a trembling hand and raised the wine to her lips. "I've always wondered if that kind of love could exist between people like us who remember. You're good, Evan. I yearn for a love that would demand that kind of sacrifice."

"They are like a family of misfits. They would take the same risk to save me."

Elsa watched him and imagined what that must feel like. "I think you should turn back now. I am not sure I can protect you."

"Do I need your protection?" Evan asked.

Elsa broke her gaze from Evan as Silvia entered with a large silver platter covered with plates. "Ah, looks like eggplant Milanese style. Silvia, can you bring me all the newspapers from my briefcase?" She remained silent until her cook was out of earshot. "Evan, I don't think you know what they are capable of doing. They're evil," she said, choking up again.

"I have to find a way to save them. I have thought about this, and I am willing to do whatever it takes to free my friends."

"You say that now, but under her dominating eyes, you may feel differently. Her whole system works on compromising people—you've seen that now. It starts with small, simple tasks that pull people down an easily darkened path." She paused for a calming breath. "I started that deputy minister of defense with a few favors to hire some of our new candidates, and that led to making some questionable allocations of resources, and that led to the first dereliction of duty that could be leveraged via exposure or blackmail. It always starts with something easy and innocent," she said, leveling her green eyes at him. "Like a simple request to deliver a message to the Cognomina."

Evan stiffened as he felt how dangerous the ground was beneath him.

"She'll find a way to compromise you too. That's what she does." She squeezed his hand and looked into his eyes. "I don't want any of this darkness for you, Evan."

"Do you want it for yourself, Elsa?" Evan challenged. "It's obvious you hate it. Now that you know things can be different, why don't you leave them?"

She lowered her head and shook it slowly. "You can't just leave a group like this. No one has ever left," Elsa said and paused as Silvia brought in the day's newspapers.

"Perhaps they don't know they can," Evan continued after Elsa's servant disappeared back into the galley.

"I haven't explained this properly," Elsa said, emotion and fear welling up in her again. "When you read the news and you see stories about war, disease, financial crises, genocides, you don't see them as related, but they are."

"What are you talking about?"

She searched the stack of newspapers until she found the *Times* of London and handed it to Evan. "Find the international section, pick a story, and read the headline. Any story."

Evan took the paper and read a headline aloud, "'Rebels Advance in the Central African Republic.'"

"That is her, working through my captain counterpart, Mr. Bousin. He manages guerrilla and Marxist movements in sub-Saharan Africa. Try another."

"'Quebec to Vote on Independence.'"

"Again hers, working through Captain Voulard, who has the conservative half of Canadian parliament under his control. If you don't go now, you will hear him report his progress at the Conclave. Read another one."

"'Russia Reinforces Divisions in Ukraine.'"

"Oh, that is one of her favorites right now. She is funding and influencing both sides of the conflict through senior La Mutuelle assets. She works the left and the right equally. She enjoys sowing discord toward her own ends."

Evan folded the newspaper closed again. "You mean to tell me that she is behind all of this? That's not possible," he said, reflecting back on Rafic's paranoid-sounding comments on searching for some hidden driver to events that kept going unseen.

"This is what you don't get," she said, placing her hand on the stack of newspapers. "Imagine that nearly every chaotic event that you read has an author, the same author. She is like an invisible hand that can reach anyone, affect anyone, accomplish anything. Evan, it's faceless, nameless, endless. It's tens of thousands of bureaucrats, bankers, CEOs, and celebrities being controlled by hundreds of corrupt politicians, officials, investors, and leaders, who are being controlled by dozens of captains like us, who are being controlled by her. It's a superstate," she said, looking out the window, weighing her words, "that has been corrupted to her control. We could run, but we couldn't hide. At least not for long."

"Are there other captains who hate this work with her?" Evan asked her.

"Yes, but we don't discuss it openly. We just don't go there."

Evan sat in silence as he absorbed her warning. "I have to see this through, Elsa. My friends are counting on me."

"We will reach Venice tomorrow afternoon. Once we are there, I cannot protect you," she said, her eyes filling with tears. "Leave now, I beg you. I will tell her that you left in the night."

"Once I get enough information to help free my friends, I will leave. But when I *do* leave, I want to take you with me. Would you come with me if I could make it safe for us?"

"You have no idea what it would take for us to be safe if I left her."

Elsa laughed nervously and wiped at her eyes. "Evan, being with you makes me realize how much I miss feeling some hope in my life."

"I have my own hopes too," Evan said, reaching across the table to take her hands into his.

She squeezed his hands as she looked out the windows of her train to the darkened countryside. "It's like we have the world all to ourselves tonight," she said, embracing the opportunity to change the subject as she looked over at his fancy walking stick. "Tell me that long story about how you got that cane in a past life."

THE AFTERNOON SUN WARMED THEM as they sat in the dining car in silence as her train crossed the narrow man-made isthmus rail line that connected the island city of Venice to the mainland. "Our captain's dinner starts at her palazzo exactly at sundown this evening, and La Mutuelle assets will arrive for the Conclave after our meeting is complete. When we were back in Milan, I took the liberty of having Silvia purchase a tuxedo for you. It is hanging in the guest cabin. It is black tie for the leaders and Carnival costumes for the invitees and selected guests."

"Do all the captains or apprentices wear the same masks?" Evan asked, admiring the formal outfit.

"No, we will not be in costume tonight. Only the guests, the assets," she quickly corrected, "will be wearing masks tonight. Lesannées designs these events that way on purpose so that every asset will know who *we* are but they will have no idea who the *other* assets in the larger organization might be. For example, Deputy Defense Minister Gorgone will be there tonight in a mask, but he will not know that two Italian generals and one admiral from my territory will also be in attendance tonight."

"Why do it that way? Wouldn't it be more effective if they knew about each other?"

"I thought that too at first, but keeping the membership mysterious protects their identities and plants doubt in the mind of the asset about how many people are involved—and who those people might be. Oscar might very well believe that his boss or even the prime minister himself might be in attendance tonight and allied with us. Everyone knows who the bosses are, but no one knows who their coworkers are," she said ominously, "opening the possibility that it could be anyone."

"Or everyone," Evan said, trying to wrap his head around the dark genius in the design.

"Now you're getting it," she said gravely before dropping into a whisper. "How am I to know that Silvia is not someone's asset?"

"I guess you don't."

"Precisely. Oh, and one more thing," Elsa said as she stared out the window as her train came to a stop. "There is a strict ban on all cell phones during the Conclave—for assets and captains. You will get me in big trouble if you don't check yours in with the others."

"Understood. I would like to go for a walk in the sun," Evan said, trying to cheer her up. "I know a great bar in Cannaregio that serves the best Venetian spritz in the city."

She smiled, but her eyes still looked sad. "I'll be the judge of that."

The streets of Venice buzzed with masks and music on the first day of Carnival. Evan led her along the crowded waterfront walkways of the normally quiet neighborhood and into the quaint Il Santo bar. He ordered two spritzes from the familiar woman behind the bar and looked around in vain for Gonzalo. He took the drinks from the barwoman, and she gave a quick nod toward the bathroom in the back. Evan excused himself and entered the dirty men's room to find Galen's boatman washing his hands in the sink.

"Good afternoon, Mr. Evan. Mr. Galen says Ramsay is almost ready in Rome and to stay with them and learn what you can. Tell me what you know so that I can tell Mr. Galen, what are their next steps?"

28

Evan slipped on the tuxedo jacket and admired himself in the mirror of the guest cabin of Elsa's parked train. The formal wear added at least ten years to his young face.

Elsa knocked on the open door to the cabin and froze in the doorway to look at her transformed young apprentice. "You look amazing."

Evan turned to her, holding the limp bow tie that dangled like an unsolved puzzle in his hand. She wore a black, floor-length evening gown with her long blond hair piled high upon her head. "Wow," he said, stunned.

"I have another item that you will need to wear tonight." She held out her hand to reveal a silver La Mutuelle butterfly pin. She reached out and pinned it through the right lapel of his tuxedo jacket. "Apprentices wear it on the right lapel and captains on the left side. I suspect you will recognize every new apprentice tonight from the Cognomina."

"Yes. I imagine a few will be surprised to see me in attendance," Evan said, struggling with the bow tie.

"Can I help you with that?" she asked, slipping the tie from his hand. She turned him back toward the mirror and stepped behind him as she started working at the knot. She fixed her eyes on him in the mirror. "I will assist you with any information I have that can help get your friends back, but I cannot help you with anything that would harm my fellow captains."

"I understand," said Evan, stretching his neck high for her to finish her knot. "What do you know about her operations in Rome and the Vatican?"

"That would be my counterpart, who runs Rome and southern Italy—mostly mafia and Catholic Church assets. Mr. Buono, Massimo Buono. You will meet him tonight."

"Do you know about the projects he is working on for La Mutuelle in Rome?"

"I don't," she replied, daintily looping his tie together. "We only know what each other are working on when directed by Lesannées to assist with information or provide help to one of our assets."

"Will he talk about his projects tonight?"

"He might. Sometimes she asks the captains for updates, but mostly she manages them in private. There, you're done," she said, finishing the bowtie.

Evan kept his eyes locked on hers reflected in the mirror. "What about Botis?"

He watched her expression, but it didn't change. "That's Zao's operation. He's running it with Dr. Ling. Those two are very close. Botis seems like a special project for her."

"Do you know what it is?"

Elsa stared back at Evan. "I do not. But I suspect it is about getting your side to join her and about what they did to your friend in Somalia."

Evan reached up and touched her hand.

"You wanted to meet our group," she said, slipping her arm around him to hold him close. "You're about to get your wish."

Evan moved his arm over hers and continued to look at her reflection. "I know more about her now. I feel prepared this time."

She quivered next to him. "No one is ever prepared for her. My advice to you is to follow along tonight," she continued as she rested her blond head on his shoulder. "Do what they ask and don't cause any trouble. That will be your best chance at getting more information about your friends."

"What do you think they will ask me to do?"

"That's what I'm worried about," she said, turning him to face her. She placed her right hand over his chest. "I sense the good in you, Evan. It's something I haven't felt in a long time." She stroked her hand over his lapel and lingered on the butterfly pin. "Don't lose that. I don't want to live in a world without hope for something good."

Evan held her and thought about the night ahead. "How do we get to the Conclave?"

"I like to go by gondola," Elsa said as her face broke into a smile.

SHE STEPPED INTO THE BOBBING GONDOLA and slipped under a heavy blanket where Evan held her close to him. The air was cool, and the setting sun cast an orange glow on the city's crowded walkways filled with masked revelers eager for a night of anonymity. The gondolier pushed them silently under the arch of the white stone Rialto Bridge, which buzzed with costumed Venetians and tourists on their way to hundreds of different parties on the first night of Carnival.

Evan felt his chest tighten as the gondola steered from the center of the Grand Canal toward a square platform of a dock that connected via a narrow wooden walkway to one of the largest palazzos overlooking the wide waterway. A large white banner with a red painted butterfly hung from the top-floor balcony. Two guards in designer suits stood at attention on the dock next to two men in black ties and tuxedos who smoked cigarettes. *Were these the first two new members of La Mutuelle he would meet tonight?* he wondered. *Was one of them Mr. Buono?*

Evan leaned forward to catch a glimpse through the crack between the tall wooden doors that filled the ancient arched doorway of the palazzo's canal entrance, and he saw what looked like a great hall illuminated inside. The towering five-story palazzo seemed to float on the water like a magic trick.

"Buona sera, Elsa," called a midsixties tuxedoed man from the dock as the gondolier steered them in.

"Good evening, Chester. How are things on Wall Street?"

"Diversified," he quipped and glanced at Evan with a squinting grin behind thick glasses. "That looks like a new face."

"This is Evan Michaels, my apprentice."

"The same Evan from the notebooks, no doubt. Welcome, Mr. Michaels," the spectacled man said, gripping Evan's hand in a firm handshake that also pulled him soundly onto the secure dock. "My name is Chester Banks, and I run finances for us. This is our associate, Mr. Gustafson. He manages the Nordics."

"I'm Arn, Arn Gustafson. That is a splendid cane you have there. Nice to meet you, Evan," said the stoutly built Scandinavian as he offered an oversized hand in greeting.

Both men turned to Elsa and smiled at her before speaking in unison. "I am my own servant . . ."

"And I serve a just master," she replied before each of them embraced her. "Let's get you both inside. You're some of the last to arrive."

Evan took one last look down the width of the Grand Canal as it turned toward its opening into wider water. Out there somewhere in the lagoon, Galen and Rafic and the rest of the Cognomina huddled over a broken and tortured Auda. He imagined them all urging him forward into this new world.

He stepped through the entrance, arm in arm with Elsa. The wooden double doors opened into a vast expanse of a hall with a soaring ceiling covered in dozens of giant historical frescoes, each surrounded by a wide gold border. A series of antique wooden tables, laid out to form a wide square, dominated the center of the giant room, and members of what looked like a uniformed serving staff placed dozens of ornately carved wooden chairs into place around the four sides. Stone stairs led up to a colonnaded balcony that ringed the room and offered passage into a dozen darkened rooms beyond.

Elsa powered off her phone, laid it in a velvet-lined tray, and slid it into a numbered slot in a rack with hundreds of open slots. Evan did the same with his simple flip phone and then walked with Elsa across the polished wooden parquet floor of the hall toward the next group of captains. "Ms. Sommers," said a tall woman with short hair who wore the same tuxedo and black tie as the men in attendance. "How are you, darling?"

"Good afternoon, Mr. Bigelow. I would like you to meet one of our new apprentices, Evan Michaels."

Evan shook Mr. Bigelow's hand and felt his excitement rise as more elegantly dressed leaders walked over to greet him.

"I am Mr. Seenft. I manage our efforts in Silicon Valley."

"I am Fausto. I run Central America. Nice to meet you, Evan."

"I am Juliana, Brazil."

"Welcome aboard, Evan. My name is Cooper, and I run our operations within the UN."

Evan scanned the crowd and saw at least ten familiar faces from the Cognomina, including Kerr, Steen, Kress, and Mr. Ing.

"Attenzione, attenzione prego!" Zao shouted in Italian to get everyone's attention. "I need the help of Mr. Gustafson, Mr. Salavetti, Ms. Rivera, and all the apprentices by the west stairs, please. We need to get some equipment in place to memorialize tonight's activities."

Most of the captains laughed as though he had told a joke.

"Go with him," Elsa said to Evan. "It's fine. They are setting up surveillance equipment in all the side rooms for our guests who will arrive in a few hours. Don't worry, I will save you a seat next to me."

Evan approached the group and saw Zao bring a hidden microphone in his sleeve up to his lips and speak to a remote observer. "All right, focus on me as we walk the rooms. Make sure you have good video and audio." The bearded captain turned halfway up the stairs and addressed the new faces from the Cognomina. "Here is how this works tonight. We invite our assets to this once-a-year party and we provide them with drinks, drugs, temptation, and freedom from the constraints and morals of the outside world. And that, as you will discover before the night is through, is a delightfully liberating combination. The assets get the time of their lives, and we get a memento of the event that we can then share back with them if we ever need to get their attention on a task," the leader said, breaking into a knowing smile. "Keep in mind that some assets are returning guests and will waste no time in getting upstairs tonight. Others will need some help getting comfortable. We will offer plenty of temptation for them in the lovely forms of our players tonight, but we need to ensure that each guest makes it upstairs and has a good time. The captains will invite them to meetings upstairs. We have hidden cameras in the rooms, but some of you will be given small handheld units later in the evening. Get faces on camera. Our players tonight have been coached on how to engage our guests so that those masks come off. If there are no questions, let's walk the rooms and make sure sofas and chairs are placed right for the cameras. Let's knock this out before our dinner meeting."

The apprentices followed Zao upstairs, where he directed groups of two and three into each room to pose and turn at his direction. Evan was directed into the third room along with fellow apprentice Steen, the short blond man from the Cognomina that he had met only once at his Ascension party.

"What are you doing here?" Steen raised his hand to cover his mouth as he whispered to Evan.

"I came to learn more," Evan answered in a hushed tone, not sure if he could trust him.

"It's a trap," Steen said in a low voice as he walked behind Evan and brushed up against him. "Did she threaten to bankrupt you too," he asked, "if you didn't embrace the vision?"

Evan smiled for the hidden cameras and nodded to Steen. "Do you want to come back?" Evan asked through tightened and stoic lips.

Steen smiled and nodded back to him. "And there might be a few others like Kress. Some, like Kerr and Mr. Ing, seem to love it here," he hissed in reply.

Evan nodded and continued his work.

"One of us who came over has already disappeared," Steen whispered into Evan's ear.

A series of four ominous single notes from a piano reverberated throughout the palazzo and repeated several times.

"She's calling us," Zao said, pausing his staging work. "Let's go back downstairs. Apprentices, please take a seat next to your captain."

Every captain was seated around the large square of arranged tables. Evan searched the crowd for Elsa's pile of blond hair and took the empty seat next to her. Elsa brought a finger to her lips as the group of over fifty captains and apprentices sat in complete silence. Evan looked around at the white china, polished crystal glasses, and took inventory of the faces he had not yet met. He found the menacing Dr. Ling among them as he sat in the seat to the left of the one empty seat that remained.

In a distant room off the hall, Evan heard the familiar click of high-heeled shoes on stone and then on hardwood as she drew closer. All eyes landed on her as Brevicepts strode into the room. She wore white pants and a jacket under a glowing white cape that trailed behind her like wings. Her black hair, fastened tight to the top of her tall head, was her only concession to color-matching her tuxedoed team. She approached the empty seat of honor in the middle of the north side of the table and stood for a moment, admiring her team. "I am my own servant . . ."

"And I serve a just master," all repeated in unison back to her as she took her seat at the table.

"As we prepare for our most important night of the year, I want to start this evening by highlighting our gains since the last time we all met under my roof." She paused as two of the male servers carried out two impossibly oversized bottles of champagne and began to fill every glass. "We have enjoyed a truly great year. We have expanded our networks and assets. We have advanced and accomplished some long-labored policies that can help protect our precious earth."

The captains applauded in unison as they looked at each other in satisfaction.

"Thanks to the efforts of every captain in this room and the foresight and coordination of our Mr. Banks and his investments, we have enjoyed record earnings this year, and I am pleased to announce that we are paying out our full dividend"—she paused for a moment—"plus 40 percent."

The captains all rose to their feet and applauded their success with toasts of champagne.

She enjoyed the applause until it died down to silence again. "But our greatest win this year is not in money, but in power and potential. Our greatest gain this year is in our numbers. Look around this table tonight, and you will see many new faces. These new brothers and sisters are just like you and me. They remember the past and are witness to the same destruction we have seen. They join us from my old family. Let us take a moment before our dinner to welcome them into our ranks. Enjoy your evening, everyone," Brevicepts said, closing her speech.

All the captains applauded again before some came over to greet Evan and the other defectors from the Cognomina.

"Hello, my name is Ms. Lutz, but everyone here calls me Opal."

"I am Mr. Pandaman. I manage our interests and influencers in Hollywood and music."

"I am Victor Cervo, call me Vic. I'm fairly new. I run social media."

"I am Ms. Lindahl, Lindy for short. I run illicit narcotic manufacturing and distribution globally. And, you be will happy to know, I am one of our party planners for this evening."

Evan felt a shiver when the Asian doctor walked up to him. "I am Dr. Ling. We met briefly in Yemen. I do wish we could have met under better circumstances, Evan, but welcome."

"I remember you," Evan said extending his hand.

"The cane is a nice touch," Ling said with a wry smile. "Very stylish with the formal wear. I don't remember you using it on the boat."

The white-uniformed serving staff brought out identical vegetarian plates for dinner along with dozens of bottles of red and white wine. The short series of high notes came again from the piano that sat in the corner among classical instruments on their stands. Conversations ceased when all heads turned to see their leader standing at the edge of the instrument with long fingers sounding the simple notes to draw the group back to order.

"Let us take our seats again and formally begin our meeting," she said, directing everyone to sit and begin eating. "In addition to our outstanding financial and personnel gains, we have expanded our reach into exciting new areas such as venture capital, influence marketing, big data, grassroots nationalism, and human life extension. These are important new areas for us to capture and influence toward our goals while they are newly developing, and our efforts now will ensure these trends serve our needs into the future. Next year, we plan to add two very promising new sectors. The first is augmented reality, and I am looking for a captain or apprentice who can own this space, and the second is artificial intelligence in autonomous robots to ensure this technology gets weaponized for inclusion in our ongoing hot conflicts—which leads me to our first report out," she said, turning to her left to nod to a middle-aged, fastidious-looking man with a stack of prepared notes. "Mr. Tannant, would you please update us on your progress in Crimea?"

The first captain thumbed through his notes and began. "Now that the shooting has started, our focus is escalating the conflict and targeting other former Soviet Socialist Republics as phase two."

"Excellent," Brevicepts replied after savoring a sip of the white wine. "Mr. Zao, what updates can you bring us on your eternal conflict?"

The bearded captain rose to address the group with his Middle East update. "Sunni and Shia relations are at their lowest since the Iran-Iraq war, and we are prepared for our next flashpoint to be Kharg Island, the tanker terminal in the Persian Gulf. Yemen is in flames and holds the possibility of spreading to Saudi Arabia when we are ready. Islamic State is shrinking but is still influencing Arab youth as we had hoped. Thanks to our newest captain, Mr. Cervo, for his help in that area," Zao concluded.

Brevicepts turned to Mr. Banks. "Please offload any policies we have on Kharg and build short positions on all those insurers who pick up our Iranian coverage."

Mr. Banks nodded behind his thick glasses, and Brevicepts motioned with her wine glass for him to report out.

"I closed out our Gazprom calls last week at a 500 percent gain," Mr. Banks stated. "We are building very large positions in Atelos Corporation, based on Mr. Serna's reliable information. And per your instruction, we have built large positions in Syntaxos and select cryptocurrencies."

"Ms. Sommers, how are things with our favorite minister?"

Elsa stood up next to Evan. "A force of Italian troops is on their way to occupy the American bases in eastern Libya, and I have coordinated with Opal on her Boko Haram efforts. He will comply on scaling back immigrant boat interdictions."

"I have four drug transport boats coming into Naples and Bari next week," Lindy interjected. "Let's talk after dinner."

"Speaking of Africa," Brevicepts continued, "Mr. Bousin, where are we on your collaboration with Dr. Ling?"

"The first tests of the doctor's samples have started the small outbreaks we wanted for your test. The next questions for me are: how big of an outbreak do you want in the Congo and where are we on manufacturing more of the contagion?"

She glanced over at her captain. "I will update you off-line about that. Dr. Ling, where are you on replicating the life-extension serum samples we procured for you?" she asked. "Our arriving guests will be most interested in hearing about your progress on that front."

The doctor rose to his feet reluctantly to give his report. "I have little progress to report to date, and cracking the complex compounds will take additional time for the required trials."

"How much time?" she demanded.

"It is hard to say, Lesannées, but I estimate I will need at least a year."

"Unacceptable," she uttered, letting each angry syllable echo about the great hall. "I need it this summer. Redouble your efforts," Brevicepts barked before turning to her accountant, who blinked anxiously behind his amplifying lenses. "Mr. Banks, please give our doctor whatever financing and infrastructure he requires to complete his duties for us."

"Mr. McCormick," she continued, "I could use some good news. Please update us on the world of genetic plant modification and how our funding is advancing terminator seed[56] development."

One after another, each captain detailed some planned disaster or managed mayhem with clinical dispassion. Evan looked at the panorama of her captains' faces; each seemed dour and somehow marred with malice. He couldn't help but reflect back to the laughter and joy and

---

56. *Terminator seed* is a protest term surrounding genetic use restriction technology, or single-use seed. It is a genetically modified organism (GMO) whose seeds are purposefully engineered to be infertile. It is considered a threat and a famine risk in some developing nations who have recently outlawed it.

humor and stories that accompanied a Cognomina dinner in the grotto below the St. Germain.

As the dining and status updates went on, he let his eyes drift to the ceiling as he focused his mind and tried to memorize the details of every project, timeline, and owner. His eyes found the triptych of frescoes on the ceiling above Brevicepts. The center scene depicted a darkened Venice with its wailing inhabitants in the throes of pestilence, and Evan assumed it was a commemoration of her deadly efforts. He listened on about planned famines and coup plots as he looked at the next fresco, which detailed long-dead peasants cowering before the lances of a menacing cavalry charge. The final fresco showed fields of denuded pine trees stretching to the horizon, each tree branch stripped and sharpened into a bloody point as it held the weight of an impaled human form.

Evan listened to the last of the captains report their disturbing plans over dirtied plates and emptied wine glasses. Galen's and Ramsay's and even Elsa's warnings rang in his ears as if he could hear no more after the last captain spoke.

"Thank you all for those reports," Brevicepts said. "I am proud of each of you for what you have been able to accomplish with your teams. One last toast before our guests arrive," she said, raising her glass. "Let us toast our assets, who continue to help us improve our world for our futures to come." Every captain and apprentice raised a glass with her as she addressed them, "I am my own servant . . ."

Evan joined in their collective pledge back to her. "And I serve a just master."

29

The pair of wide-shouldered security guards at the dock threw open the tall double doors to reveal dozens of guests already crossing the narrow walkway from the dock to the palazzo's canal entrance. Zao looked over at the assembling musicians in the corner by the piano and snapped his fingers to start them playing a welcoming waltz.

Evan stood next to Elsa and turned toward the open door to marvel at a scene right out of the seventeenth century. Masked party guests lined up in an aquatic queue of bobbing gondolas, each craning their anonymous eyes for a peek at what delights awaited them inside the palazzo. Zao and Dr. Ling greeted each guest at the entrance table.

Some guests wore simple snow-white masks with black capes and hoods; others donned elaborate feathered headdresses above sparkling gowns. Others hid behind hideous masks with grotesque grins and oversized noses. Some of the most mysterious guests wore expensive suits or dresses along with simple black or white half masks that covered only the eyes and nose.

Confident and aloof in their stations, all of them looked like they might have just arrived in Venice from a boardroom or a movie set or a government ministry. All masqueraded guests did share one thing in common: each held a silver plaque with an engraved butterfly logo. Mr.

Zao received each presented plaque and placed it neatly in a grid atop a table covered in red velvet behind him. Dr. Ling watched as guests powered down their phones and placed them in the numbered bins before he ushered them into the filling ballroom.

Masked acrobats danced, leaped, and tumbled in time to the classical music that echoed about the vast room as uniformed waiters offered the guests champagne from gleaming silver trays. Evan took a glass and touched it against Elsa's, who returned to a conversation in Italian with two masked guests. He watched the guests arrive for an hour and was surprised to see the great hall filled to capacity by the time the last of them had checked in. Evan looked at the neat rows of silver plaques laid out on the red velvet and counted over four hundred.

He walked around the room, eavesdropping among the dozens of languages that mixed with the chamber music. Most of the masked guests lingered in loose orbits around their unmasked captains, sharing stories in their shared language. Other guests tried to mingle in protected conversations that kept them occupied yet anonymous to each other.

Evan watched as Zao closed the giant double doors and walked over to the piano. The musicians watched the imposing leader with hands at the ready as they finished their fugue. Zao reached down and repeated the telltale four high-pitched notes at the treble end of the piano until the room fell silent.

"Greetings, guests," Zao shouted. "On this first night of Carnival, I would like to welcome you to our annual Conclave." He brought his hands together with their applause and waited until it died down. "I have some announcements to make before we start our festivities. For some of you, this is your first time attending one of our little fetes, and you need to know the rules. The first and only rule to a La Mutuelle Conclave is that there are no rules." Clapping and laughter rose from pockets of the crowd. "This night is a reward to you for the hard work and difficult tasks accomplished throughout the year. This night will soon be yours to enjoy—after we talk a bit of business."

Conversation in the room simmered in anticipation as Zao continued, "Our leader will join us in a few hours, and she has a special message and presentation for you all tonight, so please come back down when you hear her call. Next, I want to talk about our earnings for this year." A few cheers echoed from the corners of the room. "I am pleased to announce that we are paying out your full dividend for the year, plus an additional 30 percent." The room erupted into cheering applause and clinking of glasses. "The updated balances should land in your numbered accounts of record by end of business on Monday." The bearded leader paused for the clapping to quiet down. "If you want advice on what to do with your new reward, please share a drink or a trip," Zao said, pausing to take two pills from a passing platter of multicolored drugs, "with our all-knowing Mr. Banks."

Several masked guests burst into laughter as the La Mutuelle banker smiled between nervous, magnified eye blinks.

"Please, friends, take a drink or take several," Zao bellowed over the crowd. "Take whatever you want tonight, but partake." He raised one of his arms over his head, and all eyes in the crowd now drifted upward toward the second-floor balcony as masked and barely costumed handsome young men and alluring women began to emerge from the inviting darkness of the rooms above.

"We have many new players tonight," continued Zao as alluring bodies leaned over the balustrade and invitingly embraced the stone columns on the second floor. "And some returning favorites," he concluded as an enormous, muscled man, naked to the waist, crossed in taut leather straps, and sporting a menacing, horned minotaur head stepped out from the dark, leading two petite women dressed up as ponies by their glittering reins.

"Ladies and gentlemen," Zao said, grabbing a fresh glass of champagne from a passing tray to wash down the two pills, "we created this wonderful evening for you because, for people like us, the world is just not enough."

Zao took a bow, and the guests applauded one last time to acknowledge that they were free to enjoy themselves. Many members peered behind masks at the nearly naked bodies at the top of the stairs, and a few of them climbed the stairs and picked a playmate. One athletic young man in a tailored black suit and a red cat mask raced up the stairs and threw himself into the muscular arms of the man-bull.

Other guests below sipped champagne and sampled from the prepared trays of hors d'oeuvres, drinks, narcotics, and hallucinogens and began conversations as the quintet of musicians filled the ample room with classical notes.

Evan looked for Elsa but saw the diminutive Mr. Ing approaching him. "So nice to see you, Evan," he said, turning his bald head toward the musicians. "It's lovely, isn't it? Can you imagine how many times this music has echoed off these magnificent walls?"

"Do you know it?" Evan asked.

"It's Vivaldi," he said, looking up at Evan. "I wonder if he ever conducted it live for her in this very room."

"Do you like it here with her?" Evan inquired with the hope that he might find some discontent.

"She's a genius. She's the leader we have deserved all this time," Ing said thoughtfully before walking away toward Mr. Bigelow, leaving Evan alone to listen in on the conversations around him.

"I heard she has found a way for us to live to two hundred years old," stated a man in a half mask adorned with small pearls.

One reveler staggered back down the stairs in search of two fresh glasses of champagne, clearly not caring that his gilded mask rested on the top of his head. "This is the best night of my life. My God, what a party."

"No, it's not two hundred years old, more like a hundred and fifty," said a man behind a pig mask. "My captain said it is coming next year."

"My captain said they have figured out a way to make us like them."

"What will you spend your dividend on?"

"A new political contribution—one large enough to get an invite to the House of Lords. What about you?"

"I have been eyeing this little island in the Persian Gulf, just off Dubai."

"You might want to rethink that. My captain warned me to divest everything from the Emirates and avoid the region altogether."

"I'm going to fund a run for office again," answered a man in a black mask lined with white fur.

Evan wandered from group to group for the next hour and listened to masked conversations that became harder to hear over the distracting moans of pleasure coming from the second floor.

"Maybe we should see what's going on up there," a young-sounding woman said behind a fox mask.

"Is this your first time here? If so, you *must* go up and enjoy yourself."

"More like you must go up and *exhaust* yourself," said an older woman in a radiant sun mask.

"If she can help us live longer, here's to another hundred years of this," said one masked asset to another on her way to the stairs.

"To La Mutuelle," shouted a woman in a feathered mask as she walked up the stairs toward the seductive sounds.

Elsa nudged Evan, and they watched as a tall androgynous-looking man with a striking chiseled face accentuated in drag makeup, a thong, and platform women's boots strutted down the stairs and made one flamboyant loop around the ballroom until five of the last eight guests locked eyes with him.

"Well, what the fuck are you waiting for?" he called to them as he placed a boot on the second step. "Come on up and see what I have for you."

Evan looked at Elsa. They were the last eight people on the ground floor not wearing a mask. "Are we supposed to get the last of them upstairs?"

"None of these are mine," she answered.

"Do any of the captains enjoy the festivities?" Evan asked, pointing up to the noises on the second floor.

"Some still play," Mr. Buono said in passing, "but most are played out."

Zao put two fingers in his mouth and whistled down to them. "Elsa, new guy, up here now," he commanded.

The dark-haired captain met them at the top of the stairs and placed a small, handheld video camera in each of their hands. "Follow the last of them into those rooms and make sure the video is rolling."

Evan felt a knot of revulsion tighten in his stomach as he took the camera from the captain and followed two men into the dark labyrinth of staged rooms on the second floor. He turned his camera from left to right scanning more for naked faces than naked bodies as he walked. He captured them in their twos, threes, and fours, unmasked faces atop slapping bodies slick with sweat. Open hands and hungry mouths reached out for him as he slowly walked from room to room with only the narrow sight window of the video camera to guide him. Evan lost the trail of his targets and felt some relief in that. He froze for an instant when he thought he saw the familiar orange of a back tattoo flash in the viewfinder but was then promptly knocked to the floor by a flailing arm of the muscled minotaur in his motions.

Evan picked up the camera and walked toward the light of the open balcony. He inspected the video camera, but it no longer functioned. He looked through the columns toward the ballroom below and saw only unmasked captains sipping drinks and smoking cigarettes. Evan lit a cigarette of his own and retreated into one of the first rooms, where he sat on a dry sofa and pretended to film the flagging forms before him.

He watched for what seemed like hours as new players and new guests performed and then moved on. He watched until the haunting sounds of the summoning piano notes jolted him out of a jaded trance and sparked new stirrings in the motionless tangle of naked limbs before him.

Evan walked out onto the lit balcony and ran into Zao, who was trying to rouse the spent guests into an assembly. Evan handed the camera to the captain. "The minotaur broke it, but I got some footage."

"We got everything we need," Zao said with a satisfied smile. "Now help me get these assets downstairs, please, and make sure they take their clothes," he commanded before racing off into the darker back rooms.

Evan helped round up the last of the stragglers as the haunting series of four piano notes continued to beckon every ear in the palazzo. They slowly emerged from the darkness and descended the stairs like survivors of some elegant disaster. Some were shoeless and holding torn clothing; others steadied themselves against sturdier partners as they righted their crooked masks.

Evan looked over the railing to see the regal Brevicepts touching the keys at the end of the piano. The dining tables were gone now, and in their place stood a wooden altar and what looked like a hand-carved oak throne. Evan felt a strong hand on his shoulder.

"The serving staff and the band are gone now. It's just the committed who remain. Let's get down there," Zao said.

The summoning piano notes stopped when Zao and Evan stepped onto the parquet of the main hall.

"Good evening, all," Brevicepts began as she walked over to the raised wooden throne. Her high heels clicked on the hardwood floor as she strode gracefully through the crowd, her topknot of hair on display like dark plumage. "Thank you for joining us," she said, stopping before her elevated seat. "Some of you have been with us for many years, and I thank you for your loyalty. Others have joined us this year, and this is your first event with us. Welcome, all. This is your home now," she said, spreading her arms wide. "We created all this for you. We created it because we know you in a way that the rest of the world can never know you and can never truly appreciate you. We know that it is *you* who drive our culture, our politics, our policies, our global commerce, our very futures. We know *you* are the most important people in the world, and we celebrate you this night. We know you want to live in a world that is free from the bounds that *their* world would put on you. And now, that journey to be free from their bonds has brought you to us.

"And we," she continued, opening her long arms to indicate her captains, "have made ourselves known to you. You know what we are. You know that we are special. You know we are older. You know that we remember. Some of you know that we have worked with your families for generations, and for others, we start that generational relationship on this night.

"We are known to you, and we wear no masks." She paused as masked faces turned and studied every naked face. "But, as some of you will note, there are some new faces tonight. This is a new group of emerging leaders in our ranks. Apprentices, please step forward," she commanded.

Evan caught Elsa's eye, and he sensed her anxiety as he stepped forward with his former Cognomina brothers and sisters to the first row of spectators that ringed the altar and throne.

"These new leaders are like us—they are old and remember their past lives. Some of these new leaders might even lead you in your tasks for La Mutuelle in the coming years. I want you to welcome these new leaders into our ranks." She waited for their applause to trail off before continuing, "But there is a special addition among them, someone who agreed to work with me from the beginning, someone who desired to bring two families together—and then did." Brevicepts's penetrating eyes fell on Evan.

Evan felt the hot fear rise in him like a fever. He felt every captain's eyes on him as he looked over and saw the panic on Elsa's terrified face.

"Evan," Brevicepts said, extending a long arm to isolate him from the comforting crowd. "Step forward."

Evan felt himself moving closer to her as if the applause of the crowd somehow pushed him forward. He felt the surrounding presence of Mr. Zao to his left and Dr. Ling to his right.

"Beloved guests, my captains, friends—I know that we often ask you to do difficult and distasteful things in your service to La Mutuelle. We view these tasks as tests of your loyalty to our cause." Brevicepts paused for a moment as the masked crowd turned toward a commotion near the piano as two of her male captains carried in a young girl who struggled violently against the gag in her mouth and the ropes at her feet and hands. "And we do not exempt ourselves from these tests when they are required." Her dark eyes fell on Evan and pinned him to the floor as the two captains tied the girl to the wooden altar.

Evan trembled at the sound of Zao's whispered voice in his ear. "It's time." He felt the crushing grip on his right arm as Dr. Ling leaned in and took the cane from his right hand. "Let me hold this for you, Yousef, as you atone for that stunt in Zagreb," he hissed menacingly.

"You might find this a bit *unsavory*," Zao whispered to Evan with a manic excitement flashing in his dark eyes. The two captains walked Evan toward the girl on the altar as Brevicepts took her seat on the elevated throne.

Brevicepts looked up to address the masked crowd again. "So now we ask Evan to pledge his loyalty to us and our cause for a better world through sacrifice."

The masked crowd murmured and moved to get a closer view of the altar.

"This girl represents their hope for a better world, their hope for the future. But we know better. We are our own hope, we are our own servants, and our own masters. We are the curators of this world. We are vigilant, constant guardians, and soon we will be able to give this gift to all of you. But this responsibility doesn't come without pain, without sacrifice, without a strong will to consider the needs of countless future generations—sometimes at the expense of the current one. This girl," Brevicepts continued as she extended a white draped arm toward her, "represents our commitment to the cause, our justice for the future, and our mercy for the earth. Tonight, our newest captain will demonstrate our collective commitment if you wish it." She paused and turned to look at every masked face. "Tell me now, do you wish it?"

The masked crowd whispered in unison, and then grew stronger until they shouted as one, "We wish it!"

The crowd stepped forward again, and Evan could feel the constricting circle tighten around him. The young girl looked at Evan and struggled against her bonds on the heavy wooden altar.

"Evan," Zao whispered into his left ear as he placed a small antique dagger in his trembling right hand, "I am my own servant . . ."

"And I serve a just master," Dr. Ling whispered into his right ear.

Mr. Zao and Dr. Ling released their grip on him and took their stations at their leader's side.

"Do you remember when we spoke about commitment, Evan?" Brevicepts asked above the chant of the crowd as she broke into a satisfied smile. "This is your time to commit." She looked with blazing, excited eyes at the blade that quivered in his hand. "Show us your commitment and take your place among us."

The masked group pushed forward to see the spectacle, surrounding Evan and shoving him to the front of the altar. All fell silent except for the stifled cries of the girl as eager eyes peered out from behind the anonymity of the stoic, emotionless masks. Evan turned to Elsa. Tears streamed down her cheeks as she watched her hero face the test she had tried to spare him from.

Evan looked from the tears of his lover to the tears of his offered sacrifice. He felt his own eyes fill and begin to spill onto his cheeks. He felt the crowd closing in on him in the same way his choices for the past weeks had narrowed down to this one.

Evan's mind searched the memories of his four lives for how to act at that moment. It was not just the life of the innocent girl that hung in the balance. It was also Clovis's and Samas's and Etyma's and Dilmun's lives that were at stake. He had killed before. *How many lives had he ended with each artillery shell Vasili had loaded into the breach? Were there innocents then when he helped rain hot metal down onto Balkan villages filled with his nation's enemies? As soldiers, they told themselves they were saving the lives of their comrades by killing others in war, but was he not already in a war between La Mutuelle and the Cognomina?*

Evan looked down at the girl, and she panicked at the newfound hardness in his expression. He imagined himself remembering her death at his hands. It would be like a discovered darkness waiting for him in each new incarnation, a stain he could never clean from himself. And then he imagined himself failing his family at this moment. *What if Galen only needed another day or two to create an antidote? What if Ramsay planned a rescue tomorrow and needed just one more day from him?*

Evan looked down at her and saw all of his failures lying before him. He had failed the Cognomina when he had decided to trust Brevicepts—even just that small trust to do one task for her. He had failed to heed Clovis's warning not to trust her, his last words to him. Gonzalo's words rang in his ears: *"Rome is almost ready. Mr. Galen says stay with them."* He could not fail those who counted on him now.

The small blade felt like an unbearable burden in his hand as he raised it over his head. The surrounding crowd jostled for a view, their eyes wide in expectation behind their hideous masks. They pressed against him and the table, willing him to do it, projecting their collective hatred on him for all the distasteful deeds Brevicepts and her captains had demanded of them over the years.

He looked up at the ceiling, and his tearing eyes could just make out the menacing outline of the blade as he repeated to himself, *I cannot fail the Cognomina. I cannot fail again.*

Evan brought the knife down at its target until he could feel the resistance of flesh separating before its point. He felt the girl writhe beneath the terrible blade, and then he heard a voice cry out in pain. He felt the knife moving against some residual struggle of a life leaving. The crowd around him gasped, and Evan blinked to clear his watering eyes, not wanting to see the girl expire but unable to look away.

His eyes cleared to see his hand gripping the handle atop a mass of bleeding flesh. But his mind took a minute to process what he saw. The knife had not penetrated the flesh of the girl but instead had pierced the backs of two small, white-gloved hands crossed into a protective shield across the young girl's still heaving chest. Evan kept his hand on the knife as his eyes noticed the blade had sliced open the long silk glove on the woman's top hand to reveal the distinctive angular outline of a black Embe tattoo on a quivering hand. His eyes followed the hands to the familiar arms and up to the white-masked face to find the familiar black eyes of Poppy. Time stopped for everyone in the room as those guests next to the altar tried to make sense of what they had just witnessed. Poppy took a deep breath and looked down at her bleeding hands, still pinned together by the blade.

Evan removed the knife, and Poppy screamed just as both Zao and Ling staggered and dropped to the floor in violent convulsions, their confused eyes looking out from paralyzed bodies in search of assistance. The crowd retreated into a widening semicircle around the stricken men. Guests screamed as Mr. Banks collapsed on the other side of the altar, followed by Ms. Rivera.

"They have the serum," Brevicepts shouted as two smoke grenades popped and began filling the palazzo's great hall with billowing blue clouds. The room descended into chaos as screaming guests tore off their masks and rushed toward the exits of the great hall.

A gloved hand bent down and grabbed the cane like a weapon before taking Evan's left wrist and guiding him toward the dock beyond the canal entrance door. The man who led him had a mop of curly black hair above a pink mask complete with floppy ears and white whiskers—Rafic.

Two more captains fell, shuddered, then lay still, their eyes locked open wide. Brevicepts shouted for calm amid the chaos, and the entrance guards rushed to her side, leaving the door unprotected. Rafic raced toward the rack of phones, swinging the cane with murderous intent until he could pick up his MI6-issued chrome unit.

Evan stepped over a paralyzed and wild-eyed Mr. Buono and joined Rafic as they pushed their way through the wooden double doors and onto the dock, where a gleaming new speedboat sat at the ready with a stoic Gonzalo at the wheel. Evan looked back to see Elsa standing on the dock, the hulking Mr. Gustafson right behind her. Rafic shoved Evan onto the boat.

"No, wait!" Evan shouted as Rafic, Galen, Jens, and a bleeding Poppy landed on the cushioned seats next to him. Ignoring him, Gonzalo accelerated from the dock, speeding away into the cool Venetian night.

BREVICEPTS SHRUGGED OFF HER GUARDS. "They've escaped, you fools!" She stooped down to stroke the beard of a paralyzed Zao and noticed a handwritten note crumpled into his permanently clenched fist. She pulled it out to read it.

I can undo this. Meet me at the last place we saw each other. Come at dawn. Come alone. —Galen

30

Every mother in the Romani camp in south Rome marked the first day of Carnival by making papier-mâché masks for their children out of discarded newspapers. The children took turns wearing blue masks dyed from ink left over from luxury fountain pens picked from the pockets of politicians near the senate, and devilish red masks dyed from the remnant blood taken from the alleys behind kosher butcher shops. Ramsay walked between the warring factions of children on her way to Perez's trailer. She had one last ask of her adoptive tribe, and she knew it would not be an easy one.

She found Perez sitting with Lucca in front of his trailer. Ramsay was dressed in her janitor uniform and had packed up her one change of clothes into a tight roll under her arm. She turned the trailer key in her hand as she approached.

"Are you leaving us?" Lucca asked.

"Yes, it is time. Thank for you sheltering me."

"All is open to the daughter of Dante," Perez said over a steaming cup of coffee.

She opened her hands and motioned toward the empty chair to ask permission to sit in the respectful fashion of Romani women. Both men nodded their approval as she sat next to Perez. She reached out to drop the key into the old man's hand but moved her hand to his ear to produce the key magically as one final trick.

Both men smiled, and Perez reached out and took her tattooed hand in his. "I am near the end of my life, and it has been wonderful to meet you, my child. Tell me, is there any last thing the Roma people can do for you?"

"There is, my king." She kept his gnarled hand in hers as she spoke. "Now we need your help to free *our* people."

SMALL GROUPS OF MASKED TOURISTS POSED for photographs in the open square in front of St. Peter's Basilica as Ramsay stepped off the bus and walked to work. She showed her badge at the service entrance and began her last shift at the secluded building within the sheltering walls of Vatican City. She started on the lower floors and took her time at her tasks to ensure she worked the top floor at the end of the day, that same day when Brevicepts would be calling her assets and her captains together for an elaborate party in her palazzo in Venice.

As she completed her familiar labors, Ramsay thought about the ones who had deserted the Cognomina. She had known them for centuries, and she wondered, as she swept offices and emptied trash, who among them was happy in her Venetian palazzo and who among them had shunned her offer and might now be compromised and on their way to that impromptu medical ward behind the security guards on the top floor. She scrubbed sinks and toilets and hoped Evan was prepared for whatever might await him on that first night of Carnival.

She wheeled her cart over to the staff cafeteria in the neighboring Governor's Palace for her usual lunch break, but this time she followed the small crew of ambulance drivers back into their garage at the back entrance. She went about her sanitary tasks with a servile invisibility that allowed her quickly to disable the ignition modules on both Vatican City ambulances and take two road flares from their roadside emergency kits.

Ramsay worked her way up to the top floor as the afternoon sun crept toward the west. She followed her routine of working at the opposite end of the top floor and finished by waiting for the two guards to bring the spent refuse out to her. She retreated to the basement with her cart and carefully inspected the contents to ensure there were still only four people held captive behind those closed doors. She checked the time on the military watch discreetly hidden under the blue cleaning gloves as her cleaning counterpart came down to check on her.

"Today is my last day. I think Rita comes back tomorrow," Ramsay said to her coworker in her ancient Italian. "I took too long today on my floors. Let me take out your trash for you. You should leave now if you want to catch your bus."

The two women exchanged a gloved handshake before Ramsay walked her out and locked the service door behind her. She pushed her cart back to the center of the basement, near the furnace. She worked the access panel to the main duct open after some effort, and then she sat on a folding chair beside her familiar cleaning cart and waited for the message to come.

The burner phone buzzed just after midnight with a simple text message: *We got ours. Go get the rest.*

Ramsay resumed her mission by stuffing the discarded papers and soiled linens from both carts into a tight block inside the open heating duct. She reached into the collected bottles of cleaning solutions and brushes and removed the two emergency flares. She popped the protective caps off both and struck their starting fuses against each other to light them both at the same time. Ramsay squinted her eyes against the red sulfur smoke as she stuffed them into the trash block inside the duct, instantly setting it alight. She snapped the access panel back into place and quietly wheeled her cart back over to the elevator.

Ramsay exited into the first-floor lobby and positioned her cleaning cart near the tall glass double doors of the main entrance. She sat at the empty receptionist desk before adjusting the master thermostat for more heat. She looked from her watch to the vents as she waited for the small fire to take hold. Black smoke tinged with red from the burning flares billowed out into the lobby once the furnace fan finally kicked in. She walked calmly over to the elevators and pulled down on the red fire alarm lever, sending undulating waves of shrill sound into the quiet dark of a sleeping Vatican City.

The blue-uniformed Vatican police arrived first, followed by the ambulance drivers who sprinted on foot toward the screaming siren.

"I work in this building, and there are sick people kept on the top floor," Ramsay shouted to them as she opened the lobby doors.

"This is an office building," said the police captain in Italian.

"Yes," Ramsay protested, "but there are patients upstairs who are helpless. Go check, please. I would hate for something to happen to them!"

The youngest of the ambulance drivers stopped at the open front doors to catch his breath. "We ran here from the palace when our ambulances wouldn't start. We believe there could be patients on the top floor."

"What's wrong with the ambulances?" asked the Vatican City police captain.

"We don't know, but they are both out. If we need medical transport, we'll have to call it in from Rome."

The police captain thought for a minute and then turned to command the young driver. "Run down to the gate and tell them to let two outside ambulances into the city. I will make the dispatch call from here."

Two ambulances arrived at the gate right behind the red City of Rome fire trucks, and all were waved through on the Vatican police chief's orders. Ramsay walked out in the fresher night air to see Lucca and his team dressed in first responder uniforms in the front seats of both stolen ambulances. She smiled at the Romani men and opened her arms to invite them inside just as Cardinal Forpo, hurriedly dressed in red cardinal vestments, waddled into the lobby on his way to the elevators.

"Hold it right there, Your Eminence," said the captain.

"But I must get inside," the cardinal ordered. "I have important business on the top floor."

"Stand aside, Your Grace," said the police captain as he motioned to the firemen and makeshift medics with their gurneys. "We will handle this."

"I must enter at once!" the clergyman shouted at the police chief and his men.

The chief turned slowly until he squared up in front of the powerful cardinal, blocking the fat man's way. "Do you know about the medical patients on the top floor, Cardinal Forpo?"

The cardinal lowered his head and took a half step back as he smoothed his ruffled vestments. "What I mean to say, Chief Inspector, is that I wish to accompany you to investigate."

"Signora," the captain shouted to Ramsay, "can you show us where they are?"

"Certainly," Ramsay said, casting a sneer at a fuming Forpo. "They are on the top floor."

"Peasant!" the cardinal said to her as he shoved a junior officer out of his way and struggled up the stairs after them to the top floor that was rapidly filling with smoke. The double doors to the corner suite were open, and Ramsay could see the two guards gasping for fresh air at the opened windows past the four motionless bodies who lay still as statues in their hospital beds.

Ramsay reached out to grab the arm of the police captain, but he and the leader of the firefighters strode into the room. "What is going on here? Who are these people? Who are you?" the fire chief barked at the two security guards, motioning for Lucca and his three disguised medic counterparts to load the four catatonic victims onto the gurneys. Ramsay stepped in behind them to disconnect the attached sensors and IVs, all the while keeping an eye on the police captain as he quizzed the tight-lipped guards.

The panicked cardinal dialed on his phone again and cursed in Italian before leaving another frustrating voicemail. "Signore Buono, per favore, please answer my call. We have a fire at the college, and they are taking them away, Signore. I do not want to disappoint you—or her—but I cannot stop them. I know you are at a meeting tonight, but I must reach you. Please call me back."

The firemen helped the substitute medics carry Samas's overweight body down the stairs and into the waiting ambulance with the other three. Ramsay stepped into the back of the stolen medical wagon and stood over Clovis, whose wide, alert eyes locked on hers as joyous tears ran into the deep wrinkles on his face.

"We've got you, old friend." She snapped off her blue gloves as she reached into her pocket for the flip phone. She cradled his weeping face with an Embe tattooed hand before snapping a photo and texting it to Galen. She turned to Samas next. "We're taking you to a safe place. The doctor will meet us there. He has an antidote for this." She took photos of Samas, Etyma, and Dilmun, then exited the ambulance. "Take them to private hangar number six at Ciampino Airport," Ramsay barked to the ambulance driver. "There is a plane waiting. Put on the siren and don't stop for anyone." She held out her hand to Lucca to thank him but quickly drew it back. "Wait here for a second," she said, slamming the rear doors closed.

Ramsay walked over to Cardinal Forpo, who still spoke frantically into the phone as he paced behind the ambulances. "Please pick up, Signore. Please call me back, Maestro. They are leaving."

Ramsay dropped to one knee and reached up to grasp the cardinal's right hand with its large gold ecclesiastical ring. The cardinal instinctively relaxed his hand into the well-practiced greeting to adoring parishioners. She took the man's soft, supple hand in hers, being careful to show the black Embe tattoo as she kissed the ring. The clergyman gasped in horror and dropped his phone to the cobblestoned drive.

"Pleasure to finally make your acquaintance, Your Eminence," she said as the needle of the syringe filled with silver liquid entered the smooth flesh on the back of his hand. She kept a tight grip on the heavy ring as the red cardinal fell to the street and started convulsing.

Ramsay ran back to the open window of the ambulance. She reached her hand up to Lucca's ear, magically produced the ring, and dropped it into his open hand. "Fit for a king," she said with a breathless smile. "Perhaps you will even wear it one day."

Lucca smiled as he slipped the heavy gold ring into the shirt pocket of his stolen uniform.

"Tell your Re Zingaro that we will never forget what the Roma have done for us this night."

31

Brevicepts stepped onto the dock in front of her palazzo just as one of her guards pulled up in a vintage wooden speedboat and tied it off. She looked past the familiar Rialto Bridge toward the first light of dawn and then looked back at Elsa and Mr. Bigelow as they prepared IVs for her five stricken captains who lay petrified on the empty parquet floor of the hall.

"We would like to accompany you," said a bodyguard behind her.

"I have to do this alone," she said, motioning the first guard out of the speedboat. "See that those five are taken care of. I will return in a few hours."

"But who will take you there?" asked the first guard as he stepped onto the dock.

She shot him a look of pained disappointment as she took the wheel. "I know how to captain a boat, you dullard," she said as she idled away into the calm waters of the Grand Canal.

"Where are you going?" both guards asked nervously in unison.

"Back to the past."

SHE EASED THE SLEEK WOODEN BOAT into an idle as she glided up to the neglected dock next to the derelict buildings of distant Lazzaretto.

Brevicepts stepped out onto the dock and tried to recall the fuzzy, fever-dream memories of the last time she saw him here. The forgotten island looked abandoned, except for a single light that shone from the first open doorway. She entered to find a stainless-steel table and chairs set with two small beakers in place of wine glasses next to several dusty bottles and a moon-faced Carnival mask. Clean paths in the dirt on the floor marked the hasty removal of heavy lab equipment.

Galen, still wearing a tight-fitting tuxedo, entered the main hall from the back. "I see you got my message, Stregua. A wonderful party, I must say—shame we had to crash it."

"Is that really you, Doctor?" she asked as she stepped toward him to look into his strange face. "Or is it still physician?"

"I see you are still wearing your hair in the traditional style," he said, pointing to her neat topknot.

"It's funny, isn't it?" she said, craning her long neck to peer out through the empty window frames. "You and I dealing with matters of life and death here again in this place."

Galen reached for the dusty, unlabeled bottle and began pouring into both beakers. "The lab gear is all that I had time to bring with me, so they will have to do."

"I confess," she continued, "I get a bit of a chill just thinking about me lying out there somewhere in a mass grave."

Galen motioned for her to sit. "Oh, you're out there all right," he chuckled to himself. "I saw to that. I'm out there too, right next to you."

Brevicepts brought the lab glass to her nose and sniffed deeply. "Well, here's to us and what we were."

Galen offered a forced smile and then drank with her. He rolled a vial of silver fluid from the Croatian pharmacy across the table toward her. "I assume your good Dr. Ling hasn't been able to crack an antidote for his monstrous creation yet, or you wouldn't have made the trip out to see your old friend."

Brevicepts looked at the wine in the beaker, then turned toward the colors of the breaking dawn visible through the open double doors. "You are correct," she replied coolly, her acid words an overt indictment of her doctor's inability. "Do you wish to propose a trade?"

Galen choked on his sip and set down his wine. "A trade? For what?"

"Mine for yours, of course."

"You don't know yet," the physician chuckled and watched her stiffen as he reached for his simple flip phone and slid it across the table to her. The photo on the small screen showed an Embe tattooed hand cradling Clovis's face.

"I see," she said, taking a long drink and reaching for the bottle to refill her glass.

"Don't fret, old friend. There is still a bargain to be had here, for you *do* hold something of value."

"Pianosa," she offered flatly.

"Pianosa," he agreed. "And a return of all the assets stolen. And a truce between our sides."

She swirled the fine wine in her glass as she thought about the offer. "I could just kill my captains, you know."

"Oh, I know," the physician said before taking a long drink. "But you would have to start their influence cells over again. And if your fawning followers don't see their shepherds alive again after last night's excitement, they'll be off your team for good." He reached over to refill his glass. "I wonder if you can afford that kind of setback to your plans."

She drank in silence before answering him. "I can never let you give the world the gift of longer lives."

Galen laughed to himself as he recognized the familiar feelings of dread that came with her company. "You're the same person, the same broken and fractured person, Brevicepts. After tonight, I can see your signature on the Venice outbreak and hundreds of other disasters. *Malus bonum ubi se simulat tunc est pessimus.*"[57]

"I'm not so bad, am I? Virtue is all a matter of perspective." Brevicepts squinted a forced smile back at the doctor.

---

57. Latin—When a bad man pretends he is a good man, then he is at his worst, Publilius Syrus

"You're lucky I'm making you any offer at all," Galen snapped at her. "I should let your people suffer as you planned to torture us into perpetual madness."

She stared at him and knew she was beaten. "Pianosa can still transfer the assets back to exactly where they were before. When do you want to meet?"

"I'll get you a message about a meeting and the antidote when we are all away safely. But there is one more thing we want"—Galen checked himself—"one more thing *Evan* wants."

"Elsa," she guessed.

"Yes, he wants Elsa out of La Mutuelle."

"What does he see in her?"

"*Qui amant ipsi sibi somnia fingunt.*"[58]

Brevicepts smiled. "And if I refuse?"

"It's only a matter of time until she leaves you—in this life or the next. You know that now. Evan has shown her a better way," said Galen, swirling his wine. "I wonder how many others in your organization might be looking for an alternative family right about now. It is only by light that one can appreciate your darkness."

She drank but didn't answer for a long time. "We have a deal."

"Excellent," he said. "You are welcome to stay and drink with me for a while if you want. It might be a long time before we spill wine again."

She tilted her head at his offer so that her topknot flipped to one side. "All right, but I have a few questions."

"Go ahead," Galen said in a long yawn that betrayed his sleepless nights of work.

"First of all," she paused and considered the glass. "What *is* this wine?" she asked.

"I thought you might like this one. It's a Côte-Rôtie, from my own estate. Next question?"

"What would it take for me to get some more of your life-extension serum?"

---

58. Latin—Lovers create dreams for themselves

"What, so you could extend the lives of those that are loyal to you?" Galen scoffed. "No, I will not have my work perverted by you again." Galen leveled his exhausted eyes back at her, but she remained silent, still demanding an answer from her old friend. "What would it take?" he repeated as he took a heavy gulp of the heavenly wine and threw his head back in a laugh. "It would take a smarter doctor than you've got now."

Her stern face cracked into a slight smile that slowly widened into a forced grin. "You're exactly the same."

"Unfortunately, my dear Stregua, so are you." He raised his glass in another toast.

She sipped and savored his wine. "I hated you for voting against me," she said in a soft voice that hinted at remorse.

"I know you did," replied Galen. "I imagine you still do."

"*Acerrima proximorum odia!*"[59] she replied before finishing her wine.

"Perhaps another bottle of this would ease the sting."

---

59. Latin—Hatred of the closest is the most bitter, Tacitus

32

Evan arrived early at busy Caffè Florian, the meeting spot Galen had communicated to Brevicepts. He faced the afternoon sun at an outdoor table at the edge of the open expanse of St. Mark's Square in Venice. Masked Carnival tourists crowded the square in a benign replay of his surreal costumed nightmare from the night before. Evan looked around at the colorful twisted grins and scowls and wondered if any of those masks covered a face that saw him last night at the Conclave. He looked at the couples and families who frolicked in the freedom of anonymity, but he could not share their joy. The ambiguity that amused them only served as a reminder to Evan that the danger of La Mutuelle could be lurking behind any face, masked or not.

He watched Ramsay arrive and stood to embrace her in a silent comradery of everything they had accomplished. "Are they all safe?" he asked.

"Yes," Ramsay replied with a slight smile of satisfaction. "I have all four of them, and they are safe. I have the remaining members of the Cognomina. They are sequestered in a secure location in Paris. I will take us there right after we are finished here," she said, looking around for Brevicepts.

"How did you do it?" Evan asked.

"It was Perez. His clan returned the favor and rescued us."

"Stay on the side of the angels," Evan replied.

"Something like that, but you wouldn't have thought that if you had seen Lucca and his team in their stolen paramedic uniforms," she laughed. "Did you have a chance to speak to any who left our ranks and joined her? Do you think any of them might want to return to us?"

Evan took out a cigarette. "Elsa, for sure. Mr. Ing and Kerr seem to have embraced her vision. Steen and Kress might return to us. There might be one or two others among her existing captains. After that, I'm not sure," he said, exhaling a stream of smoke.

"I heard about your party last night. It must have been hard to face that kind of test."

"They rescued me before I had to—" He struggled to recount the horror he had been prepared to commit. "Poppy sacrificed herself to prevent me from— She protected an innocent girl."

"I heard. She wasn't the only one who stepped up to protect the innocent."

Evan nodded, thinking of Auda and Galen and even Samas sacrificing his art collection. "In the end, I don't think I accomplished much by going over to her."

Ramsay reached over and touched his arm. "That's not true, Evan. The information you were able to gather while with them will be very valuable for us now. What you learned could save us, but it could also protect many more like that girl." She leveled her steel-gray eyes at him. "We're in a war with them now. The stakes are not just us and our survival, but the survival of the world around us, the world we embrace and love. You have seen inside of her organization and how it operates. You can identify her captains and their plans."

"Some of their plans," he corrected her.

"Look around you, Evan. What future do you think she envisions for humanity?"

Evan looked around at the colorful costumes and masked performers in the square and tried to focus on the joy in their conversations and laughter.

"We're on their side. They don't even know the peril they face from her," she said, looking at the happy revelers with Evan. "We may be the only chance they have now. We, the Cognomina, are the only possible counterbalance to La Mutuelle and their dark mission." She looked back at Evan and paused until he turned back to face her. "We are smaller, weaker, and disorganized compared to her, but the risk you took is our first step to getting us onto an equal footing with her."

"Do you really think so?"

"You said it yourself, we needed more information about her and how her organization works if we are to ever have a chance of leveling the battlefield. Rafic has been able to get some great information, but even he would still be blind without you. You gave us a chance," she said, motioning to the people in the crowded square, "and you're giving *them* a chance too."

"That's her," Evan said, spotting the topknot of black hair atop Brevicepts's tall frame as she moved through the crowd. "It looks like Elsa and Pianosa are with her," he said in relief.

"Do you have it?" Ramsay asked.

Evan nodded but kept his eyes locked on Elsa as the three approached. Elsa's eyes met his, and he felt the same rush as when she had waved to him from the window of the departing jet, the same rush as when she had held his arm at the office in Paris, the same rush as when she took him on the train. Elsa smiled for an instant before resuming her leader's stern air as they approached.

Evan remembered the panicked look on her face last night when she realized she could not protect him from Brevicepts's test. Now he envisioned protecting her from the same danger.

Brevicepts sat Pianosa in an open chair next to him. Evan noticed that the caretaker's hands were bound in front of him, covered by a scarf draped between his slack arms. He looked drugged, struggling to keep his blinking eyes open.

Brevicepts looked at Evan and said nothing and then turned to study Ramsay—from her tattoo to her cool gray eyes. "Is that really you in there, old friend?"

"I would recognize you anywhere," Ramsay answered with contempt.

"I'll take that as a compliment. Well, I am certainly getting to meet a lot of my old friends recently. I assume Rome was you?" Brevicepts asked coolly.

"Ask your cardinal."

Brevicepts nodded and crossed her long legs. "I just want to know one thing, Ramsay. How did you find them?"

Ramsay turned her head slowly to each side, surveying each human face in the Carnival crowd around them. "I have a secret weapon on my side—a weapon that will always beat you."

"Oh, do tell."

Ramsay met her cold gaze and held it. "It's them," she said, motioning to the happy people around them in the piazza. "Those people, the very ones you wish to destroy, they helped me find you."

"Don't think you've won, old friend," Brevicepts said with a sneer. "You've bet against me before and lost. This is a minor digression in a long timeline."

"We're not through," Ramsay answered.

Brevicepts's eyes narrowed behind a forced smile as she turned to Evan. "Do you have it?"

"I do. Will those two leave with us?" Evan asked, pointing to Elsa and Pianosa.

"He will. Elsa," she said, placing a hand on the young woman's knee, "Elsa gets to make her own decision. But before we make the exchange, I have a question for you that has been *plaguing* me since the party," she said, smiling at her own joke.

Evan looked at her with a hardened resolve as the memories of the Conclave assaulted him again.

Brevicepts cocked her head and studied him in silence for a moment. "Right. There it is. I saw that same steely look in your eyes when you held the knife in your hand." Her cold smile warmed. "You were going to kill that girl, weren't you?"

Evan remained motionless and channeled his hatred back at her in a silent glare.

"I saw it in you last night. I saw you harden into one of us before my very eyes. You cannot undo that, Evan," she said with satisfaction. "That is part of who you are now."

"You saw my commitment last night," he said, pushing down the emotion of seeing the girl's innocent, terrified face. "What happened to the girl?"

"Kerr killed her," Brevicepts said without a second thought. "Now give me the delivery from Galen and let us go our separate ways for now."

Evan looked over at Ramsay, who nodded ever so slightly. He pulled four vials filled with clear fluid from his pocket and pushed them across the table. "Galen says to administer this every eight hours until they are normal, then administer once a day for another week."

"All right then," Brevicepts said, standing up to leave. She looked down at her young captain, who looked straight ahead, her hands trembling. "Have you made your decision, Elsa?"

Elsa sat locked in her chair, tears welling up in her green eyes as she looked up at her master and weighed her choice.

Brevicepts craned her head down from its heights to look at her. "Are you sure, little one? You know what this means, right?"

Evan reached out and took Elsa's trembling hands to stop them from shaking. "Elsa is welcome with us now."

Brevicepts stood over her young captain for a long breath and then a second. "As you wish it, Elsa." She turned to go just as Ramsay stood and extended a clenched fist toward the taller woman. Brevicepts opened her hand as Ramsay slowly released five gold coins that clinked one at a time onto her palm. "You remembered," Brevicepts said with a wry smile as she closed her hand around the repaid wager.

"I will stop you," Ramsay stated as she kept her icy gray eyes locked on her foe.

"It was nice to see you, old friend. Know that I *will* ensure the Cognomina atones for its sins against me," Brevicepts said before turning and walking through the crowded square toward her palazzo.

Elsa snapped out of her trance and turned to face Evan as tears began to roll down her tan cheeks.

"It's all right, Elsa," Evan said with a bright smile that tried to comfort her. "We did it. We got my friends back. We're out."

Elsa smiled and nodded, too emotional to speak.

"We can protect you," Evan reassured her.

Elsa reached out her fingers and stroked them over Evan's face. "No, dear one, you cannot," she said, breaking into sobs. "But I can still protect you, for now. I will know where to meet you if you rebuild the hotel."

"No," Evan protested softly. "We can start now, right now."

She stared deeply into Evan's eyes one last time. "I dreamed of a love like this," she said as she rose on unsteady legs. "I need to protect it now. I will be watching over you, Evan," she said before turning to catch up with her leader at the far end of the square.

33

Ramsay walked with Evan past the crowd of tourists toward the administrative entrance of Les Invalides, the sprawling opulent 350-year-old military hospital in central Paris that now housed the French Army Museum. She showed her newly laminated ID badge to the soldier at the gate and instructed Evan to do the same with his.

"Is this an army base or a museum?" Evan asked as they passed through the military gate into the manicured gardens of the wide courtyard.

"It started as a hospital and retirement home for injured French soldiers, but about a hundred years ago, they converted this part into the French Army Museum," she said pointing to a long three-story stone building. "This section at the back is still a working hospital today under military administration. I was able to call in some favors to get us a private space for a while. It's this way."

Evan followed her as she showed her photo ID badge to another stern-looking French soldier who stood sentry at the entrance to the old hospital wing. Ramsay passed the first checkpoint and then a second. She showed her badge again as they walked into the labyrinth of white hallways before stopping in front of an innocuous unmarked office door.

"So what do we do now?" Evan asked.

"Well, we will need help," Ramsay answered flatly. "And you actually gave me an idea on how we can get it. Come on, I'll tell you more inside." She swiped her badge on the scanner and pushed the door open with the sound of a vintage buzzer.

The plain door opened into a long rectangle of a room that housed two administrative desks, a waiting room with a small kitchen off to one side, and a row of six modern medical beds set up in a row along the side wall. Evan saw that five of the beds were occupied and that Auda was sitting up in the one closest to the familiar faces of the Cognomina members who sat in the comfortable chairs of the old waiting room. Galen looked up from his work at Samas's bed and smiled as they entered. Auda looked at Evan and nodded without speaking.

"We all have private rooms in the back," Ramsay said to Evan as he followed her inside. "I'll show you in a minute." Ramsay turned to face everyone in the long room. "I've triple-checked," Ramsay said loudly enough for all to hear. "It looks like we've lost them."

Rafic stood up from his laptop on one of the two desks. "From what I have been able to monitor so far, they don't know where we are, but they *are* searching."

"We should be safe here. While it hosts tourists all day, Les Invalides is technically still a military facility," Ramsay said, pacing the length of floor between the table and a recuperating Auda in the nearest hospital bed. "I have called in a few favors and made arrangements for us to stay here in Paris as long as we want."

"It's a bit ironic," Poppy started, "that we are hiding in the city that is the headquarters for La Mutuelle."

"We're hiding in plain sight, just like she is," Mr. Diltz countered from his seat next to the scribe, who worked at the larger desk. "I have been able to reverse all of Mr. Pianosa's transactions. You should see your balances as they were before."

"What did you do with Pianosa?" Evan asked.

"Don't ask," Ramsay and Diltz said in grim unison.

Rafic walked around the edge of his desk toward them with his chrome phone in hand. "You found the dark matter I couldn't see," he said as he threw his arms around Evan. "It's everywhere. They are into everything."

"What are you talking about?"

"Do you remember back at the hotel when I was able to pull information from your phone just by placing it next to it?" Rafic asked with a smile as he held up his sleek prototype phone.

"Yes," Evan replied.

"And do you remember me telling you that it has a mode to do that even when powered down?"

"Yes," Evan said, confused.

"Well, thanks to you and the information you passed to Gonzalo before their Conclave, I was able to get this," he said, waving his spy phone over his head, "right in the middle of that rack of checked-in phones at her palazzo where it sat and worked silently for three hours."

"And?"

"And it's a gold mine." Rafic beamed. "Only the Italian generals and one American businessman had encryption I can't break. Everyone else I was able to get. We're not blind anymore, Evan, thanks to you."

"How the hell did you guys get in?"

"After you told Gonzalo where you were headed, I ran a data analysis and searched for important people coming to Venice for Carnival, but I eventually focused on business moguls and government bureaucrats who spend way more than they make. From there, I found ten targets I thought could be assets and sent them each a text message to come to the Hotel Metropole in costume with their invitations for an urgent premeeting. And five of them showed up. Our doctor prepared a cocktail that ensured they slept until morning while Jens, Poppy, and I took their clothes, masks, and invitations, and we just went in their place. I even included a search parameter for sex and size," Rafic said with nerdy pride, "so that I could get everyone fitted—everyone except Chance, of course."

"I took care of the guards on the dock," Chance boomed from a comfortable chair near the window as he looked out.

"Keep that curtain closed," snapped Ramsay. "We can't be too careful now."

"It was my idea to get us in and get this data download," Rafic continued, "but it was Galen's idea to prepare the injections in case we needed them."

"I cracked the antidote and snapped Auda out of it earlier that day," Galen said from across the room. "Once I could reverse the effect of the injection, I knew we could use it against them if we had to. Injecting them was going to be the backup plan if Ramsay failed in Rome, but it turned out to be your escape plan in the end."

"Speaking of plan," Evan said, turning and walking over to Poppy, who sat in the leather chair next to Chance, "how did you—"

"Oh, this?" she said, holding up her hands that were bandaged into clumsy white mittens. "Well, this was certainly *not* to plan. But I couldn't let you become a murderer, could I?" she asked as she sat up in the chair. "Be a dear and give me a cigarette, will you?"

"You can't smoke in here," Galen ordered without looking up from Auda's pulse.

"Oh really?" Poppy smirked as she confidently waved Evan toward her with a gauze-covered hand. "You should check your schedule for when my next shot is due, Doctor," she growled as Evan placed a cigarette into the corner of her mouth. "Skip me again, and I'll crawl into that last empty bed to get your attention."

"Will they all recover?" Evan asked over his shoulder at Galen.

"Yes, but it might take a while. Auda here says a few words sometimes." The physician looked over at the last bed. "I suspect Clovis will take the longest. They're all improving at different paces."

"Wait, where is Jens?" Evan asked. "And do *not* say don't ask."

"He's looking into something that could help our plan," Ramsay said with a sly smile.

"So what *is* our plan?" Chance asked in a voice loud enough for all to hear but clearly directed at Ramsay.

"First, we need to heal our injured and get all the members of our core team back to one hundred percent."

"That might take some time," Galen cautioned.

"After that, we need to get our house in order," Ramsay offered, "figuratively so that we have a place to call our own, besides here, and literally if we can."

Mr. Diltz coughed to get her attention. "After I restored all your accounts, I took the liberty of making a few calls and using some of the communal funds," he started. "I was able to get the site of the St. Germain surrounded with a metal security fence yesterday. I was just on with the building commission, and we have permission to rebuild it."

"Excellent work, Mr. Diltz. I hope we can delay your retirement party for a while longer," Ramsay said with a smile. "In your follow-ups with them, you might ask if we can expand with the rebuild."

"Expand?" Poppy said, struggling to manipulate her cigarette between wrapped hands.

"Don't you mean *contract*?" Chance said, looking at the remaining faces in the room.

"Hold that question for a minute. Next," she said, pointing to Rafic and Evan, "we need to find out all we can about Brevicepts, her captains, and the plans you heard during the Conclave."

"I have some faces ready for you to identify," Rafic said with a grin.

"This should let us know how big La Mutuelle really is and might give us some additional insight into what they are planning next," Ramsay continued. "After that, we need—"

"After that," Poppy interrupted, "we need to take this bitch down."

"Take her down," Auda mumbled quietly, taking all of them off guard for a second.

"Yes, after that, we take her down," Ramsay replied.

"But how?" Chance broke in.

"We need to strike at her most critical advantage, her invisibility," Rafic added. "If we can do that, we can make it her biggest liability. We need to shine a light on La Mutuelle."

"And just how would we do that?" Chance demanded. "And with so few of us now?"

"You're right, my friend," Ramsay agreed as she walked over and ran a finger along the silver edge of the scribe's open tome. "There aren't enough of us to counter La Mutuelle, even if we could find a way to expose her. But what if both of those problems could be unlocked with a single solution?" she said, turning to look at Evan.

"What? What solution? I don't have any solution."

"You've already given it to us," Ramsay teased.

"I don't understand," Evan responded.

"I don't follow either," Chance declared.

"Evan, your narrative in the notebooks has already freed us from our secrecy. Who and what we are is no longer in the dark. You have already disclosed us, and now we are in a perfect position to expose her and La Mutuelle for who they are and their long-term plans."

"I like where this is going," Galen said, joining the conversation.

"And," Ramsay continued, "we all believe there are more Reincarnationists out there. Maybe *they* could be the help we need, but instead of setting up a system to search for them the way Brevicepts does, we could—"

"We could what? Advertise?" Chance quipped.

"I might have a more elegant solution," Ramsay mused as she looked at their faces. "We would obviously need to vote on it before moving forward, but I have asked our scribe to start work on something that could capture the whole story in a way that exposes her *and* recruits for us."

"We're listening," Poppy said for the group.

Ramsay took a deep breath. "It would involve each of you spending some time with our chroniclers where our accounts would ultimately become a new volume in our—" Ramsay stopped midsentence when the buzzer on the electric door lock announced the entrance of Jens.

He paused for a moment to catch his breath from the run through the maze of hallways. "I checked, and you were right. The writer is here in Paris. We could just leave it for him."

All eyes turned back to Ramsay, who directed Jens to take a seat. "Well, now that we're all here, I suppose it's time to vote on what to do next."

AUTHOR BIO

D. Eric Maikranz has had a multitude of lives in this lifetime. As a world traveler, he was a foreign correspondent while living in Rome, translated for relief doctors in Nicaragua during a cholera epidemic, and was once forcibly expelled from the nation of Laos. He has worked as a tour guide, a radio host, a bouncer, and as a Silicon Valley software executive. His first novel, *The Reincarnationist Papers*, was adapted into the Paramount Pictures film, *Infinite*, starring Mark Wahlberg.